The Autnor

Geoff Lee was born in the Lancashire glass town of St Helens in September 1939 on the first full day of the war, although it is believed that this was just a coincidence. He first worked at Prescot for BICC (British Insulated Callender's Cables), but known locally as the Biggest Individual Collection of Comedians. Since then he has been employed as a draughtsman in London in the Swinging Sixties, from 1972 to 1976 in Hull and since then in West Yorkshire in a number of engineering drawing offices, the source of much of the content of his written material.

His first novel, *One Winter*, was published in November 1999 to much critical acclaim and was followed in March 2002 by the sequel, *One Spring*, both written against a background of Romance, Rock 'n' Roll and Rugby League. Having completed *One Summer*, again inspired by the old saying about work, "They could write a book about this place. It'd be a best seller", he is now preparing to start work on *One Autumn*, set in the last decade of the twentieth century.

He has recently undergone quadruple heart bypass surgery but remains a leading member of the Rugby League Supporters' Association, being responsible for the distribution of its magazine, *The Greatest Game*.

To George

Yours is the greatest game

Geoff Lee

One Summer

Romance, Redundancy & Rugby League in the Eighties

Geoff Lee

The Parrs Wood Press
Manchester

First Published 2005

THE PARRS WOOD PRESS
St Wilfrid's Enterprise Centre
Royce Road, Manchester, M15 5BJ
www.parrswoodpress.com

© Geoff Lee 2005

ISBN: 1 903158 46 X

Printed and bound by Biddles Ltd of King's Lynn

CONTENTS

1.

The Double Dutch holiday fund

"QUICK, LADS. Hang up some garlic. The vampires are coming."

It was Tony Robledo, disturbing the peace and tranquillity of Wilkinson's Drawing Office. Before anybody could respond, he carried on:

"Don't you try and sneak out, Yorky. It's not safe. The bin men haven't finished collecting all the rubbish yet."

Turning to the man stood next to him, he continued: "I didn't think I'd see you here today, Charlie. I thought Tuesday was pension day or have you forgotten to go again?"

He rubbed his hand roughly over Alan's head, asked him if he had started going out with girls yet, and continued:

"Listen lads, I don't want to disturb you but Basil Brush is on his way here. So can you open the curtains, brush all the cobwebs away from the windows, find a pencil and start drawing something, if that's not too much to ask?"

Then he turned to Mick, flicked some imaginary dust from his shirt collar and said "Are all the barbers in Wigan still on strike, ewd lad?"

He cast his eye over the drawing on Mick's board and noted that in a week's time it would be two years old.

"I take it nobody's waiting for this drawing, Mick. Do you know what? If anybody ever did a painting of this place, do you know what they'd call it, eh? 'Still Life'!"

Then he looked at his watch, said "Time for me to have a lie down" and walked out of the office by the back door.

"I thought Basil was in London today," said Alan.

"He is. It's just Tony winding us up as usual," replied the office comedian, Charlie Eccleston.

A few minutes later, a young apprentice walked through the office, carrying a brass casting. Within a few minutes, he returned, telling Charlie on his way out that he had been at a party over the weekend in Liverpool and had spilled a pint of lager over Mick Jagger's crocodile shoes. Shortly after, the Planning Department Office Manager scurried through with a bundle of drawings in his hand, puffing and blowing as he usually did.

"This place is getting like a bloody railway station," complained Mick, "all these folk flying through. They keep waking me up."

"Mick, if all these people are flying through, don't you mean that this place is getting more like an aeroplane station?"

Alan's comment elicited no response from Mick or anybody else and all went quiet for a while.

Ever since the place had been built, there had been only one way into the Electrical Section of the Drawing Office. But recently the old storeroom had been refurbished and a new door into the Planning Office put in, so now that provided an alternative way to get to the Work Study Department and down the stairs to the Machine Shop.

Before long, the door burst open again and in shuffled the next person to divert their attention from doing anything productive. It was John Bolton, another of the many characters who worked at the Wilkinson Engineering Works in Ashurst.

John was a Progress Chaser. It was his job to keep up to date all the documentation associated with the work of the engineers, draughtsmen, planners, estimators, technical clerks and others who worked in the Drawing, Planning and Shipping Offices and the Machine, Wiring and Assembly Shops. It was not in his job description to understand any of the technical content involved. Essentially, he was a gofer; 'Go for this', 'Go for that' and more often than not 'Go for a Mars Bar for us, will you, ewd lad?'.

Little was known about his background, although it was rumoured that he had had a mid-life crisis when he was still at Newton Road Junior School. In 1956, at the age of eighteen, he had started doing his National Service in the R.A.F., elevating him from the depths of absolute obscurity to the heights of relative absurdity. After he had completed his basic training, he had become a pilot with Bomber Command. However he was not a pilot in the commonly accepted sense of the word. All John did was pilot the instrument trolley around the hangars, where the maintenance crews worked.

Before being demobbed, he had risen to the rank of Leading Aircraftsman. But he had only gained that title because on Passing Out Days and the Queen's Birthday, it was his job to lead the camp goat on to the parade ground. One thing he had learned as a National Serviceman was to always obey orders and particularly the last order. Back in Civvy Street, he began to realise how bad his memory was. As a result, whenever he got the details of a message wrong, John would scratch his head, smile stupidly and repeat what he had just said, but with the words in a slightly different order. When the puzzled recipient of his message asked if it actually meant something else, John would again agree. In fact he was often called Mr. Agreeable, because he always agreed with or did whatever was said to him or asked of him, ridiculous though it might be.

THE DOUBLE DUTCH HOLIDAY FUND

A typical example of this had occurred a few weeks earlier. An order for four electrical control cubicles was being processed through the factory for delivery to a steel mill at Duisburg in West Germany. As John was walking through the Assembly Shop, he had been stopped by a chargehand.

"John, are you on your holidays today?" the chargehand had asked him.

"No, I'm at work," said John with a pleasant smile on his face.

"Well, I wouldn't spend all day strolling around like you are doing. If you take my advice, you'd better get back to your own office, sharpish. The Kaiser is coming from Berlin today to inspect all the paperwork for this Duisburg job."

When John arrived breathless back at his desk a few minutes later, his section leader asked him why he hadn't brought with him the post from the General Office, where he had been sent over half an hour earlier.

"Tommy Stott told me to come straight back here. Caesar's coming."

John's boss just laughed to himself, went back into his office and put the comment that John had just made into his little red exercise book. It was his intention one day to write a novel based on the life and times of John Bolton, but not just yet. He didn't have enough suitable material, only thirty-nine totally daft comments, obtained over the last three months. He did however have a title for the intended book: 'Jack Blackburn. The Idiot Goes Forth and Comes Last'.

Although his title was Progress Chaser, it could be said that the only thing that John had ever chased with any enthusiasm were women. It was also known that the only ones he ever caught were those who couldn't run very fast and most notably Ann, who worked in the Metal Fatigue Lab and had a club foot.

He was, though, a very likeable character. Whenever he was seen walking along the corridor towards the Drawing Officer, all the draughtsmen would smile. Inevitably they knew that they would be well entertained for the next half hour or so. Not only would he agree with whatever was said to him, John would also repeat things that were said to him, like the yodelling noise that Charlie had perfected.

"Morning, John. How's your poompledomps today?" asked Yorky, the first member of the office to greet him.

"Fine. How are yours, Sam?"

"A bit grumpy. So, what bit of useless information have you brought for us this time in your little black bag?"

John smiled, turned to Charlie and said "Charlie, Arthur Young wants three prints of the Control Desk Wiring for the Rolling Mill at Lambaqaque in Peru and the Parts List as well."

"Don't you mean the Rolling Desk Wiring for the Control Mill?"

"Yes, that's it, I think."

"Well you can tell him I've drawn it, but there's just one problem with the Parts List."

"There always is when I come here."

"Yodelliao."

"Yodelliao."

"There's just been a revolution in Peru and Lambaqaque is now in the hands of the rebels."

"Up the revolution, eh Charlie?"

"Up the revolution indeed my good friend and to all who sail with her."

"So what's the problem?"

"With this new Government in power in Lambaqaque, the official language is now Bolivian. So it looks like we'll have to change all the labels we've drawn for the cubicle doors."

"You're having me on. I thought that Bolivia was miles away."

"Well, be it on your head John. You can have three prints of the Parts List first thing before the tea break this afternoon. But don't blame us if the labels get sent back."

"The other thing, Charlie, he also wants the layout of the main control panel by Friday."

"Any particular Friday, John?"

"This one I think."

It was not a bad assumption to make since it was only Tuesday morning.

"Is that Friday the sixteenth?"

"Yes, it will be."

At this point, Yorky muscled in on the proceedings and produced a previous year's desk diary, in which he kept many useful pieces of technical information.

"I think you've made a mistake there, John. Next Friday is the twenty-first. Does he mean this Friday or next Friday?"

John looked puzzled, then looked into his own pocket diary and said with a small degree of certainty.

"No, this Friday is the sixteenth. The sixteenth of March."

"What year is your diary, John?"

John looked at the front just to make sure.

"1979."

Fortunately for John, there was a typical drawing office calendar on the wall. As he looked up at it, Charlie asked him if he liked the look of Yorky's wife.

"I don't know. I've never seen her."

"You have."

"Where?"

"On that calendar, you daft bat."

"Is that your wife, Sam? She looks very nice."

Yorky smiled and said "Yodellaio."

"Yodellaio."

Then Charlie flicked through Sam's old diary and said "When you get back to your office, just check with Denise what date next Friday is, John, and give us a ring. We'll be here all day. It's better to be sorry than in a safe."

After John had left and they had all finished laughing, Colin told them what had happened when he had recently shown Mr. Bolton his holiday photographs. One was of him stood next to a weather-beaten stallholder, aged about eighty, in the Portuguese market town of Aljustrel.

"That's the wife," Colin had told John. "Don't you think she's got a nice tan?"

Later that afternoon, the Welding Shop foreman had been talking to John, who had told him that he had just seen some holiday snaps of Colin and his wife on Earlestown Market.

On another occasion, Charlie had asked John if he wanted to take part in a competition. As always, John had said yes. He rarely, if ever, said no to a request for him to do something.

"All you have to do is stand under the office clock with your arms outstretched for as long as you can. We've all done it and Yorky is winning at the moment. He stood there for four minutes."

"Four minutes and six seconds," growled the man from Mytholmroyd. And so John put his papers on a desk and did what he believed that all the others had done.

After less than a minute, the angry voice of the boss, Basil Wilkinson, was heard coming from the top end of the office and so John proceeded to perform a little bit of magic. He just disappeared. But in his haste to get away, he left his notepad and bunch of R711 schedules behind and spent the rest of the morning trying to remember where he had left them.

"So what did John want?" asked Mick, who had been on the phone for most of the time that John had been in the office. "Did he say anything about the holiday we were supposed to be having with him?"

A few weeks earlier, John's mother had passed away. She was only sixty-seven, but having had to look after her daft son for so long, had easily put another ten years on her. As her only child, John thus became the owner of the family house in Carlton Lane and the beneficiary of an insurance policy that she had been paying into for years. He also discovered that she had been buying Premium Bonds as well. He found them, one miserable wet afternoon, in a folder marked 'Something for a rainy day'.

Now John was not one to keep something like that to himself and so a week after the funeral, he told Charlie. Charlie's response, particularly where money was involved, was really helpful. In his view, the best thing that John should do was to have a holiday and begin to recover from his sad loss.

"What you need to do, old lad, is to get away for a week or even a fortnight. Have a break and sort out in your own mind what you want to do next. Don't forget that tomorrow is the first day of the rest of your life. Start as you intend to carry on."

John nodded. He really was so lucky to have Charlie as a mate. He always seemed to talk such sense and make John laugh as well.

"Have you ever been abroad before?"

John had, although it was a long time ago. It was when he was still at school and had spent a week in Italy with his parents. During his time there, they had visited the famous city of Venice. He remembered thinking at the time that it must have rained very heavily during the previous week because all the pavements and streets were flooded. Then two or three years later, he had gone to the Isle of Man with the Boys Brigade for a fortnight but he wasn't sure if that counted.

"Where would you suggest I go, Charlie, and will I need to get a passport?"

"I wouldn't suggest going too far, not for your first trip. And if you are going away for no more than a fortnight, you can borrow our Paul's passport. He's not going anywhere this year."

Always so helpful, that Charlie.

"John, here is my suggestion. Why don't you go to Amsterdam? It's a lovely city and would suit you down to the ground because you know what Amsterdam is famous for, don't you?"

"Oh aye, windmills, people wearing clogs and riding round on old-fashioned bikes," said John, quite innocently.

"You missed the best bit out, John. Yodellaio. There's plenty of that in Amsterdam, you know."

"Yodellaio."

"Did you know that all the photographs of the women on this calendar were taken in Amsterdam?"

"Really?"

"Are you interested then?"

John of course said yes. How could he even think of any other answer?

"The best way to go there John, is not on your own. The best way is to go with a big bunch of mates."

Didn't Charlie always talk a load of sense?

"Have you been left plenty dosh, then?"

"The solicitor said it was over ten thousand pounds."

"Did your mother have it all in socks and shirts?"

"She must have."

THE DOUBLE DUTCH HOLIDAY FUND

"Why don't you put a thousand quid into an account called the Double Dutch Holiday Fund, half for going there and half for coming back? You can put the rest of the money in a deposit account, where it will attract a higher rate of interest. Then, for a fortnight you can do what that woman from Castleford did; spend, spend, spend."

He really was clever, Charlie, suggesting a great way to spend money and yet have even more when he came back. In fact with all the interest, the longer he was away, the more there would be to come back to.

"So here's the deal, John. You know whenever you come in here, you always have a good laugh? Well, how would you fancy having a good laugh all day, every day for a fortnight? For a thousand pounds, you could take us lot to Amsterdam with you. It will be unbelievable. You pay for the trip and the lodgings and we'll buy the ale and after two weeks, you'll be like a new man."

John nodded keenly. He had never been on a holiday like this with a bunch of mates before. He remembered the first time he had ever gone on an outing. It had been in 1968 with the Machine Shop, down to London to watch the Challenge Cup Final. That had been the one between Leeds and Wakefield Trinity, the famous Water Splash Final, so called because of the heavy rain that had poured down during the game. His mother had suggested that as it was his first trip to the capital, he should dress well for the event and so, the previous week, he had bought an expensive suit at John Colliers. All dressed up to the nines, the group had gone to London on the Friday morning and stayed in a hotel near Lord's cricket ground. After walking round Oxford Street and Piccadilly on Saturday morning, they had arrived at the stadium in good time to enjoy the community singing and the pre-match entertainment. Their seats were on the front row between the try-line and the twenty-five, but shortly after the game started, the heavens opened and they all got absolutely drenched.

On the way out of the ground, John had got separated from the others and finished up back at the hotel, still wringing wet an hour later. He had a meal in the restaurant, during which time the waiter had suggested that he hung up his new suit in the Boiler Room, the hottest place in the hotel. Dressed in his pyjamas, John had done that and gone back to his room to wait for all the others to return. Inevitably he fell asleep and didn't wake up until seven the following morning. He went down to check on his still damp suit, returned to his room and fell asleep again.

Around half past nine, the lad he had been sharing a room with, and who had spent all night in somebody else's bed, returned. He woke John up with the news that they only had half an hour to get to Euston Station. But when John rushed down to the basement to collect his suit, it had gone. Somebody had pinched it and so he had travelled across London and then back to Ashurst on the train, wearing his pyjamas.

ONE SUMMER

At the start of the following season, the lads in the Machine Shop had invited him to go on another outing with them, this time to the Boulevard in Hull to watch the Saints play the famous Black and Whites. He had certainly enjoyed that game. Well, he had until he had fallen asleep on the back seat of the coach and finished up being turfed off at the Ribble bus garage in Preston at midnight.

"Now listen John, don't tell anybody else about this holiday. You know what them bloody mechanical lot are like. If they find out there's summat like this going for free, they'll all be wanting to come."

John now had a big grin on his face. This was going to be great but he still had plenty of work to do. So he picked up his note pad, his bunch of R211 forms and his little black bag and departed. Just as he opened the office door, Charlie shouted out.

"John, Yodellaio every night for a fortnight."

"Yodellaio," was the response.

However, by the time they all had their evening meal, talked to their wives, played with their children and read the evening paper, it had begun to sink in that the holiday was a non-starter and in the end the trip never did go ahead. It was John's Auntie Marlene who firmly put the kibosh on it, convincing John that such a large group of men heading for that den of iniquity would no doubt attract the attention of the Dutch police. They would probably be suspected of carrying drugs, would no doubt be detained and possibly strip-searched. And out of respect for his dearly departed mother, he ought to have a longer period of mourning and finish it by visiting a more suitable holiday resort like Morecambe, where temptations were not to be found stood around on every street corner. And to make sure he didn't come under the influence of Charlie Eccleston any more, she convinced him to put all the money from the will into her bank account and spend more time deciding which charities would be the best to make donations to.

"So what would you have done if you'd won all that brass?" Charlie had asked Alan, after John had told them that the trip was off.

"If I was single I'll tell you what I'd have done. I'd have gone travelling round the parts of France where I once went hitch-hiking when I was an apprentice and see how much things had changed. And I would look up some of the ladies who had fed me at breakfast time, after a night of scintillating bilingual conversation."

"Not a very good idea is that," said Mick.

"My neighbour's lad was on holiday in France five years ago. By all accounts, he had a hell of a good time. Anyway last month, he went there again and finished up one evening in the same hotel where he had once slept with one of the chambermaids. After he had had his evening meal, who should appear but this girl again, not looking quite as smart as before, since she was now five years older. She shakes his hand, kisses him on both cheeks, and asks him how long he was staying. He told her he was there for a week, and when she said 'tres bon', he was sure that what had happened before was going to happen again. Then she told him to wait there for her to return in an hour's time, after she had finished work.

"They had a few drinks. She told him that she had often thought about him and how nice he had been to her before. She now lived in a house that was only a ten minute walk away and invited him to go back there with her. So, arm-in-arm and thinking that he was due for another grand night of pleasure and passion, she took him home. When they arrived at the house, she opened the front door and ushered him into the front room. She disappeared for a few minutes before returning, holding the hand of a small boy about four years old. 'Anton, dit bonjour a ton papa.' Turning to the lad, she said 'This is your son, Anton'.

"While he was reeling from the shock, she continued, 'He also has a leetle twin brother. Pierre is his birth name. With this moment, he is on the maison de son grandmere. But in one hours he is by here'."

"So what did the lad do then?"

"I'm not quite sure. All I know is that the day after he came home, he went into hiding somewhere on t'other side of Bolton and nobody in Platt Bridge has seen him since."

2.

The tea lady from Leigh

THE FOUR MAIN characters in the Electrical Section of Wilkinson's Drawing Office, listed in terms of length of service, were Mick Henderson from Platt Bridge, Charlie Eccleston from Thatto Heath, Sam Holroyd, usually called Yorky because he originally came from Mytholmroyd near Halifax, and Alan Greenall, a local lad from Chisnall Avenue in Ashurst, a town believed by many to be the original birthplace of Western civilisation.

Mick was a bit of a naturalist. The things that he most liked to do were the things that came naturally to him, like having forty winks whenever he felt tired. This meant having a little nap just after the morning tea break and most afternoons, returning from the canteen. It was then that one of his mates would often tie Mick's leg to the leg of his reference table with a piece of string. Then, whenever he was woken by the ringing of the phone or when somebody shouted out that he was wanted on the phone, as he got up off his stool, he would pull the table with him and fall in a heap onto the floor.

He had joined the firm in 1946 after he had been demobbed from the Royal Navy. He had not intended to stay that long. It was over eight miles to travel there every day from his mother's house at Ince, not far from the centre of Wigan. But after he got married, he and his wife, a former beauty queen from Hindley Green, bought a house at Platt Bridge. Not now having to go that extra mile every day, he decided to stay and he was now part of the furniture. He was a keen Rugby League fan, having made his first visit to Central Park in 1929. Now turned sixty, he was a proud grandfather, with a daughter-in-law from the picturesque Dutch village of Volendam and a clever little grandson who could speak Dutch, French and English with a Wigan accent.

Charlie Eccleston was the office comedian. Rarely did a day go by that he didn't make somebody laugh. He was a past master at telling stories, usually with some compelling punchline. Many were about the time he had been an apprentice at the Pilkington glass works at Ravenhead. After he had got married, he had lived in the same street in Thatto Heath, in which the St Helens and Great Britain half-back Alex Murphy had grown up.

As a boy, Charlie had played in many Challenge Cup finals that had been held in nearby Taylor Park. However, his career as a Rugby League superstar had been interrupted by the outbreak of war. On returning relatively unscathed from active service in 1945, he had gone back to work at Pilks as a maintenance electrician. A year later, he had signed on for the amateur side Uno's Dabs, but, having a sidestep as good as Stan McCormick's, the speed of Frank Carlton, the ball-handling skills of Alan Prescott and the tackling style of Duggie Greenall, he only managed to get selected for half a dozen games in his first season, before breaking his leg.

This put paid to his career and he had gone back to watching the game . Before long, he began to develop an interest in the thirteen-a-side code and for the next thirty years he kept promising to all and sundry that one day he would write the most definitive history of the greatest game. Not too far off retiring, he had now decided to wait until he was an old age pensioner before he could find the time to start it.

Sam Holroyd had joined the company in 1952. His parents came from Egypt, which is quite near to Queensbury, which stands high up on the mountain range that divides the town of Halifax from the city of Bradford. A month after he was born his parents had moved to Dunkirk, which is two miles west of Halifax town centre, and later on to Mytholmroyd, which is not far from Hebden Bridge. During the war he had served in the Merchant Navy, sailing on convoys taking supplies to the Russian port of Murmansk in the depths of the Arctic winter. Not surprisingly, he had many tales to tell about those frost-ridden days and nights in temperatures that often dropped below thirty or forty degrees. After the war was over, he continued to sail the Seven Seas until he had been invited to the wedding of an old shipmate in Ashurst Parish Church. There, he had been introduced to the widow of a miner who had been killed in an explosion at the old Havanna pit in Gillarsfield. It was the first time that Sam had been in a church since he left school. It was also the first time he had set foot in Ashurst. Not long after, he went again to get married and become the stepfather of her young son.

Sam had a general interest in sport. As a merchant seaman, his opportunity to watch any sport had been limited, but after he had settled in the town, he had played cricket for the Astley Social Club Second XI, until the pitch had been taken over for the purposes of open cast mining.

Alan Greenall (known as 'Greeno' to his mates) had lived all his life in Ashurst. He had been born on the first day of September in 1939, two days before the start of the Second World War. As a small child, he frequently heard the drone of German aircraft overhead, heading for Liverpool to drop bombs on the city and its docks. He could well remember sitting on many occasions, in the middle of the night, under the living room table and at other times being taken by his Mum to the air raid shelter at the top of Martin Avenue along with his older brother Paul and sister Joan. He had become a Wilkinson's apprentice in 1955 and after a year working on the tools, he had transferred into the Electrical Section of the Drawing Office in 1962.

On the sporting front, he had played soccer for Astley United in the Ashurst Junior League, rugby for Wilkinson's Sports, crown green bowls for Victoria Park and snooker in the hall above Burton's shop in Bridge Street. Like Charlie, he was another keen Saints fan, having first stood in the boys' pen in the late Forties, and counted among his many boyhood heroes such star men as George Parsons, Duggie Greenall, Joe Ball, Ray Cale, Jimmy Stott, Don Gullick, Steve Llewellyn and Alan Prescott.

Over the years there had been many other draughtsmen who the four of them had worked alongside: firstly there was Stan, the war hero who had fought with Montgomery in North Africa and had later taken part in the liberation of the Belsen concentration camp, something which had clearly affected him and which he rarely spoke about. Then there was Len Turner, the trade union man, the one who had convinced and organised the rest of the office into joining the draughtsmens' union, D.A.T.A. And how could anyone forget Les Earnshaw, who had left in 1965 but still remained very much in the public eye, as he had later become a successful author with stories based around his own career as a sheet metal draughtsman.

Then there was Frank Stewart, with his many tales about what went on behind the scenes in the many clubs that he had performed at around the town. On the stage, he was a good singer and an even better impersonator, something that ultimately led to his downfall as he had once been found guilty of impersonating a police officer in Widnes and sent down for eighteen months.

A further blast from the past had been Billy Jones. Billy's claim to fame was that he had played rugby league for three clubs, all of which were now defunct. He had started as a seventeen-year-old with St Helens Recs during their final season in 1938. After the war, he had played for Liverpool Stanley for a season before being transferred to Belle Vue Rangers. In what proved to be his last game, a rather torrid affair against York, he had started brawling in the tunnel before the teams had even come onto the field. The referee had thus warned him, even before he had stepped foot onto the pitch. Unfortunately, Billy had continued his personal feud with the opposing prop at the first scrum and been sent off. For this piece of ungentlemanly conduct, he was banned for ten matches and never played again.

In the Drawing Office, what was particularly annoying about him was the way he used to smoke all day and even worse his tendency to leave his tab ends in the most unlikely places. This was something that Mick had discovered to his cost when he returned one day from the canteen to discover that AO drawing he had been working on had just been reduced to ashes.

More recently there had been Jake, the one who was always getting into trouble with the women. After leaving Wilkinson's, he had drifted around. It was a pity he hadn't found something a little less productive to do, because at the age of twenty-seven, he was now the father of four children, all with different women, one in Ashurst, one in Rainhill, another in Goose Green and one in Paris where he had gone to an art exhibition and spent a week painting the town red, in more ways than one. He was also currently involved in a divorce case with a fifty-one-year-old headmistress and her bank manager husband who lived in a large detached house in Chester.

Other draughtsmen from the past that they often talked about included Tony, now managing a pub in Halifax, one which his Dad had bought as a result of a large win on the pools. Tony was the social secretary, masseur and coach to a womens' rugby team, who used the pub as their headquarters and social centre. Another old mate was John, the guitarist from Prescot and one time friend of John Lennon, Noel, who used to play the trombone in the Salvation Army Band until he had become a Buddhist monk in South London, and Kevin, who, six months after he had started working in the Drawing Office, had left and joined the Fire Brigade.

One great name from the past was someone who never used to spend more than ten minutes in their office every day. It was the font of all knowledge, scandal and gossip, their old tea lady Joan. She was well known for her incorrect use of the English language, deliberate or otherwise. Her best comments included a description of an octopus in a glass tank in the museum at Blackpool Tower, which in her words, "used its long testicles to catch smaller fish with". Another of her comments was around the time that the French State Railways (S.N.C.F.) had placed an order with Wilkinson's for what, in her words, was "some railway electrocution equipment".

Back in the Sixties, just after she had moved temporarily from her home town of Leigh to live with her sister Alice in Ashurst, she had worked as a barmaid in that den of iniquity, the Hyde Bank Arms on Billinge Road. There she had really made a name for herself around the time of the start of the 1961 season. On that particular Saturday evening it had been very busy, as two of the other barmaids and the manager hadn't turned up. Dashing around to serve one person after another, Joan had been heard to utter those memorable words, "I wish this bloody place was self-service!"

Around six o' clock, two coaches had pulled into the car park, one carrying members of an amateur rugby league club from Rochdale. They had spent the afternoon at Haydock Park. The other had brought in members of a rugby union team from the Midlands, returning home after playing Preston Grasshoppers. For no apparent reason, both groups had taken an instant dislike to each other and before long it was clear that a punch-up was about to take place. If the manager Frank had been there, being an eighteen stone former professional wrestler, he would easily have sorted them all out. But he had gone to Wilderspool that afternoon to watch Warrington play Leeds and had been held up. It was later discovered that he had been held up by three policemen following a small altercation he had had with a coachload of

Loiners. In his absence, Joan, only five foot four tall and around eight stone nothing, found herself in charge. As the tension had begun to rise, she had climbed on to a chair in the middle of the bar and, flourishing her umbrella, had laid down the law, much to everybody's amusement.

As the two groups edger closed towards each other, she had jumped down from the chair and went straight towards the loud-mouthed Brummie captain. As he continued to laugh at her, she had shouted out, "They Shall Not Pass" and hit him over the head with her brolly, causing him to collapse in a heap. The reason that she had used those words was probably because the previous nights she had been watching a TV documentary about the Spanish Civil War and had been particularly moved by the fighting spirit of La Pasionaria, the heroine of Madrid, Dolores Ibarruri. Her action immediately found favour with all the Rochdale lads and most of the other team too, since none of them seemed to like their solicitor captain, Nigel. And from then on, a good night had been enjoyed by all.

That was one version of the evening's events. It had been a very drunken affair, and nobody was absolutely sure exactly what had taken place. A slightly different version was that after lambasting everyone from the chair, Joan had then stood in front of the door leading to the gents' toilet, brandishing her umbrella and shouted out something like, "They shall not pass water", or maybe the more obvious shorter version.

Without doubt, Joan was the best tea lady the Drawing Office had ever had although, as they were to discover, a younger, equally loquacious, much better looking and intellectually high-powered one was soon to appear in the shape of the lovely Hazel Hutton from Earlestown.

But of all those who had ever worked in the D.O., it was Thelma Johnson, the one time mysterious and secretive office girl and orphan from Cardiff, originally nicknamed Freckles, Ban the Bomb and, most cruelly, the Little Welsh Dresser, who they talked most about. But this was because in 1965 she had changed her name to Thelma Greenall, and was now the wife of Greeno and the mother of his two children, Rebecca and Robert.

Others whose names often cropped up in their reminiscences about the past were the various bosses they had worked under: people like Alan Groves ('Grovesy'), who had had been their section leader for years and really was an O.K. guy. Just as popular had been John Tunstall, the former Transport Manager, who was always wanting to take somebody for a ride in more ways than one. He was now living in a home in Crewe where he was driving the staff and all who lived there mad.

Most of the other bosses they had had though, were a quite different kettle of fish; Basil Wilkinson had probably been the worst, right from the time when he had taken over after his father suffered a heart attack at the end of 1962. A man with a similar inability to behave like a human was Stephen

THE TEA LADY FROM LEIGH

Williams, Basil's University chum, who Basil had made Managing Director. He had got away with murder until 1966, when he had finally blotted his copybook. While everybody else was watching England beat Germany at Wembley in the World Cup, he had run off to Blackpool with a sixteen-year-old-girl from the Wages Office. In the same league was J. Arthur (you can't do enough for a good firm) Wood, once the Assistant Chief Draughtsman and commonly known as Lurch.

In the summer of 1963, the firm had been sold, in rather strange circumstances, to the Miller Engineering and Construction Company from Cleveland in America. There had then been a strange collection of individuals running the show. The first to arrive were The Three Stooges, three aged Ivy League boys who didn't stay long and were succeeded by Mr. Winston Z. Cypanski, whose mentor would appear to have been Al Capone. He didn't last long either and had been recalled to base after the fiasco known as the Storming of Stafford Gates. Two very cultured American gentlemen, both of whom, quite independently, knew how to say please and thank you and who seemed to spend most of their time keeping an eye on what the other was doing, were next. They ran up an enormous joint expense account visiting such industrial centres as Harrogate, Stratford-on-Avon, Bath, York, Spurn Point and Morecambe. Then had come Wilbur from Idaho, the one who specialised in setting up little committees and holding meetings that never resolved anything.

But they had had more than their fair share of English-bred and educated buffoons, like Basil's two brothers, Cyril the Meddler and Norman the Do Gooder. There had also been Lady Phillipa Delcourt, whose husband worked at the Foreign Office and had important contacts all over the world. She had been given a lucrative contract by Basil for no obvious technical or commercial reason and was for a while seen as the power behind the throne, or more bluntly the power under the bedsheets. She had been made responsible for organising a wide range of publicity leaflets, most of which showed photographs of herself with technical information about the company's various products. She was ten years younger than Basil and, for a fiftysomething, a stunning beauty, a pure English rose with blondish hair that draped over her shoulders, pure blue eyes, an endearing smile and a beautiful pair of hands. These were highlighted frequently in the photographs taken in various select locations along the South Coast by a French photographer called Jules. His work was really top class although his photographs never showed Phillipa's hands dipping into the company's accounts or writing cheques to an expensive health club in Chelsea where she spent much time making contact with important people in the City and the Government. It later transpired most of these were all fit, well-spoken, young men who played rugger for teams like Wasps, Harlequins, Saracens and the Old Fartonians of Twickenham.

ONE SUMMER

One of the recurrent topics of conversation in the Drawing Office was the Second World War. Charlie had fought at El Alamein in the Eighth Army, Mick, along with another 1300 crew members, had served on the battleship H.M.S. Rodney and taken part in the hunt for the Bismarck and Sam's service in the Merchant Navy was legendary. Alan had never been asked to fight for his country; he had not even been called up to do his National Service. Well, he had been called up but had been granted a deferment until he had finished his apprenticeship. By the time he had come out of his time, National Service had finished. His family however had made the ultimate sacrifice. In 1944, his father, Arthur John Greenall, had died from injuries received in the bitter fighting around Monte Cassino, one of over a hundred thousand Allied troops killed or wounded in the liberation of Italy.

Throughout his early life, the two big influences on Alan had been his grandparents. His Grandad, Edward Holding, had been the one who had interested Alan most in knowing about the Great War. 'Ned' had many stories to tell, having been among the first men in Ashurst to volunteer in August 1914. But after only a few weeks in the trenches, he and large numbers of the South Lancashire (Prince of Wales Volunteers) Regiment, had been captured and had spent the rest of the war working down a lead mine for the enemy at Neuruppindorf, in what was then known as Prussia.

In the Second World War, his Uncle Stan had seen active service as a Desert Rat in North Africa and then had fought in the Italian campaign. His Uncle Jack had served in the Navy on the battleship H.M.S. Victorious. He had also been involved in the fight against fascism much earlier. His experiences during the General Strike and then during the Depression in the Thirties had led to him joining the International Brigade and fighting for the Spanish Republic against the dictator General Franco.

But totally opposed to anything to do with war and killing, an even bigger influence on him and the rest of the Greenall and Holding family had been his grandmother. Mary Isabella Tabern had been born in 1891. Now slowly losing her eyesight but certainly not her marbles, she lived in the Greenfield Old Peoples' Home in Dob Lane, where, in her own words, she was being treated as though she was the Queen of England.

In the past, whenever any of her grandchildren had asked her what was her job when she was a young girl, she would usually tell them that she had never worked. Did that make her one of the idle rich? Did that mean that she was just plain lazy or did it mean that she was not good enough to find employment? But her saying that she had never worked was one great lie. When she was eleven, her own mother had passed away and after that, Mary had stopped going to school and became the little mother for the rest of the family. From then on, until after she had nursed the young Welsh orphan, Thelma Johnson, back to health during the early months of that terrible winter of 1963, she had never really stopped working. Even now, living in the home, she would often offer to side the table or help with the washing up, particularly whenever any of the young care assistants looked tired or said that they had a nice young man to meet later that evening. But then, as they say, old habits always die hard.

It was not surprising, therefore, that other members of the Drawing Office or managers or men who worked on the shop floor, would often ask about her health, for it had been the way in which she had cared for young Thelma the orphan girl from South Wales, that made the name of Mrs. Holding from Silkstone Street synonymous with all that is good in humanity itself.

3.

Beware the Pattern Shop girls

THE WILKINSON ENGINEERING Works had always been the largest factory in the town since work had first started on the old Atherton Lane site in 1819. The first major bit of engineering had been the manufacture of water pumping machinery for the nearby Havanna colliery. One hundred years later, the Prime Minister, Lloyd George had officially opened the company's Newall Research Laboratory. Here Basil's grandfather had experimented long and hard on the use of gas for industrial purposes, ultimately with disastrous results, blowing both the laboratory to smithereens and himself into the next world. As a result of this unfortunate occurrence, Basil's father, Joshua Albert George Wilkinson D.S.O., had assumed full control in 1926. One of his first decisions was to buy and then have demolished the adjacent Smethurst Rubber Works, thus allowing room for Wilkinson's Copper Rolling Mill and Machine Shop to be built.

Many former employees of Smethursts had then moved over to Wilkinson's. The 'Rubber Men' as they were known, brought with them a culture that embraced innovative technical skill, above average fertility and excessive humour. One of the best known was their Managing Director, inebriated for ninety percent of the week, technically brilliant for the remainder. However, among those who didn't quite make the grade was one 'Rubberman' who was sacked after being found sleeping on night turn in the Refinery Manager's office, twice on the same night. Another had been asked to leave the company at short notice after letting two mice loose in the Wages Office, following a disagreement about his overtime. A third went out one Friday morning to pay a group of fitters who were working at a substation in Oldham. He did not arrive and, along with the money, was never seen again.

As the firm had expanded, the town of Ashurst had grown around it, although it continued to be dwarfed by the surrounding larger towns of St Helens, Wigan, Leigh and Warrington. Because of the influence of the 'Rubber Men', it had acquired quite a reputation throughout Lancashire for varying reasons, so much so that by the time Basil had taken over in 1962, it was generally known as a place where something was always happening, humorous, dramatic or just plain daft.

Due to the managerial style of most of the old guard, there was always some issue on the boil or some scandal unfolding. And like in most big

24

factories at the time, playing tricks was part and parcel of the place, all of which accounted for why Wilkinson's was also known as 'Butlins'.

There were of course tricks and *tricks*. Category One tricks were those played on a mate, ones that did not harm him, but something that everybody could laugh at. Category Two tricks were more serious, they were played on bosses or on someone who nobody liked. They were not only played within the walls of the factory either. They were often played away from work, maybe at the works dance or on an office outing or just when the opportunity presented itself, because with Ashurst being quite a small town, inevitably word would quickly get around as it always did.

Barry Lowe was an electrician in the Works Maintenance Shop. He had suffered more than his fair share of trickery over the years, but that had been all his own fault, due to the bad attitude he had always shown towards the people he came into daily contact with. One of these was the storeman, John Sunderland, who suffered with a speech impediment. Except for that, he was a good worker and got on well with everybody he had to deal with, except for Mr. Lowe, who continually imitated and embarrassed the lad in the presence of others. Finally, John was presented with a great chance to get his own back. Since he worked in the stores, he knew what jobs every electrician was working on, and so he knew who was requesting more equipment than he needed. With Barry, it was well known that he always wanted twice as much cable as any other electrician.

One evening on his way home from work, John noticed that Barry's van was parked in Carlton Lane, outside a large house that was being renovated. In the front garden was a board, which stated that all the electrical work was being carried out by Lowe Electrics. This firm was owned by Barry's brother and for whom Barry worked in the evening and at the weekend. A few days later Barry had to go to Aberthaw Power Station in South Wales to install a piece of electrical switchgear. That evening, John had stuck up a second board in the garden. On it he had written, 'All electrical cables for this house renovation have been provided freely by Wilkinson Engineering Ltd. who can be contacted at 27 Warrington Road, Ashurst'.

On another occasion Barry had nailed an apprentice's jacket to the wall. When the lad had pulled it off the hook, it had ripped in two. All the other 'sparkies' immediately ganged up on Barry and forced him to buy the lad a new jacket. A few weeks later, the apprentice managed to get his own back. On his seventeenth birthday, he had brought in a box of cakes that his mother had baked. On each one, she had put the initials of the intended recipient in icing sugar. When 'Bungalow' saw the letters BL, he grabbed it and scoffed it down. Not much was seen of him for the rest of the day because among the ingredients for his cake, and his cake alone, were three crushed laxative tablets.

Barry was indeed a rare animal. Among some people he came into contact with, he acted as though he was the champion of the underdog, the conscience of the nation and a firm believer in Christian principles. At other times, he behaved as though his political inspiration was Genghis Khan and on odd occasions he acted as though he was Genghis Khan. He was also a member of Ashurst Labour Party and when a vacancy had appeared for a candidate to stand in the local elections, Barry had put his name forward.

Along with three other hopefuls, he was asked to give a short speech to the selection committee to explain why he should be chosen. He began by calling everybody comrade, and outlined the contribution he could make for the people of West Central ward. He said that ever since he had been a child, he had always wanted to make the world a fairer place. He concluded by stating that what had guided him throughout his whole life had been his strong socialist convictions. Unfortunately for Barry, one of those present had been at school and then an apprentice with Barry and knew what he was really like. By the time Barry had mentioned his socialist convictions for the fourth time, his old school mate had heard enough. He burst out laughing and shouted out, to the amusement of all those in attendance:

"Socialist, my arse! You're not even bloody sociable. You wouldn't even help an old lady cross the street or tell somebody the time unless they paid you."

This intervention did not help Barry win the votes of the undecided members present. In fact at the end of the meeting, the only vote he received was his own.

Another example of trickery, if trickery is defined in the broadest possible way, were the incidents involving what became known as The Mystery Voice. Every few weeks a foreman would receive a phone call from what sounded like and what the foreman assumed to be, the boss. Basil Wilkinson was well known for the curt way in which he relayed his messages and instructions to those he employed. Quite often they seemed somewhat senseless or a pure waste of time, the most notable being 'his' instructions to have the old Apprentice Training School painted just four weeks before large brass castings were to be moved from the back of the Rolling Mill to the hut behind the Joiners' Shop. What was strange about this instruction, which required the efforts of two labourers and a fork lift truck for a whole day, was that for the last three years, until about a month ago, the castings had been enjoying their retirement in that self-same hut.

Tricks were also regularly played on J. Arthur Wood, who was in charge of the Research Laboratory, which was actually in two parts. The original one, built in 1923, was located in the middle of the factory. The new one, which was less than a year old, was at the far end, overlooking the Ashurst to Leigh railway line. To get from one to the other, it was possible to go two ways. The quickest was past the Gatehouse, onto Liverpool Road for four hundred yards and back into the factory through the gates, which were to Lindsay's Pie Shop. The other way was through the factory. This route was longer but a better way to go when it was raining.

All the heavy duty test machinery had been installed in the new lab, which was where Lurch spent most of his week. But many technicians were still based in the old laboratory. As a result, every day, Lurch. called in to see what was being done there. On these occasions, someone in the new lab would ring up the old lab, warning them that Lurch was on his way and informing them which route he was taking. At this point, those who had good reason to visit the new lab would do so and of course they would go by the opposite route. As a result, whenever Lurch walked into the old lab, he would usually find that the place was almost empty.

One morning, a warning was received that Lurch was coming through the factory. Immediately half a dozen technicians, all wearing their white smocks and carrying pieces of metal for tensile testing, left the building, walked past the Gatehouse and then at twenty yard intervals stepped on to Liverpool Road. Then, horror of horrors, there was Lurch on his way towards them, with a face as black as thunder. He had either changed his mind on which route to take or finally worked it out why he had never seen some of his staff for over a month. Anybody who lived on Liverpool Road and looking out of their front room window at that moment would probably have thought that somebody was making a film about the place.

The old adage, "They should write a book about this place. it'd be a bestseller" was very true of the largest factory in Ashurst. If somebody could make a film about it, they would no doubt have made a fortune. But it would have had trouble getting past the film censors, if it included any of the Pattern Shop Girls who worked in the Iron or Brass Foundry, girls like Nymphy Norma the chargehand or Rough Rita and her two sisters in grime. Two years earlier in 1977 on the occasion of the Queen's Silver Jubilee, Basil Wilkinson had sent a note round to all departments suggesting that all his employees should dress in the most appropriate way to mark the great occasion. On the day in question, a sheet of paper had been pinned up on the Social Club noticeboard, next to the foremens' office stating that:

TO CELIBRATE THIS GRATE DAY, THE PATTERN SHOP
GURLS ARE WURRING NO NIKERS

Then there had been that occasion on Christmas Eve back in 1962, just before the onset of one of the worst winters in living memory. Coming back from the pub at lunchtime, a young apprentice had been told by his foreman to go over to the Foundry Pattern Shop where one of the girls had something for him. When he walked into the place, he discovered that it was Martha, sat there on the bench all alone, idly swinging her legs.

"Have you got something for me?" he had asked a little nervously.

"I certainly have," she said, licking her lips seductively. "Come into the office. I've been keeping it in my drawers for you."

The office she referred to was not really an office. It was just a large storeroom, where the records of every wooden pattern that had been made there since 1913 were kept. As soon as the lad entered the room, six other girls appeared from nowhere and proceeded to remove all his clothes and rub Vaseline and Swarfega all over his private parts, followed by large handfuls of iron filings and wet sand. Then one had climbed up a ladder, put his clothes on a high shelf and moved the ladder out of sight.

Then there was Dolores, who was always prepared to carry out some dare, as long as there was a bit of money to be made: like the time she had bet a couple of members of the works soccer team that, for a shilling each, they would find her having a shower in their dressing room at the end of their next home game. It was no big deal really, it wouldn't have been the first time that most of the team had not already seen her in her birthday outfit. With about ten minutes to go before the end of the match, she had come out of the Social Club, where she had spent the afternoon drinking, gone into the showers and stripped off. What she didn't know was that the away team dressing room was being painted so the home team had changed in the canteen that day. Thus it was now in the dressing room of the away team that she was soaping her naked body. Her presence came as quite a shock to the members of St Luke's Parish Church team as they returned from an eight-nil drubbing and particularly shocked their centre half, a new curate who had just arrived in his new post from a well-heeled parish in Surrey.

Yes, it was true that the Pattern Shop girls were considered a bit rough by many people. Well, they probably were by those who held more socially acceptable views on alcohol, cigarettes, bad language, sex before marriage or outside marriage or anywhere else in some cases. But they weren't all bad, not by a long chalk. Three people who had more reason to thank them for their kindness and thoughtfulness were Mrs. Jackson and her two young children Paul and Simon. Their father, a self-employed window cleaner, had broken his leg playing rugby for Gillarsfield Labour Club in a 'friendly' against East Ashurst Social Club a couple of months earlier. His time off work had left the family virtually penniless, so on hearing of their plight, various organisations in the town had offered their help. Ashurst Theatrical Society decided to put on a special performance of *Oklahoma* and give the proceeds to help the family. But with a week to go, ticket sales were very poor. It was then that Nymphy Norma made her suggestion. The following day, posters were put up announcing that the show was to be renamed *Jokelahoma* and would include special appearances by Norma, Dolores and Rough Rita. Passed on by word of mouth was the news that the three girls would be getting up to some of their old tricks. Within three days, all the tickets had been sold.

During the first half of the show, the three girls had played bit parts, but it was made clear to all but the most dumb in the audience that Norma was wearing no knickers. At the start of the second half of the show a scene was included in which Norma played the part of a shop assistant. A young man had walked into her shop and, knowing what had been winked at all through the first half, asks her for two ounces of raisins, knowing that she would have to climb up a ladder to take them from a jar on the top shelf. While she is doing that, he has a quick peep up her skirt. As soon as he had walked out of the shop, his mate comes in and asks for two ounce of raisins and then looks up her skirt as she had climbed up the steps again. When he had left, in comes the main actor, who looks at the audience, tapping his nose, then turns and smiles at Norma.

In a crazy Southern American accent, she shouts out:

"Ah suppose yours is raisin' too."

"No marm," he had replied in an equally bad American accent, "marn's just a twitching at the moment."

The show had carried on with the three girls right in their element, ad libbing in such a way that made it almost impossible to complete the show in the way that had been intended. Despite this, as the curtain came down at the end, there was a tremendous round of applause with many in the audience shouting out for more.

Onto the stage came the compere again and asked the audience to welcome members of the Rochdale Harlots Rugby League team. From the left hand side of the stage came Norma, Rita, Dolores and three other female members of the cast, all wearing red and white hooped jerseys and white shorts, passing a rugby ball to each other.

The compere then asked for more applause for the members of the St. Vitus Dance Rugby League team. On came six male members of the cast from the right hand side of the stage, pirouetting and dancing about as though they were performing *Swan Lake* for the Royal Ballet Company.

The compere, who was now to play the part of the referee, blew his whistle and Norma started the game by kicking the ball to the opposition. Both sides met in the middle of the stage and what occurred then was five minutes of grovelling and messing about. In the corner, one of the men was laid out flat on the stage, as though he had just been stiff-armed. Alongside him was Dolores, giving him a long kiss of life. Then the referee blew his whistle, shouted forward pass and ordered a scrum to be formed. He put the ball in the tunnel and what followed were scenes more reminiscent of a Roman orgy than action from a rugby field.

His next act was to blow his whistle point to Dolores and one of the men, point to the back of the stage and shout out 'early bath'. She had asked where the soap was and then walked off stage with her back to the audience, but in full view was seen to remove her jersey. He blew his whistle again, shouted out "Half-time" and, as the two teams changed ends, the curtain went down. At this point the compere/referee stood in front of the curtain and announced that the next scene would take place in a famous stately home. It would be at somewhere called Thrum Hall, which was in bandit country and where the sun never shone, where the wind always blew and the snow lay six inches deep. And that was in the middle of summer!

As the curtain went up again, large bundles of cotton wool were seen lying all round the stage. The second half was as torrid as the first half had been with plenty of shouting, bawling and more orgy-like scenes. Then two of the girls started backchatting to the referee who sent them both off for an early bath. And before they left the stage, they removed their jerseys and put their arms round each other. Finally the referee blew his whistle for full time and announced to the audience that there were to be two prizes given for the two best players on the field. The first prize would be a day out in Widnes, while the second prize was a weekend in the same exotic coastal location. Then there was a great roll on the drums, followed by the announcement that the winner was Norma. As Norma kissed the compere, Rita shouted out from the back of the stage that her colleague was the best hooker in Ashurst!

Then in typical Rugby League style, the players of both sides shook hands, took their jerseys off and exchanged them. Wow! But not to be outdone and always wanting to steal the show, Dolores also removed her shorts to reveal that she was wearing nothing more than a pair of white ankle socks. Then she had waved the shorts around her head and launched them forth into the audience.

It was perhaps fitting, or symbolic or ironic or platonic, that they only reached as far as the front row and landed on the head of the sixty-two-year-old parish priest from St Theresa's Church. It brought the house down and was later condemned equally strongly by the vicar of Ashurst Parish Church, who had been sat next to him, as an example of religious tolerance and understanding.

Interestingly, a few weeks later, Norma handed in her notice and told everyone that she was going into the acting profession. Most folk thought she was going to London to work as a stripper or maybe even to go on the game, but soon after she was seen on television, playing a minor part in *The Bill*. A bit later she reappeared in *Brookside* and then had a part in the film, *Four Weddings and a Funeral*.

Then there was the incident involving the electrical inspector, Dave Crabtree. One morning, he hadn't finished checking the wiring in an electrical control cubicle before it was due to be loaded onto the back of a lorry. So he had climbed up onto the lorry and gone into the cubicle in order to carry on with his work. As it was still in the depths of winter, he had closed the cubicle door behind him to keep warm. Shortly after a second cubicle had been loaded right up against it. This didn't worry Dave too much since he knew that it was only the forklift driver Reg playing one of his usual tricks.

A few minutes later, the driver switched on the engine and drove off. The cubicle that Dave was now 'imprisoned' in was bound for the ICI chemical works at Widnes, less than seven miles away. Unfortunately a cable drum on the back of the lorry had to be delivered first to the Shotton Steel Works in North Wales. By the time Dave had been able to get off the lorry, he was absolutely frozen. Luckily for him, the second cubicle was bound for the Guandong Cotton Mill in the Chinese city of Shanghai, so with that in mind, Dave felt that he hadn't been too badly done to, although the overtime he would have claimed for a trip to China would no doubt have paid off most of his daughter's clothing debts.

If that wasn't enough, another trick was played on poor Dave on the following Saturday. Dave was approaching his fortieth birthday and over the years had played soccer on and off for his local team, Astley United. In fact, over a period of around fifteen years he had managed to get picked ninety-nine times, but with increasing old age had not been selected or available to play for the last eighteen months. Finally he had one last chance to get into three figures but only because half the team had gone to Amsterdam for the goal keeper's stag weekend. So Dave had managed it. It didn't stop him working that Saturday morning though. He brought his kit into work in a bag he had been carrying round with him for years and left it in the locker room. While he was out on the shop floor, an apprentice, who he had been annoying for weeks, took one of Dave's boots out of his bag and replaced it with something totally unsuitable. That afternoon, Dave had celebrated playing one hundred games for Astley United by slipping around a muddy field wearing on his left foot a boot he had bought in 1965 and on his right foot, an equally old slipper strapped to his foot with a great length of PVC tape!

The following weekend the same apprentice had also got his own back on the foreman of the Wiring Shop. Arthur Lyon was a keen Warrington fan and never missed a home game. He also liked his overtime and regularly worked Saturdays and Sundays. He would book until five o' clock on a Sunday afternoon, although this included the time he had been watching the Wires. Around two o' clock, he would disappear, telling whoever was around that he had work to do elsewhere. On his return, he would make sure everybody was off the premises, lock up, and get paid for those three hours and all at double time. Finally the apprentice, who only received time and a half for working at the weekend, had had enough of it. He waited until quarter to three, fifteen minutes before kick-off and then rang the ground, asking for an urgent announcement to be made for Mr. Arthur Lyon to return to work. Thinking there was a real emergency, Arthur had rushed back, only to find a note on his desk bringing to his attention the fact that his tea was getting cold.

4.

"Auntie Vera is staying
with us for a bit."

"HOW DID YOU get on, last night, Charlie?"

"Do you know that's only the second time in my life that I've ever been to Odsal and not frozen to death."

The previous evening Charlie had driven over the M62 to watch Lancashire Schools play Yorkshire Schools at the famous Odsal Stadium, the home of the Bradford Northern Rugby League club. In the car had been his neighbours, Mr. and Mrs. Harris, the parents of young Keith who was playing on the left wing for the Red Rose team, along with his 'never been known to stop talking' girlfriend, Dawn.

None of his passengers had watched a match before, neither had they ever been in a football or rugby stadium before. So walking through the only open turnstile and seeing Odsal for the first time was a bit of a culture shock for them. Charlie had been there on a number of occasions, but that had always been for a big game. Then there might have been thousands in the ground and on one occasion, the 1954 Challenge Cup Final Replay between Halifax and Warrington, there had been well over one hundred thousand people in attendance. So it was a bit of a shock for him as well to see less than three hundred people dotted around the ground. No music was being played and no announcements were made but when the two teams began to descend the steps from the dressing room, an atmosphere of sorts began to develop among the many mums, dads and girlfriends present.

As was usually the case, whenever Charlie watched a match in Yorkshire the referee would be blessed with defective eyesight or turned up without his glasses. But despite this, the guile and skill of the Lancashire lads outclassed the clumsy play of the big Yorkshire forwards and tackled their backs right out of the game. But all this had been lost on Mr. and Mrs. Harris, who were clearly bored by the whole thing. Dawn showed more interest, but it was obvious that she only had eyes for Keith, even watching him being bandaged-up off the field of play for over five minutes, while his team mates ran in two length of the field tries.

After an away game, while travelling back in a coach or in his car, Charlie would have normally engaged in a deep analysis of the game, the various stages it had gone through, who had played well and who hadn't, the fitness levels of the team, particular acts of great skill etc.

But trying that with these three was something of a waste of time, although Dawn continued to talk all the way back home, not about anything in particular, just using language as a way of exercising the muscles in her face and throat. By the time they arrived back in Thatto Heath, Charlie was exhausted.

Around ten o' clock in walked their tea lady Joan along with the engineer, Ronnie Garner. Knowing where Charlie had been the previous night, Ronnie asked him how well the three St Helens lads had played. Soon the conversation moved on to what Odsal Stadium was like now.

"I bet it's changed a bit since I was last there."

"When was that, Ronnie?"

"That Championship Final against Hunslet in 1959."

"I was at that match," said Alan. "We beat them 44-22. Vollenhoven scored a hat trick, including that great try in the first half."

"I remember that game well," said Charlie. "That try was one of the best I've ever seen and I've seen a few over the years."

Whenever Charlie talked about going to the match or watching his favourite team, he always seemed able to embellish it with some off the field, even off the ground, stories. And so this was a chance to repeat a story he had told them once before.

"We all met in The Springfield in Thatto Heath. There were two coachloads of us. It was before the M62 was built so we went up the East Lancs Road, through Oldham and over the top. When we got to Brighouse, the coach our kid was travelling in was about three cars behind us. I remember going through a place called Bailiff Bridge. It was nearly two o' clock, so we had enough time, although by now the traffic was building up. We went about half a mile further up the road and came to more traffic lights. Just as we went through them, they turned red, so our kid's coach had to stop. By the time we got parked up we could see great long queues outside the turnstiles. So we didn't wait for the other coach to turn up and by the time we got on the terraces, the teams were coming down the steps. Just on half-time, I saw a group of Saints fans pushing past, trying to find a spot. It was our kid's coach party. Just a minute's gap in getting through those lights made him miss the first half."

"I remember going to that replay when Warrington beat Halifax 8-4," said Ronnie. "What a crowd that was. I was working at Ferrantis in Oldham at the time. The lads on our section decided they'd have the afternoon off and go. So about a dozen of us went up to this lad's house and got into his Dad's van. As soon as he managed to get off the drive, we were in a traffic jam. He lived on the main road out of Oldham going towards Yorkshire and all the coaches and cars from Warrington were going past his house, it was bumper to bumper all the way. We got parked up about ten minutes before kick-off and joined the queue to get in. The lad who had been doing the driving was right at the front of us. He was the only one to pay! As he was getting his change, the whole of the turnstile housing collapsed and we all got in for nowt."

"I always liked to go to Thrum Hall for a big game," chipped in Mick. "It's a much smaller ground but whenever it was full, you could always be kept warm by the blokes stood next to you."

"Why, did they let you put your hands on their hot water bottle?"

Talking about games played in Arctic conditions, on the eastern side of the Pennines was always a source of much amusement and entertainment. Probably not too good at the time, if the truth be known, but good to remember in the warmth of the Drawing Office or in a pub or in your own front room. That was why many of the encounters up on the Cumbrian Coast at Whitehaven, Workington or a little nearer home at Craven Park in Barrow were just as entertaining.

"Imagine what it must have been like going to away games before the First World War," said Alan. "Imagine what it must have been like for York going to Mid Rhondda or Aberdare."

"It wouldn't have been that bad," said Charlie. "There wouldn't have been much traffic on the road or any motorway holdups!"

"What about after the Second World War, when Great Britain toured Australia? The players were on the boat for nearly six weeks before they got there. And then travelling across Australia as well and another six weeks on the boat coming back."

"It always amazes me how they organised that first tour by the New Zealanders in 1906. You know, when Louis Baskerville was in charge. I bet you didn't know they even brought a kangaroo with them."

"I know when they came to St Helens, it died," said Mick.

"So what did they do with it?" asked Colin. "Eat it or bury it?"

"I can remember the Aussies coming over at the start of the 1939 season," said Mick. "They only played two games and then had to go back home because the Second World War had started."

"Haven't you lot finished your teabreak yet. It's nearly eleven o' clock."

It was Joan, back to take their cups away. "I wish I was a draughtsman. What an easy life I would have."

"If you were a draughtsman, Joan, what would you wear? Would it be a frock or a smock?"

The reason for Charlie's question was because of the recent introduction of a new dress code for all draughtsmen. Now they were expected to wear a white smock at work and so, inevitably, whenever they were down on the shop floor they would hear one of the electricians or fitters or wiremen shout out:

"Doctor, doctor, I'm feeling a little funny. Can you come and feel my pulse?"

"How much are your ice creams?"

"I don't think Graham thinks any of these stories are very funny," said Mick, as he placed his cup on Joan's trolley.

"What do you think, Joan? Do you think we are funny in here?"

"Do you know what all the girls in the canteen call this place? The funny farm."

Graham had only recently started work at Wilkinson's. He came from St Albans, a town some forty miles north of London, where most of his family lived in a totally different environment to the one he was 'enjoying' now, lodging in Vincent Street in the middle of St Helens. He had been pretty quiet during his first few weeks, although, as it became clear later, that was because he couldn't understand half of what they were talking about. He was not interested in sport, didn't drink and always went out on his own at lunchtime for a long walk. But on the plus side he had replied very positively on his first morning, when Charlie had asked him if he was in the union. When he told them that he had been a member since 1949 and had once been a branch secretary, their opinion of him had gone up immediately. Later on, as they got to know him better, he had become an important member of the Drawing Office both on the technical and the social side.

"What do you think of all our tales about the old days and all the characters who have worked here? We never seem to put a smile on your face."

"I smile inwardly, Mick, both at your conversational style and your new suit."

"Nice one Graham, we've been laughing at that since 1965."

The most interesting thing about Graham was his use of language. At first they though he was a bit stuck-up because of the way he spoke, without a trace of an accent. But then that might be due to the fact that round where he lived, that's how people spoke. But on the other hand, the clever and subtle way he used words was a joy to listen to. He also had a wide repertoire of sayings, and was always defining words or just tacking them on to what the others said; like his definition of ballroom dancing as 'a vertical representation of horizontal desire' or even the word 'conversation' which he defined as a 'monologue in the presence of another'.

"To be honest, Charlie, I've only just begun to understand your Lancashire accents and the other thing is that I don't understand the first thing about rugby."

"It will be rugby union where you come from, Graham. They don't play rugby league in St Albans," said Alan.

"AUNTIE VERA IS STAYING WITH US FOR A BIT"

"I didn't even know there were two games of rugby until I came here. And the chaps who were interested in rugby down there never seemed to get as animated about it like you lot do."

"Well rugby league is more of a working class game up here, whereas it's the middle classes round your way who play rugby union."

"So what did you play when you were at school?" asked Charlie, expecting Graham to say that it had been football and cricket.

"You might be surprised to know that I never went to school after my thirteenth birthday."

"How come?"

"I caught polio and spent a year in hospital and after that my parents were allowed to teach me at home."

"I'm sorry about that, old lad. I didn't know."

"I was lucky in a way because they were both teachers. My Dad taught me Maths and Science and my mother taught me Geography, History and English Literature. Our next door neighbours were Swiss, so I also learned French and German from them and they sent a teacher to come to see me once a week to make sure everything was going all right."

"Didn't you get a bit bored being at home all day, you know, having no mates to knock about with?

"I had three good friends who used to come round every week or so. And the girl from next door often used to give me my French lessons."

"What, in French kissing?" laughed Alan.

"Oh, there was none of that. She was very religious. Later on, I heard that she had started doing missionary work in Africa."

"So you didn't have much contact with the opposite sex then, while you were growing up?"

"I suppose it was a case of 'out of sight, out of mind' at first and my friends didn't seem too interested either. One spent most of his time building model aircraft, another had a chemistry lab in his Dad's garage and was always making fireworks and the third was dead keen on trainspotting."

"Another Greeno," laughed Mick.

Their conversation was halted with the arrival of John Battesby, the Chief Draughtsman, telling them that a new system for filling out their timesheets was going to be introduced by the powers-that-be. It seemed a little complicated and was summed up adequately by Charlie, when he asked John whether he was going to give them a job number for filling out timesheets. So it was the following day, before Graham told them a bit more about his unusual education as a teenager.

"It was just after my sixteenth birthday. My general health was getting much better but my doctor thought it would be best if I stayed at home, rather than go back to school a few weeks before the exams started. And then one evening, my mother told me something that was soon to lead to my education moving into a whole new field."

"Your Auntie Vera is coming to stay with us for a bit."

With a smile on his face, he asked them if they wanted to hear about her.

They all nodded, perhaps anticipating that they were going to hear a good story. Well, they were.

"She was my mother's younger sister and had been working as a teacher in Brighton until her and her husband had split up.

"She was quite plumpish, in a nice sort of way, very friendly and prone to sitting right close to me on the settee, when the four us were watching the television. She also used to help me a lot with English Literature, which was her main subject.

"After a few weeks, my parents went to Coventry for a trade union weekend school. It was then that Auntie Vera came fully into her own, as I was soon to pleasantly discover. I had spent most of Saturday in my bedroom revising but by teatime I had had enough. She had been out shopping and then in the kitchen, preparing our evening meal and baking a cake. She told me to put all my books away and get ready for dinner. We ate the meal, talked a lot and drank a bottle of wine between us as well. Then she said that it was time for us both to relax after a hard day's work and suggested that we should play some games, starting with Scrabble.

"While I was getting the Scrabble out, she went upstairs and came back wearing a white shirt, a short red skirt, white ankle socks, black trainers and a headband. She looked great and she knew it. I couldn't take my eyes off her. Anyway we played a few games and she won every time. Then she told me to put the Scrabble away and come and sit next to her on the settee. What should we play next, she said. How about hide and seek or pass the parcel or maybe we could play Zenti.

"I told her I had never heard of Zenti. She said it was very popular in Brighton, so Zenti it was to be. I had to lie back, close my eyes and relax. Then she slowly ran her finger over the palm of my hand, up my arm and onto my face. After five minutes of this, she stood up, pulled me up and started walking me round the room, into the hall and up the stairs. But all the time, I had to keep my eyes shut. On the landing, she spun me round three times and led me into one of the bedrooms. She told me to continue to keep my eyes shut, stand facing the wall, with my hands held high and stay there until she told me to move. It seemed a strange game, I remember thinking, but very pleasant. After a couple of minutes, she told me to turn round and open my eyes and lo and behold, we were in my parents' bedroom and would you believe it; Auntie Vera was in the bed.

"'Put your clothes neatly on that chair,' she said, like a very stern schoolmistress, 'close your eyes again and come and sit next to me.' It was then I discovered that she had nothing on. I soon discovered why the game was very popular in Brighton. In fact I was still there learning the rules at half ten on the Sunday morning, when we heard the front door bell ring."

As they all laughed, Charlie asked if it was his parents come back home, without their front door key.

"No, it was my friend Michael wanting me to go trainspotting. I don't think he would have understood if I had told him what I had been doing all night or why I couldn't come with him. Anyway by the time I had run back upstairs, she was running the bath and for the next half hour we splashed around before getting back into bed for a bit more of beginner's Zenti. Unbelievable she was.

"Later on that evening, as we were all eating some scones that she had baked, my Mum said, 'Has Graham behaved himself, while we have been away, Vera?'. 'Oh yes, he behaved very well for a sixteen old,' she had replied. 'He didn't bore you with his stamp collecting did he?' No, he bored me with something else, I thought she was going to say, but she kept our little secret. And for the next few weeks we were at it most afternoons."

"A case of plenty Zenti," laughed Charlie.

"Well it was until the bloody union went and spoiled it."

"Why, did she go on strike?"

"No. The thing was that my Mum had been collecting signatures for a petition against education cuts and that afternoon the local M.P. was visiting her school. It was a good time to confront him with this petition, but unfortunately all the sheets were in her bedroom. So one of the other teachers drove her home, she came up to the bedroom and found me and Auntie Vera in her bed."

"So what did your Mum say?"

"Nothing then. But later on that evening over dinner, as we were all engaging in some rather strained polite conversation, my Mum turned to my Dad and said, 'You'll never guess what I saw today, Norman. Our dear little son Graham in our bed, fornicating with my innocent little sister.'"

"And what did your Dad say to that?"

"He just smiled and said something like, 'Well, if he is now fit enough to spend the afternoon on the job, when he's passed his exams he can go and get himself a job.'"

Before long Graham's stories began to attract more interest. And the longer he stayed, the keener he was to let the rest of the office know about his auntie. Maybe it was the way he told his stories, but then they all seemed to be true.

"I was never religious," he started off one day. "I got that from my parents. They were both agnostics and had been pretty unreligious in their youth. One thing I did know was the names of a few hymns that we used to sing when I was still at school, *Nymphs and Shepherds* for example. I knew what a shepherd was, but not a nymph, well not until I first rang Auntie Vera's bell."

As they all laughed he carried on; "A few weeks later, Mum and Dad went away again. After we had eaten the evening meal, she told me she wanted to play a different game that night. It was called Zubidoo. What I had to do was leave the house and return, after eight o' clock, and read the note she would leave on the table. So I went to see my friend Roger and played with his train set. I don't think he would have understood what I was on about if I'd told him that I would be doing some shunting myself later that evening. Anyway, I came back and read her note. What I had to do was to go into my parents' bedroom, get undressed and get into bed, but not switch the light on and not speak until I was spoken to.

"So I did exactly that. As soon as I came into the house, I noticed a strange smell. I thought it must be her new perfume. It was even stronger as I got into the bed. I lay there wondering what surprise she had in store, when I felt a rough hand stroke my face. It certainly was not Vera's hand. Neither was it Vera's tongue that started working its way round my face and into my mouth. I remained silent as a much bigger woman climbed on top of me and soon I was fighting for breath as she crushed me down. When she had finished, the woman shouted out 'Geronimo', and the light went on and there was Vera stood half-naked drinking from a bottle, and lay beside me was a friend of hers from Brighton, at least fifty years old, with no more than an inch of silver hair on her head and a mass of tattoos on her arm and back. Then Vera told me that I had just been for a ride with Denise. It was then that I discovered that many a fine tune can be played on an old fiddle and what a threesome was."

With this account of his initiation into the ways of the world, despite his posh accent and his total lack of interest in rugby, Graham, with more of his stories as a teenager in St Albans and later at a squat in Brighton with Denise and an even older lady, became another of the many characters who had graced Wilkinson's Drawing Office with their presence. Unfortunately he didn't stay too long with them. The domestic dispute that had initially driven him out of St. Albans to St. Helens, was soon to be replaced by a family reconciliation. It was all due to the persuasive powers of his eldest daughter and his wife's promise to stop spending her evenings at a so-called meditation centre in Wembley and going to non-existent evening classes. But before he handed in his notice, he accepted Charlie's offer to go with him to a couple of matches at Knowsley Road.

"I'll come with you, my friend, but I won't enjoy it. I just do not like rugby."

"Maybe you don't, but with your interest in the use of language, I'm sure you will enjoy all the humour that you'll hear on the terrace."

"AUNTIE VERA IS STAYING WITH US FOR A BIT"

And so it proved for his first game. It was the worth the admission money alone for Graham to stand in front of an old woman from Haresfinch and listen to her shouting at the referee and the away team in a most humorous way.

By the time he had gone to his second match, he had had the rules and the finer points of the game explained to him about a dozen times. It was a much more exciting game with the final result in doubt until the last five minutes. Much to his own surprise, he had shown some enthusiasm as he watched the winning try scored right in the corner where he and Charlie were stood. He had clapped, albeit in a manner more suitable for a performance at the opera or the ballet, and had shouted out to the scorer "Well done," although to those stood around him it sounded more like "Well, Dan."

After that, he thought about accepting Charlie's offer to go to an away game at Post Office Road, but he never did. Although he had thoroughly enjoyed his time living in nineteenth century Lancashire, he didn't think his constitution would stand going back to eighteenth century Yorkshire.

A few weeks after he had left, he sent a letter telling all his former workmates how he was getting on back in St Albans. He finished the letter with a note to Charlie telling him that he had seen a couple of games on *Grandstand* and was beginning to enjoy watching rugby league:

"But it'll never catch on in St Albans. I'm sure of that. All my old friends here think that I've gone a bit funny since I went up 'oop North', so I don't know what they would all make of you lot."

But it was what he had written at the end of his letter that made everybody laugh:

P.S. All that stuff that I told you about Auntie Vera and Denise and her mate in Brighton was a load of old cobblers. And you all believed me!

It was actually Chantelle
And her mother
And me
All enjoying a nice Swiss Roll.

Zenti and Zubidoo indeed!
You load of seagullibles should stick to playing Scrabble.

5.

Waiting for Harold Wilson

SPORT HAD ALWAYS played a big part in the lives of many of those who lived in Ashurst. Although no small number followed the round ball game, Rugby League was clearly the most popular. Due to its geographical position, any supporter of the handling code could easily follow one of five local teams: Leigh, St Helens, Warrington, Widnes or Wigan.

Who you chose to support was usually a family thing, sons and daughters carrying on the tradition that had been set by older relatives in the past. At other times, it was as a result of peer pressure, like with the Liptrot twins who lived opposite Alan's old house in Chisnall Avenue. Pauline, the older one by three minutes, had a boyfriend who came from Woolston and had thus become a Warrington fan after having been taken to the Wilderspool Stadium on her second date. However, her younger sister Kathleen, by three minutes to be equally precise, was a student at Wigan Technical College where she had fallen in with a good crowd of young folk who liked to spend every other Sunday afternoon at Central Park, on the banks of the River Douglas. Their separate allegiances made things rather interesting when the family was sat talking round the dinner table for their dad had been brought up in Pendlebury at the far end of the East Lancashire Road, close to the home of Swinton and whose 'A' team he had once played for and for whom he still had great affection. It was made even more interesting once their young brother Richard became interested in sport, because all his mates from school supported the Saints. Luckily, their separate allegiances did not bother their mother one bit. She had been brought up on a farm near the German town of Drensteinfurt, from where she had departed as the wife of a young National Serviceman in 1953.

Not surprisingly the rivalry between the supporters of the various teams was always intense and never more so than after the draw for the Challenge Cup semi-finals had been made. In the first few days of April 1979, the atmosphere in the town had begun to build up as the Saints prepared to face the unfancied Wakefield Trinity. The prospect of another trip to Wembley Stadium seemed almost certain as thousands of supporters set off for Headingley, the home of the Leeds Rugby League club. Many travelled in coaches, over twenty of which had been parked on Ashurst Town Hall Square. Everybody was highly confident that their next journey out of town would be to London later in the month, even when at half-time the Saints were only leading by four points. Early in the second half there was a bit of a shock as the Dreadnoughts scored a converted try. But a speedy twenty-five-yard sprint to the line by the Saints winger Les Jones soon put the Saints back in front. But with only three minutes to go, and the Saints again pressing on the Trinity line, the Wakefield scrum half David Topliss intercepted a pass, ran seventy yards before floating the ball out to the winger Ray Fletcher. His try ensured that the Yorkshire side had won the right to meet Widnes in the showpiece game of the whole rugby league season.

The game, which should have been a South-West Lancashire affair, finished up being a Lancashire-Yorkshire affair. Despite this disappointment, many people travelled down from Ashurst to Wembley on the day. It was not a bad game and not a bad day out either, although it is never quite the same when your own team is not playing. Alan, his brother Paul and half a dozen others, went down on the train and enjoyed their brief moment of glory as the TV cameras picked them out walking up Wembley Way, along with a big group of Workington Town fans who they had met on the Tube. One of them was a rather buxom sixty-five-year-old lady from Silloth. Somewhat intoxicated by the whole affair, she had playfully kissed Alan as the cameras beamed in on them. Back in Silkstone Street, when Alan's son Robert saw this in their front room, he had shouted out, "Mum, Dad's on the telly and he's with his girlfriend."

As Thelma dashed into the room from the kitchen and just missed seeing him, he went on, "And she's really old."

Many stories were told at work during the following week about what they had all done in the capital over the weekend. Many centred on the Friday evening and early Saturday morning in and around the red light district of Soho. One or two had spent an absolute fortune and couldn't remember on what. Some had been rather poorly, wearing their best clothes, others had spent the night in a police cell for what they could still not remember, but it was Billy Kenilworth from the Iron Foundry who had suffered more than anybody. Sometime between arriving at his hotel on Friday evening and eating his breakfast on Saturday morning, he had lost his ticket. Convinced that he would be able to buy one outside the ground, he had carried on regardless, and at half past two had bought one from a loudmouthed tout, paying an exorbitant amount for what turned out to be a clever fake.

Poor Billy, his bad luck didn't finish there, because when he got back home to Ross Street he discovered that his wife had run off with the milkman, a deed made even worse by the fact that on the Friday morning, just before he had set off for London, Billy had paid the man for the following week's milk!

ONE SUMMER

A few days later, the General Election took place. It was not something that could be considered as interesting or exciting as the Cup Final had been. But, as things turned out, it was going to be a lot more significant. Among the draughtsmen, Mick had expressed his support for Mrs. Thatcher, while Yorky decided that he was going to vote for the Liberals as he was fed up with the outgoing Prime Minister, James Callaghan. Charlie confessed that he had never felt less enthusiastic about canvassing for his local Labour Party, after the so-called Winter of Discontent. Alan made the comment that the only person to go into Parliament with honest intentions had been Guy Fawkes. When asked which way he was going to vote Keith had seriously asked "What Election?", while Colin in a rather disinterested way had declared that he was going to vote with his feet, "But only after I've washed them, of course."

Then John chipped in with a story from the 1964 General Election and his own embarrassing attempt to help Harold Wilson, the Labour candidate for the nearby Huyton constituency. At the time, John had been working in the BICC Accessories Division Drawing Office in Prescot. Early one morning, Phil, a fitter from the Works Maintenance Department, had told John that 'Harold' was doing a lunchtime factory gate meeting outside the Liverpool Road gates. Keen to help the party he had just joined, John went round everybody in the Drawing Office, telling all the draughtsmen to pass the word round in order to get a good turnout. As soon as it was lunchtime, he nipped out of work quickly, bought a meat and potato pie at Lindsay's Pie Shop and hurried down to the spot where he hoped to meet his great hero. Phil, on the other hand, just went up to the canteen for his dinner as normal.

When John arrived at the far end of Liverpool Road, he saw a few of his mates stood around chatting with the blonde Claire and a couple of other girls from the Telephone Cables Division. Billy Higgins was also there from the Foundry, with his *Daily Mirror* stuck in his back pocket, along with a couple of his moulder friends, although they could perhaps be better described as his mouldy friends. It was now ten past twelve and Phil had said that Harold would arrive around half-past, just long enough to get his microphone set up before speaking to the assembled throng until they all had to go back to work. As the minutes ticked by, others began to saunter down the road and by twenty past there must have been nearly a hundred people stood about. Then John noticed a journalist from the *Prescot Reporter*, looking rather important, though no doubt he had met and interviewed the great man before. Five more minutes passed and the crowd stood around was now more like two hundred. Then John looked over the railings and down into the main road that lead through the factory and saw an amazing sight, perhaps up to a thousand people all walking past the Copper Refinery towards the gates. It looked more like a crowd going to the match for an evening game, straight from work. It was now half past twelve and the pavements on both sides of the road were full of people hoping to hear the next Prime Minister say his piece.

Shortly after a police car drove by, followed by a second. By now every car that approached was scrutinised by the waiting crowd which numbered probably in excess of two thousand. But before much longer all those stood around heard the five to one hooter sound and so, slowly muttering that Prescot Labour Party couldn't organise a piss up in a brewery, they all returned to work. John kept his head down for the rest of the day. As he watched the television that evening, he wished he had totally ignored Phil, because the main item on the *Nine o' Clock News* concerned a visit that the Leader of the Opposition had made that morning to the Elysee Palace in Paris to meet the French Prime Minister.

Everybody knew what had happened. John's enthusiasm for the cause had made him forget that Phil's main aim in life was to trick the unsuspecting and the gullible and that day he had succeeded, big time. But now, over fifteen years later, it was something to laugh over, although it wasn't at the time. Not one bit.

"Didn't Phil Anderson used to be a councillor for North Ward?" asked Charlie.

"Yes," said Alan, "until they went and expelled him for wanting to wear his boiler suit."

"Eh?"

"It was when the Queen came to open Ashurst Technical College. He and other local councillors were invited to meet her, well, get presented to her. A few days before, some official comes up from Buckingham Palace to instruct them all how they had to behave, how to bow before her, what to wear and what to say if she spoke to them. That night in The Black Horse, Phil told a few of the regulars what he was going to do. He was going to wear his boiler suit and when the Queen shook his hand, he was going to get a petition about the bus services out of his pocket and ask her to sign it. Well, somebody who heard this must have told somebody else and it got back to the authorities who decided that instead of all the councillors going, just the Mayor and a few Labour Party geriatrics would be invited instead. So Phil's invitation was withdrawn 'on security grounds' it was said."

Phil Anderson came from a rather unusual family. Perhaps the oddest member had been his older brother Peter. Peter Anderson had served his apprenticeship as a joiner at Dean's, a small odd-jobbing firm in Helmsley and because of a speech impediment he never used to talk much. He was a bit of a loner, kept himself to himself unless something or someone upset him. But when that happened, he displayed enormous skill and talent at getting his own back.

A good example of that had been over a running dispute that he had had with the local councillor for Newtown Ward. Councillor Samuel Bothell had served on Ashurst Council for years. He was definitely a legend in his own head. What had aided his political career over the years, had been his willingness to write the minutes of every committee meeting that he had ever attended. These minutes always emphasised his own contribution and downplayed or ignored what everybody else had said. Towards the end of his very insignificant political career, it had been decided to have the Dob Lane Day Centre for the Elderly named after his good self. The contract to paint the place had been given to Dean's, it being a pure coincidence, that the company was owned by Samuel Bothell's father-in-law.

Peter Anderson had worked at Dean's ever since leaving school. There he had been tormented by the owner Mr. Dean and bullied by his son Angus. Finally Peter was presented with a golden opportunity to get his own back on both the Deans and on Councillor Bothell, who had consistently shown no interest in doing anything about the war in Vietnam or the withdrawal of the number ninety-three Sunday bus service to Earlestown. Peter had been given the job of painting the plaque that was to be placed in the entrance of the new Day Centre. As always happened on a Thursday afternoon, Mr Dean had left early, but not before giving Peter instructions to lock up when he had finished work. He then had to take the plaque home with him and, first thing the following morning, take it to the Day Centre and screw it to the wall and cover it with a piece of purple cloth to which was to be attached a piece of yellow ribbon.

On the following day quite a collection of local dignitaries had turned up, including staff from the Council, the vicar of St Mary's church with a few of his flock, the Assistant Chief Constable along with a photographer and a reporter from the local paper. A short speech was made by the chairman of Ashurst Round Table, who then asked his dear wife to pull the ribbon. As the cloth fell to the ground, there was a great gasp from the assembled group, when they saw the plaque. Painted in bright red against a background of green and yellow, for all to see, were emblazoned the words 'The Brothell Centre'!

Over the course of the next few days, the main topics of conversation in the office centred around what the new Conservative Government was going to do. At the time, few people could envisage how the whole industrial face of the country was going to change over the next decade. Few could even contemplate how many of the fixtures of the economy would either disappear or change drastically. Few could imagine just how bad the employment situation, particularly in the North of England, would become. It was thus somewhat ironic that one of the first companies in Ashurst to go to the wall was Greenside's D.I.Y., run by the Conservative Party Councillor for Moss House Ward, Herbert Greenside. He had for years been a great advocate of the idea of unregulated and unbridled free market competition, unless of course it meant other shops in the town competing with him.

On the following Monday morning, there had been a heated argument between Alan and Mick, which had carried on in the canteen and then on the bowling green. But as soon as they returned to work, all political discussion came to an end when Yorky walked in with the sad news that one of their old workmates had been killed in a car crash and for a time everything else was forgotten. Len Turner had worked as a draughtsman at Wilkinson's since the mid-Fifties and had retired on the grounds of ill-health a few months earlier. It had been mainly through his efforts that, when Basil had taken over the running of the company, they had all joined the Draughtsmens' Union and helped prevent Basil turning the place into a sweatshop. Over the years, Len had negotiated hard with the firm over wages, conditions and other matters of direct and often indirect interest to the members. He had also risen in the union hierarchy to the position of Divisional Council Chairman before having to finish work. After that and with plenty of time on his hands, he had turned his attention to other matters and tried somewhat unsuccessfully to set up a branch of the Old Age Pensioners League in Ashurst to campaign against the Council, the Government and the Law Lords for a decent pension and better facilities for the over sixty-fives.

The news of his death was greeted with great sadness not only in the Drawing Office but right across the factory, for Len had been well respected by most people he had had dealings with. And it was no great surprise that over fifty people took a half-day's holiday to attend his funeral.

The funeral was unlike any funeral that any of his old friends had ever been to before. The religious ceremony had been held in St Margaret's Church, where Len's wife Mary had been a regular worshipper, but in which Len had rarely set foot. Then the small gathering of relatives had gone, with some degree of trepidation, to the Boilermakers' Social Club to be greeted by a crowd of over a hundred of Len's political friends and associates. There, in a very informal way, various people had stood up and spoken in praise of their old comrade. One of the first people to make a contribution was Alan who explained how Len had saved him from the sack when he had thumped one of the graduate apprentices after the twit had described the Welsh as a load of sheepshaggers. Then Charlie told the audience how much Len concerned himself with the problems that union members, who worked at other firms in the town, faced. After that others chimed in with snippets of information about Len's life and his activities.

On one occasion, the full-time organiser of the Draughtsmens' Union, Ken Glover, had asked Len to go to a small company in the centre of Liverpool where the wages were low, where the staff were being pressurised into working unpaid overtime and where a senior manager was sexually harassing the younger women. The place was ripe for getting the union organised and Len was really up for it. It was located in a seven storey block and the staff entrance was at the rear of the building. Len hung about outside just before eight thirty, the normal starting time, waiting to join a group of people as they came in from the city centre. He got out of the lift on the top floor and walked down to the door at the end of the corridor, the entrance to Anderton Engineering Associates. He had been told that the boss only came in after nine and the person to contact was a lad called John. So he had asked the first person that he had seen to tell John that his visitor had arrived. Luckily the person he had spoken to was the lad in question.

"Ken's sent me to have a word with everybody before nine. Is everything organised?" Len had asked.

The lad seemed a bit dim and told Len that Mr. Butterworth wasn't in today but if Len wanted to speak to everybody, he had better do it before they started work. So Len had walked into the office where about thirty people looked up in amazement at him, particularly when he had stood on a chair and delivered his five minute speech all about the advantages of belonging to a trade union and being able to do something about their wages, their holidays, their conditions and the anti-social behaviour of the boss. His speech was received in total silence and when Len asked if there were any questions, no one had said a dicky bird. So he gave everybody a leaflet and left. Clearly his visit and his speech had gone down like a lead balloon.

As he waited for the lift, John had come out of the office and told him that there must have been some sort of a mistake because everybody had been expecting to hear about the advantages of joining BUPA, which was something their manager Mr. Butterworth was very keen on. When Len got out of the lift on the ground floor, his eye was attracted to a large noticeboard indicating that Anderson Electrical Engineering Ltd. were located on the second floor. He had gone to the wrong place!

The next person to speak was a lecturer from Ashurst College, a fairly young women and very attractive too. Whatever did she have to do with Len, many would have thought. She explained that Len's outlook on life stretched far beyond the boundaries of Ashurst or even Britain. His interest had been with anybody who was fighting corruption, injustice and oppression, wherever they lived and particularly those suffering under apartheid in South Africa. As soon as she had finished, she was followed by a much older woman who stood up and explained how Len had got into trouble on a few demonstrations he had attended, mainly with the police but on one occasion with his wife.

"Mary never really liked his political involvement," she explained. "So, quite a few things that he got involved with, he never told her about. One Saturday morning the pair of them went out to buy him a new raincoat, quite an expensive one for Len. Knowing him and his attitude to clothes, he would have been quite happy to have picked one up in Oxfam. That evening, a big anti-Vietnam war demonstration had been organised in Liverpool, and which Len had arranged to attend. So he goes round town quite willingly with Mary and even suggested they had lunch in the Bear's Paw, before returning home with more shopping than Len would have normally agreed to. Then, with Mary tucking into a large box of chocolates Len had bought her, it was off down to the Pier Head. When he and his three mates arrived, they discovered that the demonstration was going to be in the form of a candle-lit procession, so of course Len grabs the biggest candle he could. Now, it was a windy evening and a few hooligans threw bottles and stones at them as they walked through town. Finally, they arrived at Liverpool Cathedral Steps where a short meeting was held. By this time, it had started raining. When they had arrived back at the car, Len looked in horror at his brand new mac; it was covered in candle grease and dirt and wringing sopping wet. So when he got home, Mary went wild when she saw the state of it and didn't speak to him for a week."

Continuing in the same vein, another of his old workmates told a hilarious story. Jack Quartermain lived a couple of streets away from Len and usually gave him a lift to work. But Jack's wife, did not like this arrangement whereby some militant agitator was allowed to sit in their nice new car. So she had told Jack to stop giving Len a lift. In order to keep things sweet at home, Jack had worked out an arrangement whereby Len could continue to go to work with him without Dianne knowing anything about it. On most days, Dianne would be still in bed when Jack left the house to drive thirty yards from the wasteland where the car was parked, round the corner to pick Len up. But on certain days, Jack had to drop Dianne off at her sister's. On those occasions an alternative arrangement had to be made, and as Dianne made all her decisions on the spur of the moment, Jack could never easily warn Len to catch the bus. So they had this arrangement whereby, on the excuse of getting something out of the car on a 'bad travel day', Jack would place a large piece of wood against the garden gate and unlock the boot of the car. When Len peeped round the corner, if he saw the danger signal, he had to put into operation Plan B.

With the coast clear, he would creep up to the car and get into the boot and have an uncomfortable ten minutes ride to Earlestown where Dianne got out to visit her sister. This happened a few times without any problem. On one unfortunate day however, Dianne had told Jack that she wanted him to take her to their Beryl's. So out nips Len to put the wood in position. After they had had their breakfast, Dianne informed Jack that she would drive him to work and then go on to Earlestown because she wanted to use the car to go shopping in Warrington. Despite his weak protestations, she retained firm control of the car keys. So when the car arrived outside the firm's Warrington Road gates, Jack had to make the excuse that he wanted to get something out of the boot. To the amazement of all those hurrying into work, he had to lift up the boot to let Len out, who then had to walk in the opposite direction to make sure Dianne did not see who she had just driven to work that morning.

The last of the many contributions was made by Rita Martlew, who had taken over from Len as secretary of the union's Office Committee. One of her first tasks had been to organise a collection to buy a going-away card and present, which was then signed by all his old colleagues. On the morning of his last day, she had nipped out of work and with the money had bought two books that she was sure the old firebrand would surely appreciate: *The Civil War in France* by Karl Marx and *The Story of the Marx Brothers*. Rita then made everybody in the Boilermakers' Social Club laugh, when she told them exactly what she had said to Len as she had kissed him and then presented him with the two books:

"We all knew that you were a Marxist, Len, but we were never quite sure which sort."

6.

Tracey's last trick

BASIL WAS SAT looking as debonair as ever, wearing his awful pin-striped suit with a large carnation in his top pocket. He would not have looked out of place at a reception in Buckingham Palace itself. Sat by his side in the company boardroom was his Personnel Manager, John Thomas, looking as miserable as ever. There were thirty or so other employees sat facing them, all who knew that they might just be about to learn that they would be out of a job by the end of the month. Rumours had been rife for some time. There had already been cutbacks in various parts of the factory, all overtime had been stopped, those who had retired, been sacked or left, had not been replaced and the order book had little in it, as far as most of them were aware.

He began by thanking those present for coming to the meeting, which he had called at such short notice. Those assembled there included the senior managers, the shop stewards representing both works and staff, along with Elizabeth Kay, secretary of the now moribund Staff Association. Soon they would all be carriers of bad news to the people they ruled over or represented. He made a few comments about the state of the company and the failure to win a recent large order in India. Then he spoke about the result of the General Election; the fact that it had greatly pleased him could be seen by the smile on his face and his general body language.

"Not everyone in this room will be happy that the Conservative Party won the General Election last Thursday. Not every one in this room will think that a woman can run the country. Not every one will be pleased that Mrs. Thatcher is now our Prime Minister. But then I am sure that not many of you were very happy with Mr. Callaghan and his lot, so let's see it as a fresh challenge for all of us."

He then took a press cutting from his pocket and proceeded to read a few lines from the new Prime Minister's first public comments in Downing Street.

> Where there is discord, may we bring harmony,
> Where there is error, may we bring truth.
> Where there is doubt, may we bring faith,
> Where there is despair, may we bring hope.

Then he carried on to his captive audience, who were of course all being paid to listen to him:

"I think we should all be pleased and even happy that we now have some one in charge who has compassion, who wants to bring an end to all the strife in the country and who wants to give us all hope for the future, not just for ourselves, but for our children and grandchildren too. Over the last few months we all know how bad things have been, rubbish left rotting on the streets, buses not running, dinner ladies not being allowed to feed the school children and the dead left in the morgues because the gravediggers were not prepared to bury them. Unemployment has continued to grow. There are now over a million people out of work, thanks to Mr. Callaghan and his socialist policies."

"One point three million," grunted the Personnel Manager.

"What socialist policies?" replied Gerry Higgins, a shop steward in the Iron Foundry.

"Before last Thursday, there was no sign of things getting any better either. None of us want to see Wilkinson's go the same way as other factories in the town. We have seen Power Design, Hilton's, Shelton's and Dawson's close down, Pearson's have just announced that they are stopping all production next year and who knows what is going on at Jarratt's and now at Stephenson's? Of course you might say that we have not been that much different because there have been a few redundancies here. That's correct but the main difference is that we are still operating and most of those who have left over the last eighteen months, chose to leave."

He then went to the heart of the issue facing Wilkinson's. Drastic measures had to be taken in the short term in order to save the company in the long term. He stressed that it was those assembled before him who could determine whether the firm had any future. It was up to the managers to manage the place much better than they had ever done before. It was also up to the shop stewards to play their part, act responsibly and convince those they represented to think of their own future and act responsibly too. Then after making his usual comments about demarcation lines, excessive wage demands and incorrect filling out of timesheets, he went on to say that he had agonised long and hard over what he was going to say. Then he proceeded to inform them about what he described as his four main proposals:

PROPOSAL 1

Shut down the whole factory, sell off the profitable parts to GEC who had shown some interest, sell land that the company owned to the Council for housing and have sufficient funds to pay everybody their full redundancy entitlement.

PROPOSAL 2

Close down the Iron Foundry, the Rolling Mill, the Tinning Shop and Metal Fatigue Laboratory. Move more research, development and drawing work to Morgan Chemicals, a company who were based in Essex and had done work for Wilkinson's before.

This would enable a reduction to be made in the number employed in the Drawing Office, Work Study, Planning Office, Measurement Lab and Works Maintenance. The total result of all this would be around eight hundred redundancies. After that, as long as orders continued to be won, the annual wage negotiations could start as usual in January.

PROPOSAL 3

Close down the Iron Foundry and Metal Fatigue Laboratory, put the Rolling Mill in mothballs for six months, stop the night shift in the Brass Foundry, make redundant a smaller number who worked in the Drawing Office, Work Study and Planning Office and move those who worked in the Measurement Lab into the main Laboratory. Restructure the shop floor wages to a Payment By Results scheme and introduce Job Evaluation for the staff. Total result of this would be around four hundred redundancies.

PROPOSAL 4

Do away with the night shift in the Iron Foundry, Brass Foundry and Rolling Mill. Stop paying premium rates for overtime. Do away with the annual wage increase and hold discussions after six months about the introduction of a different payment scheme. Stop all new recruitment, cut down the apprentice intake to six and encourage voluntary redundancy. This would result in about two hundred redundancies.

He then stood up, announced that he had to leave them due to a pressing engagement in Liverpool with people from the Board of Trade, from whom he hoped to bring back some good news about the Rosario contract, and walked out. As soon as he had left the room the Personnel Manager stood up and announced that Basil had asked him to read out those jobs which would be made redundant under proposals two, three and four. Then he informed the assembled employees that they had three days in which to decide what they wanted to do.

A new Government in London, a Prime Minister advocating peace, harmony, hope and faith, and within the week more people from the town joining the dole queue. Maybe the words peace, harmony, hope and faith did not mean the same thing in Ashurst as they did in London.

Meetings were held around the factory and resolutions passed, trade union officials were brought in, while outside others who had an interest in the factory's continued presence had their say too. Everybody knew that the situation facing the town was similar to that in many other towns right across the North of England. But that didn't mean that people in Ashurst couldn't make their feelings known and try to prevent the worst happening.

The following night, Ashurst Council voted to send a delegation to see their M.P. in London. The vicar of St Luke's Church suggested that prayers be said on the following Sunday while the *Ashurst Reporter* decided it would be a good idea to make a big issue of the whole affair, with a large feature on the role that the Wilkinson family had played in the town over the years. One young reporter was given the job of talking to people who worked there and what they thought of Basil Wilkinson. She got an enormous amount of material, unfortunately little of it was printable.

One organisation that decided to take a strong lead was the Ashurst branch of the Young Socialists. At their weekly meeting in the back room of Gillarsfield Labour Club, they decided that what was being proposed at Wilkinson's, was a calculated and deliberate attack on the whole working class and had to be resisted not just in the factory itself, but nationally. After a long heated discussion they passed the following resolution.

"Ashurst Young Socialists deplore the action of the Wilkinson management, aided by the reactionary Thatcher Government, to attack their workers and close the Ashurst factory. It demands that the TUC immediately call a 24-hour General Strike and declare its complete support for the overthrow of this Tory Government and its replacement by a Labour Government committed to a policy of nationalisation without compensation, the introduction of a thirty-five hour week, four weeks holiday for all and M.P.s to be paid at the same rate as a skilled fitter. It also calls for full official trade union support for the reinstatement of the Belmount Young Socialists into the Labour Party, an end to all witch hunts of the revolutionary Left and the re-instatement of the lollipop man at the bottom of Wigan Lane."

For this proposal, four votes were cast for, one against, and two abstentions, one on the grounds that they didn't have a quorum and the other on the grounds that the issue was political.

Over the next few days, many meetings of the employees were held and decisions taken to deal with the situation. There was general agreement that Propor. Morgan Chemicals did not have the capacity to handle all the research work and no way would Basil close down the Rolling Mill, after all the money that had been invested in it. In the end, a compromise was put forward by the Ashurst branch of the General and Municipal Workers Union. It was to accept only voluntary redundancies, stop all overtime, accept the closure of the Metal Fatigue Laboratory, and demand that the

Company sells its prestigious office block in Mayfair and relocate to a more suitable location on the outskirts of the capital. It also asked the Company to explain the annual financial contribution made to the highly profitable Isle of Man Electrical Design Company, with its offices in Douglas.

At first it seemed a rather strange way of fighting the issue. However what many people did not know was that the chairman of the Ashurst branch of the General and Municipal Workers Union had a daughter called Frances, whose best friend was Tracey, Basil Wilkinson's shapely secretary. Tracey had always given Basil the impression that she was no lover of trade unions and was a great admirer of all that the Wilkinson family had done for the people of Ashurst over the years. Not surprisingly, she knew all about Basil's scheming and conniving. She had made it her mission to help him to set up his filing system and keep his office tidy, something which he was incapable of doing. As a result she knew of his plan to knock down the old Metal Fatigue lab and sell the land it stood on to the Council, move the company offices out of Mayfair to within a hundred yards of Wembley Stadium in North London. And most importantly she knew just how money, made by people employed in the Ashurst factory, found its way into the bank accounts of the Isle of Man Electrical Design Company, via another smallholding company based on the Isle of Jersey.

All that she had discovered, she had told to Frances, who like the good daughter she was, had passed it on to her Dad, who then used it to work out a plan to fight any compulsory redundancies.

When this information became common knowledge, the general mood throughout the factory turned to anger as people discovered that Basil was up to his old tricks again, seeking to protect his own bank balance while blaming the enforced redundancies on the general world economic situation and the absence of orders. When Basil heard what soon became public knowledge round the factory, he went ballistic. If he had succeeded in his plan, he would have, at one swoop, cleared all the company's debts, got rid of all the shop stewards and troublemakers, done away with the annual wage increase and made the company a leaner and fitter organisation, much more capable of being able to handle a large contract in the Middle East that he was on the point of signing with the Government of Saudi Arabia.

As soon as Tracey walked into work the following morning, he shouted at her to come into his office. There he accused her of going through his personal documents, listening to his telephone conversations and prying into his private affairs. She listened quietly while he ranted and raved. When he had finished, she opened the door and asked one of the other girls in the office to act as a witness to what she had to say.

"Sharon," she said, "Mr. Wilkinson has just accused me of going through all his private papers, listening to him when he is on the phone and prying into his private affairs. I just want to say publicly that for the last three months I have been sorting out all his paper work, just like he asked me to. Secondly, whenever I have been in the room, he has never once asked me to leave when he was on the phone. Thirdly, I have never passed any comment to anyone about his private affairs. In fact I know of only one private affair that he has had all the time I have been here. That was with Mrs. Billington in the Wages Department who I am sure will be able to confirm that. Finally I want to know, why does he keep looking up my skirt when I am taking shorthand notes, why on two occasions has he put his hand on my backside and why did he ask me to spend a couple of nights with him in Whitehaven, while he was at that important meeting at Sellafield?"

Basil was dumbfounded. She had totally fooled him, with a clever combination of half-truths and lies. It was true that she had access to all the papers that came into his office, but he was so sure she was on his side, not a bloody troublemaker like the rest of his employees. It was the same with the telephone calls although he usually made his most devious ones from home. She knew full well about his little fling with Mrs. Billington, because she had actually signed the invoice for the company to pay the bill for their three night stay at the Grosvenor Hotel in London. As to him looking up her skirt, well the way she sat you would have to be blind not to see what might be on offer. And touching her backside, well it had been the way she had smiled as she squeezed past him on more than one occasion. As to a dirty weekend in Whitehaven of all places, that just was not true.

Before he could respond, John Thomas came into the office with two visitors from the Board of Trade. Basil thus only had time to tell the women who worked in his office not to breathe a word of what had just been said and left the room. A few days later, the compromise that was put forward by the General and Municipal Workers Union was accepted by Basil. Among the hundred or so workers who finally took voluntary redundancy later that month was Tracey, who had been intending to hand her notice in anyway.

Soon after Tracey and went hitch-hiking in France. On her third day she got a lift with two American sailors heading south out of Bordeaux. When they stopped in a quiet country lane and tried to force their attentions on her, she flattened the pair of them, left them tied up in a field and drove a further one hundred kilometres until the car ran out of petrol just outside Lourdes.

The rest of 1979 went along slowly in some ways, quickly in others. Soon it was December 23rd, the last working day of the year. In the past, they had always worked on Christmas Eve until lunchtime, then gone down to the Worsley Arms to have the Drawing Office Awards ceremony. When the landlord had been Kenny, a one-time prop forward first with the St Helens amateur team Vine Tavern and then Liverpool City, they had always been made welcome. But now the pub had been taken over by a trendy couple from Chester, who wanted to change its old fashioned character in an attempt to attract a younger clientele. All the walls around the place had been knocked down, thus removing the four small rooms and a very loud jukebox had been installed. For the last Christmas do, they had gone to The Mountain, a good pint but no food. And with the departure of a large number of men from the Mechanical Section of the Drawing Office, the ceremony had fallen by the wayside.

A few of the old timers came into work that morning to reminisce. But somehow the heart had gone out of the place. As always at these gatherings, much of the conversation was about the good old days and asking those who had left if they knew what had happened to others who had not turned up or who hadn't been seen or heard of since they left.

Quite a few of those who were seriously worried that they were soon about to lose their jobs, were contemplating taking early retirement. One or two of the younger ones were thinking of putting their redundancy money into a business venture, like a chip shop or. Colin declared that if it wasn't for his daughter having to go into hospital early in the new year, he would up sticks and emigrate to Perth in Australia where his brother lived. Then to everybody's surprise, Mick said that he was also seriously considering volunteering for redundancy.

The place would just not be the same without their favourite Wiganer. Over the years, he had been the butt of so many cruel, though humorous, comments; about his team, his clothes, his work, his propensity to sleep and snore, being a grandfather, being left out of his rich Uncle Ernie's will and whatever. But it had all been done in good spirit and in a very typically Lancashire way.

He had worked at Wilkinson's over thirty years; going right back to the days when the Electrical Section had been made up of him, Stan and Horace who produced all the parts lists and who, some would say, Mick had modelled himself on. Horace was actually sixty-seven when he finally finished work in 1959. If it could be said that Mick spent an hour a day asleep, then it could equally be said that Horace spent an hour a day awake. This was partly due to the medication that he was taking for his angina. Little was known about his life outside work after his wife had died. He just continued to turn up and old man Joshua Wilkinson hadn't had the heart to tell him that his services were no longer required.

One Thursday evening, Stan and Mick had both left on time, leaving Horace slumped over his desk. The following morning the two had walked in together and seen their colleague apparently out to the world again.

"He's starting early," Stan had jokingly said.

Mick said nothing. He was getting sick and tired of the way Horace seemed to get away with it. He picked up his pad and went down to the

Assembly Shop where he had spent most of the previous afternoon. Stan collected a couple of prints from his reference table and walked down to the Refinery where he was due to start checking the wiring of a Circuit Breaker. An hour later and, in the absence of any of the bosses, two of the apprentice draughtsmen from the Mechanical Section, bemused by Horace appearing to have been fast asleep all morning, began to throw things at him from behind one of the Drawing Office's cabinets. When one bounced off Horace's head and did not wake him, they decided something was wrong. It was then discovered that Horace had been dead for nearly a day!

Time began to drag during the last few weeks of the year. Tea breaks were no longer the oasis they had once been. Since the departure of their tea lady Joan, with her endless stories of factory gossip, there had been no end of replacements with the current one being Tina, who only ever spoke to the younger lads and who seemed to derive enormous pleasure by using the word 'it'. But even her days seemed numbered since, as part of the latest costcutting exercise, it was rumoured that Basil was considering installing vending machines, another example of machines replacing humans.

In many respects Wilkinson's had continued to exist despite the antics of its management, since the death of old man Joshua Wilkinson in 1962. But inside and outside of Ashurst, the world was facing rapid change. Soon, decisions taken in the corridors of power in Westminister by the new Conservative Government would, within the following decade, change forever the industrial face of the country. Nowhere was that to be witnessed more acutely and bitterly than right across the industrial regions of the North of England, as the employees of the Wilkinson Engineering Works and the general population of Ashurst were soon to discover to their cost.

7.

Our man in Brazil

"HAPPY NEW YEAR, my cockatoos, and let me be the one to tell you about your first big cock-up of 1980."

It was Tony Robledo, with one hell of a big smile on his face, as per usual.

Nobody said a word. It was too soon after all their Christmas and New Year celebrations to try and get their heads round the troublesome issue of work.

"Well listen up lads, Basil Brush has just found out about what's happened on that job in Brazil at Corumba and he's on his way here, as we speak. So my advice to the guilty party is to fill out a holiday form for this afternoon and disappear as quick as you can."

Still more silence from his audience.

"Anyway, it won't be one of you lot. It never is. So I'll go and see what His Royal Highness, Mr. Groves, has to say about it. Where is he today?"

"He ran off to Warrington with a woman from Malaga," said Charlie.

Alan Groves had been their section leader until the previous September when he had had a blazing row with Basil Wilkinson. It had been one of many disagreements they had had. But this one had been the last straw. 'Grovesy' just packed his bags, walked out of the place and was never seen in the factory again. In October, his house in the Warrington suburb of Grappenhall was put up for sale and the next communication they had from him was a postcard from Malaga, on which he had so eloquently written:

'I am very pleased to tell you lazy bastardos that my lunch breaks are now even longer than yours ever were.'

It was signed from 'Grovesy and Elaine', who used to work at the Gas Showrooms in Warrington.

Since then the Electrical Section had not officially had a leader and had reported to John Battesby, the Chief Draughtsman. All the jobs they had worked on had gone through without any real problems, until now it would appear. There had been some rumours about difficulties on a large installation at Corumba, a Brazilian town that was close to the Bolivian border. Now they were going to find out that if a big cock-up had occurred, who exactly was to blame for it?

Half an hour later came the dreaded, though expected phone call, with instructions for the four senior draughtsmen, Mick, Sam, Charlie and Alan, to go over to Basil's office immediately. It looked serious.

Basil never wasted words and certainly not on this occasion. As soon as he had slammed his office door shut, he started on at them:

"I want you four to drop whatever you are working on, no matter how urgent it is and sort this fucking Corumba job out quick. Somebody has dropped a great bollock and if it is somebody here, the penalty clauses will bankrupt this company. I want you to double check the whole design. This is top priority, so get started on it straightaway. It is so important that I have had to tell our Senior Sales Engineer, Harvey Roebuck, to come over from Rio. He'll be arriving tomorrow to tell us everything that he knows about it."

"So where do we start?" asked Charlie. "It was a very complicated job. We were on it for weeks and how do we know if it's an electrical problem?"

"Harvey will know more. He's the one to talk to first. He'll have all the details. Liase with Tony Robledo. He'll know when you can meet up with Harvey. Hopefully tomorrow afternoon."

Then, contradicting all what he had just said, he proceeded to tell Sam to spend the rest of the day making sure that the Block Cable Diagram for the Control Room at Tilbury Power Station was finally checked off and half a dozen prints be in the hands of the Sales Office and ready for the post at four o' clock. Then he almost smiled and said, "I'm relying on you lads. I'm sure you won't let me down."

Half an hour later, Tony Robledo returned.

"Well, my little cockatoos, I suppose Basil has told you all the gory details. Somebody is for the high jump. I wonder which one of you beauties it's going to be."

Then he pulled a piece of paper out of his pocket and with a dead straight face read out the following bit of useless information:

"Michael Angelo Henderson 3-1 on
Alan Greenall's Brewery Evens
Samueltine Holroyd 2-1 against
Charlemaine Eccleston 4-1 against."

"And that, gentlemen is the current odds on who is going to get the chop."

"Why me?" moaned the Wiganer. "I hardly did anything on that job."

"Maybe you didn't Mick, but you still booked over two hundred hours on it, including four Saturday mornings. But don't let's fall out. Let's see if we can get the blame shifted on to that American subcontractor, or maybe that old tea lady you used to have, you know, the one who used to check all Greeno's drawings."

The last comment was actually true, well, partially. Joan had once been asked to settle an argument between Alan and the Wiring Shop foreman over whether a cable number on one of his drawings was 163 or smudge63. But in her view it looked more like smudge83, which resolved little.

"Anyway, you'd better all come in your best clogs tomorrow. I've arranged for us to have Harvey for lunch in The Crimea."

"Have you got a job number for it?" said Alan somewhat disinterestedly.

"Don't I always have a job number for anything I want you lot to try and do?"

"Then, we'll all be there, mon capitaine."

So the following day, in the oldest pub in Ashurst, they met the company's South American Sales Engineer. Harvey Roebuck had the appearance of an executive member of the Confederation of British Industry at a banquet in the Mansion Hall. In his plush office in the Brazilian capital of Rio de Janeiro, dressed in a pin-striped suit, he would have looked just the part. But in the company of four untidy draughtsmen in The Crimea in Canal Street, he definitely looked out of place. They all sat round, pints on the table in front of them as Harvey explained the situation as he saw it.

"In the opinion of my site engineer Pedro, there is a fault on the design of the water control system. The motors can't handle the load at peak times, the 33kv transformers keep tripping out for no apparent reason, no one can switch the lights off in the meter room and on top of that there are no spare ways on the main fuseboard?"

Nobody said a thing. They each knew that the more that any of them said at this point, the more likely they would be the one to be blamed, so they let him continue.

"What I want you four to do is to check that everything has been drawn and designed to the latest Brazilian Electrical Standards and my memo of 7th January this year. Then I want you to check what date every drawing was sent from here, who signed for it on site and when the Delivery Confirmation Note was returned."

"A lot of that checking can be done by Simon Clegg," said Charlie, it'll all be in his Quality Control system."

"I don't want that jumped-up clerk anywhere near this job. He's a bloody idiot. I want you to do it. I want it done right and I want it done this week, not next month. As soon as you have finished, you can tell Tony what you have found out. He'll know where to find me for the next week or so. I've got to go to G.E.C. at Trafford Park tomorrow and then I might have to go to London for a couple of days."

Then he rubbed his hands together and asked Charlie what he recommended.

"Try the Desperate Dan Pie. That's what I'm having. That's what we are all having. That's all there is today."

For the next hour, as they devoured their lunch, Harvey proceeded to tell them about his most recent escapades in Brazil and Bolivia, the women who he had met, which casinos he had visited and which Embassies organised the best receptions. It was quite clear that he had a very high opinion of himself. It must have been something to do with his upper class background and public school education. After they had eaten, at his suggestion they played dominoes and, over an hour later and nearly eleven quid better off, he left them.

The first thing Tony said surprised, nay, even shocked them.

"Clever move on your part, lads, to let him win, but it won't change owt."

None of them said a thing. That had been the last thing on their minds, cocky little bastard; well, cocky little six foot three bastard.

"That was a bloody farce," said Charlie. "We might have a major design fault on this really important job, one that might even bankrupt the company and what do we do? Eat the last supper, play dommies and listen to him tell us about all the women he's shagging over there."

"I thought it was quite a pleasant way to spend an hour," laughed Yorky.

"What would you have done?" asked Mick.

"We should have worked out how best to check the whole scheme to make sure the fault isn't an electrical one. We should have asked Graham Healey and Dave Rogers to get looking for possible faults on the mechanical and civil side. Then we should have started sorting out our passports and travel documents, enrolling for a crash course in Portuguese and getting some practice in at riding a llama at Belle Vue."

"I didn't like him," said Mick. "Too smooth and cocky with it."

"There's not many that do like him and even less who trust him," said Tony. "You see, it might just be another of his devious plans to get some work done by that Brazilian firm that one of his girlfriends owns."

That was something that had long been suspected but had never been proved. However it wouldn't have been the first time, if it was true.

Back in the Drawing Office a few minutes later, as they were all waiting while their latest apprentice was making them a drink, Charlie said, "Tony, there's something I've been wanting to ask you for ages. You know how whenever you visit our humble little office, we always make you very welcome? You drink our coffee, eat our bacon butties, look at the panoramic view out of our windows and sit in the best chair. Well my question to you is this, when are you going to invite us to your place?"

"You mean my new bungalow in Wigan Lane?"

"No, you pillock. That office you spend so much time at in Vista Alegre."

"It's only small. You wouldn't all get in it."

"Well, we wouldn't all come at once," laughed Yorky.

"Actually, you might be pleased to hear that before all this trouble blew up, Harvey was talking about a draughtsman coming out to help us for a bit. There's loads of drawing work on the electrical side that needs sorting out ."

That looked promising for at least one of them.

"So who does he want?"

"Well first of all, whoever it is must be prepared to stay for a minimum of two months and be fully acquainted with the B.E.B.S. system."

They all were.

"Secondly, he must have worked on the Lambaqaque or the Rosario job."

That ruled out Mick and Alan.

"He should have had at least six months' experience working out on site with the O.C.D. lads."

"That's ruled me out," said Yorky, leaving Charlie with a big grin on his face.

"And finally he must be fluent in Portuguese."

"You bugger," laughed the office comedian.

He had tricked them again. He was always doing it. But before anymore could be said, in walked Albert Cunliffe, a planning engineer wanting to talk to Mick about some cabling changes at Kearsley Power Station near Bolton. As he was about to leave, the phone went, but as Charlie picked it up, Albert said, "If it's Jack Kershaw for me, tell him I'll give him a Meucci this 'avvy. I've no time now. I'm as busy as Bob Forrest." And before anymore could be said, Albert had disappeared.

"What the hecky flump is a Meucci?" asked Colin.

"According to Albert, the telephone was actually invented by a guy called Antonio Meucci in 1860. It turns out the man was a distant relative of his grandmother who had been brought up in Florence as a girl."

"And who is Bob Forrest?"

But before Mick could tell them, another visitor was seen approaching. It was Kimberley, Basil Wilkinson's new secretary, slowing working her way through the top half of the Drawing Office and being stopped and chatted up by just about every mechanical and civil draughtsman under the age of sixty-four.

Finally she reached the Electrical Section, where she immediately gave Charlie a large folder with instructions from Basil to read through it straightaway. Then she sat on Yorky's stool, giving them all a good look at her legs, and proceeded to tell them all and Keith in particular that she had been at a party in Manchester over the weekend with members of the Boomtown Rats.

After she had gone, Charlie made the point that he reckoned that she fancied Keith.

"Do you think so?" said the lad, with a big smile on his face.

"Yes. I think she's heard about what you keep hidden in your trouser pocket."

"I see she still likes to do a bit of name dropping," laughed Mick.

"Well, it's not the only thing she likes to drop."

"You'd never think that both her parents were Sunday School teachers."

"Well, there's one religious lesson she has obviously learned from them: love thy neighbour, particularly if he is young, fit and able."

"Is that how she got the job as Basil's secretary, after Tracey left, specially as her typing speed is about five words a minute and she can't do shorthand."

Suddenly the five to twelve hooter blasted out all over the factory, informing all Wilkinson's employees that it was time to get ready for the four hundred yards race to get to the front of the queue in the works canteen.

Ten minutes later, sat at their usual table, Keith asked rather innocently if anyone knew where Kimberley had her dinner.

"I've never seen her in here for ages," said Charlie, "I think she must stay in Basil's office and have a bit of a nibble of something in there."

"I bet she's leading him a right merry chase," laughed Yorky.

"He hasn't a chance with her," said Charlie "unlike young Keith here who I reckon is evens-favourite for Kimberley's next star performance, like she had with that Cockney bloke, Wilf."

Then turning to Keith, he carried on:

"It was last year when she was working in the Wages Department. All the girls went on a night out in Liverpool. She gets chatting to a bloke in a pub on Lime Street, who told her that he had just moved up from London. One thing leads to another and he finishes up taking her back to his place. He told her he was in the upholstery business, which was why there was so much furniture in his very large flat. Well, before too long he got her into one of the double beds. When she woke up in the morning, the first thing Kimberley saw was a woman in a uniform, chatting to a middle-aged couple. Shortly after, she discovered that her new friend was a shop manager at T.J. Hughes. Well, he was. The next person to arrive on the scene was the senior manager, who sacked him on the spot for misuse of the company's property and shortly after the bed was considered shop soiled and sold in the sales."

"Summat liked that happened to our kid, last month," chipped in Colin. "He was working on a job building a block of flats at Parrs Wood in Manchester. One afternoon he decided to have a bath in this right posh flat. The only problem was that the joiners hadn't finished what they were doing, so there was no lock on the door. Our kid didn't know that that afternoon, an estate agent was taking prospective buyers round. He'd only been in the bath a few minutes when a woman suddenly burst into the room, pulls down her kecks and has a pee.

"It was quite a large bathroom and at first she didn't see him. Then another woman shouts out 'Hurry up Celia. I'm bursting. Have you got a man in there?'

"By this time the first woman was washing her hands and it was then that she saw our kid in the bath. She must have had a good sense of humour because she goes over to him, looks down into the water, says something like 'What are you hiding in there? It must be pretty small' and walks out.

"Then her friend went in and as she sits down, she sees our Ronnie straightaway and emitted the loudest scream you'd ever heard."

"Did he get the sack for it?"

"No, but on his next wage slip, in the deductions column, somebody in the Wages Department had included the amount of twenty pence (Soap)."

"You've made that up," laughed Charlie.

Then Alan joined in. "I remember when they were building those new houses in Penketh Drive. We often used to go in there after the builders had gone home and mess about. One night we discovered the water hadn't been turned off at the mains. So we turned the tap on in the bath and waited till all the water came flooding into the kitchen downstairs."

"You little hooligan."

"Oh, I bet you were a right little goody-goody as a kid, Mick. I bet you never did anything like that."

"The only reason Mick never did anything like that was because they didn't have running water in Wigan when he was a kid."

"And they still don't," laughed Yorky.

Humour was an ever-present feature of Wilkinson's Drawing Office. Punning, deliberate and subtle misuse of words, retelling stories from the past with the inevitable long drawn-out punchlines, were all part and parcel of the place. Frequently the stories were told for the benefit of the graduate apprentices, some of whom came from such delightful places as Chipping Sudbury, Little Much Binding-in-the-Marsh, Stowmarket and Stow-on-the-Wold. But quite often such tales were lost on those bright young things, who either had no sense of humour, or a quite alien sense of humour, totally unlike what had been bred into the people of Ashurst and district.

One such character was Rupert who had recently obtained a degree at Liverpool University and had been brought up in the Cotswolds, or Costworld as Mick usually called it. One evening after work, Charlie had given him a lift back to where he was lodging at the YMCA in St Helens. Driving through the fields approaching Bold Power Station, they had seen a young woman stood next to a Mini van, with its back door wide open. She appeared to be struggling with a pony on the grass verge. Charlie had slowed down and said to Rupert, "Should we stop and give her a hand?"

"To do what?" the young gentleman had asked.

"To get that horse into her van. She'll never do it on her own, will she? It'll bang its head."

And on another occasion, humour had been used to put in his place one Jason Montgomery Helston-Giles. On the morning of the first of April, Charlie had told the young graduate apprentice to go down to the Machine Shop and speak to Maureen who worked in the office there. As soon as she saw him, she asked him if he was the draughtsman she had just rung up for.

"Yes," he had replied in the usual aggressive manner that he employed when dealing with members of the lower classes.

So she picked up a feather from her desk, held it against a small crack in the wall and as it fluttered in the air, she went on:

"Well, can you do summat about this draught?"

8.

The spy who came in with a cold

EVERY YEAR IN early September, in addition to twenty trade apprentices, the Company took on six graduate apprentices, giving them an opportunity to gain practical experience in industry to add to the qualifications they had obtained at University. They came from a wide range of backgrounds and for most of them, working at Wilkinson's, was one great culture shock. On odd occasions, one of them might have had a similar background to that of a typical draughtsman. But more often than not, they came from a totally different world. Among the 1979 intake for example, four had been to a top public school, the father of one had for a time been a member of Ted Heath's Cabinet, another drove to work in a Bentley and, at the tender age of twenty-two, the one they called Rockafella was so well off, he owned his own house in the stockbroker belt of Surrey.

The worst of that particular group had been Simon King. He didn't have a home town as such, because when he was not at boarding school he lived at the family home at Tunbridge Wells, or at other houses that his father owned, one of which was located quite close to the town of Llanfairpwllgwyngllgogerychwyrndrobwllllantysiliogogogoch (St Mary's Church in a dell of white hazel trees, near the rapid whirlpool, by the red cave of the Church of St. Tysilo) in Wales. Daddy made his money in property development and also had offices in London and New York as well as owning an apartment in Monte Carlo, which his son often flew out to for the weekend.

On his CV, Simon had listed chess, cross-country running, throwing the discus and rugby among his sporting interests. On the last point, he appeared to have something in common with Mick, Charlie, Alan and Colin, although very little else. His CV also indicated that he could speak five languages, had a degree in Electrical Engineering, was a committed Christian and concerned himself with environmental issues, and world affairs.

So the Electrical Section waited with great interest for the arrival of their new colleague, who would spend four weeks with them, to be followed by a fortnight with the Mechanical Section. But when he did arrive, he didn't quite look the part. He was certainly no Charles Atlas, and it was unfortunate for the lad that he had obviously caught the virus that was doing the rounds, for he brought with him a very bad cold and cough. Despite this, on his first day, wanting to make an immediate good impression, he had told all within earshot, that he was a keen rugby player, his club was the Harlequins and that he was a regular member of their second team. Then, he asked if anyone else in the office played rugger.

"I used to play for Uno's Dabs," said Charlie proudly.

"Mick used to be a referee," said Alan. "Colin had a couple of games with Swinton and I played for the Works' second team for a season."

Simon had never heard of Swinton, and clearly didn't have much time for works' teams and quickly went on to say that he had been at Winchester with three members of the current England Rugby Union team.

This initial discussion was interrupted by the arrival of an engineer from the Outside Contracts Division, wanting drawings for a design change to a job in Belgium and rugger was not mentioned again that day. The following morning, Simon was taken by a Sales Engineer up to Blyth Power Station in Northumberland and only returned on the Thursday afternoon, having spent the previous night in a bed and breakfast at Whitley Bay, which must have been quite nice for the young gentleman.

On Friday morning and just as they were waiting for the tea girl to serve them, Charlie quite pleasantly asked Simon whether he was going home for the weekend.

"No, I'm staying here. Father has some important business to attend to in Scotland next week, so he's coming up here tonight and staying at the Helmsley Hilton for a couple of days."

"I can make a list of all the beauty spots that are worth having a look at round here," said Yorky, with a big smile on his face.

"There's only one beauty spot in Ashurst," said Charlie. "That's the field at the other side of Mount Everest, where you catch your first glimpse of Bold Colliery and the road into St Helens."

"Ashurst is full of secret places of outstanding beauty," butted in Alan, keen to defend his hometown.

"The Town Centre is well known for its ideal location, particularly for the many tourists who flock through its highways and byways. And you may be interested to know, Simon, that you can get to anywhere in the world from Ashurst Bus Station."

"The only things that flock to Ashurst are the flock of sheep that Billy Fairclough has on his farm up Helmsley Green, the ones that have to be locked up on a Saturday night, just before the pubs shut," laughed Mick.

"Wigan is a better place for any tourist to visit," chipped in Colin, "particularly for any students of history. I mean, if you want to know what the 18th century was like, go and spend the afternoon in Abram."

That was where his mother-in-law lived.

"I tell you where it might be interesting to take your ewd fella, particularly if he is interested in wildlife," continued Charlie.

THE SPY WHO CAME IN WITH A COLD

"Just drive up to the end of the East Lancs Road, go through Oldham and after that you'll come to Yorkshire. It's full of dinosaurs, ancient and modern."

"If you don't want to go too far, you could take your Dad to Platt Bridge and maybe Mick will treat you to a pea wet for thi' tea," said Alan.

The humour however was quite lost on Simon. It had soon become clear that when his new workmates started going on like this, he didn't have a clue what they were talking about. It was also obvious that he wasn't very impressed with, what seemed to him, their childish form of behaviour.

"Why don't you take him to Knowsley Road on Sunday afternoon? They're playing Workington Town in the Cup. It should be a cracking game. Just a pity they weren't playing that new team, Fulham, else he could have shouted for them. And there'll be a big crowd there as well."

But when this suggestion was put to him, Simon virtually spat out his response: "I don't think that my father would want to waste all his precious Sunday afternoon watching rugby league. I'm sure there are many better ways for him to pass the time."

"Has your father ever watched a game of rugby league?" asked Charlie.

"I'm sure that he hasn't."

"Have you?"

"No. It's not my cup of tea. It has little entertainment value, in my honest opinion."

That was not a very clever way to speak about something that many of those around him felt such great passion about.

"I would have thought that professional staff people like yourselves would have preferred to associate yourselves with rugby union. Surely rugby league is just a game for shopfloor types and other losers."

"What makes you think we are professional people? We are just a bunch of draffies," said Charlie. "Anyway league is a much better game to watch than kick and clap."

"Do you know that the fitters get paid better wages than we do and yet they can't even start work without our drawings?" chipped in Colin.

But that economic fact of life was not something that Simon had any interest in knowing about.

Over the next few days, the lad demonstrated that he had no idea of the culture of the area in which he was temporarily residing. He was a real snob, arrogant with it as well and despite his irritating posh accent, not very eloquent with his use of the English language either. But he carried on as he had started, behaving as though the rest of the people around him were idiots, uneducated members of the working class for whom he clearly held such great contempt.

ONE SUMMER

Despite his superior education, background and grooming, but probably because of it, he held some pretty reactionary views. On general political questions, they soon discovered that he greatly admired Mrs Thatcher but had no time for the previous Conservative Party Leader, Ted Heath, who he thought should have stayed on his pathetic little yacht. He did not like trade unions and most certainly not the union, which all the draughtsmen and most of Wilkinson's technical staff were now members of.

On the following Monday morning, by which time they were all sick and tired of him, Charlie decided he could not stand his coughing any longer. He told him to go down to the Works Surgery.

"I'm sure that Sister Broadbent will have something for your sore throat."

"Aye, a big carving knife," Mick uttered under his breath.

Simon didn't seem too keen to learn about the noble art of drawing and spent a lot of the day talking about his time in America, his interest in the environment and the general laziness of the average British worker. He did not like the French, despite going to the South of France every year for three weeks' holiday. One morning, he had been chatting with, or rather talking at the young apprentice Dean, who had been waiting in the office, while Alan was searching for a drawing in the Print Room. As he returned, Alan heard Dean say, "I can't stand the Germans either."

It was obvious that Dean's comment had been in response to some poisonous remark that Simon had just made to the lad. Dean was a keen Saints fan and so Alan decided to have a little go at him and at Simon at the same time.

"I'm surprised you saying that about our European neighbours, Dean," he said quietly and diplomatically.

"Alan, the Germans killed your Dad. You are not saying now that you like them, are you?"

Alan proceeded to make the point that he often made, a brave one bearing in mind the circumstances around his father's death at Monte Cassino in Italy in 1944.

"Dean, you can't blame young German men and women who are only as old as we are for what their parents and grandparents did in the war."

Dean nodded. "Maybe not."

"And with you being a big Saints fan, I'm surprised at you slagging off people like Herman the German either."

"Who's he?"

"I thought you knew a bit about the history of the Saints. Clearly not."

"Go on then, tell me. I'm listening."

"Back in 1873, it was the interest and enthusiasm of a German chemist named Herman, who worked at Pilks, who called a meeting in The Fleece and started the original club going."

THE SPY WHO CAME IN WITH A COLD

Before Alan could say any more, Simon butted in and showed his complete ignorance on two fronts.

"So that's where your rugby league team comes from. It certainly wouldn't have been started by any true Englishman, either then or now."

With no bosses around, and now sick to the back teeth with the pillock, Alan decided to have a right go, listened to attentively by the rest of the section and particularly Charlie, Mick and Colin.

"Simon, are you saying that there wouldn't have been a rugby league team in St Helens today if it hadn't been for a German?"

"Yes. That seems fairly obvious to me."

"So you don't know that in 1873, there was only one version of rugby and it was not until that big meeting at The George in Hull in 1897 that rugby league got started."

Charlie looked at Alan a little puzzled, since he appeared to have given Simon some duff information.

"Yes, I know all about that meeting in Hull and how a few Northern teams wanted paying for playing and were going on strike over it and all the rest of it."

"What Herman did was to start the St Helens rugby club, over twenty years before the great split. To be absolutely accurate, Herman's team began its existence as what you and I would correctly call a rugby team, not league or union, just rugby."

"Alan, I'm not interested in all that history rubbish. Rugby league people have had a chip on their shoulder ever since 1897. You just can't accept that you made a mistake when you broke away to play your game in a few insignificant Northern villages and towns. But I don't want to discuss it any further. I thought we all came here to work rather than to spend all day discussing the past."

Then Charlie chipped in.

"Simon, ewd lad, do you know since you clocked on this morning, I don't think that you have drawn one fucking line. But you have coughed sixty-seven times. Are you going for some sort of a world record?"

Luckily at that point, the telephone rang for Charlie and while he was discussing a problem with the Wiring Shop foreman, Ronnie Garner arrived to sort out a design modification at Skelton Grange Power Station in Leeds. By the time Ronnie had left, it was almost hometime and so no more history was discussed that day.

Early the following morning, Simon rang in to say that he had just been to the doctor's and would be off for the rest of the week. Sat having their Friday lunchtime drink in The Horse and Jockey, the draughtsmen were laughing and joking about other graduate apprentices they had known, when young Dean walked over with a pint in his hand and sat next to Alan.

"Greeno, are you going to tell me a bit more about Herman the German? I'm interested."

Alan laughed.

"Can I just say two things to you, Dean? Number one, you can often judge a bloke by the company he keeps, so I hope we are not going to see you chatting with that bastard Simon again."

"No, problem, Alan, what's the second thing?"

"Do you know much about law?"

Dean shrugged his shoulders. He was a likeable lad, though at just turned seventeen, still pretty wet behind the ears.

Alan stood up, grabbed hold of his boilersuit, pulled Dean towards him and shouted loudly in his ear for all to hear,"You have to be eighteen to come in here."

As all the draughtsmen burst out laughing, Alan carried on.

"You know how you said you didn't like the Germans?"

"Well, you know what I meant."

"I bet you don't like the French either do you?"

"The ones I've met were all right."

"I'm glad you said that Dean. You see, Herman was the club captain for the club's first three seasons. After that he handed it over to another foreigner, the Frenchman, Monsieur Le Peton, who also worked at Pilks."

"I'm not being funny, Alan. But how do you know all this? I didn't think you were that old."

"A lot of it I've read about in various books and old papers like the *St Helens Sentinel*, the *St Helens Lantern* and the *Ashurst Globe*. I've also got some of it from listening to Charlie because he actually is that old."

Then he carried on, making a general comment, one that all the rugby league fans in the factory would no doubt agree with, irrespective of which team they supported.

"Rugby League history is fascinating and really interesting. It's real David versus Goliath stuff. It makes you proud to be a fan of the greatest game, despite some of the incompetents who have been in charge of it in the past. You should read about it sometime, instead of all them mucky books you've got in your drawer."

Then Mick chipped in.

"I don't often say this about Greeno, Dean. But he's right, although I must admit I don't really know much about how rugby league first started myself. I'll have to read up about it when I retire."

"Does that mean you'll be starting next Monday?" laughed Colin.

"Here's another bit of interesting information for you."

It was Alan again.

THE SPY WHO CAME IN WITH A COLD

"In that first season, did you know there were twenty players in each side, thirteen forwards and seven backs? The only method of scoring was through kicks at goal. The try existed simply as a means of winning the right to try for a kick at goal."

"You really are a clever bugger, Greeno," laughed Charlie, "And you were pretty clever when you told Simon about that 1897 meeting in Hull. I thought you'd got your facts wrong."

"I don't get things like that wrong, Charlie. It was at a meeting on Thursday, August 29th 1895 at the George Hotel in Huddersfield, at half past six in the evening. That was when rugby was irrevocably split into two different games."

"You are not quite right there, Greeno." It was Charlie again. "The meeting actually started at twenty-five to seven, but I won't quibble with your relatively accurate account of that great day."

Alan smiled, turned back to the lad and went on, "Here's another one for you, Dean. Do you know when the Saints first played a floodlight match? It was in 1889 against Wigan. They played it at Dentons Green and over seven thousand people turned up and to help them watch the game, the ball was painted white."

"Well, I never," laughed Dean, "I bet my Auntie Jenny would like to know about that."

"Why?"

"She lives in Dentons Green, at the bottom of Hard Lane. She will be pleased."

"You can tell her this as well, the first time the Saints played at Knowsley Road was in September 1890 and they played against Manchester Rangers."

"She'll be pleased about that as well."

"Why?"

"She's going shopping in Manchester next week."

"With all your great knowledge, Greeno, can you tell me when St Helens Recs first started?"

It was Colin wanting to know something about the team that his grandfather had once been the kit-man for.

"In 1879, Pilks formed a team just for their employees and they started playing at Boundary Road, near where the Baths are now."

"Er, Professor Greenall, can I ask your good self a question?"

It was Mick, either taking the piss or asking a question about a game played in the past that Wigan had won. Surprisingly it wasn't either, well not quite.

"When was the first derby game played under the old Northern Union, how many people watched the game and what was the final score?"

"This must be something that Mick read on the back of a beer mat last Saturday night in the club," laughed Colin.

ONE SUMMER

"November 16th 1895, played under the old rugby union rules and it finished nil apiece."

"How did you know that, Mick? You've just made it up."

"He was there!"

"My neighbour's lad is at University doing Sociology. One of the things he has to do is write a dissertation on some aspect of social history. So he chose 'The changing face of sport in the final decade of the 19th century'. He let me read it before he handed it in. Really interesting it is. Anyway here's another one for you. Who scored the first try in a Northern Union Wigan v Saints derby game, when and where was it played?"

Nobody said a word.

"Wigan won ten-nil, the game was played on March 21st 1896 at Frog Lane and a guy called Webster scored a try which was worth three points, scored a conversion for another three points and the winger Ted Flowers dropped a goal and that was worth four points."

"Was that on page one, Mick?"

"When are you going to read page two, Mick?"

"Why was it played at Frog Lane, Mick?"

"Were you still at school then, Mick?"

"Eh, Mick. You like poetry don't you?"

Mick said nothing. Whenever they were all having a go at him, more often than not, one of them would refer to that poem written by Alex Murphy following Wigan's 21-2 defeat at Wembley in 1966. But that was not what Colin was referring to. It was another little story from the past.

"Saints used to have a committeeman called Alf Critchley. I knew him because he used to live next door to my auntie. He was a fish merchant in St Helens and on one of his blackboard outside his shop, he had written this little bit of poetry."

But before he could say any more, they all heard the five to one hooter blow, giving Mick the opportunity to finish his pint in one gulp and lead them all back to work on time, without having to run.

Back in the office later that afternoon, it was time to have a big clear-up. The painters were due in over the weekend, but before they could start, a couple of desks, an old drawing board and a reference table had to be removed. They would later form the centrepiece of a bonfire that Ashurst Round Table was intending to build over the weekend. One of the desks was the one that Simon had used. The drawers were locked and so with the aid of a large screwdriver, Charlie had forced them open. There was nothing in the top drawer of any significance other than a copy of B.I.C.C. Cables and Tables, a sheet of Critchley cable markers and a folder full of timesheets. The second drawer was something of a revelation.

74

THE SPY WHO CAME IN WITH A COLD

They had all been a little surprised when, within ten minutes of arriving in the office, Simon had put a wad of papers in the bottom drawer, but only after asking whether there was a key for it. With that drawer now open, the contents were there for all to see. They included a couple of A4 notepads, the property of the East Sussex Private Detective Agency, In the first pad was a list of around thirty telephone numbers, including the Head Offices of the Engineering Employers Federation and the Economic League, two junior Conservative M.P.s, Brighton Police Station, Scotland Yard, the Help the Aged Charity Shop in Camden Town along with three London clubs, The Gay Hussar, White's and Churchill's. Obviously Simon moved in rather unusual circles. It was however what had been written in the second pad that revealed what he had really been up to.

Sam had been very suspicious of him ever since he had arrived. It was just a gut feeling he had and one that he had initially kept to himself. He decided that if there was something a bit dicey about the bloke, then he would find out what it was. It would require a bit of subtle investigation and one way to do that was to behave in a very friendly way with the lad, something which Alan and Charlie had soon picked up on.

Within a few days, Simon had begun to ask him questions, about their union and who were the militants. Sam had led him to believe that the main troublemakers were George Pennington and Ernie Broadbent, both Jig and Tool draughtsmen who worked in a little office next to the Sand Wash. He told Simon that all the other draughtsmen called that place the Kremlin. It was where George and Ernie schemed and plotted all day long. It was they who controlled everything both at work and at the monthly meetings of the Ashurst branch of the union. Simon seemed really keen to know as much as he could about them and so Sam fed him loads of duff information, like Ernie being chairman of the Merseyside All Action Workers Committee, who were currently planning to bring the whole of the North West out on strike next month. George and Ernie were actually the worst members in the office, like a pair of old washer women Charlie called them, not even man enough to be members of the Mothers' Union.

It was of course all lies. and so when Simon's notebook was opened up, not only were the names of George Pennington and Ernie Broadbent listed, along with a couple of other more likely candidates, there was also a note that Maurice, whoever he was, had been informed along with the name and telephone number of a detective in Warrington C.I.D.

So had Simon been an industrial spy? Well, not a very good one, obviously. Who had he been working for? Trying to find that out proved difficult, particularly when Mrs. Foster, who was in charge of Staff Wages, told Charlie that Simon was paid monthly on a different account than all the other graduates. Was this an example of the Government's new industrial relations policy? Had it been an attempt by the Engineering Employers Federation to undermine or infiltrate the union? Were agent provocateurs being put in place? Or was it just some cunning plan by Basil; well, not that cunning because it had been a complete failure. That was never discovered, although a couple of years later Alan was sure he had seen Simon at a picket line outside Parkside Colliery in Newton-le-Willows, liasing with a high-ranking police inspector.

They were all pleased to see the back of him for he never returned, not even to collect his possessions or to spend time observing how members of the Mechanical Section drew and dimensioned brackets, flanges and cover plates. Perhaps he realised that his own cover had been blown, but then on the other hand, maybe it really had been the Ashurst Flu that had laid him out.

And so that was how the so-called 'graduate apprentice' Simon King had earned his nickname, the one by which he would always be remembered by Wilkinson's draughtsmen: 'The spy who came in with a cold'.

9.

The funeral of Auntie Doris

FUNERALS ARE GENERALLY such sad affairs. They are occasions when someone who has been known for a long time, who has been a part and parcel of your life, is no longer with you. Sometimes the person who has died has been plucked away suddenly without the slightest hint that they would never be seen again. At other times though, a funeral can be a relief, particularly for a person who has been suffering for years with a painful illness or from a dreadful accident or horrific war wound. Sometimes a funeral is an occasion to celebrate the life of a person whose time has come and who will be remembered by the whole nation for what he or she has done with their life. But at other times the person who has died may only be remembered by a handful of relatives or friends, and sometimes the only person present at the funeral would be a vicar or a priest.

However, on a few occasions a funeral can be quite a humorous affair, like that of Tommy Forshaw who had 'looked after' Charlie when he was an apprentice at Pilkington's factory at Ravenhead. Tommy had arranged for what he had called his last bill and testament to be read out immediately after he had been buried in Hard Lane cemetery at Dentons Green. In it, he had begun by saying that by the time those present heard these last words, he would be on with his first job up in Heaven: welding the Pearly Gates shut so that none of those present would ever get in. Then he had proceeded to make a few comments about those of his relatives who he had never liked, like saying of his cousin Councillor Todd that his secret about him once being in prison for stealing was safe with Tommy!

For Alan, the departure of his Auntie Doris was a very sad affair, although if there was such a place as Heaven, then the good thing was she would soon be reunited with his Uncle Jack. In his family, growing up as a child in post-war Britain, there had been many other pairs of relatives around; most importantly there had been his Granny and Grandad, Uncle Billy and Auntie Kitty, Uncle Stan and Auntie Sarah, though unfortunately a Mum but no Dad. His death at Monte Cassino in 1944 had meant that his father, Arthur John Greenall, would never be able to enjoy watching his three young children Paul, Joan and Alan grow up or spend time with the quiet love of his life, Doreen.

It had been during the war that Alan could remember making his first visit to the house in Rivington Avenue where Auntie Doris had lived for years. It was something of a horror story, something to laugh about when he was older. His Granny had pushed him there in his old rusty pram. It was about a twenty minute walk away from her house in Silkstone Street. He still vaguely remembered Granny taking him past a long grey wall and then down a pathway to the brightly painted house. Then she had knocked on the front door and lifted him out of the pram.

Auntie Doris had opened the door and straight away her eyes lit up as she took him in her arms and proceeded to kiss him, saying "Ee, it's my little boy. Ee, aren't you a lovely little thing." Then she hugged him before putting him in the hallway and helping Granny bring the pram into the house. She took hold of his hand and walked him into the living room: so far, so good. He had always liked her, she was forever tickling him whenever she came to Chisnall Avenue and she always had a bag of sweets for him. If this was where she lived, maybe there would be more here, he might have thought. Then, what an awful fright! Sat in a chair in the living room was a very, very old woman, with piercing eyes, just one tooth in her mouth and a mass of pure white hair. As he stopped in his tracks, she held out her wrinkled hand, touched him and began to sing:

> Here we are again,
> Happy as can be.
> All good friends
> And jolly good company.

It was Great-Auntie Nelly, at the time approaching her ninety-first birthday and looking twice as old. Straightaway he had turned to run away from her. He headed for the first door he could see, ran through it and pulled it behind him. It was quite a small room he had entered, and had only one door. At first he thought he would be safe there from whoever had just touched him. Then he screamed out in even greater fear. Hanging on the wall in the room that he had just entered was a fox, its eyes staring at him. It was the cloakroom he had entered, a rather grandiose title for the smallest room in the house. And the new object of his fear was Auntie Doris's scarf, the height of fashion in wartime Britain.

He spent the rest of the afternoon sat on Granny's lap, holding her hand tightly while looking at this old lady and continually asking Granny if they could go home now. If he had not been so frightened, if he had been able to listen to her and if he had been able to understood what she said, he would have learned a lot for she had been born in 1853 and had seen life in the raw. Granny took him there a few more times, despite his protests and then one day when they went, she wasn't there. At that tender age, he didn't understand what death was. He was just pleased that now whenever he went to Rivington Avenue, there was never a very old lady there to frighten him.

THE FUNERAL OF AUNTIE DORIS

It was nearly forty years later that Auntie Doris passed away, almost a year to the day that his Uncle Jack had died. The service was held in Ashurst Parish Church, a rather sombre affair led by a vicar who had probably never known her and who acted as though she had been one of his flock for years. Coming down the aisle at the end of the service, Alan recognised a couple of familiar faces. He didn't smile at them, he just half-nodded. You don't smile at a funeral, well, not in the church or at the cemetery. Some of those he saw, he hadn't seen for years. But one thing they all had in common with him was the fact that they were all much older than when he had last seen them.

The funeral party travelled up to Windle Steps cemetery in three large black cars. It was a miserable day. It had been trying to rain all morning. Finally, as the coffin was laid to rest, the heavens opened. There was no time to hang around, so everyone hurried back to the cars, which then proceeded to drive the mourners back to Alan's house in Silkstone Street. Once upon a time, it had been the house of his grandparents. His Grandad was now dead, but Granny was still alive and living like royalty, she would often say, at the Greenfield People's Home in Dob Lane.

While they had been at the cemetery Alan had seen another familiar face from the past. It was Bob Matthews, who had been his Grandad's pal for years. He had always been known as Old Bob, now he really was looking old and sad as he stood apart from everybody else. But as soon as Granny saw him, she hobbled over to him, aided by her new walking stick and asked him to come back to the house with them.

Old Bob had shared a lot of his life with Alan's Grandad. They had gone to the same school, then had both worked at Bank Top Colliery, now a dim and distant part of Ashurst's past. They had both answered Kitchener's call to arms in 1914 and been captured early in 1915 and spent the next three years working down a lead mine at a place called Neuruppindorf in what was now East Germany. During the Thirties, they had stood in the same dole queue at the Labour Exchange in Nelson Street until Old Bob had been fortunate to get a job in Widnes, where he had gone to live with his wife, Agnes. But they had never settled and returned to live in Orrell Street. They had also shared a sporting interest, cross-country running. And while Grandad was still alive and until old age had begun to creep up on them, both would frequently be seen at events across the North of England, team manager and assistant team manager of Ashurst Harriers.

It was clear that Old Bob was not well. His wife had died a year earlier and they had never had any children. So now his Grandad's old pal really had no one left. But back in the house in Silkstone Street, which he had visited so many times before, he suddenly perked up. Maybe it was the large brandy that Granny had told Thelma to give him that had helped. Maybe it was just being sat in the room where he had spent many hours discussing team tactics with Ned that did it, because suddenly he turned to Granny and started talking about his old pal and happy times. And it was then that they all learned a little more about Grandad's time in that German prison camp.

It was probably the first time that Old Bob had been in company for quite a while. Maybe it was just being among other friendly folk. Maybe it was just remembering bits about his own younger days, which had been so strongly dominated by that terrible war and then the unemployment, who knows? But as soon as he started to reminisce, the others went quiet and listened with great interest.

It was partly a response to Alan's comment about Grandad's time at Neuruppindorf that sparked it off. It was how the two Ashurst lads first heard about the end of that terrible war, that those present would now hear.

"Do you know how we found out the war had finished, well it wuz Ned really. We wuz all billeted in big huts, about six there wuz. We shared 'em with the Scottish Highlanders and some lads from the Somersets. Now, every morning two of the guards used to open the hut door, bang their rifles on the wooden floor and shout 'Raus, Raus'. Then you had about five minutes to gerr up, get thi'sel washed and dressed and out into t'yard with thi plate and spoon for thi brekky.

"Then they lined us up and marched us about a mile to that lead mine. We worked every day bar Sunday and them as wanted to, could go to a church service. Ah never went, I allus thewt God wuz on t'German side.

"Anyway one morning, I woke up first as usual. Ned wuz in t'next bed. Well it wusn't a bed, more like wooden planks on legs. He wuz always heavy sleeper, and a loud snorer too and he was allus the last to gerr up. It was usually me that woke him, otherwise Jerry would come down and poke him with his rifle. I lay there for ages, wondering what time it wuz. Anyway Ned wakes up, so we knew it must be late and summat wuz wrong. Then this lad from Oldham in t'next bed says to Ned, 'Eh, Ned, wheer's us breakfast? I'm starving.' Now I don't know why he asked Ned but he just did. Mind you, he wuz a bit of a rum bugger, that lad. He had to be, he come from a place called Mumps. He never looked very healthy either.

"Ned wuz a lance corporal and a bit like a shop steward for us all. So he decides he would go and find out what wuz gooing on. I went with him and a couple of others went as well, a lad from Atherton and one of the Somersets. I don't know why he come with us, we could never understand a word he said. Well, there were no guards anywhere. We walked over to the gates, which were allus locked and guarded and there wuz nobody there either and they were open. So we walked out o' t'camp and up this little brow to the road that led to the mine. Then we heard a load of noise, it sounded like men singing and cheering and from round t'corner came about two hundred soldiers, mainly our lads but a few French soldiers as well. As they got near us, Ned shouts out 'What's gooing on?' A little guy with his cap on back to front, shouts back 'The war's over, all the guards have scarpered. We're gooing wom. Tha can come with us if tha wants.'

"Nah Ned wasn't going anywhere until he had had his brekky, so he said nowt. But this other lad from Atherton wanted to be off. So he shouts out 'Are you going anywhere near Bolton.' Ee, it made me laugh."

Then, fortified by another large brandy, Old Bob carried on with more tales from the past, including the time when he and Ned were both A.R.P. wardens during the Second World War. It was the time they thought they had uncovered a secret nest of German spies in the clubhouse behind Mather's Foundry. They had been on general patrol and seen a light in the distance. As they approached the hut, with the intention of telling whoever was there to turn it off, they heard what sounded like an argument. As they got nearer, they listened and thought they could hear German being spoken. Ned being the faster runner of the two ran down to the police station to get help, while Bob stayed nearby. His hearing wasn't too good, but he could definitely hear voices yakking away and it certainly wasn't in English. About twenty minutes later, Ned comes back with four soldiers. One of them was a sergeant and being a pretty big lad too, he tells the other three men where to stand while he creeps up to the wooden hut where the argument was still going on. He kicks open the door and the next thing they heard was him laughing. They all rushed over to see why and there they saw him with four British soldiers. It turned out that they were all from Newcastle and none of the Ashurst lads could understand a word they said.

At this point, Old Bob turned to Granny and said, "Put some slack on t'fire Mary, else we'll all freeze," smiled at Thelma and nodded at the bottle of brandy on the table and carried on.

"Ee he was a rum bugger wuz Ned, but I couldn't have wished for a better pal. I wish he wuz here now. We could go t'Earlestown Races, if they still have 'em."

It was clear that he was enjoying himself and although it was a funeral they had all been to, why did it have to be a sad affair? Granny appeared to be enjoying herself too, even though it was her sister who they had just buried, for she kept tugging at Thelma's sleeve and telling her to listen to Old Bob and discover what Ned had been like as a young man.

Before long, it was time for those present to leave. Uncle Stan took Granny back to Dob Lane in his car but, on the way, dropped Old Bob off at the bottom of Orrell Street. As he had got out of the car, he looked sadly at Granny and said, "So nice to see you Mary. I've enjoyed me'sel today. Nice to be in your company and in your old house."

"Look after yourself Bob," Granny had replied sadly.

"Aye and you look after yourself too."

Then he had turned away and slowly struggled up his street to number seven. Two old people who had known each other through hard times, one through her late husband, the other through his best pal and now each urging the other to look after themselves.

But that was not the same for them. In the Greenfield Old Peoples' Home, Granny had all the staff to look after her and more than a dozen relatives who would frequently call in to see her. Old Bob had no one. Even his neighbours were of little use; on one side was a woman who was older than him, who rarely went out of the house and was stone deaf. On the other side was a man who worked nights and shared the flat with a little dog that barked all day. Upstairs was a young man who played loud music all through the night and did not appear to have ever had a job.

A week later the Gas Board man had come to read the meter and been unable to gain entry, Social Services had been informed and the police and when the front door had been opened, Old Bob was found dead in his bedroom, still wearing the clothes he had worn at the funeral of Auntie Doris.

A few days later Alan and his older sister Joan went up to Rivington Avenue to sort things out. After his Uncle Jack had died, Auntie Doris hadn't been quite as tidy as she had once been, but both Alan and Joan knew there would almost certainly be some hidden treasures to be found. And they were not disappointed, finding in the pantry in a biscuit tin over fifty pound notes, an emerald ring in an envelope in a wardrobe and a photograph of Uncle Jack with Bob Hope, on the back of which was written 'All my love to your charming wife'. And tucked inside one of many old copies of the *Ashurst Reporter*, along with a dozen or so cooking recipes was the most interesting discovery of them all: four typed sheets titled *The Memoirs of Annie Delaney*.

He hadn't a clue who Annie Delaney was. Maybe she was an old friend of Auntie Doris, although Alan had never heard her mention her. But despite that it was still a fascinating account of what life had been like for one young woman, growing up in the inter-war period. Whoever she was, her life had been typical of the lives of hundreds, maybe thousands of women who had been been brought up on the South Lancashire coalfield and the way it was written brought to life vividly someone who, like Auntie Doris, had just been laid to rest.

My maiden name was Annie Delaney and I had three brothers and one sister older than I and four sisters and a brother younger, all of whom were attached to the pits in some manner. I was eight years old when the 1926 coal strike occurred and I was very frightened to see the Mounted Police guarding the men who were working and dealing with the miners rioting for more pay. It was sad to see neighbours fighting for their rights.

THE FUNERAL OF AUNTIE DORIS

I was fourteen years old when I left school on 6th January 1932. Later that year my eldest sister got married and I had no choice but to go and work on the pit brow for the simple reason that 'Richard Evans' needed the rent money for 73 Juddfield Street and my sister had paid out of her wages so I had to follow and do the same.

My father and three brothers worked in the pit at the time which was not owned by Richard Evans so I was the only one to have the rent money taken out of her wages. The top rate of wages was 9/6d, the rent being 3/8d and I also had to pay 1d union fees.

On my first day at work, my mother got me out of bed at 5.45a.m. to a mug of tea, sugar but no milk and bread porridge with no milk. I was ready to walk to the pit at 6.15a.m. in order to start at 7.00a.m. The coal started winding at 7.0a.m. and lo and behold if you weren't in attention for 5 minutes to 7.00 you were in trouble. The finishing time was 3.30p.m. with a twenty minute break at 11.00a.m. to go to the toilet and have a snack. This usually consisted of jam or corned beef and a can of tea, all of which you brought with you. The toilet was a hole that was covered in chloride of lime to burn the contents and there were no sinks or baths. I would take a cloth soaked with soap and water in a small tin and use it to clean my face before walking home.

When I first started work it was on the screens, a cold draughty place with no heating whatsoever, you worked to keep warm. It was situated underneath the pit brow, nearest to the coal going into the wagons. At fourteen years of age, in company with a few more girls, with bare hands I had to take anything other than pure coal from the revolving belt. There was no sitting or talking and you were standing from 7.00a.m. till 11.00a.m. The machinery noise was deafening and there was black dust everywhere; you had no gloves though you could wear a pair of mittens if you had any. Many a time you put your hands on dead mice, and the other, as the men underground had to do it on the coal they had dug, even more so on a Monday morning after a few pints the previous night.

I went to work in thick, black stockings held up with elastic garters and clogs with 'polished' irons on heels and toes. We had to wear suitable items of dress to keep warm so I wore a black linen pinafore with pockets and a handed down man's coat. Headgear was a gent's big red handkerchief tied with knots at the four corners to cover your hair. We also wore a shoulder shawl. Now this was the pit brow lasses work of art; you got a cardboard lid from a shoe base cut to the shape of your face and rolled it round and put it into a pint cup that we used in those days. This would be left overnight, then we pinned it inside on the edge so that the cardboard fitted over your head and protruded over your face but inside the shawl. This kept some of the black dust off your face but we had to walk home in this gear though we tried to make ourselves presentable, hoping some fellows would whistle after us.

When I got to the age of fifteen I moved to the pit brow, that was promotion earned because of your ability for work. Here you worked alongside the men, you had more responsibility but it was still very hard work. At the 'Southport Edge' pit, there were two working shafts, one open and the other closed up, a little frightening when you see and hear the cages working up and down. One of my jobs was helping the onsetter, the man in charge of winding up men and coal. When the heavy boxes of coal came out of the cage they went along a track, three boxes being linked together. I was told to undo the box links with my feet as only one box could go over the weighing machine. Each box had a metal tally number representing the name of the man who had filled it. Only the checkweighman knew this. If it was too heavy and contained dirt and not coal, then the miner didn't get paid for the dirt. Quite a few things I could mention about 'cutting corners'.

The miners underground finished work at 2.30p.m. but we had to carry on until 3.30p.m. and clear up, such as spading dirty coal, etc into the wagons. I was in collision with a spade at the age of 14 years and cut my forehead open. I still have a blue mark on my forehead so I have always had to have a fringe to hide my pit brow injuries - no compensation for me.

I worked for six hard years after leaving the pit brow and got married to a miner. I was offered a job peeling pit props at the time my husband was sick. This was much easier and cleaner work though it was outdoors. My photograph was taken in the 1950s showing me peeling the pit props and this is now in Ashurst Museum.

The reason women working on the pit brow didn't enclose information in my time was that we were supposedly low class, but circumstances altered cases and I had no choice being a member of a big family. My mother brought us up respectably to be clean and hardworking with no smoking or swearing and I have done the same with my family.

Thankfully my three children all passed their scholarship and moved away.

"I suppose you'll want to keep that," said his sister. "Another bit of paper to add to your collection, eh?"

But there was another side to it as well for Alan could remember working with a young man called Delaney at Fidler's Ferry Power Station a couple of years ago. Maybe it was one of his relatives, and since Glen used to live quite near, after having made a copy of the document, Alan decided to call round on his way home to see him after work But when he met his mother, Mrs. Delaney, Alan discovered a quite different side to the young man, whose company he had enjoyed in the meter room at the power station.

10.

The unluckiest lass in Ashurst

GLEN DELANEY HAD SPENT most of his apprenticeship in Wilkinson's Maintenance Shop. He was a right Jack the Lad, always chasing the girls, a regular drinker, a bit of a gambler and well able to look after himself when the need arose. For a while he had also been on Warrington's books but managed just half a dozen games in the 'A' team. He lived in what had always been known in Ashurst as Bug Row, a small cluster of streets tucked in between Wilkinson's and the two adjacent pubs, The Chapel and The Besum. The Delaney family were quite well known in that little community of around one hundred houses, because both Glen's parents, his brother, his grandfather, and his auntie all lived there. They occupied houses in Agnes Street, George Street, Fanny Street and William Street, all modelled on that Victorian cosy assemblage of two up and two down with shared outside lavvy. The houses in the adjacent Montague Street had obviously been built for the hoi polloi back in 1870, for downstairs they had two rooms and a back kitchen with pantry and three upstairs bedrooms. Despite that degree of luxury and comfort, the occupants still had to brave the elements when they wanted to follow a call of nature: unless, of course, they possessed a guz under.

Glen's elder brother Tommy lived at number two. On one side of his house, at number four, lived the six members of the O'Hanlon family. On the other side, separated by a ginnel during the day could be found anything in excess of well over forty people, though as evening approached this number would usually drop down to one. There was nothing strange about this situation. It was just that Tommy's house shared a wall with Wilkinson's Wages Office.

Glen lived at the opposite end of the street at number twenty-seven. He had perfected the art of getting out of bed as late as possible while never being late for work. His alarm clock was the work's seven forty-five hooter. He knew that if he was halfway through his breakfast when the five to eight hooter blew, he was on time. As long as he was outside their Tommy's house when the two minutes to eight hooter blew, he was still on time: all that without breaking into a sweat either. All the time that he had worked at Wilkinson's, ever since leaving school, he had the proud record of never having once been late for work.

THE UNLUCKIEST LASS IN ASHURST

Tommy also worked at Wilkinson's. But despite living nearer, he did not have such a good timekeeping record because he had been late, though only once, although in rather unfortunate circumstances, it must be said.

In 1958, he had been sent for two days to work on an installation job at a factory on Hedon Road in Hull. You wouldn't think that Wilkinson's would have changed much while he was away during those two days. Well it did in one small way, because when Tommy turned the corner into the Winding Shop at bang on eight o' clock on the next day, he discovered that the wall on which the clocking-in machine had been fixed to, ever since the relief of Maefeking, was no longer there. The machine had been moved only another fifty yards down the shop, but by the time Tommy was able to punch his card, instead of the blue 8.00 he always saw, there was a red 8.01.

'Quartered'. It had never been known before. Then, despite appealing first to his chargehand, then his foreman, then his mate who was the foreman in the Welding Shop, his shop steward, Mrs. Billington in the Wages Office, his local councillor, the chairman of Ashurst Trades and Labour Club, the Citizens' Advice Bureau, Vic Feather at the T.U.C. and finally the Pope, all with absolutely no success, Tommy decided he had had enough. And so began a new way of thinking in the lad's mind, which five weeks later saw him hand in his notice and start work at Shelton's Foundry, exactly three weeks before it was unexpectedly closed down.

Following this experience, Glen had modified his early morning travel arrangements. Now he aimed to be outside their Tommy's at five to, just in case. Bizarrely, three weeks later he arrived in work to discover there had been an accident on the night shift. The new forklift truck driver, the one who reckoned he could do the job with his eyes closed, had driven into the wall and dislodged the clock which was now permanently stuck at 5.08.

Early in 1978, Glen decided that he wanted to travel the world and so had taken the afternoon off and gone for an interview at British Insulated Callender's Cables factory at Prescot. Well, it was at least five miles away, laughed his mates. But it was not for a job at Prescot but one working for the Contracts Department that Glen had successfully applied for. He then worked on cable installations all over the place, his first job being in Aberdeen, followed by one at Fidler's Ferry Power Station, King's Cross Railway Station in London and at the small Mary Tavy Power Station in Cornwall where the site foreman had fallen in love with a local barmaid and so conspired to make a three month contract last twice as long.

Then Glen had been put on his first job abroad, working in the Alps, installing a High Voltage transformer in a substation. Strangely, he had been made late on his very first day by a large group of cyclists, though it was no ordinary group of cyclists, the substation being witness to stage thirteen of the Tour de France. He worked there for three months before being sent to a job in Iceland, followed by another at the docks in the Belgian city of Antwerp.

On his return to Prescot, he discovered that he had three weeks holiday due, rather a strange thing really because the way his gang had been allowed to work made many days working with them seem like a holiday. So Glen decided to spend a week at home, then go up to Aberdeen to see some of the lads he had worked with, before his next contract started. This would be at a town called Weesp, not far from the centre of Amsterdam, another place he knew that he could spend a lot of money and have a good time.

His first day at home was spent talking to his Mother and Granma, telling them about some of the things he had seen or done and about which they hadn't a clue what he was talking about. Then, exhausted by having to repeat everything twice to his increasingly senile grandmother and slightly deaf mother, he called in at The Seven Stars. Unfortunately none of his mates were in there and he finished up talking to an old neighbour, whose only topic of conversation was what was running at Haydock that week.

Friday morning was spent in bed overcoming 'delayed jet lag' and too much beer, then a visit down town to The Volunteer, where he was sure he would bump into somebody he knew, but didn't. An hour was profitably spent in Lands' bookies, where he walked out one hundred and thirty pounds better off. He thoroughly enjoyed his tea: his mother had made his favourite liver, onions, chips and beans, followed by her speciality, jam and syrup Penketh Tart, but it was still hard work telling his Granma exactly what he had told her the night before. Then it was up to Onderman Street to see his old mate, Terry Shaw. No doubt they would have a night going round Ashurst and, if his luck was in, he might well finish up with some old girlfriend who just happened to want to hear about his exploits around the world, hopefully in the peace and tranquillity of her bedroom.

As he knocked on the Shaws' front door, he heard the sound of children and wondered if, while he had been away, his mate Terry had finally decided to take the plunge and marry his long time girlfriend Maureen. But as soon as Mrs. Shaw saw him, he learned that he would not see Terry that night. In fact he would now have to go halfway across the world if he wanted to see his old boozing partner again. Two months earlier, Terry had decided to go travelling too and was now working on a building site in Salt Lake City in America. It was something that Terry had always said he would do and once Glen had left town, Terry had gone and done it as well.

As Mrs Shaw was telling him this, two children came into the room followed by a young woman whose face seemed vaguely familiar. She nodded to him politely though sadly, took the children by the hand and said thank you and goodbye to Mrs Shaw.

"Who's that?" he asked, after the woman had shut the front door.

THE UNLUCKIEST LASS IN ASHURST

"Do you remember Mr. and Mrs. Morris who used to live in Naylor Street? Well it's their daughter, Sally."

He did remember the Morris's, not so much the parents but their two lads John and Geoff. John had played football with him for Astley United and Geoff was a couple of years older. John had been killed working at Gillarsfield Colliery when the roof had caved in and, a year later, Geoff had died in a car crash on the East Lancs Road at Haydock. Their younger sister he had remembered vaguely, although he had hardly spoken to her, even though she had often been in the house when he had been there.

Then Mrs. Shaw said a few words that made Glen change his plans for the next few days and weeks and even years.

"She must be the unluckiest lass in Ashurst."

"Why?"

"You know her two brothers were killed in accidents, don't you?"

"Aye."

"Well just after you went away, her husband was knifed in a fight down Liverpool."

"Did he die?"

"Yes. Mind you it might have been a good thing. He was a right waste of space, although I would never let her know I thought that."

"So what was she doing here?"

"I look after her two kids a couple of nights a week while she goes to work. She's got a packing job."

Then Mrs. Shaw continued with the poor girl's tale of woe.

"I don't know how she manages, poor thing. She hasn't two ha'pennies to rub together. She's got that job at Kenton's, she does a bit of cleaning at the Fleece and another job at home packing envelopes. And all she's got for a light in the house is a candle."

"What do you mean?"

"There's something wrong with her electric. She hasn't got any. I don't know how she's going to manage. I wish I could help her, but I've no money. Do you want a brew while you're here?"

While she was in the kitchen, boiling the kettle, Glen thought about what she had just said. Really it was a sad situation the girl was in, though nothing to do with him. Over the last few years he had often accused those who ran big business of being heartless in their dealings with the majority of the population. And he had always argued that the working class should stick together and help each other. And for the next few days all he was intending to do was go round the town getting drunk, talking to whoever would listen to his fairy stories and then he would go and work in Holland. There it was his intention to earn loads of money and spend a lot of it on Amstel beer, wine, women and song. In the meantime, a young widow in Ashurst would continue to bring up two children and struggle simply to survive. And on top of that, she was also the sister of an old mate.

"Do you think she could do with a bit of help, Mrs. Shaw?"

"I'm sure she could, Glen. But what could you do for her?"

"I'm an electrician. Maybe I could sort her electrics out."

"I'm sure she'd be really grateful, though she couldn't pay you. It'd be too much money."

"I wouldn't do it for the money. Don't forget, her brother John was a mate of mine. Maybe I owe her one for him."

And so he decided that was what he would do. Well, the least he could do was have a look. Wiring houses was something he was good at. He knew he could easily make a couple of hundred quid rewiring a house over a weekend. Though, as Mrs. Shaw had made it quite clear, there wouldn't be any money made on this job. But then money isn't everything in life.

He left the house soon after and walked up to Sally's house in Ashcroft Street. The house looked shabby on the outside and although he could hear voices inside the house, there was little light. She came to the door holding the youngest in her arms with the other child holding onto her frock.

"It's Sally, isn't it? We just met in Mrs. Shaw's. She's just told me about your electricity. I hope you don't mind but maybe I could help you."

Then, seeing that she seemed almost frightened of him, he went on to say that he and her brother John had been best mates when they were younger and both had played football together for Astley United.

She asked him to come into the house. He looked around the room but couldn't see that much, the solitary candle was not throwing out much light. She then told him that the house needed rewiring and she just didn't have any money to pay someone to do it.

So carefully choosing his words, he told her that he could rewire it for her. He didn't mind doing it, certainly for the sister of his old mate. He didn't mind giving up the time to do it, though as he talked it dawned on him that he would certainly have to buy all the gear as well. But then his win on the horses would help pay for it and if it didn't, well what the hell. And so it was agreed that he would call round in the morning and get started.

On his way there he called in at Sam Ellison's place. Sam's father had once been a spiv in Manchester and had taught his son all he knew. Sam liked to tell people that he was in the Import-Export business. Well, he was in a way. He used to import things from places they shouldn't have been removed from. Then he would export them to people who didn't want to know where they had come from. It was no use telling Sam why he wanted the cable, sockets, plugs and a Consumer Service Unit. Sam had no heart or conscience. He was an entrepreneur, someone on the way up and his price for anything that you wanted from him was the first price he gave you.

THE UNLUCKIEST LASS IN ASHURST

Having got Sam to agree to deliver the goods later in the day, it was down to the bank to get some money out and then up to Barrow Street to see an old mate who owed him a favour. It was John Mellor, whose house he had rewired one mad weekend and for which he had received six cups of coffee, three jam butties and a red hot tip for the 2.30 at Haydock on the following Monday. John was a plasterer by trade and his skills would be more than useful patching up the chipping-out that Glen knew he would have to do.

Back at the house, Sally began by protesting that he didn't have to do it. But he was now determined, though he had to tell her three times that Land's betting shop would be paying for it all. By the end of the afternoon, he had ripped out all the old wiring, sockets and fuseboard. Going round the house, he soon saw that there was not very much in the place, although he was pleased to see a few books from the library by her bed, good quality reading he thought too. By five o' clock he had had enough. He was exhausted with more than a few cuts and scratches on his hands where he hadn't used his Critchley knife too cleverly. He was starving too and so when she asked him for about the tenth time did he want another cup of tea he declined, gave her a five pound note and suggested that she get fish and chips for the four of them. While she was away he had a look in the kitchen. Not very much quality food in there, just tins of baked beans, tomatoes and soup.

After they had eaten and while he was wondering whether he now ought to leave, her little boy gave him a very good reason why he should stay, when he asked Glen whether he would play Ludo with them. After Ludo, it was Snap, then Animals, Snakes and Ladders and by then it was time for the kids to go to bed. And by that time, Glen's head was in a whirl.

The following morning he was there as promised at ten o' clock on the dot. By lunchtime, he managed to get the lights on. By teatime, except for the plastering, which could be done later by John, the job was done. It was then that the little lad said a few words that literally changed Glen's whole life.

"I wish you lived here, Glen. I wish you were my Daddy."

"I'm sorry," said Sally. "I think he's quite liked having you here. We don't get many people coming to visit us."

By this time Glen's whole attitude to what constituted pleasure was changing. He had enjoyed playing with the lad and his little sister. He had felt good putting power and lighting in the house and making sure a widow and her two children would be kept warm and safe. And in a very honest and honourable way, he had enjoyed doing what he had done, but perhaps most of all, he had enjoyed being in the company of Sally. She wasn't that good looking, but she was easy to talk to, once she had got over her awkwardness of him being there. The way she treated her children and the bond that existed between the three of them, was quite touching. They were really well behaved and it was clear she had done a fine job bringing them up. And despite having a sad face and lines on it that indicated what a hard life she must have led, when she smiled, well it just knocked him out.

Before he said good night to the three of them, he told Sally that he still had change out of his winnings. It was actually a lie, but it was a lie he was not ashamed to tell. On that false basis, he convinced her that she should let him put a new sink in her kitchen and repair the floorboards, on which it would stand. And by the time he had finished doing that three days later, he was not looking forward very much to going to work in Amsterdam, despite the many attractions that he knew would be stood around in various shop windows and on the street corners.

By this time, Liam had virtually attached himself to Glen: no matter where Glen went or no matter what he did, Liam would go with him and watch him closely. He was so keen to help, either to pass him the pliers or hold the screwdriver or a rawl plug. So when Glen asked him if he would like to go and play football in the park, a couple of afternoons later, the little lad's eyes had lit up.

"Go and ask your mum if it's all right," and, just as the little lad got up to run downstairs, Glen had continued, "Tell them that they can come as well, if they want to."

Within minutes, Liam returned with a great smile on his face to inform Glen that his sister and his Mum both wanted to know if they could play too. Well one thing led to another and despite working in Holland for the next two months, Glen started coming home to Ashurst every other weekend. Soon, he was turning up for work on his very last day at Weesp, when he was called into the office by the Works Manager who proceeded to thank him for everything that he had done and for his co-operation. Then he had invited Glen to return for the official switching-on of the water treatment plant that he had installed and commissioned.

"Come back as a guest of the company and bring your wife with you, and if you are not married, bring somebody else's wife," the Works Manager had said. When Mrs. Shaw heard the news, she said she would be very happy to look after the children for a couple of nights and so Sally was able to make her first ever visit to a foreign country. On their return to Ashcroft Street, she then told Liam that she had brought him and his little sister, Cheryl, a nice present.

"What is it? Where is it?"

She told him it was in the front room, but although he looked everywhere he couldn't find it. Almost on the point of tears, with his sister continually looking in the same places, Sally had told him to stop searching as she would now tell the pair of them what the present was.

"Holland is over the sea and a long way away, but when I was there, I found something I know that you would both love to have and play with."

THE UNLUCKIEST LASS IN ASHURST

Liam looked very puzzled, this searching for his present and not finding it had really upset him.

"Do the two of you promise to share the present and look after it?"

Both the children nodded and said yes. Whatever could it be?

"Your present is a new Daddy. Glen wants to come and live with us. What do you think?"

Much jumping up and down by the two children. A bit of a surprise though when they discovered that Glen would now be sleeping with their Mummy every night, but something they soon got used to. Then, there was another surprise for Liam when he discovered that his Mummy, him and Cheryl were going to go to a wedding and after that he would be changing his name to Liam Delaney. A month later, with all the changes and improvements that Glen had made to the house, it was put up for sale. Three months later the four of them made a complete fresh start to their lives when they moved into a new house on the Rose Bank Estate, which had recently been built on the site of the old Bank Top colliery. And who should be their very first visitor but Mrs. Shaw, with a nice symbolic present for them; an ornamental pair of candlesticks and a pack of 100 watt light bulbs!

11.

Horse manure and a large fan

''YOU'LL NEVER believe this.''

It was Mick returning to the Drawing Office, with a large bundle of marked-up prints in his hand and an enormous smile on his face.

"What?"

"It's hilarious."

"What?"

"It's the best I've heard for ages."

"Mick, what is it? What's happened?"

"Oberfuhrer Hitler. He nearly got drowned."

It wasn't the one-time failed Austrian painter and decorator that Mick was referring to but their boss, Basil Wilkinson, who by his actions over the years had earned that particular nickname. Not only was he disliked by almost every single one of his employees, his company was not particularly enjoyed by most of his relatives either. In fact it was often said that even when he was on his own, he was not the most popular person in the room.

Now looking more and more like an old age pensioner, Basil was invariably in one of three moods: a bad mood, a very bad mood or an absolutely foul mood. However on a few rare occasions he could be quite charming. This was when he was at his most dangerous. As a result most people made sure that they kept well out of his way. But they all liked to hear of any scandal that involved him and since Basil was often his own worst enemy, there was always plenty of that for half of Ashurst to laugh and joke about.

That morning, he had taken two American visitors to the Copper Refinery. Because it was raining heavily, they had used the short cut through the old Shower Room, totally ignoring the large NO ENTRY sign that was screwed on the door. Of course, Basil didn't think that the warning applied to him. He knew full well that the sign had been there for weeks and the chance of any of his lazy, overpaid employees working on the complete refurbishment of the place was pretty slim anyway. Unfortunately one of the plumbers was and quite keenly too, for just as three immaculately dressed gentlemen reached the middle of the room, he had turned the main water supply back on. As a result, Basil, Mr George Senior from Baltimore and Mr J. Roland Bush Junior from Houston in Texas were absolutely drenched.

"Who did it?" asked Yorky.

"Little Ernie Case."

HORSE MANURE AND A LARGE FAN

"He should get a gold medal for it."

"He'll probably get his cards."

"So what did Basil do next?"

Mick laughed and continued: "Well, according to Eric Kenyon, the three of them rushed back to Basil's office and Basil tells Kimberley to find some dry clothes for them to wear. So she gets football shirts, shorts and socks from the Social Club and then takes their suits to the launderette in Platt Street. And just as the three of them were sat drying out in front of an electric fire, a high-powered executive turns up from the Midland Bank to discuss the company's overdraft."

"Telephone call for Mr. Eccleston. Telephone call for Mr. Eccleston."

It was the sexy seductive voice of the delightful, though slightly overweight receptionist Stephanie booming out over the work's tannoy system that interrupted Mick's tale. Charlie heard it as he was climbing the stairs that led into the Drawing Office. As he walked quickly past the members of the Mechanical Section he was informed about twenty times that there was a phone call for him, probably from the Saints coach Kel Coslett, offering him a place on a park bench.

"Charlie, where have you been? Have you been hiding again and who was it with this time?"

Before he could think of a suitable response, Stephanie went on: "You've got a visitor. It's a Mr. Earnshaw from Manchester."

"Well this looks good, lads. It looks like Les is back in town, though I can't really imagine him as a salesman, not unless he's just flogging ice cream or something for the weekend."

Over two hours later, he reappeared with a bunch of catalogues in his hand and a big grin on his face. It was obvious that he had been drinking.

"So how is my old mate?" asked Mick. "And what's he flogging?"

"It wasn't our Les," replied Charlie. "It was another Earnshaw, but clearly one from the same mould."

"And where have you been since half eleven?" asked Yorky.

He threw the catalogues down onto his reference table, sat on his stool, burped loudly, turned to Alan and said, "Say excuse me when you do that, have you no manners?"

He continued, "He took us to the Crimea. Do you know I have never seen a bloke eat like he did. He started off with a bowl of soup and a barmcake, then he had Desperate Dan pie with beans, chips and gravy, rice pudding and peaches, two coffees and three pints of bitter and as we came out, he bought a pork pie and put it in his pocket. Then when we got back to his car, he gets an apple out of the glove compartment and tells me that his wife is always urging him to eat more healthily so when she asks him what did he have for his lunch, he could honestly say it was just a bit of fruit."

ONE SUMMER

He stretched his arms, yawned loudly and went on: "As soon as I saw him I was sure I knew him from somewhere. Anyway, he shook my hand and I took him into the interview room and the first thing he said as we sat down was 'Has your mam bought you a cozzy yet?'.

"Before I could say anything he went on: 'I can remember you swimming in the Hotties in your bare nack.' It turns out that he used to live not far from us in Owen Street and his sister was in our class at school, so we had quite a bit in common."

"Like eating food and drinking beer that you don't have to pay for," laughed Alan.

Their conversation was interrupted by the arrival of the wiring shop foreman, Harry Potter, who told Charlie he couldn't get hold of any LDZ 240 Volt relays anywhere for love nor money and needed twenty by Friday.

"Well I've got none in my pocket old lad, but I know a man from Swinton who might have some. Leave it with us."

"So was he any relation of Les, then?" asked Mick.

"No, but he might just be a distant relation of yours, Greeno."

Then he turned to Alan saying, "We talked about technical stuff for about ten minutes and then he started on about what Thatto Heath was like in the Thirties. He told me about a few people I used to know and then he started telling me about his wife, making the point that she had had a troubled upbringing because she came from a mixed family.

"I thought he was going to say that the problem was religious with half being Catholic and the other half Protestant but it wasn't. It was much more serious. Her Mother's side all lived round Dodd Avenue and Mulberry Avenue and were Saints fans, but her Dad came from Windle City and their lot all followed the Recs. He also told me that one of his relatives was a lad called Johnny Greenall, who played at scrum half for the Recs. He would appear to have been something of a super star man in his day. Do you know ewt about him, Greeno?"

Alan didn't. He had managed to draw the family tree going back to 1791 when his great-great-great-grandfather had been born in a tiny colliers cottage at Collins Green, but it was all based on his mother's side of the family. Very little was known about his own father's background, other than he had been brought up in Preston by a distant auntie after his mother had died when he was only six months old. And Greenall was a very common name all over South Lancashire.

"He knows loads about the old days," Charlie went on. "Did you know that the Recs and the Saints both started off playing at Boundary Road and the Saints were first known as St Helens Rangers?"

"One thing I did know from those early days," said Alan, "the two of them met in 1927 in the Lancashire Cup Final at Swinton and the Recs won 33-0. I would have loved to watch that game."

"Couldn't you get time off work?" his mate flatly asked.

"So what was he flogging?"

"The usual stuff, relays, contactors, terminal blocks, push buttons, nuclear warheads and secondhand submarines. He's working for Klockner Moeller."

Then he laughed loudly and went on: "I don't know if he talks to everybody else that he meets, like he talked to me, but he was hardly a typical sales rep."

"What do you mean?" asked Yorky.

"When you meet a rep, you either expect them to talk posh or at least in pretty standard English. But not him. He was a typical Sintelliner. Not that there's ewt wrong with that. It's just that you don't expect it from a bloke in a pin-striped suit and a carnation in his top pocket.

"After he had told us a few tales about swimming in the Hotties and collecting cig packets on that slagheap near Eccleston Water Works, he started telling me where he had worked before he had gone into selling. But he had that typical St Helens way of saying 'me' at the end of his sentence, like 'I worked at U.G.B. me, before I did my National Service' and later on when I asked him how far did his area cover, he said 'I gerr up as far as Carlisle on this job, me'.

"You know it sounded really funny said by a bloke in that posh suit, like after he had suggested going for some lunch, he said 'Do you have fo' go back for your coat?' And when we were in the pub, they put the television on for the News and when a big fat woman stood right in front of us, Arthur shouts out 'Eh, love, you weren't born at Pilks were you ?' The funny thing was she knew him, so she turns round and says to us, 'Go and shove ducks up North Road', just like your Mam used to say to you when you were a kid."

Charlie turned to Yorky and translated what he had just said.

"If you don't know what that means, Sam, it means get out of my sight."

Charlie's account of his lunchtime entertainment was halted temporarily while the Planning Department Office Manager scurried through the office, puffing and blowing as he usually did. After the door had closed behind him, Charlie imitated the noise he made and then carried on:

"He showed me this new contactor they've designed. It's very compact, and when I asked him how do you change the current settings, do you know what he said? It was a very distinctive explanation, short and to the point. 'Ya fo pull this little plastic bit out and turn it'."

"So what other useless bits of information did you get from him?" asked Mick.

"He told us about how they used to play the Grand National."

"How do you play that?" asked Alan.

"You can only play it in a terraced street where the houses have front gardens with a hedge separating each garden from the next one. You and your mates start at the top of the street outside the wall of the first garden. Then it's one, two, three, go and you have fo' climb up and over the first hedge, run across the garden, then over the next hedge and garden, right down to the bottom of the street."

He burped again, looked round pretending to see where the noise had come from, then went on, clearly enjoying himself, being paid to make the rest of them laugh and so maintaining his well earned reputation as the office comedian.

"Well he's certainly going down on my Christmas card list, a real character and a red hot Saints fan as well. He told me he can easily get us tickets for next Sunday's game. How do you fancy coming Greeno and sitting down for a change? You could even come in your beddies and pretend you are sat at home in front of the telly."

"What's his background, Charlie? Most of the reps that have come here have been a right bunch of plonkers. None of them ever seem to have worked on the shop floor," said Yorky.

"He served his apprenticeship at U.G.B., then he worked at Crone and Taylor's for a bit, Hilton's and finished up in Dawson's Drawing Office before it closed."

"What was he doing there?" asked Alan. "Drawing bars of chocolate?"

"Anyway what have you lot been doing while I've been away representing the company?"

"Have you heard what happened to Basil and his two visitors?" smiled Mick.

"I heard that Ernie Case thought they were from the Water Board and wanted to make them feel at home."

"No doubt, when the real Les hears about it, it'll appear in his next novel. Has anybody seen him recently?"

"Jack Campbell told me he saw a photograph of him in the *Radio Times* a few weeks ago."

Sam's comment made Charlie make a factual comment about another old workmate with the same name, when he said, "This must be the only place in the North of England where you could have somebody who had been dead for nearly a day in a drawing office and nobody noticed it."

"Do you mean Horace Campbell?" laughed Mick.

Quite innocently, the Wiganer said to nobody in particular,"I wonder where he is now."

"Do you know, one of the funniest things I ever saw here was when Norman Wilkinson tried to design a paint mixer that used compressed airlines."

HORSE MANURE AND A LARGE FAN

Norman was the younger brother of Basil Wilkinson. He was known around the factory as the Meddler because of the way he continually interfered with things that he knew little or nothing about. He was forever talking with the mechanical draughtsmen about his various harebrained ideas, although he never came into the Electrical Section because he just could not understand how electricity worked.

"To try out his idea he got a fitter to replace the four paddles from inside an old paint tank and fit four compressed airlines and then cut a piece of metal from the front of the tank and fit a small window in its place. As luck would have it, the day on which the experiment was to be tried out, a group of students from Manchester University were being taken round. So Norman gave them a fifteen minute talk about the principles behind his idea. Then he told the fitter to go upstairs and pour paint down the chute into the tank. Once it was full, Norman switched on the four airlines and slowly turned them up to full pressure. Suddenly the glass window cracked and paint spurted out all over these students, the three lecturers and department head.

"I know it doesn't sound that funny," continued Colin, "but I almost pissed myself when I saw it happen."

It was true. Sometimes things that are witnessed are hilarious to watch, but not that funny to tell. But then other things are more humorous when told than actually seen, particularly when told in a pub after the first pint has been drunk. Maybe that was why there was so much laughter every Friday lunchtime in the Horse and Jockey. One great teller of stories was Billy Atkinson, better known as the senior of the Yorkshire clowns. This was because he worked at Wilkinson's depot in Leeds and was a regular visitor to Ashurst along with his sidekick who everybody called Einstein.

The following day as they all trooped into the Horse and Jockey, Billy was sat by himself, demolishing a large meat and potato pie, covered in gravy and surrounded by a huge mound of chips and baked beans.

"Nah then Atko, whur's thi mate?" asked Charlie.

"He can't find his passport," laughed the Loiner.

"Have you come about work or have you just come early for Sunday's match?"

One of Billy's great interests in life was following the Leeds Rugby League team and on Sunday they were playing the Saints at Knowsley Road.

"I know a very good five star hotel in Thatto Heath, where you can stay if you want to."

"Actually I've come to say goodbye to you all. They're moving our office from Bramley to Nottingham and making me redundant."

"I'm sorry to hear that, ewd lad. I thought you had plenty work on."

"We do. It's just that the accountants think it will be more cost effective if there is just one office and depot for the Northeast region."

"What, in Nottingham? Sounds about right for an accountant. Anyway are you going to fight it?"

"No, I want out. We've got a new manager and I can't stand the bastard. I'll take the money and run."

"'What about Einstein? Are they finishing him as well?"

"No. They have made him up to depot foreman, so he's going to travel there every day."

"Where does he live?"

"A place called Hanging Heaton. It's between Batley and Dewsbury. Do you know what he said when he heard he was being moved? 'Where I live it's on the way'. Mind you, knowing him, he would have probably said the same thing if they had moved him to the Norwich depot."

"Well, we'll miss you Billy with all your riveting stories about Yorkshire and its impending entry into the twentieth century."

"They got a new lad starting on Monday. He's taking over all my jobs."

"Where's he from?"

"Brighouse."

"Can he read?"

"He can read a meter though I think he might struggle to get through the *Ashurst Reporter*."

"Is he a rugby man?"

"Oh aye. He's a season ticket holder at Thrum Hall."

"We'll soon put him in his place."

"He also used to prop for Siddal."

"Only kidding!"

Back in the office that afternoon, they talked about the departure of their old mate. They would all miss him, even though most of the contact they had had with him had been over the telephone. Then Charlie became a little nostalgic about the various people he had known and worked with in the past.

"It's sad really. You work with a bloke for years, day in day out. Then one of you leaves, you both promise to keep in touch, but more often than not, you don't and you never see or hear from him again."

But that wasn't how things worked out on this occasion, for less than forty-eight hours later, Charlie's Law of Coincidence popped up. Stood in the queue behind Mr. Eccleston on Sunday afternoon was a large group of very noisy Leeds fans. And amongst them, yes you've guessed it, was the self-same Billy Atkinson!

During the course of the following week, another coincidence occurred. On Tuesday morning, Alan told the rest of them that going home from work the previous night, he had seen a dog run across Dob Lane and nearly get run over by a car driven by the former Wigan centre, Eric Ashton.

HORSE MANURE AND A LARGE FAN

"That's weird," replied Charlie. "There was almost a bad accident at Toll Bar last night, a little girl ran out of Stafford Road and was nearly run over. I don't know how the driver missed her. And do you know who it was eh, Ray French."

Two famous local international rugby league stars, both avoiding what could have been a serious accident at almost exactly the same time.

Then on Thursday Yorky told them that he had seen the widow of their old workmate Stan in Earlestown at the weekend. This prompted Mick to say that he had seen Les Earnshaw's wife Maureen stood in a bus queue in Ashton that morning. And then on Friday, both Alan and Charlie quite independently said that they would be passing through the Lake District on Sunday. But that didn't really count, as both were going to Derwent Park to watch the Saints play Workington Town.

Mick's comment about Maureen Earnshaw quickly led on to a discussion about what her husband was doing these days. Les had worked in Wilkinson's Drawing Office in the early Sixties. After he had left, he had taken up writing as a hobby and a few years later his first novel, called *The Draughtsman's Tale*, had been published. It was all based on his own experiences working as a draughtsman and on the old saying about work, 'They should write a book about his place. it'd be a bestseller.' Some time after, he had written a sequel called *The Actress Goes to Heaven* which included one storyline in which his main character Albert Entwhistle, a one-time scaffolder from Wigan, saved Brigitte Bardot from being kidnapped by the Mafia at the Cannes Film Festival. After that he managed to appear on a television programme hosted by David Frost, after which the literary world had begun to take notice of this rising star.

Anybody who had never worked in a drawing office or at an engineering firm like Wilkinson's or who had never lived in a town like Ashurst, would dismiss his writings as sheer fantasy, even ridiculous in parts. But those who knew him and particularly those who had worked with him knew that his seemingly far-fetched stories were all between eighty and ninety per cent based on real life incidents.

Typical of Les was the time he had been sent to work at Rugeley Power Station in the Midlands for a month, in order to redesign the control system for the coalhandling plant. Every morning he had to spend the first couple of hours in the coal crushing plant or boilerhouse, taking measurements. Then for the rest of the day, after having had a shower, he would work on his drawing board. For some unknown reason, the Power Station Manager had taken a dislike to Les and kept complaining about the time that Les spent washing himself. Then one morning someone had moved the plastic box that Les had put all his clothes in and so he had spent the rest of the day wearing a boiler suit and a pair of clogs, until the plastic container and his clothes were located in the Wages Office.

ONE SUMMER

Les had used this true story but modified it a little. One of his characters was having a shower, when an apprentice had hidden the man's clothes for a laugh. As he was searching for them, his boss shoves his head round the door and tells 'Jonty', the station draughtsman, that if he was not back at his board in five minutes he would be sacked. So Jonty had walked back upstairs with just a towel wrapped round him and spent the rest of the morning waiting for his clothes to be found. After an hour, the Machine Shop foreman rings him up with the details of a bracket that he wanted drawn. This meant that Jonty had to hold the phone in one hand and his pencil in the other and so as he is writing the measurements down, the towel around his midriff falls to the floor. Just at that moment, the new sixteen-year-old tea girl pushes the tea trolley into the office and sees a totally naked man stood in the middle of the office behaving as though he was a draughtsman, which of course is what he was.

Then there was the idea that Les had taken from the time when Wilkinson's maintenance electrician, Joe Atherton, had dropped pellets from a hole in the ceiling onto a table in the Hyacinth Room in the canteen where high powered visitors from the Board of Trade were having their lunch. It was Joe's protest about the pigeons and sea gulls that were forever flying around the Main Hall of the canteen, where the shop floor personnel ate.

In Les's first novel, *The Draughtsman's Tale*, the firm, where much of the action took place, always held a Christmas Dance to which only senior and middle managers and their wives were invited. It was held in the Town Hall where another of Les's characters, Stan the Man, was the caretaker. There were two large fans set about a foot below the level of the ceiling and were always running at full speed during the summer to keep the temperature down. During the week before the dance, Stan had collected a load of horse and cow droppings from the field at the back of his house and hidden them in the rafters. That evening and ten minutes after the dancing had commenced, he slowly lowered these droppings on to the blades of the two revolving fans which cut them into shreds and whizzed them all over the assembled hoi polloi, clearly giving new meaning to the old saying 'When the shit hits the fan'.

Another bizarre story, but one based on a real life incident and a typical example of the Leslie Earnshaw literary school of neo-classical industrial realism.

12.

The Yorkshire ponytail tale

"LOOK AT MICK. He's fast asleep," exclaimed Paul, a young apprentice on only his second day in the Drawing Office.

"Is he all right?"

"I'm not asleep," growled the man from Platt Bridge. "I've just got something in my eye."

"Mick, you are all 'my eye' and Peggy Martin too."

"Actually, I was just thinking about my holidays."

"It'd make a change if you were thinking about work, for once in a while."

"Where are you going Mick, or more importantly are you coming back?"

"Not if I can help it."

"And can you help it?"

"Probably not, so you'll have to put up with me for another few years yet."

"Mick, do you never worry that someone might do something to you when you fall asleep in here?"

It was Shaun, the latest addition to the Drawing Office, a bit of a whizz kid in the field of industrial electronics. He originally came from Leeds, but had just returned to England after working for a year in the Italian city of Milan. There he had fallen in love with a Gina Lollobrigida lookalike, who actually came from Gillarsfield. Seduced by Maria's charm, he had easily been convinced that their future was back in England, once her student days in Italy were finished. This explained why they were now living together, over the brush, in a flat above a chip shop in Dob Lane.

"I think after I tell you this little tale, you might try and stay awake a bit more."

It was going to be another story of what it had been like working at the Cross Fields Engineering Works where he had served his apprenticeship, a place that clearly had as many characters as Wilkinson's had over the years.

"We once had a new draughtsman join us, called Scott. He was a right dope. Mind you I think he was on dope. Everything in his life was cool and every sentence used to end in the word 'man'. In his spare time, all he ever seemed to do was listen to music and chill out. He had a great long ponytail and used to wear the strangest clothes I've ever seen on a draffie. He always looked as though he had just come from an all-night party, which was probably true because, like Mick, he was always nodding off, particularly during the lunch break. Well, one Friday afternoon, we'd all come back from the pub and there he was fast asleep, with his head on his drawing board.

"So my mate, who couldn't stand him or his stupid ponytail, gets a pair of scissors and cuts about six inches off it and leaves it lying on his board. After a bit, the lad still hadn't woke up, so Chris decides to sellotape it back on with bits of drafting tape and paper clips stuck to it as well. Then he gets somebody to ring up to ask the lad to go down to the Machine Shop. Well, they must have been all pissing themselves when he walks in there. But when he got back to the office, it had gone. Nobody said anything about it and he never said a thing either. And the following Monday when he came in to work, he had had all his hair shaved off."

As they all laughed, Shaun continued, "So we started calling the lad Yul Brynner, which didn't seem to bother him and a few days later we found him fast asleep again. So we poured red ink over his bald head and believe it or not, he never noticed that either. Going home on the bus, a little old lady tapped him on the shoulder and said that she thought he was on the wrong bus, because the one that he was on didn't go past the hospital."

"So where are you going for your holidays, Mick. Is it the Wigan Alps again?"

"Looks like Holland again to see the grandchildren."

"Don't you mean Up Holland?" laughed Charlie. "With excursions thrown in to Roby Mill, Orrell and Rainford. It'll cost you a fortune. There'll be no change out of a fiver if you go for a week."

"No, it's the real Holland and there'll be no change out of a fiver, if he ever gets to the bar," said Alan.

"I take it you and Charlie will be doing what is de rigeur for the rich middle classes now, houseswapping for your holidays," replied the man from Platt Bridge.

"Do they do postcards of Thatto Heath, Charlie?" asked Alan.

"The camera hasn't reached Thatto Heath yet," laughed Sam.

Then turning to Alan, the Yorkshireman continued, "So where are you going, Greeno?"

"We are off to an island called Hvar. It's off the Dalmatian Coast."

"I didn't think you liked dogs."

"How are you getting there?"

"Plane from Manchester Airport to Ljubljana, coach down to Rijeka and then the boat to the island. It's right off the beaten track. It should be good. My neighbour Phil went there last year."

There are three good things about a holiday. The first is the planning of it, asking the kids what they would like to do and where they would like to go; then comes the holiday itself, though sometimes it is a bit of a disappointment, though at other times for various reasons it is great. Then there are the memories of it, added to by the large collection of photographs, though there is often great disappointment when some of the snaps don't come out or greater disappointment when all the shots do come out perfectly but of somebody else's fortnight away from home.

Then Shaun chirped up again.

"My mate Vic had the right idea about holidays. He was a fitter and always used to arrange them to coincide with when he had finished working on a job abroad. The firm once sent him to the Phillipines, the job was supposed to last for a month and then he had to come back home, have the works fortnight and then go on to his next job, which was at a mill in China. So he wangled it that he would go direct to China, if he got the equivalent of the air fare in his pocket. And that's what he did. He had a week in Manila and another in Hong Kong. And on top of that, the boss asked him if he could call in to see the company's agent in Kowloon as soon as he arrived in Hong Kong to sort some spares out and they gave him a day's pay for it and he was only there for an hour. He used to get away with murder, sometimes."

"Did you go out much when you were there, Shaun?"

"Quite a bit, mainly in Europe though. Rochdale, Bolton and Cockenzie Power Station in Scotland, I seem to remember for all the wrong reasons. Mind you one of my best trips was to Portugal."

It was going to be a good time for listening to stories and so they continued to drink their coffee, while Shaun continued his tale. "On all my schematics, I always used to make the number of my neutral, ninety-nine. Usually there were never more than fifty or sixty numbers. But on this particular job in Portugal, the highest number, except for the neutral, was seventy-one, which was still no problem. After it had been installed, the mill wanted to add a couple of extra limit switches. There was one of our fitters out there and so the boss said that he could do it. I sent him a print and rang him up to tell him what to do. He only had to make four connections, even Mick could have done that.

"Well, he had all sorts of problems, sometimes the main fuse would blow, then the machine would only run in slow speed, sometimes all the lights came on at the same time. Every time I rang him, I couldn't get any sense out of him so finally the boss sent me out. He was in a right bad mood about it, so when I picked up my tickets, I discovered he had booked me on an economy flight; you can't come back before eight days and you can't stay longer than twenty-eight days.

"The fitter met me at Porto Airport, we had a few beers, went back to the hotel about twenty miles away, had a meal and a few more beers, which wasn't a bad way to start off with. The following day was even better. As soon as I walked into the mill, I met the mill manager who was very angry that this expensive new machine wasn't working. He told me to have it all sorted out by the end of the week, or else. As soon as I opened up the control panel door, I saw what the problem was. On some cable tags, number 66 can look like number 99 upside down. Every time the fitter had connected what he thought was sixty-six into the terminal block, it was ninety-nine, which explained it all. I fixed the thing in about ten minutes flat. The owner thought I was a genius. I couldn't come home for at least a week so I spent a day repairing another old machine they had there, the rest of the week on the beach and came back with an order for ten thousand pounds worth of equipment to get this old machine fully operational again."

"And we all thought you were just a pretty face."

"Well it made up for the previous time they let me out."

It sounded like another good tale, and as they had now discovered, Shaun liked to talk and joke about places where he had worked, guys he had worked with and countries he had visited and so he then carried on with his first visit to Belgium.

"They once sent me to a paper printing works near Brussels. All I had to do was take a couple of contactors and a print showing their electrician how they were to be connected. It was a big rush job. I'd worked all over the weekend to change the drawings. When I got there the owner treated me like some long-lost relative though all I had done was speak to him on the phone a few times. When I had done what I had gone out to do, he asked me to check the rest of the machine. I suggested then that it would be a good idea to get rid of the belt arrangement they had on what was a fairly old machine and replace it with one of our new electronic gadgets, which would cost him about two thousand quid. He agreed with me but then when I got back to work, I got a right bollocking. The Chief Engineer told me that the company salesman was just waiting for an ideal time to advise the bloke to scrap the whole machine and buy a complete new one, which would have cost about twenty thousand quid. So after that, whenever I went anywhere I kept my mouth shut."

"So what's happened to the firm now, Shaun?"

"It closed last year. They are building a hospital on it now. There were some great lads who worked with us but a fucking awful boss."

"Like Basil!"

"Worse. The Drawing Office Manager wasn't really a technical man. He'd just crawled his way up the ladder. All he'd do was watch everybody all day, making sure there was no talking, no lateness and never more than two lads round one drawing board at the same time. Still, we had a good time there. One of the lads was always whistling pop tunes, usually ones that related to something that was going on in the office. One day, Rocky, that was his nickname, was in a meeting in the side office with a couple of engineers from Siemens. We must have been making quite a racket, one of the sparkies had come up from the shop floor and we were just messing about with him. Suddenly the side office door burst open, and Rocky shouts out "Make less noise. It's like a bloody carnival in here," and slams the door. Half an hour later the visitors leave and Rocky goes back to his desk, with a face as black as thunder. It was absolutely silent in the office and then from the corner of the room we heard Brian whistling that hit record by the Seekers, *The Carnival Is Over*.

"About ten minutes later, Rocky went out for a couple of minutes, just as the teagirl arrived. She pours all the teas out and leaves. While Rocky was still downstairs, Brian put about six spoonfuls of sugar in his cup. When he comes back up to a silent office, he puts half a spoonful in, stirs it and sits in his chair, takes one big swig and then spits it out all over his notes from the meeting he had just been in. I don't know how Brian kept a straight face, because he then started whistling again. And do you know what it was? It was a hit from a few years earlier called *Sugar, Sugar* by a group called The Archies. You could cut the atmosphere with a knife and all went dead quiet for a minute, then Brian starts up again, only this time it was one by The Rubettes called *Sugar Baby Love*. I had to put my hand over my mouth and cross my legs to stop pissing myself. It was hilarious and then a few minutes later, the final straw. He started whistling *I'm Working My Way Back to You* by the Detroit Spinners.

"Anyway Rocky finally boiled over. He walked up to Brian's board and told him to go home. So Brian didn't say a thing, he just put his jacket, winked at me and as he walked out of the office, he started whistling that one by The Three Degrees, *When Will I See You Again*?

"Brian came back into work the following morning and Rocky had a right go at him in the side office and told him that he was on a final warning for insolence and would lose a day's pay. So Brian didn't say anything and went back to his board and all went quiet for a bit. But the following day, the Union's Divisional Organiser rang Personnel to ask for a meeting to complain about Brian losing a day's pay. Well, the Personnel Officer didn't know anything about it so he asked the Organiser to call round for an informal meeting. They had the meeting, that afternoon. It wasn't really that informal, there was the Organiser, the Office Committee Chairman and Brian on one side and the Personnel Manager, his secretary, the Chief Engineer and Rocky on the other. It was probably the first time they had ever had the union involved so they didn't want to set a precedent.

"The Personnel Manager started off by asking the Organiser why had he seen this as an industrial issue, clearly the Chief Draughtsman had the right to manage the office as he felt was in the best interests of the firm. So then the Organiser said he didn't want to make a big issue of it and just wanted to ask Mr. Fairbrother a question. 'You say that my member was sent home for insolence.' Rocky said yes. 'Could you define the word insolence?'

"Well he couldn't, and so the Organiser gets a dictionary out of his briefcase and reads out its definition. When asked if being 'offensively contemptuous' described Brian's position, Rocky had said 'not really'. Then the Organiser had made reference to what Brian had sounded like on the occasion of his first musical performance, one that was supposed to be 'offensively contemptuous'.

"'Will you whistle it for us, just to make sure we all know what is at the heart of this serious allegation against one of my members'. So they then had the ridiculous situation of Rocky trying to whistle this tune. I'd loved to have been there. And then Brian went and spoiled it for us all."

"Why?"

"He handed his notice in, but he went out in style. Rocky was in another meeting, when Brian left about half an hour before finishing time on the Friday afternoon. He put all his stuff in a bag, said goodbye to us all then went over to where Rocky's jacket was hung up, got a bag of sugar out and poured it into all his pockets. And as he went out of the door, he was whistling that tune, *You Can't Get Me, I'm Part of the Union*.

With that tale, Shaun became accepted as a full member of DOOTOFS, Wilkinson's own Drawing Office Official Teller Of Funny Stories.

But his next tale, early the following week in the canteen was all about the sporting scene at Cross Fields.

"You would have liked it there, Charlie. There were a load of rugby league fans there: half of 'em followed Bradford Northern and the other half Leeds and one lad played for Bramley as well. They used to have a seven-a-side competition every year, there must have been about a dozen teams in it. Rugby mad, the place was."

"We used to have that here," smiled Alan. "When I made my debut for the Drawing Office back in 1963, there were actually sixteen teams in it."

"Don't ask him if he scored a hat trick," said Charlie, "or we'll never hear the end of it."

"And the following day, the lovely office girl Janice asked him for his autograph," laughed Yorky.

"She actually believed that he was going to sign for the Saints."

"I wonder whatever happened to her," said Mick.

"You might be surprised to hear that I saw her outside Lane Head school with her children the other week. She was taking them across the road. She had at least six with her," said Alan.

"You're joking."

"I'm not. She's a lollipop lady."

THE YORKSHIRE PONYTAIL TALE

"It's a shame we don't have that seven-a-side competition now. There was always some entertaining rugby played." said Charlie.

"Another thing that's gone with the wind," said Mick. "I can remember when every firm in the town had a team in the Ashurst Factory Cup. There must have been nearly twenty teams in it in its heyday. I can still remember Mather's Foundry beating Stevenson's Pneumatics in 1950. There must have been nearly a thousand watching."

Just about every firm in the town had once had a thriving social club. Wilkinson's of course had had the biggest one, but never seemed to win that much. Dawson's Chocolate Works always won the snooker and billiards competitions, Pearson Engineering were the kings of the bowling green while Jarratt's always won the cricket knockout trophy. But with the progress of time, Dawson's had been demolished to make way for a bypass, the old Pearson bowling green, famed throughout Lancashire, was now somebody's back garden on the Prince Charles Estate and Jarratt's Social Club, had been sold off by the company and was now a Doctors Surgery and Health Centre.

The demise of many of the town's industrial landmarks was often a topic for discussion. Some of the recently departed firms in the town had been engaged in manufacture in the nineteenth century. Some, like Davis Pumps, were operating like it still was the nineteenth century. Well, they were. Once the Health and Safety people saw how much rubbish they were pouring into the Stinky Brook and how much chemical waste they were dumping, they closed them down. Not one person raised the slightest objection, least of all any of the staff. Strangely nobody ever added any humorous or dramatic stories of that company's history. Maybe the chemical fumes that wafted through and out of their factory in Binns Street had deadened their brains and their senses. But now the place was gone, along with Binns Street and the adjacent Rose Petal Lane. Never was a street more incorrectly named!

Another landmark that had now almost disappeared was Mount Everest, the once enormous slagheap that had grown up behind the old Everard chemical works in Ward Street. It must have been the biggest health hazard in the county in its heyday but still attracted dozens of kids in search of cigarette packets and bits of old machinery to mess about with. What finally killed the place off as a place of 'entertainment' was the war. Not the First World War or the Second World War but the war between the Martin Lane gang and the Dob Lane lot, led by one Alfonso Sidebottom. There had always been tension between the two gangs, nothing that serious, until one day it was mutually agreed, after many of them had seen a war film at the Hippodrome one Saturday afternoon, to re-enact some of the battle scenes.

The following Monday had been the first day of the school holidays and it was agreed that for the next two days, both gangs would spend time digging trenches, constructing army headquarters out of wooden planks, making large catapults using old rubber tyres and erecting observation posts in trees. It all seemed quite harmless, even pointless to a degree, at least until Alfonso's elder brother Fernando got involved.

Finally on Wednesday morning it was agreed that the battle would start on hearing the bells of St Lukes Church at ten o' clock. The Martin Avenue Army were well dug into their various trenches, which were protected by sheets of corrugated tin from the rotten apples and oranges they were led to believe their enemy would use. They had accumulated a large quantity of pebbles, wrapped in large sheets of newspaper, tied together by elastic bands and dipped in wallpaper distemper. Their enemy however were much more serious. Their arsenal included cardboard boxes full of half-opened tins of paint that would splatter on hitting the ground, homemade rockets that were lethal both when lit or when they landed, fire bombs in the shape of fireworks wrapped in petrol-doused paper and, most dangerously, Big Bertha, named after an enormous gun used in World War One.

Behind the Martin Avenue trenches had been illegally dumped large bundles of cotton rags, probably by someone from Stevenson Pneumatics. Unfortunately it was one of the first targets to be hit by a Dob Lane firebomb. While it was smouldering, Big Bertha had been brought into play. It was actually somewhat like a large catapult and the first piece of ammunition used was a large brick. The boy in charge of it had no concept of distance and so the first attack on the Martin Lane Army landed over thirty yards behind their line. It actually landed in the adjacent garden of Mr. Martlew, well actually it landed on one of his tomato plants in his greenhouse. The second 'bomb' went even further, landing a couple of feet away in the garden of his neighbour Mrs. Kenyon, frightening her large Alsatian dog which was lay fast asleep on the lawn. None of this could be seen by Gunner Morrison, who had come out to play without his glasses. Then came a couple of even stronger pulls on the rubber, which led to it tearing and so calling for a hasty repair job. With newer and stronger material was launched an even bigger brick. If it had landed on one of the 'enemy' it would probably have killed him. Luckily it landed well away from any child. It did however land a couple of yards away from Mrs. Martlew, who was actually having a bath at the time. It landed in her toilet, accompanied by glass from her smashed stained glass window. It was not something that Gunner Morrison saw, although he did hear the sound of breaking glass. It was heard and seen by all the others who, knowing what Mr. Martlew was like on a bad day, scarpered. As the brave boy soldiers ran from the battlefield, the petrol-doused paper finally ignited, the flames spread to a pile of cotton packages, dry as tinder, and within three minutes the battlefield was alight.

THE YORKSHIRE PONYTAIL TALE

No working public telephones were available in the area, mainly as a result of night time anti-social behaviour by the Pemberton Street Mafia (under-nines chapter) and so by the time Ashurst Fire Brigade turned up, a great fire was raging. After that incident, the Council finally took action and by the end of the month, Mount Everest had finally been flattened. During the next few weeks, Mr. Martlew stalked around hoping to decapitate any suspicious looking child under the age of eleven. Luckily most of the young people stayed in for the first half of the school holidays or only went out with their mother to help her carry in the shopping, a wise move on their part otherwise they might never have moved up to secondary school.

A month later, a property firm from Manchester bought the land and proceeded to build twenty tightly crammed together, individually designed detached houses. Rather bizarrely, one of the first people to buy a house, on what became the New Hill Estate, was an Indian doctor at Ashurst Hospital who as a child had lived in a village a few miles north of Kathmandu, and within sight of the real Mount Everest. But being new to Ashurst, it took him a long time before he fully appreciated the link between that world famous landmark and his new house in Daffodil Gardens.

13.

The Unified Church of the All Fearful

OVER THE LAST ten years, the town of Ashurst, like many other towns in the North of England, had witnessed great changes. Many of its famous landmarks had gone and in some cases the smells associated with them had gone too. Anyone returning to the place after a long period of living elsewhere would be in for one great culture shock. That was certainly the case for Frank Bacon, on the occasion of his brother's funeral. Frank had joined the Army on the outbreak of the war in September 1939. For the next six years he had seen active service at Dunkirk, in North Africa, at the Normandy landings in 1944, after which he had fought his way through France right into the heart of the Nazi beast and where on the banks of the Rhine he had survived a fierce battle where three of his mates, stood alongside him, had been killed. On being demobbed, he had decided to make a whole new life for himself and had emigrated to Newcastle, on the east coast of Australia. In the mid-Sixties, he had returned for a holiday and, on departing, had made the comment that the town hadn't changed much since 1945. It was quite an accurate statement, not that surprising, bearing in mind the unimaginative attitude shown by Ashurst Town Council over anything that involved the spending of money. Fifteen years later he returned a second time to bury his older brother John, who except for his wartime service had rarely left the town. On this occasion, Frank's main comment about the place was that he just did not know it any more.

For years Ashurst had four main landmarks. The first was the Town Hall, built in 1899 to replace the original one that had been destroyed by fire, five years earlier. Directly opposite it was Victoria Square, so called because right in the centre of it stood a large statue of Queen Victoria, looking as miserable as ever. Around her were a dozen bus shelters under which people could shelter from the elements as they waited for buses to transport them to some of the most important centres in the Western world, like Billinge, Earlestown, Leigh, Newton, St Helens, Warrington and Wigan. If they were patient and waited long enough they could also get a bus to both Manchester and Liverpool. If they were patients, they could also get a bus to Whiston, Peasley Cross or Billinge Hospital. Different arrangements were made for those heading for the mental institutions at Winwick and Rainhill. Now the whole area was traffic-free. Most buses departed from the new soulless bus station, built where the old Rivoli cinema used to stand. Even Queen Victoria couldn't keep her spot either, as the Council had now decided to move her one hundred yards to where the old Crown Inn used to be. She would not have liked that. But then, not being a local ratepayer, she didn't have any say in the matter.

The second famous, now sadly departed landmark, was the Co-op Hall. Within a hundred yards of the Town Hall and occupying the space of a football field, the ground floor had once housed a wide collection of shops, with the first floor being divided between a dance hall and a restaurant. Now it had all been demolished to make way for a Woolworths, ironically another Wilkinson's (the D.I.Y. store that is), a newsagents that appeared to have more under the counter than on the shelves, and a furniture shop which specialised in bargains for the discerning, but with special one-off deals that always finished at five o' clock on a Sunday afternoon.

The third landmark had been George Street Railway Station, built in 1894. In the early Sixties Lord Beeching had tried to close it down. Fortunately a small number of "hotheads, militants, Communist troublemakers, anarchists and folk from out of town", to quote Councillor O'Grady, had organised a campaign to prevent this happening. It was a highly successful action to keep it open. However, as a result of other and bright ideas by whizz kids in Whitehall who probably didn't have a clue where Ashurst was, and if they did, had never visited it, the station and railway line to Leigh had been closed in the late Seventies. The excuse given was that mining subsidence threatened the safety of the travelling public. The same excuse could well have been used to close all the main public highways, including the East Lancs Road as well.

The fourth great landmark had towered over the town for years. It was the gas-holder at the bottom of Ash Lane, demolished one Sunday morning by a demolition firm, led by a man from Bolton called Fred, and watched by hundreds of residents, many of whom had been moved out of their houses on the new Ullswater estate, just in case.

Other places that had disappeared included the last two pits in the town and many of the factories where the people of Ashurst once earned their living. Around the time that the coal industry had been nationalised in 1947, Bank Top, Havanna, Prince of Wales, Southport Edge, Montagu and Gillarsfield had all been working. Now all except Gillarsfield had gone, as had many others in and around the neighbouring towns of St Helens, Wigan and Leigh. Among the factories that no longer existed were Dawson's Chocolate Works, Smithson Power Design, Hiltons, Fosters and Stevenson Pneumatics. Wilkinson's had survived despite the quality, or rather lack of quality of its management, although some of the land it once occupied had recently been sold off for housing.

ONE SUMMER

Large parts of the town centre had also changed. The old market had been knocked down, as had the four pubs that looked onto it, The Volunteer, The Clarence, The Branch and Nelly's. All the town's cinemas had either been demolished or turned into supermarkets except for one. This was the Plaza, which was now called the Multiplex and had been divided into two units, so that you now could pay to see one film and hear two. One church had collapsed, due to mining subsidence, two others had been demolished to make way for the new link road to St Helens and Helmsley Parish Church had been bought by a man from Manchester and been transformed into a carpet warehouse called Ali Baba's Flying Carpets.

However, little had changed at the bottom end of Billinge Road where the Sacred Heart and Ashurst Parish churches continued to glower at each other. Before the great slum clearances that had been enacted under the reign of Mayor Preston, there had been two miles of terraced houses on either side, accompanied by many famous and infamous public houses, including The Lamb, The Shepherd, Old Joe's, The Wigan Arms, The Barrel, The Griffin and the most notorious one of all, The Hyde Bank Arms.

Some of the town's schools had also disappeared from the landscape. Central Modern had been pulled down in 1959, to make way for the Prince Charles By-Pass, which now ran right across where its playground had once been. But perhaps one of the most controversial acts of educational vandalism had been the decision to close Newton Road Junior School.

Many of Ashurst's most famous sons and daughters had spent their early formative years at this centre of educational excellence. One of the town's many characters was the teacher of Class Four, Miss Skidmore, a veritable pillar of the community, who had been there since 1944. She was a lady of great contrasts, with the ability to combine Biblical Studies, religious certainties and democratic principle with over-excessive use of the cane. During her reign, she had introduced her little charges to what she called General Studies. Every week she had informed her class of her ten and eleven-year-olds about a wide range of subjects and topics, of which they had little understanding or comprehension. Her view was something like that of the Jesuits; "Give me a child until he is seven and I will mould him for ever'. She believed that, even if only for an hour a week, her pupils were given the briefest introduction to the major events and discoveries that had shaped the world, they would, in later life, develop interests that would help them transform their environment for the good of humanity. Not surprisingly, most of her pupils became somewhat confused about issues that older children at secondary school would have had problems with.

One day in her absence, Miss Shuttleworth, a young trainee teacher from Manchester, had asked the children to tell her what they did in General Studies. She was soon amazed by the immediate response of those present.

"We learn about famous people from the past and things what happened to them in the old days, Miss," answered one young boy.

"We get told about things that nobody else knows about," said another.

"Well, let's go round the class and you tell me what each one of you can remember," Miss Shuttleworth had replied.

"The Greeks were very clever people. Before they came, there was no such thing as history."

"Ancient Egypt was inhabited by mummies who wrote in hydraulics."

"Socrates was a famous Greek teacher who went round people giving them advice. They killed him and after that, he stopped helping them."

"Julius Caesar extinguished himself on the battlefield. Then the Ideas of March killed him because he was going to become their King. When he was dying he said, 'Tee Hee Brutus'."

"Tell me more. It all sounds very interesting," Miss Shuttleworth had said with a big smile on her face.

"When people get married in the Bible, it is called holy acrimony."

"Gravity was discovered by a man from Newton-le-Willows. It is usually seen in the autumn when apples fall off the trees."

"When you breathe, you inspire. When you do not breathe, you expire."

"The nineteenth century was a time of many great inventions. In those days, people stopped reproducing by hand and started reproducing with machines."

"Beethoven wrote loud music because he was deaf."

"Why did the sun never set on the British Empire, Miss? It's because it was in the East and the sun always sets in the West."

"The first book in the Bible is called Guinness."

"A circle is defined as a line which meets its other end without ending."

"Christians are only allowed to have one wife. This is known as monotony."

"Marie Curie did her research at the Sore Bums Institute in France."

"During the Renaissance, America began. Christopher Columbus discovered it when he was cursing about the Atlantic."

"Queen Victoria was the longest queen ever. When she died, her reign was ended by the Government."

If Queen Victoria had been on the throne for the longest time ever, Miss Skidmore had surely taught at the school for the longest time ever. It certainly seemed that way. Because she had often been seen coming out of the building around five o' clock, many who had seen her had assumed that she was still teaching there. Well she wasn't. In fact she wasn't all there any more, though at the age of ninety-two that was not surprising. She was now living in the Anchor Housing Trust on Billinge Road but frequently managed to escape the grasp of her captors until one day, in the middle of winter, she had entered the old school playground wearing nothing more than her nightie. It had then been decided to move her to a different state institution and she had been taken the short distance to Rainhill.

Another odd character was one of the residents who lived in the Salvation Army hostel in West Street, John Ball. He had been there for years, having arrived during 1964. For the first few years of his time in Ashurst, he had worked at Mather's Foundry as a labourer, where he became known as The Silent One. He frequently went for days without engaging in conversation with any of his workmates. When he did speak, he did so very quietly and in an accent that nobody could properly understand. Most people thought he was from Eastern Europe, and was possibly Polish or even Russian. At work, one of the few people who got to know anything about him was another labourer called Tommy. Every summer, he would go down to Taunton for his holidays and, with his subsequent knowledge of West Country life and language, he reckoned his workmate was a Cornishman.

Every evening John would be seen walking around the town on his own. He also went out every Sunday morning after breakfast and was frequently observed sitting in Gillarsfield cemetery or on the White Bridge over the dual carriageway at Moses Bank. On odd occasions, he would be seen catching the bus to Manchester but other than that, little more was known about him, other than in December, he always received a letter from South Africa.

When it was decided to close the hostel, the occupants were given two months notice to leave. Mr. Ball had been asked on a number of occasions where was he moving to and when. But all he said was that he had made arrangements and would not inconvenience anyone. Through all the time he had lived in the hostel, inconveniencing others was something he had never done. On the night before the closure was to be put into effect, he went out for his usual lonely trek around the town and was never seen again. Neither was anybody the wiser about who he was, because he had taken with him all his possessions, few as they were.

Was he a displaced person? Had some grievous accident occurred in his earlier life? Had he been traumatised by some terrible event in the war, maybe witnessed some horrific atrocity? It was something that no one would ever know. However, later that year, a little more was discovered about him. After the hostel had been closed, an arrangement had been made to have all mail delivered to a P.O. Box in the Town Hall. From there most of the mail was redirected, but obviously only to those people who had left a forwarding address. Few of those who had lived in the hostel, had ever received any mail. In fact, except for his regular copy of the *National Geographic* magazine, Mr. Ball's letter from South Africa was the only thing that ever came through the post for him.

THE UNIFIED CHURCH OF THE ALL FEARFUL

So when the letter from South Africa arrived in December, the clerk whose job it was to redirect the mail had opened the envelope. In it was a moving letter, short but poignant to the extreme, but sadly with no forwarding address.

I was twenty-seven today, Dad. We had a small party and left a place for you at the table. Early next year I am going to become a mother and you will become a grandfather. I hope your grandchildren will meet you one day, despite all that went on between us. It doesn't matter now what you did.

Your loving daughter, Heidi

Tucked inside the envelope were three photographs; one was obviously Heidi, one was a photograph of half-a-dozen people sat at the table around an empty chair and one was of a gravestone, with the words carved out in Afrikaans. But that was the last letter that was ever sent to Mr. Ball. It was a story without an ending, although there might have been a happy ending. He might just have gone back home, but who in Ashurst would ever know?

Not much more was known about a quite different group of people who lived in Ashurst. It was the small number of devotees of the Unified Church of the All Fearful. The way they led their lives meant that they had little contact with the rest of the population. So it was from those who had left, that any information about their beliefs and lifestyle was discovered. But since any of those who did join and then left rarely talked much about their experiences, only snippets of information became public knowledge. But all this was to change with the arrival of Davinia, one of a new breed of the church's missionaries, sent from their headquarters in North Dakota.

Davinia was an absolute beauty, well-proportioned, intelligent, articulate even if she did have an annoying Kentucky drawl. She had come to Britain to help start a recruitment drive right across the North of England. She brought with her a whole fresh approach to the work of the church, although her ideas did seem more appropriate to the backwoods of Dakota than the South Lancashire coalfield. She began to put herself about the town, and soon began to attract the attention, of two lads who worked in Wilkinson's Machine Shop. She had met them outside the Library, where she had started to hand out leaflets on Saturday morning. The following week, they told her they wanted to know more about her church. Of course, if the truth was known, their intentions were not totally honourable. They both wanted to get into bed with her.

So she invited them to a study meeting, which proved to be rather boring. They were each given a pamphlet to read and discuss the following week. It had been written by the Great Leader of the Church, who lived at a place called Grand Forks on the border between North Dakota and Minnesota. At this stage, one of the lads decided it was all a load of old rubbish and left but the other stayed on. The following week he learned more about the main principles of the church. These were known as the Five Two Theory of Life and Love. Members were expected to spend the first five days of the week engaged in carrying out five good deeds of work amongst the people. For the last two days of the week, their time was to be divided between the pursuit of knowledge and the enjoyment of the company of the rest of the group, in what was hinted at as being a totally uninhibited and physical way. Some of the members of the group seemed weird, but Davinia was an apprentice's dream. And so the lad had said that he was now keen to know more, although he still felt a bit suspicious, despite the lure of the blonde bombshell. It was a bit like being invited to a party and discovering when he arrived that he was going to be brainwashed into signing up for a timeshare agreement.

By the end of the month, Davinia asked him if he was ready to be initiated by her. When he declared that he was, she told him that the first part of the initiation ceremony would be on Saturday afternoon in the house of Mr. and Mrs. Shelton, a couple who had been introduced to the church while on holiday in America. On the day, there were around a dozen other members present. As High Priestess, Davinia was in full charge wearing a tight-fitting dressing gown. She started the service by holding her hands up in the air and asking the lad if he was willing to join the church and carry its message forth into the world. He was. She asked him if he was willing to make a small donation to the church each week until the Coming of the Third Day of Inspection. He was. She asked him if he was now ready to be initiated by her into membership. He was. He was really up for this now. The next day, he would be able to tell his mate he had won the bet and was now owed a fiver.

She lit a candle and turned off the light. Then she undid the cord around her robe to reveal the beauty of her well-tanned body and asked him to repeat after her the following:

> Pain before Pleasure,
> Work before Leisure.
> Love will not wither
> For our God will deliver
> To those who serve and wait.

Then she mumbled something in Latin and stated that the first half of the ceremony had now been completed and the second half would take place between her, as the High Priestess of the Ashurst Chapter, and him on the following Saturday, starting at midnight in her flat on Dob Lane.

118

THE UNIFIED CHURCH OF THE ALL FEARFUL

Well it was going to be a long week for the lad. It seemed an absolute age even until the Wednesday evening when he turned up for the weekly study meeting. There he was greeted with some good news. The Great Leader was particularly pleased with Davinia and had decided to move her up to Burnley for a month, before crossing into Yorkshire, in order to set up a new group in Keighley. This meant that the High Priestess of the Ashurst Church was now Mrs. Shelton's sixty-eight-year-old, sixteen stone sister, who would take over all of Davinia's responsibilities.

Whether this was all true, or just another typical story of Ashurst folk, based on someone's fertile imagination, was never really established. But it was a story that was told all over Wilkinson's the following day and all over town the following night. And on Saturday afternoon, the lad went to Blackpool and deliberately missed the last train back to Ashurst, just in case Mrs. Murgletroyd had come looking for him.

14.

Hazel is the killer

"DID THE SAINTS win yesterday, Charlie?"

It was Mick, asking the same question for the third time, one that he had no real need to ask because he knew full well what the answer would be, that is if he ever managed to get one.

Charlie totally ignored him, no doubt hoping that a large hole would appear in the middle of the office and remove the Wiganer from his sight. But there was no earthly way that that was going to happen and so, a few minutes later, Mick said to Alan who had just walked back into the office:

"Greeno, I'm a bit worried about Mr. Eccleston. I think he is going deaf. Three times I've asked him what happened on the green grass of Knowsley Road yesterday and he hasn't heard me once. Do you know, by any chance?"

It is bad enough when your favourite team loses, but even worse when it happens on a day that your bitterest rivals win. It was however good for drawing office productivity, because for the next hour Charlie became fully engrossed in drawing a control panel that would soon find a home in the Meter Room at Pembroke Power Station in West Wales.

Peace and tranquillity was finally broken with the arrival of the tea girl, Hazel. Having worked at Wilkinson's for nearly a year, on the trolley round and in the works canteen, it was now her aim in life to raise her standards. She had decided that she would like to become a teacher and had applied to go on a teacher training course starting in September. She was an avid reader, and included among her favourite writers Albert Camus, Ernest Hemingway, Stan Barstow, James Joyce, and Les Earnshaw. It was no coincidence that she came from Gillarsfield and lived less than a mile from Les's old house in Morley Street. She had great talent for the subtle use and deliberate misuse of the English language, one of the things that gave her a large fanbase throughout the factory.

"Sorry I'm late, lads. Our tea break went on a little bit longer than normal. It won't happen again this morning."

As they all moved towards her like iron filings attracted to a magnet, she carried on:

"Would you all like serving in alphabetical order today or would you prefer to form a circle?"

As she began to pour the tea out, she carried on:

"You'll be pleased to hear that my Auntie Ada has come back home."

HAZEL IS THE KILLER

Hazel's Auntie Ada used to work in Wilkinson's Tinning Shop until she had been retired on the grounds of general depression. Being at home all day had only made things worse. Not long after, her doctor had suggested that she moved into the mental hospital at Rainhill as a voluntary patient. During her first month there, her husband Norman had passed away. At first, that seemed a real sad story but actually it was the very opposite. Norman had been the cause of most of her depression and shortly after his funeral, she decided to leave the hospital and return home. The first thing she did was to light a bonfire on which she put everything which reminded her of their disastrous twenty-one years together. Then she had walked into town and joined the Empire Bingo Club. Later that afternoon, she had joined the Library and enrolled at Ashurst College for a night school class in Yoga and Medication.

"She hated being in Rainhill. It was driving her mad."

"A bit like the Tinning Shop, then," said Charlie, as he picked his cup up from her tray. Then he carried on, "I see one of your lot has been writing again, Hazel."

At the bottom of Hazel's street in Gillarsfield was Belton Bridge. This had been constructed in 1899 to enable cars and pedestrians to cross over the Ashurst to Helmsley railway line. Just after the war, the line had been closed, so it was now a bridge over a non-descript piece of wasteland. During the early Sixties, some political activist had painted the words AMERICA. HANDS OFF VIETNAM on the left-hand side The previous month, on the other side of the road, another person, or maybe the same person twenty years later, had painted the words RUSSIA. HANDS OFF AFGHANISTAN. Over the weekend, some joker had added a few more letters, so it now read RUSSIA HANDS OFF AFGHANISTANHALL IS A NON.

No one knew who had done it. No one knew what it really meant although they could guess. The person may have run out of whitewash or maybe had been spotted doing it and run off. But it provided a lot of public comment about the said Stan Hall, who had just started a six month sentence in Walton Jail. He was the dark side of Gillarsfield, a petty thief, a person disliked by all of his neighbours, capable of frightening both child and adult simply by looking at them. He also owed money to various people around the town and so maybe the whitewasher was trying to tell the world that Stan Hall was a nonentity, or a non-payer or a nonce. Or maybe he was trying to say that he was all three, which was probably true.

"I never wrote that," said Hazel.

"But I guess I know who might have done it."

"Who?"

"Almost anybody who lives within a mile of our house."

"Does that mean he wasn't a good neighbour?"

"You could say that, but then you could say that the earth was flat, but that wouldn't disprove Copernicus."

"Is that what you are wearing today?" laughed Charlie.

Then to everybody's surprise, she unzipped the top of her jeans and showed them that it wasn't. She then told everybody that it might be best for their blood pressure if they all sat down for a few minutes and then zipped up her jeans again, saying, "I wouldn't have been able to do that yesterday."

As she collected together the money that she had just taken from them for their tea, bacon butties, buttered scones and Blue Riband biscuits, she went on:

"Three more days like that and I'll have enough to buy my first text book for college."

"And what will that be?" asked Mick. "Ten ways to overcome a hangover after spending all day in the student bar?"

"No, probably the *Origins of Philosophy* by Plato and Aristotle, that is unless any of you lot can lend me your copy."

"What use will that be in learning how to teach kids to read?"

"Mick, do you know that the mind is a bit like a parachute? It's only useful when it's open."

"Is that your saying of the day, Hazel?"

"Whose desk diary have you been reading? You can't fool me," laughed Charlie.

"Well, there's no fool like an old fool."

"So when do you know if you've been accepted on this course."

"Any time now. I'm really excited about it."

With that she pushed her trolley up to where all the mechanical lads were waiting for more words of wisdom from her good self.

A few minutes later Charlie was called down on to the shop floor to sort out a problem on one of his drawings and when he returned he found an envelope lay on his drawing board.

"Who's left this?" he asked as he slowly slit it open with his finger.

Nobody said a word.

Inside was a large piece of paper which had been folded three or four times. Finally he smoothed it and read the message, which asked, 'Did the Saints win yesterday?' and signed, 'a hidden admirer'.

"All right, Mick, we got beat. It's happened before. Not that often, so are you happy now?"

"Every time I am in your company, Charlie I am in a happy frame of mind. It's just that sometimes, my state of euphoria is higher than normal."

"Well I'm glad to have brought a little bit of joy into your sad life."

"I wish you could bring a little bit of Hazel into my life. I must saw that it's a long time since any young lady showed me the colour of her knickers."

"I'll bet there'll be no end of students offering to carry her briefcase, when she gets to college," muttered Sam

"Or her briefs," laughed Charlie.

Then the apprentice electrician Paul chipped in with his first words of wisdom for the day.

"Wow, she's a killer that Hazel."

"What do you mean?" asked Hamish, a young graduate apprentice from Aberdeen, spending a week in the office.

"You won't understand that," said Alan. "It's an old Ashurst saying, it means she's a bremmer or a belter or a woman that you really fancy."

"How easy can you understand all these Lancashire hot pots?" chimed in Yorky.

"Well, whatever you Sassenachs call her, I think she's great."

Then the sheet metal draughtsman Billy Mulholland told them a bit about Hazel when she was much younger.

"She was in the same class at school as our Claire but if you'd seen her then, you wouldn't think she was the same girl."

"Why?" asked Charlie.

"She was as thin as a lat, spotty, suffered with impetigo, had them purple patches on her head and used to smell summat rotten. I know they didn't have a washing machine in their house; I don't think they even had any running water either. Her mother was a complete waste of space and her Dad was always working away. I used to feel really sorry for her, she was someone who had never had a chance. Then her mother died so you'd think that was another bad episode in her life, but within a couple of months, her Dad's girlfriend moved in and it was the best thing that ever happened to Hazel. It certainly disproved all the bad press that stepmothers have ever had. When she moved up to her final class, they had a new teacher there and he obviously took a shine to her. He went out of his way to help her with her writing. He encouraged her to enter the Ashurst Short Story Competition and she came third! It obviously boosted her confidence no end and with a bit more encouragement from him, she got interested in athletics and to look at her now or listen to her, well, as we say here in Ashurst, Hamish, she's a killer."

"So you've known her quite a long time," said Charlie.

"Yes, she often used to come to our house and play records with our Claire. We always made sure she got a bit of something decent to eat as well. I think her mother's idea of providing her with a meal was to give her threepence to go and get a bag of chips."

"I often wondered why you always got such big portions on your plate when she was serving. Now I know."

The general good mood in the place however was shattered a few minutes later, when Billy returned to tell Charlie that he had just had a phone call from his brother, telling him that another load of redundancies had been announced that morning at the Triplex glassworks in St Helens.

"Where is it all going to end?" said Charlie, whose sister-in-law and two of his neighbours worked there.

"Ask Mick. He voted for it," said Alan. "Didn't you, Mick?"

Mick said nothing. He had been a strong admirer of Mrs Thatcher, although since she had come into office, three people in his street had joined the ranks of the unemployed as well as his cousin in Ramsbottom and a couple of old school mates, one of whom later committed suicide when he was informed that his house in Chorley was going to be repossessed.

"It's like we are living in a different world to folk in London," said Keith, whose own dad was now working only three days a week. "There are buggers down there who get more for a day's work in the City than I get working five days."

To divert attention from what Alan had just said, Mick then added to Keith's comment by saying:

"There are buggers down in London who even earn more in a day than I do working five days and Saturday morning."

"Mick, when did you last work on a Saturday morning?"

"You didn't quite say that correctly, Greeno," said Charlie. "You mean, when did Mick last come in on a Saturday morning?"

It had been before Easter. Sam, Alan and Mick had been working on a rush job that had to be ready for wiring on the following Monday. They had finished checking all the drawings by half eleven. Sam had clocked out straightaway and gone home, while Alan had stayed until half twelve. Mick had gone into the Print Room, ostensibly to put some drawings away but Alan knew he'd gone there for a nap in the comfy chair. Five minutes after Alan had clocked out, the security man had walked through the office, seen no-one about and had locked the office door. Mick, in the absolute peace of a deserted Drawing Office, hadn't woken up until turned two o' clock and had to ring the gatehouse to be let out.

A few days later, Hazel appeared with a big smile on her face. She had heard that she had been accepted onto the teacher training course at Bradford College in the unfair county of Yorkshire.

"Do you know what really clinched it for me?" she said. "At the interview they asked me whether I had had any experience of working with young children. So when I told them about feeding you lot three times a day, they were very impressed."

"So when will we enjoy the pleasure of your absence?"

"I'll finish on the Friday before the Works Shutdown. I'm going on my holidays to Ibiza for a fortnight and then I've got a job working at a holiday camp in Devon for a few weeks. Just for a break."

HAZEL IS THE KILLER

"From one holiday camp to another," laughed Charlie.

"And before I start on my course, I'm going to my friend's wedding in Wales."

"It's not anywhere near Tonyrefail, is it?" asked Alan.

Tonyrefail was where his wife Thelma had spent the first year of her life, just before her mother had died, around the time of the Normandy Landings in 1944 and after which she had been taken to Cardiff, where she was then brought up in a home.

"It's something like twenty miles away from Llanfairpwllgwyngyllgogerychwyrndrobwllllantysiliogogogoch."

"I bet you couldn't repeat that again.."

"Llanfairpwllgwyngyllgogerychwyrndrobwllllantysiliogogogoch."

"What can anybody say after that?"

"She's behaving like a bloody student already," said Mick.

"I bet none of you knew that Mick was once a student. He majored at Platt Bridge University and received a second class Honours Degree in joined-up writing."

"With chalk."

For the next few weeks, whenever Hazel appeared, it was time for discussions about teachers, education, homework,, smacking, psychology, sociology, philosophy and kidology. She really was good company and now shared with Joan from Leigh, the title of Wilkinson's best-ever tea lady. Finally, on her last day, she almost shed a tear as she kissed each one of them. Then she did shed a tear as Charlie presented her with an envelope in which were book tokens to the value of £15, collected by the electrical section and a fitting tribute to a good workmate, one of the best.

"Don't forget to come and see us," were Charlie's parting words as she sailed off into the sunset, which was an unusual way of describing the top half of the office.

Sadly, on their return to work after the Works Shutdown, they came into contact with Hazel's replacement. It was Nancy, or Nancy the Never as she soon became known. She never came on time, she never had any change, she never had a good word for anyone, she never brought any scandal for them to listen to and laugh about. She only had one good point, she never stayed a second longer than was necessary.

1980 continued to roll on. The Soviet Union continued with its occupation of Afghanistan, while in September the growing tension between Iran and Iraq broke out into open hostilities when Iraq, under Saddam Hussein, invaded its neighbour. In Britain, the unemployment, which had reached 1.5million in April, had soared up to nearly 1.9 million , the highest figure since 1936. Two events of significance also occurred towards the end of the year. Ronald Reagan was elected President in November and a month later, Mark Chapman, a twenty-five-year-old security guard with a record of mental illness, shot dead John Lennon in New York.

In rugby league, one feature of the 1979/80 season was the falling level of attendances. It had started quite well when nearly 8,000 spectators had turned up for the first game, a friendly against Pilkington Recs. The following week over 8,000 had seen the Saints beaten by their neighbours from Widnes in the first round of the Lancashire Cup. But by the end of the year, less than 5,000 had seen them play Workington Town. The first game in 1980 against Salford had drawn only 4,100 and for the last home game of the season, no more than 5,200 had paid to see them lose 19-0 to Widnes, this time in a League game. The size of the crowds watching the game had by now become a cause for concern and a regular topic of conversation.

"I can remember the Saints playing Barrow in the Ward Cup at the start of the 1959 season. It was only a friendly, yet there were over 11,000 there. A few weeks later, they played Blackpool Borough and the crowd was over 14,000," said Charlie, some time later that week.

"Wasn't that the season that over 30,000 saw them play the Australians one foggy afternoon?" said Colin. "And a few weeks later there were over 21,000 for the game against Wakefield."

Then Mick made the comment that he had been on Central Park for the Good Friday game that year along with some 49,000 other spectators.

"I was there that day," said Alan "I didn't know you were there as well, Mick. I didn't see you."

Falling attendances were no laughing matter, even though Mick laughed as he said that Alan had probably been stood in the Hen Pen at the time, along with all the other schoolchildren.

"They are going to have to do something about the way the game is run," said Charlie. "I still love going to the match, but I don't get the same buzz as I used to in the Fifties and Sixties."

"Maybe it's just because you are getting older. Maybe it's because the older you get, the better things seem from a long time ago. Think how exciting it was going to the pictures, or collecting bus tickets or going out building a den on the back fields or collecting cig packets on a slagheap. You wouldn't exactly enjoy doing that now, would you?"

"I don't know," laughed Yorky. "Greeno still gets turned on when he goes out trainspotting."

"I think they should switch to playing in the summer."

"Not that old chestnut," said Charlie.

"And they should try and expand the game, get it played in Wales and up in the Northeast and in Scotland."

"That won't help. If the crowds are falling in the heartlands, what chance has it got miles away. It'll just bankrupt the game."

HAZEL IS THE KILLER

"Don't you think Fulham coming in has been good, Mick? Oh I forgot that them soft Southern jessies beat you lot didn't they? Sorry, old lad."

"They were all second-rate Northerners. They weren't Londoners."

"Maybe they were for starters, but give it time and folk down there will soon realise what a better game we've got. And even if they were all has-beens, they still hammered you."

"Well all I can say is no matter how small the crowds are getting, I'm just glad that I've got my memories."

"You might have a good memory for what happened thirty years ago, Charlie. But you've a bloody poor memory for what happened this week. I lent you a fiver on Monday. Has it found a permanent home in your back pocket?"

As Charlie took it out of his wallet along with five pence for the interest, Colin came into the discussion.

"I agree with Greeno. The first thing we have got to do is change from a winter to a summer game. Then we won't have to compete with either soccer or rugby union or the vagaries of the English weather."

"That will make a big difference to the Saints, won't it? Attracting the one man and his dog who watch Moss Lane and the 300 who watch St Helens Town, especially since they both play on a Saturday."

"Don't be a cynic, Charlie. We can't live in the past, good as it was. And we've got to get the teachers interested again and encourage more children to start playing it at school again."

"Well Thatcher won't be interested in the last bit, she has just started selling all the playing fields off for housing development."

"Over to you Mr Henderson for a personal comment on that contentious issue."

He didn't have one. In fact, whenever the Government did something that in any way affected the world in which he lived, he was increasingly finding that he could no longer easily support it or defend it.

But on issues in the high world of international politics and economics and in the field of relationships with other countries, he wholeheartedly felt that The Iron Lady was standing up for Britain. But it was which part of Britain or which group of people in Britain that she was standing up for or looking after, that was the main thing on which all the arguments in the office raged over and would rage over for the next ten years.

15.

That terrible winter of 1963

ON THE FIRST DAY of February 1981, the people of Ashurst awoke to a heavy fall of snow. Not surprisingly, many were late into work that morning and so it was the major topic of conversation, particularly when it was heard that a wages clerk had come off his motorbike outside Bold Colliery and had been rushed to Peasley Cross Hospital. As the day went on and blizzard conditions hit the town, comparisons began to be drawn with those terrible winters in 1947 and 1963.

Whenever conversations about bad weather began, it was always the cue for Yorky to start talking about what it had been like when he was in the Merchant Navy taking supplies to the Russian port of Murmansk, in the Arctic Circle. The way he told his tales seemed to lower the temperature in the office and sometimes Mick or Charlie would rub their hands together to keep warm as they listened open-mouthed to tales they had heard so many times before!

One person with fond memories of both winters was Alan. When he was seven years, he could remember fighting his way to school through the snow that, at one stage, had reached up to his bedroom window. Much better was what had happened in 1963. It had begun on Christmas Eve to be precise. The draughtsmen had worked until ten o' clock, tidying up the office and returning all the 'lost' drawings to the Print Room. With the arrival of Joan, their tea lady, the Christmas celebrations had begun, drinking coffee laced with whisky, eating crisps, pork pies and mince pies and hiding the Sutton Rock cakes that Anne, the slowest tracer in the West, had baked for them.

Around half eleven, the Chief Draughtsman, John Battesby gave his usual Christmas address which always ended by him reminding those present that on the first day back in the New Year, work would begin at eight o' clock, not one minute past or half past. Then it was time to get to the Worsley Arms, before the rest of the factory were let out. The pub was well known for its speciality, meat and potato pie with chips, beans and gravy, a solid Lancashire dish that would stick to your ribs. This was followed by the Drawing Office Annual Awards ceremony. That year there had been six awards, The Biggest Cock-up of the Year, the Daftest Statement of the Year, the Meanest Act of the Year, King Overtime, Mr. Romance and The Holder of the Golden Pencil. This went to whoever had managed to get one over on the hated Assistant Chief Draughtsman, Lurch. As always, special hats had been made and each winner had to wear his for the rest of the day.

128

THAT TERRIBLE WINTER OF 1963

After that, it was back into work, more drinking and sneaking into somebody else's party, if they could find one. 'Work' finished at four, giving everybody time to get home, sober up and have something to eat. By half past seven, he was in the Nags Head with his mates, Ken, Roy and Geoff. Each had a story to tell about what had happened at work that day. By the time they had finished, it was nine o' clock and they decided would go to The Co-op Hall for its Christmas Eve Dance. Although it was an all-ticket do, not having a ticket was never a problem for Alan, because his Uncle Stan worked there as a doorman. With him, Alan had a special arrangement. He would walk up the steps to the entrance and ask him whether there were four tickets reserved for Greenall. Uncle Stan, not giving a glimmer of recognition that it was his nephew, would say no. At that point Alan would walk back down the steps to the other three.

Five minutes later, the four of them would go back up the stairs, Geoff or Ken would ask the other doorman if there were four tickets on the door for Greenall. By that time, the name Greenall had been written along with the number four in the reserved tickets book. That was how Alan often sneaked into the place. Unfortunately, as they approached the entrance, one of Alan's old flames, had lurched over and insisted on giving him a big sloppy kiss. By the time he had managed to get out of her grip, another old friend in the shape of Eric Yates had joined Ken, Roy and Geoff and sneaked in for free.

By now Uncle Stan was nowhere in sight and the other doorman had been joined by two policemen, one of whom had eloquently told him, "I don't care if you are Duggie Greenall. You're not coming in here tonight pal. So you might as well buzz off home."

Slowly he had walked down the steps, out onto the pavement, wondering what to do next. Then he had seen the number five bus pull up right alongside him. As he looked inside, he had seen Thelma, the mysterious and secretive office girl from work. He had waved to her, telling her to join him and had taken her to Mario's new Italian coffee bar. Certainly being with her would be a lot better than being on his own for the rest of Christmas Eve, he had thought. It was then he discovered a little more about Thelma's unknown past. She told him quietly that she was an orphan and had been brought up in a home in Cardiff. He also discovered that she had nowhere to go all over Christmas and so he had invited her to come to his Granny's on the following day. That was where his family would gather to enjoy the day's festivities. But by the end of Christmas Day, she had fallen ill and for the next two months she had been lovingly cared for by his grandparents. By the time she had recovered and was ready to go back to work, his Granny and Grandad had virtually adopted her. Now, she was his wife, the mother of their two children and living in Granny's old house in Silkstone Street.

Yes, Alan would always remember with very fond memories that terrible winter of 1962/63.

Over tea, while talking about the weather, Alan had asked Thelma if she could remember that memorable period in her life. She just smiled. Later that evening, while doing the ironing, Thelma's mind went back to that Christmas Eve. At work that morning, she had begun her day by helping tidy up all the 'long lost' drawings, delivery schedules, parts lists, machine installation lists and maintenance procedure orders that had been in the wrong place for the last few months. At lunchtime, she had gone with a few other girls to the Bottle and Glass for their Christmas drink. There she heard everybody talking about what they were going to do over Christmas. It made her feel how lucky they all were having somewhere to go and people to spend time with. She knew that once she left work that afternoon, and visited her friend Beryl to see her new baby at Nook End and given it a little present, she would be on her own until she returned to work five days later.

After leaving Beryl's house, she had stood outside Gillarsfield Labour Club in the freezing cold, waiting for a bus. She had seen all the people laughing and joking, going into the club and had wished that she could be part of a group of friends going out to enjoy a good time. Finally the bus had turned up. It was the number five which meant that it would stop outside the Co-op Hall for a while. It was there, while the bus was changing drivers, that she had seen Alan waving to her. She couldn't believe her luck. She had always liked him, right from her very first day at Wilkinson's, but it always seemed as though he was going out with somebody. So she had gone with him to the coffee bar in Bridge Street, run by the Italian Mario who spoke English with a broad Bolton accent, because that was where he had always lived. At first they had just talked about what they had done at work that day. Then, Alan had asked her what she was doing over Christmas.

"Are you going to any parties?"

She remembered shaking her head.

"No, I'm not going anywhere."

"So what are you doing tomorrow? Falling asleep in front of the fire after you've had your turkey and your Christmas pudding, eh?"

"No, not even that. It'll have to be something out of a tin. I'm hopeless at cooking anything."

Then he had asked her if all the rest of her family were still living in Wales.

"No, there's only me, Alan. My mother died when I was a baby. I was brought up in a home in Cardiff."

Seeing the look of shock on his face, she had continued, "Don't look so worried. As long as I've got enough shillings for the gas, I'll be fine. I've just started reading a great book. The time will fly by."

THAT TERRIBLE WINTER OF 1963

Right out of the blue, he had asked if he she would like to spend Christmas Day at the house of his grandparents. The following day she had been taken to number fourteen Silkstone Street. She remembered how nervous she felt, having to meet all his relatives, never before having spent a whole Christmas Day, or any other whole day, with a family.

She remembered most vividly, in fact it was etched on her mind so clearly, her first meeting his Granny. As they had walked into the living room. Granny had quickly scurried in from the kitchen to meet them. She had smiled as she wiped her hands on her pinny and said, "Hello Thelma. I'm very pleased to meet you. You are very welcome love."

Straightaway Thelma could tell those words came from the heart and she knew also that she was going to like his Granny. Then, that evening, she had fallen ill and stayed there for the next two months while this old Lancashire lady who didn't know a thing about her, had nursed her back to full health.

She didn't remember much about her first week there though, only an old lady continually coming up the stairs to see her, ask how she was, stroking her brow and more often than not bringing her a hot drink. After a few weeks when she was better, she would go downstairs for a cooked breakfast and spend the rest of the day in the back kitchen, chatting away with someone who she now lovingly called Granny. While they chatted, she could remember how warm she felt and how cold it looked through the kitchen window, where she could see the snow falling heavily and the blizzard raging.

Yes, Thelma could remember vividly those terrible first few weeks of 1963; well, terrible from the point of view of the weather, but quite the opposite from the point of being looked after so caringly for the first time in her life by a wonderful old lady. She remembered also the first time that she had gone up to Alan's house in Chisnall Avenue one Sunday morning, being driven there by his Uncle Stan in Ashurst Corporation Plumbing Department work's van. And it was there that she found in the shape of Alan's Mum, another person who wanted to help look after her.

Now living in the Greenfield Old People's Home in Dob Lane, Granny too would often sit in her room and look out at the weather and feel glad that she no longer had to go out in such bad conditions to bring the coal in. She also remembered that Christmas Day in 1962. She remembered how Alan had called round late on Christmas Eve, to ask if it would be all right if he brought a girl from work. And when Granny had heard that she was an orphan and had been brought up in a home in Wales, she had told Alan not only was it all right for Thelma to have her Christmas dinner with them, "She can stay for her tea and her supper as well, if she wants to."

Granny had seen some of the girls Alan had been out with before and she hadn't been impressed by his choice. Trollops she had called some of them.

Then, as she was preparing the meal in the kitchen that Christmas Day morning, she had wondered what this one was going to be like. As the living room door had opened, she had scurried in to greet her guest, wiping her hands on her pinny as she did. First impressions are always important and Granny's first impressions of the person who was going to spend the day with them were that she looked a nice girl, but a little on the thin side and wearing clothes quite unsuitable for the depths of winter. Before the rest of the family had arrived, she had started to get to know her young guest.

During the course of the meal, Granny remembered how quiet Thelma had been. After the meal was over they had played cards and slowly their young guest had become more relaxed, almost noisy as the various moves in the daft game that Alan's Uncle Eric had invented were played out. Then it was time for the presents to be given out. Granny remembered how quiet Thelma had become again, sat in a chair in the corner of the room with Alan sat on the floor next to her and now somewhat inebriated. No doubt Thelma hadn't expected that she would take part in this Holding family ritual, but Granny had made sure she got a present. It was only a 1963 pocket diary, but it was nicely wrapped up and with a label that said 'To Thelma from Granny'. As soon as she had opened it, Granny remembered how she had rushed across the room and run up the stairs.

Alan had made a move to follow her, but his Mum had restrained him.

"Leave her a few minutes, Alan. Perhaps it's all been a bit too much for her."

Everybody began saying what a nice girl she was and how well she had done. Then Granny had slowly climbed up the stairs and found her young guest sat on the floor in the bathroom crying.

"I'm sorry, I'm sorry, I couldn't help it. You've all been so nice to me. I've never been to anything like this before. I'm sorry I've gone and spoiled it. I'm sorry."

So Granny had done what she was so good at, looking after children, grandchildren and other members of the Holding family too. Of course Thelma was no child, she was turned nineteen, but then she was an orphan, she had been brought up in a home and she had never been to a Christmas Day dinner with a family before. So Granny had led her into the spare bedroom, covered her with a blanket, stroked her brow and told her it didn't matter. By the end of the evening the young girl was in no state to go back to her home in Grasmere Avenue. So she had stayed the night and by the following morning was so ill that Granny had to call Doctor Jackson out. He had declared that she would have to stay in bed for at least a week and moreover was very run down and under weight. That was how Alan's Granny and Grandad had begun looking after a young girl they knew hardly a thing about, and it was nearly two months later before she had fully recovered and was well enough to go back to work.

Granny had remembered this all so well and now, through her loving care, had acquired another grandchild, for that was what Thelma had become as she was married to her youngest grandson and a regular visitor to see her in the Greenfield Old Peoples' Home.

"Bad winters will soon be a thing of the past." It was Ken Moss, a wages clerk, who had come to see the apprentice Damien about half an hour ago but for the last twenty minutes had been listening to all the chat about the past, something in which he was still living. Ken was known as the joiner not because he had ever worked with wood, but because whenever he heard an interesting conversation going on, he had the uncanny knack of being able to join in. He was also a bit of an unusual lad because of his two main interests. The first was weather, weather patterns and meteorology, the second was astrology coupled with his ability to predict future events. Because of this he had acquired the nickname of Mosstradamus.

"Who rattled your cage?" asked Charlie.

"I'm just saying that in the next twenty years, the temperature of this planet will keep rising due to all the carbon monoxide emissions from America and as far as this country is concerned, the average temperature will rarely reach as low as freezing point."

"Haven't I heard that gramophone record somewhere before?" said Mick.

"Don't let us get on about what is going to happen in twenty years time," said Alan. "You reckon you can predict things, well, clever dick, predict this. What am I going to have for my tea, what's going to win the 3.30 at Haydock tomorrow and when are you going to go back to where you are supposed to be?"

"You mark my words."

It was Yorky, predicting what Ken was likely to say next. But then Ken always did, whenever anybody began to have a go at him and his unusual obsession with the weather.

As soon as the lad had left, to find somewhere else to pass the time of day and pass on more of his predictions, Charlie said, "That lad is either a genius or a complete idiot."

"I think he's a bit like you, Charlie old lad. So it must be the latter," laughed Mick.

"He's always on about this great theory. What does he call it, 'global warming' or summat? I think it's a good idea," said Charlie, "though I don't suppose the miners will think that if we don't need so much coal and they start closing all the pits."

"Aye, but what Ken reckons is that global warming will mean that the icebergs in the Arctic will melt, causing the level of the oceans of the world to rise and cause floods everywhere. He also reckons that one effect will be the path of the Gulf Stream that brings warm air from the South will change and by 2005, Britain will enter a new Ice Age."

"I haven't heard that one from him before," said Yorky. "Maybe he's only just read about it in that American magazine he gets."

"He's daft as a brush," said Mick. "He must be or he wouldn't be going out with that Elaine who works in the Pattern Shop: the one who lives at Clock Face and comes to work on a moped."

"That's the one with blue hair and John Lennon glasses, isn't it?" said Charlie. "Do you know who her mother is? Do you remember that right gormless one from Helmsley, the one who used to work for Bill Riley and spilled ink all over that job he had been working on for weeks? It's her."

"Was that the one who looked like Helen Shapiro?"

"Aye. And as soon as she opened her mouth, she sounded like Billy Eckstein. She was absolutely hopeless. Bill reckoned that it was the day after she started working for him, that his hair started falling out."

"Her name was Linda. Loopy Linda was what Bill used to call her. The first week she was here, she was late the first four days for one reason or another and by late I don't mean a couple of minutes," said Mick. "So Bill told her that if she wasn't on time the next day, she'd get the sack. Well she made it and during the tea break, Keith Sanderson congratulated her for arriving on time and do you know what she said to him and everybody else in the office? 'I hope you are all pleased. I didn't even have time to have any breakfast or even find a pair of knickers to put on.'"

"She didn't stay that long, did she?" said Sam.

"Long enough for Bill to go bald," laughed Charlie.

"Do you remember the next girl they had working in there, that Norma from Ashton?"

"No, the next one was that prim young thing. Penelope, the one who complained about being called love."

"You're joking."

"Oh, she was really posh. They came from Canterbury, I think. Her Dad had got a real top job at I.C.I. and they lived in that big house at the end of Carlton Lane. I think she'd been to public school, but failed all her exams. That didn't stop her having ideas well above her station, but I don't think she could bridge the gap between being at Roedean and working in Ashurst."

"I take it she didn't last long."

"No. That's when Norma started. She was here for years and then we had Marilyn Monroe," said Sam. "Bill said that she was twice as efficient as Loopy Linda, which meant she was still hopeless."

""Do you remember Peter Starr? He went out with her for ages. She was as daft as him, but a lot better looking," and then, to the utter amazement of

Hamish, the graduate apprentice, Charlie went on to say that he had often seen the pair of them in bed together.

"You won't believe this, old lad," said Alan, "but it's true."

Then he went on to describe all the fun and games that used to go on at number two in the now demolished Smart Street.

"And it was all thanks to Michael Angelo Henderson and his binoculars, that we were permitted to watch it all."

"Aye, and we must have done no work for a month," laughed Yorky.

It had been while Vikki, another former employee of Wilkinson's, had been living there and looking after the house for her Auntie Janice. Once it became known that Vikki had her own place, many of her wide circle of friends had begun to call round. As long as they brought booze and something exotic to smoke they were made welcome, no matter what time of day or night it was. And because Smart Street was near enough to be seen from the Drawing Office with a pair of binoculars, what went on there could be watched. There had been morning shows, afternoon shows, shows involving three, four, five or even more people at a time. Fun and games had carried on for ages until the great finale, one Saturday evening when, with the house full of happy people jumping up and down, the house and later the whole street had collapsed due to mining subsidence above the old Southport Edge colliery.

"Does anybody know whatever happened to Vikki?" asked Yorky.

"Is she still living in Ashurst?"

"Look out. Here's Basil."

Immediately the office went silent, each one wondering who would be at the end of one of his next outbursts, but it was not to be. He walked halfway through the office and then without a word to a soul, turned round and walked back through the top half of the Drawing Office.

"He must have come to see Alan Groves and forgotten that he left over a year ago," laughed Charlie.

"Maybe he heard us talking about Vikki and wanted to find out where she's living now," said Charlie.

"You're joking," said Alan. "Is he in her fan club as well? I thought he only fancied women who weighed over fifteen stone."

"Well there was a little rumour going round that he'd been seen with her in a pub in Ormskirk about a month ago."

"Well, he wouldn't be the first person from Wilkinson's who has seen the sun rise over her shoulder," said Yorky. "And I don't suppose he'll be the last."

16.

Oldham versus The World

"GARY HAS BEEN looking for you, Charlie," said Yorky. "He wants a list of all the drawings for that job in Yugoslavia that he's going to next week."

"I hope he said please."

"He said summat but I can't repeat it; not with a lady in the room."

"Why?"

"It was in Welsh."

Gary Jones was a bit of a whizz kid: that is to say he was always whizzing around the world. Over the last three months he had crossed international borders into Hungary, Zambia, East Germany and on the previous day he had been into the fair county of Yorkshire. But that was only to Post Office Road in the village of Featherstone, not far from the ancient town of Pontefract, centre of the country's liquorice mines whereas his other visits had included the cities of Budapest, Lusaka and Leipzig.

Gary originally came from Bangor in North Wales but had been attracted to South Lancashire for 'religious' reasons. While at school, he had followed the beliefs of his family who were strong Chapel people. Around the age of sixteen, he had discovered the attraction of alcohol, firstly cider, which soon led on to drinking shandies and then the real thing in the off-licence of a public house on the outskirts of the town. By the time he had reached the age of eighteen and been permitted to enter the tap room of the same pub, he had lost his beliefs in the basic tenets of Christianity and, during the rest of his apprenticeship, behaved in a manner that brought much dismay to his parents. Then, at the age of twenty-two, in rather bizarre circumstances on a trip into England to watch Bangor City play St Helens Town in the preliminary round of the F.A. Cup, the coach he had been travelling on had finished up at Knowsley Road by mistake.

It was then he was introduced to a new religion and had started following the Saints. Shortly after, he moved to Ashurst and found employment in the Electrical Wiring Shop. A couple of years later, he had transferred to the Outside Contracts Division and begun to travel the world. His first visit abroad had been an overnight stay in Brussels; this was followed by a week at Dolgarrog Hydro-Electric Power Station which was about twenty miles from his old house and then he spent three months in Alesso in Iceland, installing electrical control equipment in a fish-canning factory.

Following a few more successful trips, he had been promoted to site supervisor, although he still retained the appearance of a man who had just come to empty the bins.

"He's done well, that lad," said Charlie.

"He'll go far with this new job he's just got."

"That's right," laughed Mick. "He's going to Yugoslavia next week."

"What I like about him is that whenever he finds a mistake on one of your drawings, he doesn't tell the world about it. All you get is a quiet telephone call from him to check it out and nobody else ever knows about it. Not that I ever make any mistakes but for people like Greeno or Mick here, he's like the Angel Gabriel."

"I'll tell you something I've just heard about him. Every time he goes abroad on a job, he writes a story about it. It might be about the geography of the place, journeys he makes at the weekend, some of the characters he gets to know, or different cultures he has witnessed. He's a real rough diamond."

"I've read some of his tales," said Alan. "Some of them are brilliant. He should try and get them published. The last one I read was about a woman he met in Istanbul, who handcuffed him to her bed for two days."

"Was that true?"

"Not really. She let him go after a day."

"One of his stories is about the first rugby league international played in Bulgaria," said Colin.

"I haven't heard about that," said Mick.

"You were probably asleep when he told us," said Alan.

"Oldham and District versus the Rest of the World it was. It happened when he was on that job at Kavarna. There were three lads from the O.C.D., a gang from Ferrantis at Hollinwood installing a transformer and four Aussie fitters. Staying in the hotel, there was also a group of French teachers on some cultural exchange visit with a local school. The Oldham lads had a rugby ball with them and one evening they were playing touch and pass, when one of the Aussies asked if he could join in. It turned out that he used to play for Balmain and he also knew that one of the French teachers had played league for Albi. So they organised a match. Ferrantis versus a team made up of Gary, another Welsh bloke who had only played union, three Aussies, two French teachers, two Bulgarian waiters, one who looked like Vinty Karalius and an American they met in the bar, who thought that rugby league was a cross between basketball and soccer. They passed the word round, put notices up in the hotel and in the end, over five hundred people turned up to watch."

Colin laughed and carried on. "The only unfortunate thing was that at half-time, they all went in the hotel for a drink and when they came back some kids had pinched the ball. If that hadn't happened, rugby league might have become the national game by now."

"He wrote a really interesting piece about when he was working near Valencia in Spain. He lodged with a guy who had fought in the Spanish Civil War and had seen all his family killed when the Germans bombed the town of Guernica. It was a real imaginative piece of literature."

"That was posh words for a Wiganer, Mick. I thought they'd barred you from Platt Bridge Library."

"This might make you smile," said Yorky, "but one of Gary's first jobs was at Hickson's Chemical Works in Castleford. He was lodging in Leeds and caught the train to work every day. I don't know if you have ever travelled around that part of the world but one of the most visible sights for miles around is Ferry Bridge Power Station. It's a stunning view, particularly when there's steam rising from the cooling towers on a summer's day. The way Gary described the journey, you would have thought he was on the Trans-Siberian railway."

"He likes writing poetry as well," said Yorky.

"Rather him than me. I used to hate it at school."

"Do you like poetry, Mick?"

But before the Wiganer could provide a suitable response, or find an excuse to walk out of the room, Alan continued.

"My favourite poet is Alex Murphy. I remember vividly one of his best known pieces, written I do believe, during his red and white period.

> Roses are Red,
> Violets are Blue,
> St Helens Twenty-One
> Wigan Two.

Ignoring the last four lines, Mick then surprised them, saying, "I like reading William Wordsworth. I've even been in his cottage in the Lake District."

"The hidden side of the Henderson man," laughed Charlie.

"I'll tell you who I like," said Alan. "John Milton."

"Is he the guy who wrote *Paradise Lost*?"

"That's right, he wrote it just after he got married. Five years later, so the story goes, his wife left him, which he celebrated by writing *Paradise Regained*."

It was at times like this, sat around the office during the lunch hour, with nothing better to do than talk, that life at work can seem so good. The next contributor was Alan again, who said one of his favourite poems had been written in Latin:

> Caesar adsum iam for te
> Brutus eterat

OLDHAM VERSUS THE WORLD

Caesar sic in omnibus
Brutus sic in iat.

Before any more verses could be uttered, they were interrupted by the arrival of Tony Robledo and, as expected, he had a few tales to tell from his recent visit, to Butler's Machine Tool Works in Halifax. But he began by talking with Charlie about work, discussing how to remove all the equipment in an old control panel and mount it in a Wilkinson cubicle that had been installed in the wrong place. A few minutes later, a wireman walked in with a marked-up print, full of comments that he could not understand. Yawning loudly three times in as many minutes, it was soon quite clear that he was not getting enough sleep.

"Too much bed and not enough sleep, ewd lad."

"You can say that again, but it's not what you think."

"It never is."

"It's next door. The amount of noise they make when they are at it. I wouldn't care, but they are not even married."

"What the heck has that got to do with it?"

"And he's on the club as well."

"What's up with him?"

"He's got a bad back."

"What a surprise!"

Then the lad carried on and said: "He's a right daft bugger. He used to be a meter reader for the Gas Board. I'll tell you how daft he was. About once a week if he was somewhere in town, near the shops or where there were plenty people about, what he'd do would be to stand on the pavement near a building and look up. To anyone walking past, he'd say to them, 'Can you see that?'. Then when he'd got a few people looking up, he'd walk away. He was daft as a brush."

"I used to do that when I worked in London," said John. "It was dead funny. I once had half of Oxford Street doing it, including three coppers. In fact one time there was a photograph of me in a group splashed right across the front page of the *Evening Standard*."

"Well all this is very interesting but it won't put any bread on the table," said Tony. "I'd better get off onto my next job."

"Where's that?"

"Warburton's Bakery in Bolton."

After Tony had left, John carried on talking about the time he had spent in London. The drawing office that he had worked in was quite unlike Wilkinson's. The place did not have a shop floor, so all the engineering work was carried out at small jobbing shops around North London. Despite this, there were still a few characters in the place. One lad was a keen photographer and used to spend his lunch time walking round Bloomsbury, King's Cross or Euston, hoping to see a famous person or witness an accident or some bizarre scene, which he would photograph and take down to Fleet Street to sell to whichever newspaper was interested. Another regularly tried to worm his way into receptions or seminars that were held in many of the large hotels around the area, just to enjoy a buffet at somebody else's expense, while a third used to frequently sit in a laundrette and chat up rich tourists, offering to take them round the city at night.

Just as interesting were John's tales about when he lived in Camden Town. On the rare occasions when he didn't go out, he would spend the evening watching life go by in Arlington Road outside the pub opposite. On one occasion he had seen the start of a turf war. It had started just after closing time on the Monday evening when there had been a punch-up between two drunken men. The following night, there had been another punch-up involving about a dozen men. All had been quiet on the Wednesday night, the calm before the storm, no doubt. On the Thursday evening, a lorry carrying enough grass to fill Lord's cricket ground had appeared and two men had thrown lumps of turf at the regulars as they all stood outside the pub on the pavement after closing time. The following day he had discovered the reason for the attack. One of the regulars was believed to be a grass and so symbolically all his drinking partners had been bombarded with it. Quite bizarre really, quite humorous too to watch from the safety of his room; well, it was somebody who had been hit had seen John laughing at the antics and thrown a large stone through his window.

Later that evening Alan had been telling Thelma what had happened at work that day. Although it was over eighteen years since she had last worked at Wilkinson's, she was still keen to know how her husband had spent his day and how some of the people she knew, were getting on. In passing, Alan had mentioned that Tony Robledo was still in fine form, earning plenty dough working out on site, his present job being at Warburton's Bakery in Bolton.

"Oh, that reminds me," she said, "I've found something in the attic that will interest you."

Ever since they had moved into Granny's old house in Silkstone Street, she had been finding all manner of things up in the attic. Some things had been left by Granny and Grandad, other things had been left by Granny's parents and possibly her grandparents as well. Some had been stashed in cardboard boxes, some had been wrapped up in blankets, other things had been put in bags that were hanging on nails and there were also other items in shoe boxes, 'hidden' under the floorboards. So Thelma, always keen to miss nothing of the Holding family treasure trove, had decided that when she ever had the time, she would uncover it all. And that morning, she had brought down an old suitcase and begun to carefully remove its contents.

"I found this notebook up there today. I don't know who wrote it, it might have been Granny's brother Eric. Have a look at it."

It was the reference to Mr. Robledo working at Warburton's Bakery that had reminded Thelma. Alan looked at it with great interest. Immediately, he sunk back to the turn of the century as he proceeded to learn a little more about what life was like when Granny was a small girl.

When I was nine, my mother used to make bread dough in a huge sloping earthenware bowl and proved by the side of the fire. It would be mixed and left to prove for an hour, then knocked back (all the air knocked out of it), proved again for thirty minutes, put in a floured sack and I would have to carry it to the baker's shop, where it would be weighed off, moulded and put into tins for baking. The tins would have a tally slotted in the end of the tin with same number on it and a round tally with the same number given to me to take home until tea time when I would have to go back with the tally and cash to bring home the baked bread.

Sometimes it would be baked without tins, called oven bottom bread and of course, as they baked, they would join together; when they were brought out of the oven, you could peel bits of hot bread from the soft part where the join had been - lovely. Sometimes the oven bottom loaf arrived home with a hole in the side delivered by a boy with warm bread in his tummy.

But the next time Thelma called round to see Granny, she didn't know anything about it. Maybe it was her sister Doris or her brother Eric who had written it, she said. Giving her the paper and asking her to look at the writing was not much use either, because sadly her eyesight was now fading.

"Ee, if I remember, I'll ring you up on the telephone," she laughingly said as she held Thelma's hand. It was a rather strange thing for Granny to say, for she had never used a telephone in her whole life.

Then she carried on, quite uninterested in someone's breadmaking activities many years ago; "Do you use the telephone, Thelma? What do you talk about? Why don't you wait until that grandson of mine comes home?"

Then she smiled at Thelma in that very special loving way that she had and asked her how the children were getting on at school.

"Are they going to get a job? Robert isn't going to go down the pit, is he? You tell him to get a job like his Dad's got. All fun and games and they give him money as well. Ee, it must be a funny place."

Clearly in fine form, she asked Thelma if she had been up in the attic recently.

"That's where I found this paper."

ONE SUMMER

"Did you ever find Uncle Stan's holiday tour to Africa during the war?"

Before Thelma could say anything, the bell went indicating that it was time for the guests to leave to allow the residents to go for their lunch.

Back home, Thelma went through the cardboard box that she had removed from the attic earlier that day. She rummaged through it for what Granny had asked about. Whenever she mentioned anything about her old house, Thelma would always see what she could find. And yes, there it was in a large envelope. The first thing she saw was a photograph of Granny's son, Stanley. Behind him was a great expanse of sand, which might just have been at Southport. But it clearly wasn't, as the accompanying piece of paper indicated.

		1943
April	11th	Left Liverpool on the Franconia
	13th	Greenock
	23rd	Algiers
May	15th	Ghardimmoli
	26th	Medjes-El-Bab, Camp at Chassart
	29th	Hammamet
June	1st	Korba
	2nd	Tunis Air Port
	4th	Kairouan Air Field
	20th	Monaster, Les killed
July	2nd	Kairouan
	7th	Battery H.Q, Monaster and Kairouan
	22nd	Troop H.Q.
August	1st	Sousse
	6th	Monaster
September	16th	Bixerta
November	14th	By boat to Naples to airfield at Pomigliano
		1944
February	25th	Naples H.Q. behind Naples station
June	5th	Salerno, Montercorvino, wounded
July	12th	Naples, Areo Felice
		1945
January	21st	'B' Transit Camp, Afragola Transfer to Royal Engineers
February	3rd	Capua Prisco, San Angelo, Mule Training and Bailey bridge
March	25th	Taranto

April	4th	Greece 30 Reception, Pireus
	5th	Aliatus 1238 Field camp R.E.
	7th	Lamia No. 2 Platoon
	10th	Volos
	11th	Ladhavia
	17th	Pelasuia
	19th	30 Reception, Camp Athens
May	30th	Taranto Transit camp
June	3rd	Castel le Mare, 11th field Battery
	14th	Naples, No. 3 Transit
	18th	Bari
September	12th	Barletta
October	2nd	Bari
	22nd	England LEAVE
December	2nd	Bari
	23rd	England RETURN ON B RELEASE

It was a graphic description of where his Uncle Stan had spent his war years, serving in the British Army in the war against Nazi Germany. Strangely it was a part of his life that he had never really talked very much about. He had answered any questions that relatives or workmates had asked him, but had never talked much about those bad times. Perhaps the entry of June 20th in 1943 might explain why. But who was Les? Probably some old pal of his from school or maybe someone he had got to know during the war. Something for him to keep to himself maybe, just like the entry for his time at Salerno. As far as Thelma knew, he had never said anything to Alan about being wounded, but why should he, if he didn't want to?

17.

"Do you expect me to ring up in the dark?"

ALTHOUGH CHARLIE was now approaching the age of retirement, in many ways he still continued to behave for most of the time as though he was only half his age. Now and again he would behave as though he had just come out of his apprenticeship and on rare classic occasions, usually fuelled by the consumption of too much alcohol, he would act as though he still was an apprentice. Oddly, combined with this trait, he also displayed some of the characteristics associated with the onset of old age, like collecting and trying to swap football programmes, reading comics, looking at nostalgic photographs of old St Helens and spending time in Thatto Heath Library, flicking through books about steam railway trains. Fortunately, he had not yet resorted to playing stonies in Elephant Lane, but that was mainly because he couldn't find anyone who would play with him!

He also continued to hero worship various players just like he had done when he had first stood in the boys' pen at Knowsley Road in the late Thirties. Then his favourites had been people like George 'Porky' Davies, so named because he had a butcher's shop at Sutton Manor, Jack Waring, who lived a stone's throw from the ground in Doulton Street, Albert Butler and the Welshman Stanley Powell. Now they were the likes of Paul Loughlin, Peter Gorley, Chris Arkwright and Roy Haggerty. The big difference was that the former were all adults while he was still a boy whereas now most of the current Saints team were young enough to be his grandchildren.

Having lived in Thatto Heath for most of his life, it was hardly surprising that he knew many famous rugby league players, after all, the place was full of them. He also knew Bill Foulkes who had played for Manchester United and had survived the Munich air disaster of 1958. And having lived in Sunbury Street for a while after he had got married, he also knew well one Alexander James Murphy and his brother Billy. So from time to time their paths would cross and inevitably the following day, Charlie's first comments of the day would be something along the lines of:

"I was talking to my mate Alex yesterday (or last night or over the weekend)". It would of course be a true statement, just like the time Charlie had been in Prescot Labour Club with an old workmate from Pilks, who was now a local councillor in Whiston and had introduced Charlie to Harold

Wilson, who had been there on his constituency business. The following day Charlie had informed all who could hear that "I was having a chat with the Prime Minister about all this trouble in Rhodesia last night."

Then there had been the time when Charlie and his wife had been on holiday in Italy and visited Rome for a day. It must have coincided with some important religious ceremony because large crowds were assembled all round the city centre to see the head of the Roman Catholic Church pass by. Of course, Charlie couldn't actually say that he had been talking to the Pope while he had been in the Vatican City, but he was absolutely certain that the Pontiff had seen Charlie in the crowd and waved to him.

So, namedropping was something that Charlie had thrived on, not in a bigheaded way, but in a way that made all the other draughtsmen appreciate just what an important person, with connections, he really was. And for anyone who ever visited Charlie's house, if they were fortunate enough to go into the front room, they would be told that the sideboard and shelves had been put up not by any old tradesman but by Bob Dagnall, who was a local joiner, but more importantly, the Saint's hooker in the early Sixties.

Then there had been the occasion one Saturday morning in 1961, when Charlie was driving home from work. As he went past St Helens Junction railway station, he saw a familiar figure heading towards the telephone box. It was the famous referee Sergeant Major Eric Clay, obviously going to ring for a taxi to take him to the St Helens ground where he would later be refereeing that afternoon's game against Workington Town. So Charlie had stopped and offered Eric a lift to Knowsley Road, which was less than two miles from Charlie's house in Thatto Heath.

There was no happy end to this little tale though. The game had been something of a torrid affair, not handbags at ten paces, more like J.C.Bs right in your face and, with two minutes to go and the Saints pressing on the visitors' line, but losing by three points, there had been yet another flare-up. This had just about been the last straw for Mr Clay. He blew his whistle and sent off Dick Huddart and Vinty Karalius, two St Helens forwards and two of the most gentle, well-mannered and decent people to have ever pulled on a pair of rugby boots. Charlie's 'passenger' had then given Town a penalty, which they took an absolute age to kick over the new stand and onto the old railway line that used to run down to the nearby Triplex factory.

Charlie's view on the matter had been summed up in his comment to his brother-in-law. It was something along the lines that that man in black, whose parents were not married when he had been born, had better make his own arrangements to get back to bloody Yorkshire.

After quite a while, without having met anyone remotely interesting, Charlie had come into work with a cracker of a story, one that he had heard the night before, right from the mouth of the great Alex.

At the time, Murphy had been the coach at Leigh, where it had been the practice for the club to pay the coach's telephone bill because of the amount of time that he would be expected to spend at home on the phone on club business. On the previous day, Alex had walked into the club chairman's office and placed on his desk his telephone bill and his electricity bill.

The immediate response of the chairman had been that the club would pay the first as it normally did but had queried why the club should pay the second. Murphy's reply to the chairman, which he had told Charlie later that night, was a classic.

"Surely you don't expect me to ring up in the dark."

It was a story well worth repeating, which Charlie proceeded to do for the rest of the day. Straight after lunch, as he was about to pick up the phone Billy Mulholl and walked into the office and announced that Mr. Murphy was due for the high jump. Charlie immediately put down the phone, expecting to hear that Alex's quick quip had lost him his job, but it wasn't. It was Jimmy Murphy, who worked mainly on site for the Outside Contracts Division.

Jimmy was the younger brother of Stan Murphy, who had also worked in the same department for years. Stan was nearing retirement when he had been sacked for incorrectly filling out a timesheet. Actually it was incorrectly filling out a timesheet three weeks running, while working on an job in Carlisle. Each week, Stan had booked eight hours for Saturday and Sunday, when he actually had been at home in Ashurst. What actually had been his downfall had been a photograph of him, stood outside St Luke's Church in Gillarsfield, at the marriage of his nephew, who was famous for having played cricket for Lancashire. Short of much material that week, the photograph had been blasted right across the front page of the *Ashurst Reporter*.

A month later, Jimmy Murphy had discovered that the boss had arranged for him to go to Portugal, to wire up a control cubicle at a cotton mill near Lisbon. Unfortunately this would coincide with a nice little job he had organised for himself, rewiring a hotel in the Lake District. What Jimmy had intended to do was go off sick for a few days and miles away from Ashurst, do this job at his leisure. But his boss had made it plain that he had been keeping his eye on Jimmy and if this Portuguese job wasn't done on time, then just like his brother, he would be in for the chop.

But this hotel job was a doddle, the new owner hadn't a clue what was needed and Jimmy knew exactly how he could make a small fortune. And the other reason he wanted to do the job was because the said hotel owner was a forty-two-year-old widow, who was clearly worth a fortune and very beddable too.

"DO YOU EXPECT ME TO RING UP IN THE DARK?"

So Jimmy and his elder brother Stan hatched a crazy plan. Stan and Jimmy looked alike, there was only three years difference in age between them. Both sounded alike, certainly on the telephone and Jimmy could easily tell Stan what had to be done on site. So Stan went to Lisbon, obviously with his own passport, but with all the paperwork from the firm that indicated that it was his younger brother Jimmy who was there. No one at the mill knew any difference so that did not present a problem either. Even Wilkinson's Sales Engineer knew neither of the Murphy brothers personally and so Stan proceeded to work for a fortnight in Lisbon, while his brother Jimmy spent the same amount of time in the Lake District, re-wiring a hotel, while gradually edging his way towards Christine's bedroom.

By the end of the fortnight, by arrangement, Stan rang up Jimmy to tell him what time his flight would be arriving back in Manchester and asking him to pick him up. Then he could fill him in with all the details of what he had done in Lisbon and give him the prints he had marked-up for Jimmy to pass on to the Drawing Office. With that satisfactorily accomplished, the following day Jimmy had gone into work, happy in the knowledge that his stay would only be a short one, as he was now booked in for his next job which would be at a substation near Preston, some twenty-five miles away.

Unfortunately what Stan hadn't told his younger brother was that during his time in the Portuguese capital, he had rescued the works' cat. There wasn't too much to tell really. It had climbed up into the rafters and couldn't get down. Always keen to impress an audience, Stan had shinned up a stanchion, and retrieved Pedro, much to the delight of the Managing Director's secretary, Alfesa. That lunchtime, she had invited Stan to have his lunch with her in the canteen. From their conversation, Alfesa had put together a story that went in to the mill's monthly staff magazine. She also took a photograph of Stan, although of course she knew him as Jimmy.

Later that week, Wilkinson's Sales Engineer, having been told that the job had been completed on time, had called in to claim all the glory. He had been shown a copy of the magazine, which included the photograph of Stan. The Sales Engineer decided it was a nice bit of publicity for Wilkinson's too, and sent it to Mary in Technical Publicity who was responsible for producing Wilkinson's Staff Magazine. Rarely having anything of interest to include, she had splashed the photograph right across the front page of *The Link*.

Of course, when it went round the shop floor, most of the Murphys' old workmates pissed themselves, Stan masquerading as his younger brother Jimmy and making a meal of it too. When Basil Wilkinson found out, he sacked Jimmy, who then tried to get his union to defend him, because as Jimmy rightly said, he was being sacked for something he hadn't done.

ONE SUMMER

A few days later, Charlie was to hear what for him was some equally disturbing news about the real Mr. Murphy. Alex had not played for the Saints since 1967 when he had been involved in a dispute with the club. It was all water under the bridge now and currently he was coaching Leigh and doing it very successfully too. Meanwhile the Saints and Wigan continued to be bitter rivals and accordingly, while in work, Mick and Charlie would always be engaging in lively banter, in the 'nicest' possible way of course, as befitted supporters of two of the greatest clubs in rugby league. What gave each the most pleasure usually occurred on a Monday morning when their team had won and the other's had lost. It was enjoyable for one or the other to so innocently ask 'How did your lot get on yesterday?'

One afternoon that week, Charlie had been out on the shop floor, checking on the wiring of a piece of machinery that would soon be starting a long journey to a place called Alegrete in the Rio Grande in the south of Brazil. On his return, he had flopped down onto his stool as Mick said, with a big smile on his face:

"I've just heard a bit of interesting news while you've been observing other people at work."

"What's that? Have some more secondhand clothes arrived at that charity shop in Abram?"

"Actually I don't know if I should tell you this, Charlie. I'm not sure if your old heart can stand it."

"You're not going to come in them tomorrow as well, are you?"

"It's nothing to do with clothes. It's about your mate Murphy. He's just got a new job. Do you hope that he does well in it?"

"I've wished Alex well in every job he's ever had and I've always told him to his face. But I didn't know he'd left Leigh."

"Well he has. He's come to Wigan. How about that?"

It was true Alex had been made an offer he couldn't refuse by Maurice Lindsay, the chairman of the Wigan Rugby League club. And so for Charlie, it was something that he could never hope that Alex had too much success with. But for the next two seasons, it was something Charlie and a lot of other rugby league fans had to put up with.

Later that evening Charlie had called for a drink in The Springfield. The main topic of conversation in the bar was inevitably Murphy's move to coach the Saints' arch-rivals. Then one of the old timers made the comment that he had seen Murphy play his first game for the Saints when he was just seventeen. Billy was the source of many tales about the old days, and with him making his first visit for a while, the others were more than pleased to be given the benefit of his historical knowledge. Billy also knew that the longer he kept talking, the more free beer would land on his table.

"DO YOU EXPECT ME TO RING UP IN THE DARK?"

"It was against Whitehaven towards the back of the 1956 season. As soon as I saw him I could tell he was going to be a good 'un, and I wasn't far wrong."

"I bet you've seen them all, haven't you Billy?" said one of the younger regulars. "How old are you now?"

"Too old, ewd lad."

He took a large gulp from his glass and went on.

"I saw Alf Ellaby play his first game as well. That was in 1926 against Keighley, we beat 'em though it wasn't the best game I ever watched. Then a few weeks later I went to my first derby game at City Road. Alf got carried off, three got sent off and they beat us 33-0. What a game that was! It was the League Championship Semi-Final. There were over 19,000 there that day and quite a lot were locked out. Can you imagine 19,000 there now?"

"Folk were all a lot thinner in them days," said another young man. It was probably true for in the days of the Great Depression, the general population didn't eat as much food like many did now.

Ignoring the comments, Billy carried on, as another pint of mixed appeared before him.

"I remember that we played them at Warrington that year in the Lancashire Cup, but I never saw it. I didn't have the money for the train fare."

"So why didn't you walk it there, it's not that far?"

"I can't remember, I know we won 10-2. My uncle Joe went and told us all about it."

Billy was nearly eighty. If there had been any work around then, he would have been working for there were many mouths to feed in his family. But there wasn't any work at all, so like many other people who lived in places like Thatto Heath, Clock Face, Blackbrook, Haydock, Platt Bridge, Billinge and Ashurst, he was just a Government statistic. He had watched the Saints for years, though for a long time he had only seen the second half of matches, because that was when they let the unemployed in for free. Then with the approach of war in the late Thirties, he had been able to find work and saved up enough money to make his first trip ever to London to watch Widnes beat Keighley in the 1937 Challenge Cup Final.

There were now about a dozen of Saints diehards sat around him now, all keen to hear him talk and learn about the past and keep him well supplied with ale.

"I remember the last time I ever went to City Road, the last time we played the buggers. New Year's Day in 1939 it was. We beat 'em 5-3. What a battle that was, in the slush as well. I walked it there and back. Mind you it was midnight before I got home."

"You weren't walking all that time, were you, Billy?"

"No, one of my mates used to live in Seddon Street, so I nipped round to see him after the match and have a drink. He used to brew his own, it wasn't half strong. I don't know how I got home that neet. I know I fell asleep on a bench in Taylor Park for a bit."

"What was Alf Ellaby like? Was he as good as Vollenhoven?"

"We used to say that he was the only man in rugby league who could give the Royal Scot a start. I'll tell thee what, they liked him in Australia and that's saying summat. He went on tour later that year. Him, Les Fairclough, Alf Frodsham and Ben Halfpenny from the Saints, Frank Bowen, Oliver Dolan and Albert Fildes from the Recs. There were some good players in town in them days."

"You've got a good memory, Billy."

"I have for some things and not for others. I can tell you the names of all the kids that were in my class at school. But whenever our Maud used to send me for some shopping, if there was more than three things, I could never remember it."

It was a bit of a sad comment that he had just made, for his wife had been dead over a year now and he now lived on his own in Myrtle Street.

"I'll tell thee one thing, I can remember from them days. It used to be an advert they had in the programme. One of the committeemen was a bloke called Alf Critchley. He was a fish merchant. He had a stall on the market. And there was this little rhyme he made up, it always used to make me laugh."

He took a gulp from his glass, put his hand to his face, stroked the stubble on his chin and then said "Oh aye, that's it.

Best Thing for Today,
Saints to Win and Alf Critchley for a Plaice.
If it's triers - Saints have 'em,
If it's triers - Alf gets 'em,
But if it swims - Alf's got it.

"Well it was summat like that."

Then one of the younger lads, who had said nothing so far, chipped in. "I still can't believe that they ever got 19,000 on City Road ground."

"Eh lad, that's nowt. They once played Huddersfield in a cup tie just after the war and there was over 23,000 there. They had to shut the gates and thousands got turned away. I know because my Dad told me. He was there."

"So is the game as good now as it was then, Billy?"

"Don't ask an old timer like me that question. You see the older you get, well, you only remember the good bits. Probably not. It was unlimited possession then, great if it was your team that had the ball. Then it was a

150

much heavier ball, and it always seemed to rain more than it does now and the rain was heavier too. And another thing, there were no substitutes. I once went to watch 'em play at Leeds in a cup tie. Saints had a man carried off in the first minute. It ruined the game. We got hammered. Even the Leeds speccies agreed with us."

"Have you been on many away grounds, Billy?"

"A few. After my first visit to City Road, we went to watch 'em at Liverpool Stanley. It wouldn't have been a bad ground if it hadn't been for the speedway track and the greyhound track. It was worse than Odsal for the speccies, at least at Odsal there was plenty banking. I never liked Rochdale's ground either, but I loved it when we went to Oldham. There were loads of pubs there and always a big crowd. Swinton was good an' all, and Leigh as well, when they played at Mather Lane. Well, I thought it was."

He carried on in similar vein, pausing only to quench his thirst and clear his throat. It was like a history lesson for all those sat around him. Sometimes he repeated himself, sometimes he forgot the point he was making, but it didn't matter. He was good to listen to and not just about rugby. He had many a tale to tell about his former neighbours and particularly about things that had happened where they had worked. Sometimes they were sad stories, usually related to the poverty that existed then right across the town. More often than not though, they were stories that included a humorous element to them. And quite often they would make reference to one particular Mayor of St Helens, who Billy had clearly once had a run-in with a few years earlier and had never forgotten. Unfortunately it was a pity that no-one ever recorded his 'Springfield' tales or wrote them down, because a few weeks later, he suffered a stroke stood in a chip shop in Nutgrove Road and was never able to speak clearly or audibly again.

18.

"Obey my rules and you won't go far wrong"

THE VIEW FROM Wilkinson's Drawing Office hadn't changed greatly over the years until subsidence caused by the workings of the old Southport Edge pit had led to the whole of Smart Street having to be demolished back in 1977. Previous to that the main changes to the landscape had been the demolition of St. Oswalds Church, the flattening of the old Salvation Army hostel and the building of a featureless block of flats in Preston Street.

The Drawing Office was situated on the first floor of the main building, above the General Assembly and Wiring shop. Adjacent to that was the single storey Welding Shop. This had a roof sloping away from the main building, on the top of which was what the draughtsmen had christened Seagull Alley. The gable end had acquired this name because seagulls would frequently gather in a line, always looking south towards the nearby town of Widnes. Often, a draughtsman might throw them a few crumbs or the remains of a bacon butty, though at other times they were attacked by apprentices, firing leccy bands. The birds were always good for a laugh, particularly their leader who had been given the name Harold Spicer. That was because it was the spitting image of the foreman who worked directly below them.

On the far side of the Welding Shop had been the sports field. You couldn't see the football pitch from the Drawing Office, only the bowling green and the hut where the groundsman kept his tools and spent much of the day, reading *The Star* or *The Sun*. Further on were the iron railings that separated the factory from the world outside. For years that had also been the back entry to the houses in Smart Street, famed for the orgies that had once taken place there.

On the other side of Smart Street had been Albion Street, Peter Street and Herbert Street. Behind them could be seen the roof and chimney of Stevenson Pneumatics and the slag heap that was all that remained of the old Beswick colliery. That had broadly been the picture of Ashurst that any Wilkinson draughtsman would have cast his eye over as he looked out of the window.

Now it was a much changed scene. The Welding Shop and its collection of birds was still there, so was the bowling green, now vandalised by kids and unusable. The Social Club hut had gone too, burned down probably by the same kids who were either bored with life or just plain anti-social in their attitude to life. The football pitch was now a car park, still protected from the world outside by the iron railings. The houses in Smart Street, Albion Street and Herbert Street were now history as was everything that had once been Stevenson Pneumatics. The Beswick colliery tip had been levelled and was now a pleasant little cul-de-sac, home to about a dozen detached houses. Strangely Peter Street hadn't been touched, probably because the mother of the Town Clerk still lived at number seventeen along with her cats and goldfish.

One thing that still remained in view was the company flagpole. It had first been erected to celebrate the Coronation of King Edward in 1936. After the arrival of the American socialite Mrs Simpson, he decided he didn't want the job and soon after his brother was crowned King George the Sixth. The flag had flown at full mast that day, and then a few days later as well, to celebrate another important event in the life of the nation, the birthday of one Joshua Albert George Wilkinson D.S.O., who since 1926 had been in complete control of the company until December 1962.

The flag was also flown at half mast when any member of the Royal Family or an important former member of the firm had died. It was a tradition that had been observed as long as anybody could remember. And being so near to the pole, the draughtsmen were always the first people to learn of someone's demise and departure to another place.

On the ninth day of October 1982, it was Alan who had shouted out "Flag Up", as he had first observed the string moving slowly up the mast. They all waited to see if it would go to the top of the pole, which for the royalists among them would be cause for celebration. But it didn't and so it was in this way that they first learned of the death the previous night of an old stalwart of the company, Jack Critchley.

Jack had been the Apprentice Training Officer, appointed back in the early Fifties, when the apprentice intake each year was two dozen keen young lads. It had been Jack's job to make sure that both they and the company benefited from their work over the next five years. Alan remembered well his first meeting with the man, when within minutes of introducing himself, Jack had told the 1955 intake about his famous Golden Rules, the first one being the Three B's:

"Be here on time. Be safety conscious. Be prepared to learn."

Over their next five years, Jack would keep his beady eye on them all. And whenever any of Jack's rules were broken, the offending apprentice would be suitably punished, but in a way that ensured that he learned from his mistake and never did it again.

Three days later, St Theresa's Church was the setting for his funeral, an impressive occasion, which over two hundred people attended. Many were former apprentices, who Jack had helped, encouraged, or just sorted out over the years. Some still worked at Wilkinson's, some in the Drawing Office like Alan, some on the shop floor while others had become middle-management team. Others had moved to other firms in the town, firms such as Jarratt's Machine Tools, Dawson's, Mather's Foundry or further afield to Pilkingtons and U.G.B. in St Helens, B.I.C.C. at Prescot, Thames Board Mills and Crossfields at Warrington, Fidler's Ferry Power Station on the north bank of the Mersey and Gullick's in Wigan.

But although almost every Wilkinson's apprentice had benefited from their association with Jack, quite a number of them were now no longer working in the engineering industry and in some cases were no longer working at all. Unemployment and market forces had no heart, none at all for former apprentices. If your skills were not required, tough. Go and get on your bike and find some other way to put food on the table for your kids, was the general attitude of the government now.

If there was one word in the English language that summed up Jack, it was probably the word 'respect'. Other words that could be associated with him were 'loyalty', 'skill', 'knowledge' and his favourite phrase, 'all in the fullness of time'. No-one had ever been asked by him to do something that Jack couldn't do himself, whether it was welding, brazing, soldering, operating a lathe, a milling machine or climbing a ladder to a great height and clearing out a gutter or painting it.

He had also been well respected in the world of sport. In fact if he had concentrated on just one sport, he would no doubt have been good enough to play it at a professional level. Around the town, he was well known as a tennis and badminton player, he had run with Ashurst Harriers and played soccer with Southport Reserves for a season. He had even been known to try his hand at boxing, although on knocking an opponent's tooth out, had decided that this could not really be classed as a sport.

Living in Ashurst, it was not surprising that he had also played rugby, and in his case, both codes. Being an old boy of Ashurst Grammar, after leaving school he had moved played the fifteen-a-side code for Ashurst Old Boys, a natural progression in those days. But then shortly after the 1939/1940 season had started, he had been called up. On his return from the war, he had gone to work in Cumberland. He had started playing rugby again, though this time it was the thirteen-a-side code, for a Working Mens' club in Cockermouth and where one of his teammates had been a cameraman during the war. With the help of some 'redundant' camera reels a film had been made of various places around the town. This had included a ten minute coverage of a game between the Cockermouth team and a team from Whitehaven. One of the outstanding bits of action in this game had been a forty-yard burst by the only non-Cumbrian on the pitch, sidestepping around at least six local lads to score a fine try.

"OBEY MY RULES AND YOU WON'T GO FAR WRONG"

When Jack returned to settle in Ashurst with his young Cumbrian wife a few months later, he had brought a copy of the film with him. In this way, his skills on the rugby field had been captured for posterity, adding another dimension to what he had been doing over the previous seven years that he had been away. Within a few weeks of being back home, Jack had decided to start playing rugby union again. It was more of a social thing for Jack, as he had always enjoyed playing every sport he had had a go at and this would be a chance to meet some of his old pals from school again. That was when Jack discovered that despite having been away fighting for his country., he was no longer a welcome member of the Ashurst Old Boys Rugby Union Club. For as soon as the committee discovered he wanted to start playing again, they decided that because he had played rugby league, he was barred.

"If it was up to me, I'd turn a blind eye," the secretary of the club, Arthur Halton, had said. "It's just that it's in the rules and we can't upset them that make these rules. We've got to keep to our amateur status, you see. If we don't the County Committee will be down on us like a ton of bricks."

The decision of the committee caused a big stink among many of the players but what came later was even worse. Following a lot of pressure, the committee had met to try and resolve the situation. Finally it was announced on the Thursday evening in the bar, straight after training, that a compromise had been reached. Instead of being banned for life from playing rugby union, as was normally the case in these situations, the committee had unanimously agreed to petition the County Committee to show clemency and permit Jack to restart playing after a year's suspension.

Talk about rubbing salt into a wound. It did not come as a complete surprise to those present and, almost spontaneously, a good third of those present had walked out of the bar and returned to the changing rooms. There they had gone back onto the playing field and proceeded to play rugby league for half an hour on the hallowed turf, Halton's Hypocrites versus Bedford's Bigots being the name of the two teams that had faced each other. The second name had been chosen because Norman Bedford was the club delegate to the County Committee and well known for his dislike of rugby league, despite him having been raised less than one hundred yards from the Wilderspool Stadium in Warrington.

As it grew dark, Naylor's rebels, as they were later to become known, had walked off the field having acted in such a way as to court mass expulsion from the cloistered world of rugby union. As they were changing once again into their working clothes, Norman Bedford had walked into the changing room and told them all they would no longer be welcome in the bar.

"Who's going to stop us then?" one lad had shouted.

"I am," declared Mr. Bedford rather foolishly.

"You and whose army?" another had laughed.

"I'll fetch the police."

"Tha can fetch the bloody Gestapo too, if tha wants," a third had said. "I pay my tuppence every week to the Social Club. Bloody Twickenham doesn't make the rules here."

Muttering something along the lines that the club would be better off without such ragamuffins, Mr Benson had then beat a hasty retreat leaving all the lads to make their way back into the clubhouse.

Arthur Halton was in there having just finished playing a game of snooker with his next door neighbour, who didn't even work at Wilkinson's.

When challenged, he agreed that Norman had been out of order saying what he had, and had tried to calm things down in his own stupid way.

"I don't have any objection to any of you playing any other sport. It's a free country and you all have the freedom of choice. But on the other hand rules are rules. As your official, I've got to obey and follow the rules, all of them, even if I don't like them."

At this point the mutterings from most of the assembled group were growing louder.

"All right then, I'll tell you what I'll do. Nobody saw you lot outside playing that other game, so we can forget all about that. What I'll do for Jack is I'll write to the Committee, explain there were extenuating circumstances and suggest that he be allowed to start playing at the start of next season. So it will only be a short punishment. We've only got another four games left this season."

"Punishment? Is that what you call it for playing another sport?" It was John Naylor, all six foot four and fifteen stone of him, a former sergeant in the South Lancashire (Prince of Wales Volunteers) Regiment and who, as part of his wartime experiences, had been involved in the liberation of the Belsen Concentration Camp.

"That's what the camp guards said: 'We were only obeying orders'. Is that what you are doing, Arthur? Only obeying orders? I never thought after all I've been through and everybody else in this room for the last five years, that I would hear one of our own in this club say the same thing."

As a result of this whole affair, quite a few either transferred their allegiances to other rugby union clubs in the area, or switched over to playing for the newly-formed Helmsley Hornets Rugby League club and a couple switched to playing soccer. Meanwhile, the man at the centre of the whole affair, Jack Critchley, had literally run away from the whole thing because, by the time September and the new football and rugby season had started again, he had returned to cross-country running.

Not surprisingly, the story was retold in the pub after Jack's funeral and it was from this and the general chat about him that the idea that someone should write a book about Jack surfaced. This was partly influenced by Jack's love of using little sayings to emphasise a point he wanted to make to any of his young charges.

"I remember the first time I met him," said Alan. "It was on our first day at Wilkinson's and he had all the new apprentices in the Education Department meeting room. He spoke for half an hour, telling us what was expected of us, going to night school and all the facilities we could use by joining the Social Club. Then he finished up by saying that today was the first day of the rest of our lives, so we had to start as we intended to go on. Then he finished up by warning us not to forget to treat those who we might pass on the way up with respect, because one day we might pass them on the way down."

"'What's the difference between genius and idiocy? Genius has limits'. That was another one he often used when he was telling you off," said another young man, "and 'the mind is like a parachute. It's only useful when it's open'."

"If a man had half his wishes, he'd have twice the trouble," laughed Charlie, and then various others in the room chipped in with other sayings that Jack Critchley had employed, in order to drive home a point he was trying to make.

"The fool speaks because he has to say something, the wise man because he has something to say."

"There is nothing more impressive than ignorance in action."

"He once told me that I appeared to set myself very low standards and then consistently fail to achieve them. And then he said if I didn't try and learn something useful at night school I would finish up like a gross ignoramus, 144 times worse than an ordinary ignoramus."

The man who said that was now in charge of the Metal Fatigue Laboratory.

"You are as bright as Alaska in December, he once said to me. I didn't even know what or where Alaska was, so he told me to go to the library and find out and come back and tell him."

"One I always remembered was a little poem he had pinned up behind his desk," said another:

> Yesterday is history,
> Today is a mystery,
> Tomorrow is to be arranged
> By you.

Then Brian, a welder, spoke. He had known Jack ever since he had joined Wilkinson's in the early Fifties, although he knew little if anything about Jack's earlier background.

ONE SUMMER

"I was walking through the cemetery one Sunday morning, to go to our kid's house. There was the usual collection of people at various graves, some were the regulars, there every week and some there maybe for the first time. In the distance I saw Jack. He was almost stood to attention in front of a grave. I hung back for a few minutes. I didn't want him to see me. I don't like talking to people in the cemetery. I just don't. Then he walked away, down past the little church, so I went over to see what he had been looking at.

"It was clearly the Critchley family grave. There were the names of five or six people who had died at the end of the last century, probably some were his grandparents and then below that, there was a really moving bit of poetry. I've always remembered it. It said something like:

> Wishing your absence was just a dream
> The light will shine again one day
> When we can hold you in our arms again.
> Edward Critchley. Killed in action. 1917.

"And underneath was written, something like 'From your loving wife Agnes and the child you never knew'.

"Then in much brighter letters were the details about what must have been his mother who had only recently died. I can't remember the exact dates but it just said .

> Agnes Critchley.
> Born 1889
> Died 1978
> Reunited after many years

"They never had any kids did they?" said another former apprentice. "I think that was why he treated all us lot as though we were his own."

"Well it doesn't matter why he did what he did. He sorted me out," said another. "I'm sure I would have finished up in Strangeways if it hadn't been for him."

And quite out of character for Wilkinson's, a note was sent to the Wages Office the following day indicating that all those who had taken a half day's holiday to attend the funeral, should be paid as normal for the time they had been away from work.

19.

Drinking in the Brown Edge

"BLOODY HELL. I had a good night last night."

It was Charlie, late into work, definitely an unusual thing for him, and looking much the worse for wear.

"Why, didn't your Maud have a headache?" laughed Mick.

Ignoring the Wiganer's comment, the lad from Thatto Heath went on, "I was in the Brown Edge all night, we didn't half sup some ale."

"And what was the reason for this celebration?" continued Mick. "Have the Gas Board given you another seven days to pay your bill?"

Charlie smiled and continued to talk as he struggled to remove the cover off his drawing board. He sat on his stool, looked at the drawing on his board, decided he couldn't face adding any more lines to it and said: "Did I tell you that an old mate of mine who emigrated to Australia in the Sixties was back here on holiday and fancied a night out with me and some of the old gang from Ravenhead?"

"Yes," said Alan, "about ten times."

"Well, it was last night so we all met in the Brown Edge. It used to be his local when he lived here."

"It would hardly be his local, when he didn't live here, would it?" laughed Mick.

"There were six of us turned up, so we started off telling him what had happened after he'd left, and what each of us were doing now. Then he started telling us what he'd done."

"Where did he move to?"

"Brisbane to start with. He worked as a fitter at first, then he and another English bloke he knew set up their own machine shop. They'd only been going a few weeks, when they won a contract from a large engineering company, which kept them busy for a year. Then the bloke got killed in a car crash, so Dave ran the place on his own and the guy's widow took over the secretarial side and not long after he moved in with her. She was worth a small fortune, running a couple of hairdressers and a beauty parlour. Things went along pretty well for a couple of years and then this firm made him an offer he couldn't refuse. They bought him and his wife out and gave him a job in their Quality Control. So by the time the pair of them had reached fifty, they were worth over a million between them, he reckoned. So he retired with the intention of going travelling round the world."

"And I suppose their first port of call was Thatto Heath," laughed Mick.

"Not quite. They drew up a list of the places in the world that they wanted to visit and six months later they set off on a grand tour. First stop was the Taj Mahal, then the Seychelles Islands, sailing up the Nile, Cyprus, Amsterdam followed by a week in Paris, by which time his wife had had enough and went back home. So she missed the best part, staying at his sister's in Clinkham Wood."

"She was obviously a woman of taste," smiled Sam.

"Do you know what his favourite saying was? 'I can't believe it. I can't believe it, Charlie.' He must have said that twenty times. I couldn't believe it either. When he worked at Pilks, he never had any money and he was always in debt and now he's rolling in it."

"Did he get the first round in then?"

"Oh aye, and the crisps as well."

"So did you tell him about us lot and how poor we all are?"

"I told him what a poor draughtsman you are Mick and how you are still wearing your demob suit."

Then Charlie told them that Dave was still a keen rugby league fan and had been very pleased to hear that Wigan were just about good enough to have got back into the First Division. Dave had told his old mates about three other sports he now enjoyed watching, Australian Rules, cricket and speedway racing, what the Aussie idea of a good night out was and how he and his wife had driven nearly a thousand miles north to visit her sister who lived in the town of Cairns, and had sailed out to look at the Great Barrier.

"He told us about watching a cricket match, while he was at Cairns. It was only a friendly, and more out of politeness, Dave had asked where the away team were from. He couldn't believe it when her brother-in-law told him they were from Atherton. So he said, if you don't believe me, go on the car park and look at their coach. So Dave did, half expecting to see a Lancashire United bus. He felt a bit of a fool when he came back. Atherton is a small town about fifty miles inland from Cairns.

"Now while he was talking, I noticed that he kept looking at his watch and then he said something really strange. He told me to close my eyes and stand up because he had a surprise for me. When he was at Pilks, he was always playing tricks, so I guessed he hadn't changed much. I did what he asked, stood up and closed my eyes. Then he told me to turn round, stick my hand out and shake hands with his mystery guest, but keep my eyes shut. I had no idea who this guy was but I did what he asked and stood there holding this man's hand. And do you know who it was?"

"Alex Murphy," said Alan.

"Billy Boston," said Mick.

DRINKING IN THE BROWN EDGE

"The Pope," said Colin.

"The Mayor of Ashurst."

"Jeremy Thorpe."

"No, you are all wrong as usual. It was Mal Meninga."

Mal Meninga was one of the key players in the Australian Rugby League team, who were currently touring Britain, and he was there because not only did he once live no more than five minutes walk from Dave's house in Brisbane, he was also a big mate of Dave's stepson and so had visited their house on many occasions. Before Dave left Australia, Dave had rung Mal and invited the big fellow to Thatto Heath.

Mal had also brought two of his team mates with him. One had used the opportunity to visit the house where his Grandfather had once lived in nearby Rainhill, before he had emigrated in 1920. The other wanted to take photographs of St Helens Town Hall, Horace Street Library and Knowsley Road School for another neighbour who had once lived in Eccleston before he had emigrated many years ago. It was however not the first time the three players had been in the area. Three days earlier, they had been on the turf at Knowsley Road ground and taken part in the Kangaroos' easy victory over the Saints.

"They stayed about an hour although they were under strict instructions not to drink too much. After they had gone, the rest of us just carried on drinking and it must have been about half one before we finally got thrown out of the place."

"I suppose that you told Mr. Meninga about you playing for Uno's Dabs in its heyday," laughed Mick.

"No," replied Charlie, shaking his head.

"Lucky for him," laughed Mick.

"There was no need to. He already knew about it. It must have been on the Aussie News before they left Sydney."

"And why did they leave Sidney?" asked Mick. "Didn't he fancy having a pint in the Brown Edge? He must have heard about how bad the beer is in there."

"Just before they left to go back to their hotel, Mal gets out an Aussie jersey, signed by all the team and gives it to the landlord for a raffle. It was one that the pub was organising to send a little girl from Ackers Lane to America for some special treatment for osteoperosis."

For the rest of the day Charlie walked round with a smile on his face, a bounce in his step and a story to tell anybody who would listen. He had started off with just reporting the actual facts of the previous evening. But by the end of the day, the story had been developed to the point whereby Charlie had convinced the big man that St Helens would be a great place to live and the Saints a great team to play for.

"You mark my words, Mick. Meninga will be signing for the Saints within the next six months."

Despite the timing being a little bit out, in October 1984, the number three St Helens shirt was worn for the first time by a former policeman from Brisbane, making his home debut against Castleford.

Dave stayed for a month at his sister's house in Clinkham Wood. He travelled round most days on the bus, looking up old friends, former neighbours and workmates. Unfortunately some had died, some had left the area, and some of those who he did meet had changed so much that they hardly seemed the same people he had once known and worked with. One day he borrowed his sister's car and drove up to Chorley where he had his lunch with a distant relative. On his way back, he decided to call in at Skelmersdale, where he had once courted a farmer's daughter. She was quite nice was Sheila, almost certainly married now with a family. But it would be nice to drive past the old barn, where she often took him to roll around in the hay.

There was no chance of that as he soon discovered. The farm had disappeared completely. So had most of the old Skem that he had once known. Now, a completely new town stood there, full of people who had been moved to it from Liverpool. And if it came as a shock to him, how must it have hurt people like Sheila? So he came back onto the bypass, drove through Rainford and Crank, which hadn't changed that much he was pleased to note, and then through Moss Bank and back to his sister's house. Three days later, she drove him to Manchester Airport, where he boarded the plane that took him right across the world to his wife and home in Brisbane.

Back in work, things went rather quiet for a while in the run-up to Christmas. The Kangaroos continued to play rugby to a level that had never been seen in England before, as they went through their tour of the Northern Hemisphere undefeated. Their performance demonstrated just how much the game in England had to do to catch up. Over the next few weeks, many comments were made about how talented, skilful and fit were those who wore the Green and Gold. Something had to be done to the game in England to meet that challenge. Among some of the ideas that circulated included the top teams going professional, studying in depth the training methods the Aussies used, expanding the game and switching to a summer season, although this was not something Charlie agreed with.

In late November, rumours began to circulate round the factory that the annual pay increase was to be done away with. But nobody on the Office Committee could find out if there was any substance in the rumour because, like everybody else, none of them could ever find out where the boss was. Basil Wilkinson was now away from Ashurst for most of each week and whenever he was on site, he was always in a meeting with various unknown personnel and difficult to pin down. In fact during the previous ten weeks, he had visited Hungary, America twice and Belgium and during the time he hadn't been abroad, he had been in London and Brighton, 'on business' although what sort of business was anybody's guess.

The shop floor was still fairly busy, as was the Sheet Metal Section of the Drawing Office. The Electrical Section was ticking over but some of the draughtsmen in the Mechanical Section were getting worried, as they only had another month's work on the books. The Planning Office had enough to do but that was only because two of their members had been off sick for over a month, while the Work Study didn't really have much work to study at all. In the Estimating Department, young Tony Ramsbottom spent much of each day estimating how much redundancy pay he would receive if he got finished before Christmas and how much he could sell his house for if he were to emigrate to New Zealand!

Then in the course of a four week period, the whole of the Sheet Metal Section disappeared. Literally. It had all started on the day after Cyril had been to the funeral of his wife's sister. It was there that he and his wife discovered that they were now the owners of her large house in Southport, where she had lived alone for months. So overnight they decided to sell their own house in Gillarsfield and move to be near the sea. Never one to hang about, when his wife had decided what she wanted, the following day Cyril had handed in his notice.

The second to leave was Michael. He knew in 1952 that, if he hadn't won the pools before then, he would be finishing work on November 30th 1982, the day on which he would become an old age pensioner. His section leader Percy was happy to see the back of him. Michael had spent all his working life in the same office, drawing brackets, door assemblies and panel cutouts and was still only good enough to be classed as a detail draughtsman. On his last Monday he announced that he would be fetching cakes in for everybody on the Friday morning. Doing this was his way of letting them know that he wouldn't be taking anybody to The Horse and Jockey for a drink at lunchtime. He then walked through the Mechanical Section to have a word with the Chief Draughtsman John Battesby.

On his return ten minutes later, he saw all his workmates gathered round Ernie who was lying on the floor. Whether it was the thought of having to eat one of his wife's scones, Michael didn't know. Ten minutes later an ambulance arrived and took Ernie to hospital and later in the week Ernie's wife phoned in to say that her husband would require quadruple heart bypass surgery. At the age of fifty-nine, it would probably be at least a year before he would be fit enough to start work again. As events unfolded, Ernie was one of many people in Ashurst who, for one reason or another, retired early.

Percy was quite pleased with this turn of events. His section had lost the least productive members of the office. There was now more than enough work in the office to keep his other three draughtsmen busy. But on the following Monday, none of them turned up. On Tuesday, the youngest walked in at about ten o' clock with a big smile on his face. Percy immediately called him into his office.

"Where the hell have you been and those other two reprobate friends of yours?"

"Sorry, Percy."

"What do you mean, sorry?"

And with that Percy proceeded to tear a strip of the young lad. He finished, almost frothing at the mouth by asking the lad what did he have to say for himself. This was an opportunity that Kevin had been waiting a long time for.

"Percy, I have been here nearly two years and in that time I think that despite being the youngest, I have pulled my weight as much as anybody else. I have also seen how you have run things. So this is no hasty judgement on my part. I think that I am totally within my rights to say this to your face. You are an absolute pillock. I've known a lot of people over the years and I have to say that you are the most self-opinionated, arrogant, miserable little bastard that it has been my misfortune to have to stand near or work for. So it gives me great pleasure to tell you to go and fuck yourself."

And with that Kevin went back to his desk, opened the window and emptied all the contents of his drawer onto the roof of the Welding Shop. As he walked through the Mechanical Section, he shouted out.

"Friday lunchtime, lads. The drinks are all on us."

"Why, what have you done?"

"Won first dividend on Vernons. Four hundred thousand smackers, me, Pete and Geordie."

With that he went down to the Electrical Section, told Charlie the good news and walked out of the factory, never to be seen in there again.

As a result of their departure, the firm had to get hold of a couple of contract draughtsman quickly and also draw on the talents of some of the draughtsmen from the Mechanical Section. On the following Monday, two contract draughtsmen arrived. As soon as the first one opened his mouth, it was obvious he was from Glasgow. The accent of the second was a little more difficult to decipher. But after Percy had brought him into the Electrical Section and introduced him, it became known that he had once lived in South Africa. His first job would be to work with Charlie on the design of two control cubicles for installation in a power station in Dubrovnik in Yugoslavia. So Charlie's first act had been to take him onto the shop floor to show him a similar cubicle that had just been assembled.

While they were away, the issue of apartheid reared its head. What would this new draughtsman be like? Would he be a spreader of hate, would he help bring out the worst in those around him or would he keep his ideas to himself? They were to be pleasantly surprised, when Charlie returned to the office, on his own, and declared, "He's all right, that lad. He's certainly not a typical South African. And he's in the union as well, which is a bit unusual for a contractor."

"So what is he like on questions of a broad political and philosophical nature?" asked Yorky, with a smile on his face.

"He has a post-modernist approach to issues of a multi-flavoured content and comes from the pre-modernist school of neo-classic Marxist pieology. He's a bit like Greeno, though with a capacity to laugh in an existentialist manner."

"He won't if he finds out he has to buy the first round on Friday," laughed Mick.

Peter had had a bit of an unusual upbringing. His parents were originally from Sevenoaks in Kent and had emigrated to South Africa, three months before Peter was born. A week before he had reached the age of sixteen, they had departed rather hastily. If they had waited to celebrate his birthday, they may well have had to do it as guests of the government, in prison. On their return to England, the family lived in Oxford, where Peter had served his apprenticeship. Later he had worked in London as a draughtsman for a while before getting married and moving to live near Sale in North Cheshire.

At the end of the week, Charlie invited him to join them in the Horse and Jockey at lunchtime. Shortly after they had all sat down, Alan had asked him where did he come from. Peter's answer was somewhat unexpected.

"I was born in Bethlehem."

"The last bloke I ever heard of being born there was Jesus Christ," laughed Jason, the apprentice.

Peter continued smiling.

"You aren't the first one to make that comment."

"It's in the Orange Free State, isn't it?" asked Alan.

"That's right," said Peter, surprised that Alan knew that.

Turning to Charlie, Greeno said, "That's where Voll comes from."

Then turning back to Peter, he continued, "One of the greatest wingers who has ever played rugby league came from Bethlehem. Tom Van Vollenhoven. Have you ever heard of him?"

They were totally amazed by Peter's reply.

"I knew him vaguely when I was at school. He was a couple of years older than me. I seem to remember reading somewhere that he was the first person from Bethlehem to play for the Springboks. Well, what a surprise, I haven't heard his name mentioned for years."

Peter had been a rugby fan of sorts in his younger days, although when his family had come back to England, he had become soccer mad. He also knew vaguely that there were two types of rugby and that the other version was played in parts of the North of England, in the area where he was now working.

"It would have been rugby union he played at home. I guess he must have switched to rugby league when he came to England."

"That's right, Peter," said Charlie. "Do you ever watch any rugby?"

"I sometimes watch Sale. My brother-in-law plays for them."

"Do you prefer it to league?"

"I'm not sure. I haven't seen that much league yet."

"Did you ever play the game?"

"I played at school in the second row."

"So you won't have had much experience at handling the ball or passing it," laughed Alan.

Peter smiled and asked how long it had taken Voll to adapt to the thirteen-man code.

Charlie responded to the question by explaining how the great winger had been first introduced to rugby league.

"When he arrived at St Helens, he had never played the game before. But those who had seen him play union could see that he had great potential. In fact, Wigan had someone there looking him over, though as usual they weren't as fast as the Saints. Anyway on his first day at training, the Saints coach Jim Sullivan asked my old mate Alex Murphy to show Voll how to play the ball. That's something they don't have in rugby union."

"I know that," said Peter, "I've seen a few games on *Grandstand*."

"Now Alex has never been short of a quick response, so he said something like 'You want me to show him how to play the ball? I signed for this club for eighty quid and he has signed for eight thousand. I think for that kind of money he can teach himself how to play the bloody ball'."

"So how popular is rugby league then?" asked Peter. "Most people I ever seem to talk to about it, tell me it's a dying game."

Before Charlie, Alan, Mick, Colin or a few more in the pub could answer the question, they heard a very loud explosion outside. If it had come from the factory, a quarter of a mile away, it must be serious. But it turned out that it was just some kid messing about with a firework right outside the pub window.

As soon as they all arrived back in work, John Battesby came out of his office to tell everyone to stop all work they were doing on the Dubrovnik contract. Basil Wilkinson had just phoned up from Belgrade to say there was a major design change to be made but they would not be able to see what this meant until the middle of next week. So John suggested they tidied the place up and kept out of trouble for the rest of the afternoon.

"We might as well have an intellectual discussion about something interesting," said Yorky, after they had put all their drawings back in the Print Room and destroyed all the scrap paper that lay over all their reference tables.

"What, and leave Mick on his own?"

"Oh well, if we have got to include Mick, it'll have to be I-Spy again."

Soon after, Peter walked into the Electrical Section to find out what he should do, now that a stop had been put on what he had just started working on.

"Don't bother. We don't normally do much on a Friday afternoon, so you might as well stay here, while Mick tells us a fairy story," laughed Alan.

"I'll tell you another story about Vollenhoven and Murphy, although. I know you won't know much about my old mate," said Charlie.

"You will do pretty soon, if you are going to spend any time in here," chipped in Yorky.

"In rugby league, players are part-time. They only get paid when they play, so much for a win, less for a draw unless it was away and even less if you lost. That was the norm. But at the end of Vollenhoven's first season, Alex heard that he was going to be paid through the summer. So he goes to see the chairman of the club, to ask for the same arrangement. 'So do you think you are as good as Vollenhoven?' was how the chairman, Harry Cook had responded. And Alex is said to have come up with a corker of an answer; 'I am in the chuffing summer'."

Later on that afternoon the conversation moved back to when Peter was still at school. Discussing things that had happened over thirty years ago had obviously jogged his memory.

"A couple of other things that I remember about Tom was that he was very good at both athletics and cricket and he used to go out with a girl that lived near where we lived, called Leonie Lawrence."

"Fancy you knowing her. She's his wife now," said Charlie, "and they have both gone back to live in South Africa."

"Unbelievable, maestro. Another one of your great coincidences of our time," laughed Mick.

When Peter asked what was the significance of Mick's last comment, the Wiganer explained that despite being just a lowly person from Thatto Heath, Charlie Eccleston was at the same time an internationally renowned philosopher. He was respected by intellectual gurus from Harvard to the Sorbonne, from Berkley to the London School of Economics and from the Mining School in St Helens to Wigan Technical College. This was all because it was he and he alone who could lay claim to having discovered the Great Universal Law of Coincidence, one which was known locally from Toll Bar to Elephant Lane as Eccleston's Law Unto Himself.

ONE SUMMER

"You'll have to go and see the plaque the Council have just put in the lake at Taylor Park.

"'Charlie Eccleston, O.N.C., a legend in his own head and in his mother's old house in Emily Street'."

20.

Checkpoint Charlie and Accrington Stanley

WITHIN DAYS OF the return to work after the 1982 Christmas holiday, rumours had started to circulate about widespread redundancies right across the factory. But every time any of the managers were asked just what was going on, their response was always the same.

"We know as little as everybody else does about this place. Basil treats us all like mushrooms. We are kept in the dark for most of the time and then he drops a load of unmentionables on us. His father would turn in his grave if he knew how his son was running the show now."

Their fears were made worse when it was announced one Friday morning that no overtime would be worked anywhere on the site, over the weekend. So it came as a bit of a shock to anyone driving past the factory over the weekend to see lorries coming and going through the Warrington Road Gates.

Back in work on Monday, it appeared that the only change to the place had been that a large load of bricks and breezeblocks had been deposited at the back of the Foundry. On Tuesday, Basil reappeared and was in the most charming of moods, an indication that they must soon be going to hear bad news. Shortly after a general note went round that Basil was going to hold a "State of the Nation" meeting. All the managers, foremen, shop stewards and Elizabeth from the now moribund Staff Association, were instructed to attend this meeting which would be held on the following morning.

"It'll be closed by next Christmas."

"They're shifting all the work to the Far East."

"The Drawing Office is being moved to that firm down South."

"They've sold it all to a German company."

"Norman Wilkinson is taking over as Managing Director."

Most of the rumours were nothing more than rumours, although in such situations there was always an element of truth in them, no matter how small it might be.

For example, early in December, Basil had instructed all his managers that this would be the last year they would be expected to send Christmas cards to their counterparts in other companies that they dealt with.

ONE SUMMER

The company had just won a substantial order to refurbish a large power station in Bangkok and had also put in a bid to do the same at other power plants in the Far East, including one in the Burmese city of Rangoon.

The draughtsmen who worked for the Morgan Chemical Company, that had recently done some design work for Wilkinson's, had just been moved to a brand new drawing office at St Albans in Hertfordshire.

At the same time, the Asda supermarket in Dob Lane was running a European food promotion month, commencing with various selections of German frankfurters, bratwurst and sauerkraut.

However the idea of Basil's youngest brother Norman taking over as the Managing Director was completely out of the question. He couldn't really manage a hot dinner or even manage to cross Warrington Road without causing traffic chaos.

On Wednesday morning, Basil walked into the meeting with a smile on his face. He was clearly in a good mood. He even addressed everybody he spoke to by their first name, that was if he knew it. One absentee from the meeting however, was the senior shop steward Billy Higgins, who was off work, recovering from a splash of hot metal. As a result the representative from the Foundry was his assistant, Jack Rotherham, known throughout the factory as 'Big Dingo' on account of one of his physical attributes.

It would have been hilarious to hear Basil say 'Good morning Big Dingo'. However it was unlikely that Basil was aware of the lad's nickname, he certainly didn't even know his real name and so he ignored him. It would have been a little unfortunate if Basil had addressed him in that way, since Jack would probably have returned the greeting, using one of Basil's many highly uncomplimentary nicknames.

"Well, gentlemen and Elizabeth, I know that you have all been wondering about what has been going on over the last few weeks and why I have been away so much. Let me put your minds at ease. Despite what you may have heard, I have not brought sad tidings for you today, quite the opposite in fact. There are to be no redundancies for any of my long-serving loyal staff. However I have to inform you that there are to be some changes. They are all necessary to help ensure the long term prosperity of this company. Some of our operations will be expanded, some will be upgraded while others will be slimmed down in order to meet the exciting challenge of the 1980s, particularly in the Far East and in South America."

So far it had all been typical Basil Bullshit: Did no redundancies for his long-serving loyal staff mean there would be redundancies for those who were not loyal or who hadn't worked there more than thirty years? How do you define loyalty, Basil had never been very loyal to his employees before. The use of the word 'slimmed' only meant a reduction in something and what was the difference between some things being expanded and others being upgraded? They all listened in silence as he continued.

"I have negotiated an arrangement with a Japanese finance house which will put us on a much more secure financial footing. It will also help the company gain access to the Japanese market and help us to diversify our range of products and become more competitive in Europe. It will enable us to pay much attention to what is going on in South America and particularly in Brazil and Bolivia. In the medium term, things look very promising although in the short term, things might be a little tough for all of us."

Yes, this really was typical Basil Bullshit. Jam for tomorrow as usual.

He paused for breath, almost expecting a round of applause for what he had said, drank from his cup and then got down to the nitty gritty.

"To remain competitive, we need to make a complete fresh start. We have to organise our methods of production differently. We have to become more efficient and more cost effective in order to become more profitable. We have to plan for expansion and weed out the dead wood. This means that we have to re-organise the whole chain of command and bring in people with new ideas and experiences. As a result, it has been decided to divide the whole company into three completely separate divisions.

"Accordingly, the Ashurst site will be split into two and a new company, which will be called Wilco-Allison Products Ltd will be created, with a completely new management team in charge. This company will be made up of the Iron and Brass Foundries, Pattern Shop, Metal Fatigue Laboratory, the old Research Laboratory and the old Rolling Mill and Tinning Shop, which will be completely revamped. It means that around three thousand employees will transfer over to this new company. For the rest of us, what is at present known as Wilkinson's will become Wilkinson's PLC (1982) with my brother Norman as a non-executive director assisted by Mr. Miles Darlington and Mr. Anthony Holmes who will assume the position of Technical Co-ordinator. These are two men who both have a proven track record in industrial management."

So that rumour was true. Now it was certain that there was little future for them. Norman's only experience in a management role had been in his early twenties as a Sunday School teacher. But it was only five-year-olds that he had been in charge of, and luckily their mothers had sat with their little dears. So intellectually, it hadn't extended him too much. Now he was going to be in charge of around five thousand employees. Would they even reach next Christmas? Well it would be a laugh, if nothing else, that was for sure.

"The third part of this new company will be the Morgan Chemical Company, who are shortly moving into new premises at St Albans in Hertfordshire. As for myself, I will be fulfiling a slightly different role, acting as the International Sales Manager as well as overseeing the general co-ordination and work of all three divisions. A lot of my time will be spent abroad and particularly in the Far East, where there are some excellent prospects for us all."

So there was something to look forward to; Basil out of the way a lot more of the time was indeed good news. But Norman in charge of their destinies wasn't too clever and how good were these two new whizz kids? Darlington and Holmes sounded like a second-rate pair of comedians.

Basil then continued to wax eloquently about the future, which would be very bright for them all as long as everybody pulled together. He then asked if any of those present had any questions.

"What about the terms and conditions of all those who get transferred to this Allison Products company?" asked one of the shop stewards.

"The terms and conditions will remain exactly the same for them as they are now, except in a few instances where they will be the same as at Morgans, if their conditions are better."

"So Allison Products is not a new company then?"

"Well it is and it isn't. Making this split here has been dictated by certain financial considerations and restraints. There has to be tighter controls on the accounting side of the business, in order to assist our separate operations . Creating two medium-sized companies, with Wilco-Allison Products directly linked with Morgans, is the best way to ensure that both are successful. But basic wage rates will be the same on both Ashurst sites, broadly speaking."

More typical Basil Bullshit.

Then he put his foot in it when he carried on: "One advantage for those who transfer to Wilco-Allison Products will be that they will immediately benefit from the bonus system and redundancy agreement that are in operation at Morgans, which is a slight improvement than exists here at the moment."

"Redundancy agreement," growled a second shop steward. "You never said owt about any redundancy."

"More a slip of the tongue," replied Basil quickly. "What I mean is that whatever employment problems we may face in the future, any agreements that exist now will be respected. At this moment in time, no widespread compulsory redundancies are envisaged. However in view of the whole world economic situation, I cannot say anymore. It all depends on how the whole new company performs."

This was typical of Basil, saying that no widespread compulsory redundancies were envisaged today, but as to tomorrow, who knows? He was too clever or devious to deal with that question just at present. He already knew how many employees he wanted to get rid of, but he hadn't yet decided how and when to do it. So he put his answer in a wider context, one which meant absolutely nothing.

"This new company can not defy the international laws of economics. Every other company in the town that is still in business has had to restructure itself, make difficult decisions and even lose some of their valued staff. In my honest opinion, the main asset that this company has is its staff. I can say little else, other than I want to keep all my staff, if that is economically possible."

Then he trotted out two of his favourite sayings; "It's a tough old world out there and we've got to be tough to survive" and "There's a lot of money to be made. What we have got to do is get organised and find a bag big enough to put it all in."

When all else failed to convince whichever audience he was addressing, he would remind those present that everything was all down to one thing, Market Forces. Or Market Farces as things were soon to turn out.

At this point, he announced that he had to leave to go to a C.B.I. meeting in Manchester and that his Personnel Manager would try to answer any other questions. He finished, in classic Basil style, with another of his little sayings; "Don't forget, we either all hang together or we'll all hang together."

The whole thing then became something like a performance of *Hamlet* without the Prince: in this case the Prince of Darkness. All that John Thomas could say was that redundancies could not be completely ruled out over the next couple of years, but it was the company's intention to keep them to an absolute minimum, and hopefully they would be voluntary rather than compulsory. Then Jack Rotherham asked a question that the Personnel Manager could hardly be expected to answer.

"What useful role will Norman Wilkinson play? Will he be the Minister responsible for disasters and fiascos?"

John smiled but made no comment. He knew as well as everybody else in the room what a waste of space Norman was. But then giving him some responsibility might just make a man of him. Unlikely, but possible, maybe. But then he would be working closely with the two new bosses, Messrs Darlington and Holmes, who he was able to inform those present, were intending to start work on the following Monday.

"This guy Miles Darlington, what is his title and responsibilities?"

This was a question that John could not answer; it appeared that Miles was going to fulfil some general administrative role, but only Basil knew the actual details of the position.

Within a week, an indication of what Basil had meant by dividing the Ashurst site into two companies became clear for all to see. Over the weekend, a gang of brick layers were brought in to build a wall between

ONE SUMMER

Wilkinson's PLC (1982) and Wilco-Allison Products Ltd. The way Basil had told the meeting what was going to happen was quite different from what actually did happen. He had stressed it was mainly an administrative thing, whereas clearly it wasn't. Knowing what Basil was like, there was bound to be something stupid about the whole affair. Those who wanted to laugh at his organisational skills went home on the first Monday after the wall had appeared with their sides aching.

Wilco-Allison Products, was to be based on the east side of the site, although it wasn't quite like Basil had indicated. Certainly the Iron and Brass Foundries, the old Rolling Mill, the Metal Fatigue Lab, the Tinning Shop and old Research Laboratory formed the main part of the new company. But it also included the top end of the Works Maintenance shop and the two floors above the Copper Refinery. It was more of a division that had been made by accountants in a hurry, and was soon to become a recipe for disaster, with the first problem being the electrics.

John Day, the Iron Foundry Manager, always the first in every morning, turned the lights on, as normal. There was nothing different there. Then he walked into the Battery Room and turned the main power switch on, only to discover it was completely dead. He knew full well that the main power supply came from the substation on the other side of the wall. What he didn't know was that on the previous Friday afternoon, one of the instructions given to the Wilkinson (1982) Maintenance Shop by the new Technical Co-ordinator, had been to disconnect that supply.

Meanwhile on the other side of the wall in the Copper Refinery, the labourer who always turned the lights on first thing in the morning, couldn't. That was because the lighting supply came from a distribution board in the Brass Foundry, a distribution board that had been disconnected in order to allow extra cabling to be run. It was indeed a bright start to the future. Water was also a problem, because there wasn't any. The main supply to the foundries was from a stopcock located in the new Rolling Mill. But major changes had been made there over the weekend too. It didn't look as though much work was going to get done on the first day of the new regime.

Another thing that the new wall separated were the two Unsworth brothers. Dave was a chargehand in the Iron Foundry, his younger brother John worked in the new Rolling Mill as a handler. Dave had always looked after his brother when they were younger and continued to do so now even though both were on the wrong side of thirty. John lived on his own but still relied on Dave's wife to make his sandwiches. So every day just before the morning tea break, Dave would walk the hundred yards to make sure his bachelor brother was all right and give him his dinner. So on the first day in question Dave had to borrow a ladder, climb up it and shout to one of the labourers on the other side to tell his brother to collect his snap.

This arrangement wasn't very satisfactory, particularly three days later, when Dave discovered that a painter had borrowed the ladders and so the hilarious sight of Dave at one side of the wall shouting to tell his brother that his butties would be launched from ten yards east of the end of the old Training School. On the other side was John with another labourer holding a large sheet to catch his dinner, tuna sandwiches, which prompted some wag to declare that it must be the first time in a hundred years that anybody had caught a fish for his dinner at Wilkinson's.

Other problems soon surfaced too. The first was the use of the works canteen. Wilkinson's canteen was an enormous place, but divided into five sections, each with its own name and catering for a different group of employees. The Rose Room was reserved for the top brass and most important visitors, the Bluebell Room for the Senior Managers, the Hyacinth Room for the middle-management, the Small Hall where the junior staff and the foremen ate, all these being waitress service, and the Main Hall where all the shop floor personnel had to queue for their food. The Rose Room had been unaffected by the recent division of the company into two, but in the Blue Bell Room, the Hyacinth Room and the Small Hall, there was soon to be further division, so that from the end of the month, Wilkinson's (1982) staff would not be permitted to eat at the same table with anyone who worked for Wilco-Allison Products. This plan however was never put into practice, following an enormous protest by some of the most unlikely members of the staff.

No immediate plans had been made for the Main Hall, except in one respect. Those who worked for Wilco-Allison Products, who would now enjoy slightly better conditions than Wilkinson's (1982) workers, would now have to pay St. Albans prices for their food, a good ten per cent more. So whenever anybody approached the till girl with a tray carrying their lunch, the girl had to say, Wilkinson's (1982) or Wilco-Allison Products, before being able to work out the cost of the meal.

Then came the big one: Wilkinson's rail link with the outside world. Over the years, most of the materials brought into the factory had come in on the back of a lorry. But every now and again, an extra large load would arrive by train. As a result one day the inevitable occurred. An old steam loco, with five wagons in front of it, came down the line from Liverpool, through St Helens Junction and on through to Ashurst Junction, after which it turned left into what the locomen always used to call Dodge City. It was called that because Wilkinson's had always been known as a good place to dodge if you could do so.

That day the driver had been a loco-man who had first driven into Wilkinson's over thirty years ago. Almost sixty-five, he was due to retire on the Friday and aimed to go out with a bang. He worked up a good head of steam, intending to go rushing through the works, blowing his hooter and pretending something was wrong. As he came round the corner he turned his back to shovel more coal into the fire grate and so when he finally saw the wall it was too late. He went right through it, only at around twenty miles an hour it has to be said, but through it no less. Five minutes later two labourers who worked in the Brass Foundry were seen running through the gap in the wall, shouting 'Freedom, Freedom.'

As a result of this episode, a decision was made to remove this arbitrary division between Wilkinson's and Wilco-Allison Products and so the rest of the wall was removed. In its place was put up a portakabin, which immediately became known as Checkpoint Charlie and manned between 7a.m. and 5p.m. every day of the week by Accrington Stanley. Well, that's what everybody called the gatehouse man, mainly because his first name was Stan and he came from Accrington. Not that he had any interest in football or any other sport except perhaps for athletics, which was restricted to running after women and, in his teenage days, running away from the police.

Meanwhile, Norman Wilkinson began to appear more frequently in the Main Office. He even began to make the odd useful suggestion and spent much less time talking about how well the cactus in the Wages Office was performing. Despite Basil indicating that he would be away much more from the factory, he now seemed to be spending even more time in the place. It appeared that he was now grooming his brother Norman for a more responsible role, perhaps in forty or fifty years time! Meanwhile Mr. Darlington, who still didn't have an official job title and his sidekick, Mr. Holmes, who soon acquired the nickname, 'Sherlock', began to involve themselves more and more in the running of things.

Mr. Darlington was a powerful character, but quite out of place in a town like Ashurst. His mother must not have been thinking clearly when she gave her dear little son the full name of Miles Anthony Darlington. He certainly wasn't mad, just a well-spoken man with very fixed ideas on how employees should behave and little knowledge or interest in how the majority of people in Ashurst and district lived or worked.

In his late teens, he had made a name for himself as a member of his University rowing team and equally as a climber of mountains, having once reached halfway up Mount Everest. His intellectual prowess did not rise very high though, like the time he had made the stupid remark to a colleague, who was studying the 19th century history of the British Raj, that, "You don't have to speak Indian in order to rule India."

One of his favourite sayings was "Time is money." It was rather strange for him to use those words, bearing in mind the amount of time he wasted, holding meetings. Meetings for the sake of it, a meeting for every occasion, meeting mad: that was Miles, with a good example of what a waste of space he was, being a meeting held in early March. It was on the day that coincided ironically with the entry into the charts of the group Duran Duran with their hit record *Is There Something I Should Know*?

The agenda was as follows:

Item 1	Apologies for Absence
Item 2	Minutes of Last Meeting
Item 3	Matters Arising from Minutes of Last Meeting
Item 4	Proposed Cancellation of Fire Committee Meeting on 21st April
Item 5	Date of next meeting
Item 6	Any Other Business

Attached to the agenda that was circulated to all his managers and other 'interested' parties was the minutes of the previous meeting, at which the main item for discussion had been whether to change the date of the monthly meetings from a Thursday afternoon to a Friday morning, whether to include discussion on the Production Manager's quarterly report at every meeting and whether to invite a representative from the Merseyside Health and Safety Executive to the August meeting or leave it until after the holidays.

No better was Mr. Holmes. One of his roles as Technical Co-Ordinator was to co-ordinate the work of the different sections in the Drawing Office. In the past, if an electrical draughtsman had come up with a non-electrical problem, he would have just walked to the other end of the office and sorted it out with the mechanical or sheet metal draughtsman involved. If no agreement could be easily reached, the two draughtsmen would have taken the problem to either the section leader or the Chief Draughtsman, John Battesby. No formal record would have been made of what was discussed, the two draughtsmen would just have gone back to their drawing boards and got on with things.

But that was not good enough for Mr. Holmes. A little meeting had to be held, with him in the chair, minutes had to be taken, and submitted to about half a dozen other 'uninterested' people and then filed in a cabinet in his office. It soon became apparent that Sherlock's appointment as Technical Co-ordinator was a rather strange one for a man whose only qualification was a degree in Business Studies. Despite this, it was on his recommendation that it was decided to contract out much of the Drawing Office work, to a design company in Brighton called Southern Power Design Ltd. This was a decision fully endorsed by Mr. Darlington, the main reason being that S.P.D. had specialist knowledge of International Electrical Safety Standards. The second reason came from Mr. Holmes's view that there would be a great improvement in productivity if primary design was split from general detailing when submitting tenders for overseas contracts!

ONE SUMMER

As a result there arose the need for regular meetings to co-ordinate the work on all major new design schemes. This meant that Sherlock spent a great amount of time travelling up and down the M6 in his Jaguar. But since he had little knowledge about such simple things as designing and building power stations, he always had to take a design draughtsman with him. As a result he soon became known as the best paid taxi driver on Merseyside.

It was this relationship between Wilkinson's PLC (1982) and Southern Power Design which ultimately led to one of the biggest cock-ups that anybody in the firm had ever known, and that was saying something bearing in mind the antics of some of the salesmen and managers they had had over the years. But of course, before all the details of the Bella Doroni affair leaked out, Sherlock had been allowed to resign on grounds of ill health and return to his large cottage in the Cotswolds to look after his equally sick racehorse. Few were sorry to see him go and nobody contributed to his going away-present, not surprisingly since on resigning, the company had agreed to pay him for the remaining four months of his contract.

During the first seven months of that year, he certainly left his mark at Ashurst. In 209 days, he actually went to 109 meetings of one sort or another. It was all recorded on his weekly timesheet and monthly expenses claim. Twenty had been held at S.P.D. in Brighton, sixteen with various Government bodies in London and others in Exeter, Cardiff and the new offices of the Central Electricity Generating Board in Harrogate. These were nearly all technical meetings to which he always took at least another person with him, and at which he rarely made a useful contribution.

Mr. Darlington's style was different. He was always going to meetings as well, but since few were technical, he always felt confident enough to go on his own. Less than half of them were held on Wilkinson's premises. Some which could have been held on the premises took place in Helmsley Hilton and were invariably followed by a slap-up meal. Some of his meetings involved Health and Safety, organisation of the factory for a visit by some bigwig, planning for the office Christmas meal and party, consideration of various papers from the European Community, discussing whether to reintroduce a suggestion box for each section or just have one in the main reception area and, on one occasion, in a roundabout way, to attempt to find out who had put one of the cleaners in the club.

But many of his meetings were held in London, at Douglas on the Isle of Man and at the small seaside town of Seahouses on the Northumbrian coast. But what puzzled most people were the regular trips that he made to America, for nobody in Ashurst could ever find out what he had discussed.

21.

Sorting out the draughtsmen

BEFORE THE ARRIVAL of Mr. Darlington and Mr. Holmes, all the design and drawing work would have been done in Wilkinson's Drawing Office. From time to time, like when the place was very busy, some detailing work might have been contracted out, or a couple of contract draughtsmen might have been brought in. But that had happened very rarely. It was one of Basil's good points, he only wanted Wilkinson's work drawn up by Wilkinson's staff. It was just his way of keeping a firm grip on things.

Generally on large contracts, anything between four and a dozen draughtsmen from the Electrical, Mechanical, Sheet Metal and Civil Engineering sections could have been involved along with their respective section leaders. In overall control would have been the Chief Draughtsman, John Battesby, who spent his day going round making sure deadlines were being met with everything fitting together nicely.

In the past, technical co-ordination meant the draughtsmen all co-operating and working to the same instructions, deadlines and standards, all of which John Battesby made sure happened. But with Mr Holmes as the Works Technical Co-Ordinator, tried and trusted practices and methods of work began to be rejected as being out of date and unsuited to the demands of the new economic world order. In fact, John began to feel that his presence was now only required to make sure that the timesheets were signed, the stationery cupboard kept full and locked and all technical memorandums were seen, read and understood by everyone under his control. This actually wasn't a bad thing for him, as he was slowly preparing for retirement, which was only six months away.

Previously when a big new job was started, he would have called together the four section leaders, agreed an overall plan and timetable and decided which draughtsmen would be involved. Attention would be given to such things as the overall layout of the plant, access facilities, power supplies and availability of compressed airlines. After that, agreement would be reached on identifying the main pieces of equipment, which is exactly what had happened on the next contract, the supply and installation of four textile machines for the Gyelo Marnsch cotton mill in Western Hungary. Initially these would be given temporary numbers, which had little meaning outside the Drawing Office. They were just a convenient way of allowing some general work to get started by those concerned. Inevitably there would be changes made, probably by the mill. However, until the Sales Office issued an M12 Document, the Drawing Office could do what it wanted to, as long as John Battesby was kept informed. But as soon as John Lynch had finalised matters with the senior engineer involved and John Battesby had declared an end to all temporary numbering arrangements, no changes would be permitted unless written permission had been received from the Mill Manager.

As far as the Electrical Section was concerned, in order to get off to a quick start, every drawing produced in the first couple of weeks was given a PL number. PL actually standing for Pre-Lynch, to be exact. This arrangement seemed a little anarchic to most other people, but it had worked satisfactorily over the years for those who were directly involved in the work and knew what they were doing.

But that was until Sherlock had started sticking his 'nebby' in. He didn't really understand much about electrics, other than how to mend a fuse, stick a plug into a socket and alter the settings on his electric blanket, in the dark it must be said. Three-phase power generation and distribution, were beyond him, like they are beyond most people who don't appreciate much more than Ohm's Law or understand that power factor rarely rises above the figure of one, no matter how hard you try.

One thing that Sherlock had learned over the years from observing other people working, was that draughtsmen were absolute masters at dragging a job out, having to work weekends to complete a job on time and quite frequently engineering a situation whereby they had to go on site to sort something out that could just as easily have been done over the phone. After having been at Wilkinson's for less than a month, he decided that if he and his colleague Mr. Darlington were to profit from their time in Ashurst, their first priority was to sort the draughtsmen out.

Sherlock was also a snob. As he was soon to discover, he was much more comfortable with the people who worked at Southern Power Design Ltd. They were his type of people, able to put much more emphasis on the importance of getting round problems than talking about problems. He also felt that they behaved in a way that emphasised that work was something to be done at work, whereas most people at Wilkinson's seemed to spend much of their time at work trying to have a laugh at somebody else's expense or misfortune.

Take Mick for example: in Sherlock's opinion, he looked as though he had just got dressed in an Oxfam shop; and Charlie, who called everybody 'ewd lad' and used such strange sayings as 'it'll be all reet, lad' and 'fair do's', although the way he spoke English, it sounded more like 'furr doos'.

SORTING OUT THE DRAUGHTSMEN

But with the aid of the Brighton chappies, Jeremy, Humphrey, Grant, and young Donald, Sherlock was going to feel much more comfortable. With their assistance and co-operation he was going to get the Gyelo Marnsch job done in a way that would make it the standard for all future contracts. So with the words 'Start as you intend to carry on' firmly in his mind, he and Charlie had travelled down to Brighton for their first official meeting with Southern Power Design.

To get the ball rolling, Charlie and the Mechanical Section Leader Graham Healey had agreed that the four textile machines would be initially numbered one, two, three and four. Quite a simple decision really. But shortly afterwards, the mill decided to add an extra machine, which they wanted positioned between the original first and second machines. Since Yorky had started work on the second machine, this additional machine was given the number five, making the machine layout one, five, two, three and four, measuring away from the North Wall. A few days later the mill had rung up to ask if the space reserved for number two machine could be widened to include a secondhand Pallatini machine they were buying from an Italian mill in Genoa. As a result this was given the temporary number, six.

And so at their first meeting, Charlie had indicated that the numbering for the machine layout in the mill was one, five, two, six, three, four. This would do for a month or so until the civil engineering lads had completed their main layout drawings and by which time the mill would hopefully have finalised all their requirements. Then any other changes could all be incorporated and a decision made with the agreement of the mill manager over the permanent number of each machine. Maybe it was the flippant way Charlie had described the situation. Maybe it was the way these stuck-up consultants had got up his nose right from the moment he had been introduced to them. And no doubt Charlie had got up their noses too, which all played a part in creating a very tense atmosphere in their palatial office, within sight of Brighton Pier.

"I don't like this numbering system," Humphrey, the section leader declared, in his upper class vernacular when he had looked at the overall plans for the mill layout.

"I agree, Humph," said his sidekick, Jeremy. "We need to be clear from the outset which machines are going where and in which order. Otherwise there are bound to be misunderstandings later."

"It doesn't really matter, ewd lad," Charlie had replied. "These numbers are only for our convenience. It'll help us get some idea about how many drawings we'll need and whether we can use any of our existing assembly drawings. We can change them later after John Lynch has released his M12 documents. Doing it this way also helps to us work out how much cable and equipment we'll have to order as well."

"I don't like it. In my opinion, that's not how we ought to do this job," said Humphrey, with great emphasis on the word 'we'. "If there are six machines in the room, why can't we just call them one, two, three, four, five and six? This is our first meeting, so what can be wrong with us doing that? Surely our task is to make everything clear and simple enough so that any idiot can understand what is needed."

"Cheeky bugger," thought Charlie. "This is fuck all to do with them."

"I agree with Humphrey," butted in Sherlock. "We should agree on the numbering system here at our first meeting. Then we can put it in the minutes, inform the mill and politely tell them that we are running the show and they must stick with what is written in the minutes."

"That seems pretty sound to me," said Donald, who looked more like a clown in Billy Smart's circus, than a draughtsman.

"But you can't do that," protested Charlie. "The Mechanical Section have already used these temporary numbers on some of their detail drawings."

"Surely they can change them," offered Sherlock. "There's enough of them always stood around talking whenever I walk through the office."

Charlie thought quickly that if he argued, it would be as productive as having a conversation with a deaf man. He was also conscious of the fact that everyone else in the room was clearly singing from the same hymn sheet. So he decided to use a different approach, which would cover his back and throw any potential problems back at the others.

"Well if you insist, we can change the machine numbers but we will have to indicate it very clearly in the minutes of this meeting, so there is absolutely no chance of any confusion anywhere."

"I'm sure that we can do that," said Sherlock, thinking he had won an easy victory. "What do you propose exactly, Charlie?"

"Well something like this: original number one remains as original one, original number five becomes new two, original number two becomes new three, original number six becomes new four, original number three becomes new five and original number four becomes new six. And you'll have to give us a day for us to alter all the numbers of the power cables on the drawings that we've have already done for original machine numbers three and five, which are now new five and new two."

"Why?"

"Because each cable on our original machine number three has the prefix three and every cable on our original machine number five has the prefix five. So on original machine number five, which is now your new machine number two, all the prefixes of five will have to be changed to two. And on original machine number three all the prefixes three will have to be changed to five."

SORTING OUT THE DRAUGHTSMEN

"Does it really matter?" asked Sherlock. "Surely the cables don't know or care which prefix number they have been given."

"And what about when all the cables land back at the main control board and have to be connected to the terminal blocks?"

"Honestly, I just don't know why there are always problems with the electrics on these jobs."

But at that point Sherlock thought he had got the better of Charlie. Every time he had had to deal with draughtsmen, he had had grief. But by putting his foot down right at the start, he now felt that he had changed what could have been a problem into a non-problem.

Or so he thought.

All the way back to Ashurst, the following day, Sherlock seemed very pleased with himself. Maybe it was because he thought he now had assumed full control of this contract and had beaten Charlie hands down. Maybe it was also because tomorrow he was going to have another day out, though this time only at Trafford Park.

Unfortunately for Sherlock, when he walked into the Drawing Office on the Wednesday morning, he soon realised that things were not that simple when Charlie told him that he had opened up a parcel of drawings that had just arrived from Hungary. In it was the latest proposal for the layout of the mill, which now included a refurbished machine from West Germany, which they wanted located between the machines that he had originally called one and five. However, following yesterday's meeting, this would be between original one and new two. But this now meant that there would be seven machines in a row and the new problem was how to number them.

"It's obvious. One to seven," said Sherlock.

"We can't do that, because the minutes of Monday's meeting will have been written up and are probably in the post by now. So the six machine numbers we agreed on at Brighton won't line up with the seven machines that the mill now want."

Then, suppressing a smile, he continued, "If we use your system, we'll have to re-number them a second time and send a memo down to SPD. It will mean that original machine one remains as number one and this West German machine will have to become machine number two. That's all right, but the third machine will now be the old new machine number two which will have to be called new new machine number three and the next machine will be the old new machine number three, which will have to be called new new machine number four."

"All right, Charlie, all right. I'll look at it tomorrow."

"We could do with a decision pretty soon, otherwise we are going to get into a right state with the detailing of new machine number five which was my original number three, because Keith is now waiting to put the prefixes on his wiring drawings."

Such a complicated problem was more than could be handled there and then by Sherlock. But an hour later, after discussing the issue on the phone with Humphrey, he returned to suggest that the order of the machines should be one, two, three, four, five, six and seven, and when all the minutes of the meeting in Brighton arrived, they would have to be shredded and a new minutes written up and sent out.

"Well don't forget that we can't use the number seven, because that has already been reserved for the Dutch machine they are putting next to the chute feed upstairs and all the drawings for that machine have been done."

"Do we have to have these complications, Charlie? My God, you people don't half know how to spin a job out."

"That's the way we've always done jobs here and it has always worked before but, if you want to change things, you're the boss."

"Thank you Charlie."

"So what do we do next? And what should the Mechanical Section do. Dave Hollinghurst has finished all his work on machine number two, er sorry new new machine number three, or is that now going to be old new machine number three?"

It was clear that Sherlock was fuming. Time to put the boot in.

"Can I make a suggestion? Why not ask somebody from Brighton to come up here and help us sort it out?"

"Yes," said Sherlock without really thinking about it.

"You organise that then and in the meantime I'll get started on ordering the gear to go in the control cubicles."

"Good idea."

"And I think, to avoid any further problems, I'll call the cubicles A, B, C, and D."

"If you must."

"One other problem though. Originally, we only needed four main control cubicles for the original four machines, but with these three extra machines we will need another cubicle and I'm not sure where it can be positioned. And I don't know how to number the cubicles because if we follow your system, we might have to change the lettering sequence we've just agreed on."

"You'll have to leave this with me for a bit. I've got to go to a meeting in ten minutes."

Half an hour later, Sherlock reappeared with more unfortunate news that he had just received by telephone from Wilkinson's agent in Budapest, informing him that the mill had changed their minds yet again. They had decided to knock the North Wall down in order to provide enough space to put another machine in the main hall. They hoped to put it between where that wall had been and what they knew as machine number one. But they were also considering putting it upstairs on the first floor. It would be a new tandem machine with the speed control unit taken from an existing machine they had been intending to scrap. How would the addition of an eighth machine affect the layout drawings and the numbering of the machines?

Charlie looked at his notes to refresh his memory and said "We'll have to put on one side what we agreed half an hour ago and come up with a second new numbering system. The first new numbering system will have eight machines on the ground floor and the second new numbering system will have seven machines on the first floor and the eight on the first floor. If we call the first system Plan One, then off the top of my head it will be something like one, old new one, old new two, new old three…"

"Hang on, stop there Charlie, we will have to have a meeting about this. It's getting far too complicated."

"All right, you organise a time and I'll be there but don't forget we can't use the number seven, as I've already explained, and I must warn you that we have already taken out number eight for the tandem machine that the OCD lads are transferring from that mill at Kausin Nonpoly next week. So can you let me know if we can use number nine for the eight machine?"

"We'll discuss it as soon as possible. I am totally confused. I'll ring you later, when I've thought about this."

And with that he stormed off.

"Charlie, however did you keep your face straight when you were reeling off all them numbers?"

"He's an absolute pillock. He doesn't understand the first thing about our job. He doesn't have the foggiest idea about how to make a complicated job as simple as possible. Bloody hell, he would have had a heart attack if he had seen how me and Greeno did that job in Belgium."

"Do you mean at that mill at van Oostretyan?" chipped in Greeno.

"Aye. There were five or six different companies on site and they all had a different set of numbers for the layout of seven different machines. There were guys there speaking French, Dutch, Flemish and German. So to make things simple and foolproof, I suggested that we gave each machine the name of a famous sportsman. I don't think any of them had a clue what I meant so I drew the layout of the plant on the blackboard, added the name and they all agreed to it. So from then on the different machines were called Ashton, Boston, Foster, Greenall, Holmes, Murphy and Sullivan and every cable was given the related prefix A, B, F, G, H, M and S. It was an absolutely unique numbering system but it worked, daft as it sounds."

He smiled as he continued telling what was a completely true story.

"A few months later, a fitter called in to make a few changes in the main cubicle and to his surprise he saw that someone in the mill had painted these

185

names in gold on each machine. And to crown it all, the shop foreman asked the lad if they were all names of members of the British Royal Family."

Then Charlie went on,

"Well, I'm doing no more on this job until he tells me what I'm supposed to be doing. I can see this being one hell of a cock-up and I'm not going to get all the blame for it."

"So what did you and him do in Brighton at night, Charlie? Did you go clubbing?" asked Yorky

"I don't know where he went. He said he had a friend to visit, so I left him to it. I'd rather be on my own than with him."

"So what did you do?"

"I had a walk along the seafront and then went for a pint in this olde worlde pub and got chatting to a bloke who was in there."

"What, in Brighton? You wanna be careful there, Charlie."

"Do you know what attracted me to him?"

"We don't want to know."

"It was what was written on his jersey. It clearly explained where he was coming from, his outlook on life and how easy it would be to form a meaningful relationship with him."

"So what did it say, 'Freud, I am a battered child, looking for love'?"

"No, much simpler than that. Whitehaven Rugby League Club."

"So what did you do?"

"I just nodded to his shirt, said 'I didn't think I'd see a League lad down here,' and then when I said I was from St Helens, well it was just like two distant relatives meeting. He had a face like Vinty Karalius and looked like a typical Cumbrian half-back, you know, six foot two and fifteen stone. He knew Dick Huddart and John Tembey, and he'd played a couple of times with Barrow a few years back. Anyway, after we'd been talking for a bit, four Yorkshire lads staggered into the place, all Bradford Northern fans on their holidays, so we had a right good laugh with them."

"Meanwhile Sherlock was nowhere to be seen, I take it," laughed Yorky.

"He was the last thing on my mind because just as they called last orders, this blonde comes up to me, tells me that she had heard us talking about rugby and wondered if I could explain the difference between rugby league and rugby union. Before I could work out where to start, she told me that she lived in a flat about ten minutes walk away. So we went back there and I told her all I knew about the game, you know, how to warm up before you start playing, how to tackle round the legs, how to make a pass, give a stiff arm and then what you had to do to have an early bath."

"Aye, and then she told him she was a hooker and he owed her fifty quid," laughed Mick.

SORTING OUT THE DRAUGHTSMEN

"Did you watch any television while you were down there?" Alan asked.

"No. Why what's been on? I've not even seen the news."

"Your old mate, Les Earnshaw, was on. They were discussing his latest book."

"Really! What's it called?"

"You'll never believe this. It's called *Put Your Vote on My Backside* and it looks like they might be making a film of it as well."

Les Earnshaw had been a draughtsman in Wilkinson's Drawing Office back in the Sixties. Since leaving the firm he had had two highly successful novels published, *The Draughtsman's Tale* followed by *The Actress Goes to Heaven*, which had featured Brigitte Bardot having a night out in Wigan. After that Les had started writing commercials for TV and written some material for *Coronation Street*. Now he had returned to his theme about life in the North based on a fictional town called Garsdale, which was located vaguely between Ashurst and Wigan.

"What's it about?"

"All the corruption that was going on among the councillors on Garsdale Council and what happens when it gets exposed and sparks an anti-political political revolt throughout the whole country."

"That doesn't sound like Les."

"Oh, it is. It's typical Les, set in the Earnshaw genre of hysterical neo-realism, I think the interviewer called it."

Mick then proceeded to describe one of the storylines in the novel, which clearly looked like being another bestseller.

"When the local paper exposes these corrupt councillors, they all resign and a new council is elected to replace them. It's made up of a large group of right wing Christian fundamentalists, four Green Party members, the Garsdale Freedom Party and two independent candidates, one whose main demand was for a brothel to be opened in the Town Hall and another demanding that rugby union is banned in the schools. But it's the Moral Majority group who are in control. They begin by introducing some pretty weird policies, like no buses running on a Sunday and no shops or pubs allowed to open either. After they had been in power for a few weeks, they decide to use the Town Hall for a big evangelical meeting and arrange for their great leader in California to speak to them via a video link-up onto a large screen. But some militant members from the Garsdale Freedom Party decide to spoil the party. They hide in one of the offices upstairs and then, just as the meeting was starting, lock all the doors from the inside and go up to the projection room and kidnap the projectionist. Then instead of a religious broadcast, they show three solid hours of hardcore porn."

Then Yorky chipped in and told Charlie that Les had also been on Granada, and had talked at length about the incident in his first book, based on the shenanigans involving Peggy and Gordon. Those two actually used to work at Wilkinson's in the Sixties. Gordon was in charge of the High Voltage Test Bay and Peggy was a chargehand in the Accessories Division. Every day she had to take a couple of glass insulators to the lab for a High Voltage test. He used to take her into the Test Bay, lock the door and turn on the red lamp so anyone outside would think there was a test in progress. Everybody knew what was going on. It must have been the biggest non-secret of the year. One Friday afternoon they were in there together for ages. Usually the old punching machine was banging out brackets so nobody nearby could hear what was going on. But that particular afternoon, it had broken down. The only other person in there at the time was a young apprentice. He was working away on the bench when he heard Peggy moaning and groaning and then scream out. He was only sixteen, didn't know much about anything and having a bit of a vivid imagination, thought she was either being electrocuted or murdered. So he picked up the phone and rang all the emergency numbers. About five minutes later, Gordon and Peggy had emerged from the Test Bay looking a little flustered to an audience made up of the Works Fire Brigade, two nurses, a security guard and a St John's ambulance man. And that story is as true as I am stood here."

"I used to know Peggy. She was a Sunday School teacher, believe it or not," said Colin. "She lived near us in Helmsley."

"I bet I know what her favourite hymn was," laughed Mick. "Nymphs and Shepherds, come out to play."

"There's some right funny bits in it early on, just before the old Council get found out. The Mayor is a right conman, called Arthur Dale. He's only a labourer at the Gas Board and one day he's given the job of painting the floor of the storeroom, where he works. Well, the daft bugger starts at the door and works his way into the room and then when he's nearly finished, he has to spend a couple of hours waiting for the paint to dry before he can get out. And while he's stuck in there, the Finance Sub-Committee are waiting for him to start the monthly meeting in the Town Hall."

"That's a true story," said Charlie. "Les based it on Joe Small, when he used to work in the Machine Shop. That's just what he did."

"There's another one when Arthur and his wife get invited to a banquet in the Free Trade Hall in Manchester along with a load of other civic dignitaries. On the table there were quite a few unusual bits of food, like pickled walnuts. Arthur was always keen to try new things to eat, especially if they were free. So he tries to lift a walnut with a pair of silver tongs, but he can't get the knack of these tongs and it finishes up with a large walnut flying across the table and into the soup of the Lord Mayor of Manchester. And then his wife, whose only experience of eating out was in the Bears Paw chippy in Dob Lane, bawls out 'That wouldn't have happened if you hadn't used them stupid pliers. Why don't you use your fingers like you do when you're at home?'"

"Another true story," laughed Charlie. "That was based on Tony Hanson who used to be a chargehand in the Foundry and his wife Alma, who once clocked a bloke in the Colliers' Arms after he had accused her of breaking the mirror in the ladies toilets, by looking at it."

"That's why his material is so true," said Mick. "It's all based on real people."

"Do you remember when he was on that TV programme with David Frost?" said Alan. "When he started off talking like John Snagge and then completely changed and finished up sounding like Mick."

"I can still remember right at the end of that programme, just after David Frost announced that the following week, they would be looking at the contribution made by women writers," laughed Yorky. "And the next thing everybody heard was Les shouting out 'I'll fetch the wife'."

A few minutes later Billy Mulholland walked in with another story to go into Wilkinson's One Hundred and One Best Cock-Ups. An apprentice had just done a drawing of the proposed extension to the Machine Shop Stores. No one had checked it and when it arrived in the Works Building Department, it was discovered that if none of the dimensions were altered, the new extension would be thirty yards long and two foot wide.

But all conversation on the matter suddenly came to a grinding halt with the news that two police cars had just pulled up outside the entrance to the General Office and an inspector from Manchester C.I.D. had told Mrs. Billington to have the door to Basil's office locked.

22.

A strange story from America

IT IS QUITE amazing just how quickly news can travel round a large factory. By lunchtime, everybody knew that the police had locked the door to Basil's office, that he hadn't been seen since Friday lunchtime and that his two brothers Norman and Cyril had been interviewed by a detective who looked like Inspector Barlow out of *Z Cars*.

Then just after he had returned from the canteen, Charlie had received a phone call from an old workmate.

"Charlie, what are you doing tonight?"

It was Ray Hewitt, who had worked in Wilkinson's Drawing Office until twelve months ago when he had retired early on the grounds of ill health. He was well known among many of the older members of the office, having done much to help the other old stalwart and now deceased Len Turner, get the draughtsmens' union, D.A.T.A., started after Basil had assumed full command in 1963. A man with a fine analytical brain, always able to put things into their correct historical context and with contacts all over the place, he had always been recognised as the real power behind the throne of 'King Lennie the First'.

"Why, are you having another beer festival in your shed?"

"Listen, I need to talk to you about something important."

Charlie knew that Ray always chose his words carefully. He also knew of the high quality of Ray's homemade beer, the strength and the quantity which would be on offer.

"Get Sam and Greeno to come as well, but don't tell anybody else. You'll understand why when you get here. And don't have much for your tea either. I've made some Ashurst Hot Pot to tantalise your tastebuds."

As soon as they walked into his house they could sense that he was enjoying his retirement, although sadly he no longer enjoyed the company of his late wife Beryl, who had passed away six months earlier. They looked at the many photographs on the walls and passed a few pleasantries with him, as he poured out four pints of his latest brew, one which he had called his Donkey Common Hofmeister. They sat down in his front room, as he proceeded to tell them a weird story from far across the Atlantic Ocean.

He began by asking them if they ever remembered a lad called Joe Platt.

"I do," said Charlie. "He used to work in the Chemistry Lab and lived at Hyde Bank in a prefab. If my memory serves me right, I think he also played in a rock 'n' roll band called The Hideaways."

"I remember him," laughed Alan. "I remember him very well. He still owes me seven and six. He was once a suspect in a murder trial in Bolton and couldn't provide an alibi for where he was on the night of the murder, even though he was with a senior police officer."

"Why not?" asked Sam, who had never heard of him.

"Because he was in bed with her and shouldn't have been."

Ray smiled, "Yes, that's the one. He was a right ladies' man. It used to get him into all sorts of bother. Well, he came here last night."

"I didn't know he still lived round here."

"He doesn't. He's been living in America for years but he had quite a lot to tell me about, which I am sure you will be very interested in."

He wiped his lips with the back of his hand and went on. "About ten days ago, he learned that his brother, who had lived in Helmsley all his life, was dying of cancer so Joe came back to see him. Sadly he only arrived in time for the funeral, so now he's helping his widow sort everything out. Yesterday, he heard about Basil's strange disappearance and so that's why he came to see me. He also told me what he'd been doing for the last twenty years. I must say, if only half of what he told me is true, it's still an amazing story.

"Anyway, I'll start by telling you about that first, and to coin an old phrase of mine, it will help to put things into their historical context. Then I can tell you about the dark side of our Mr. Wilkinson. And in between, we'll have summat to eat."

This certainly sounded a good way to spend an evening, good beer to drink, Ashurst Hot Pot to eat and what sounded like an intriguing story to listen to, as told by an old workmate who had always been able to tell a good tale.

"Joe left Wilkinson's after it was sold to that American firm, the Miller Engineering and Construction Company, in 1963. He told everybody that he was going working down South but that wasn't true. He had got this job with Miller's but on the condition that nobody in Ashurst knew about it, for some strange reason.

"They wanted him to carry on working on that X21 Project he had been on with for ages, which he did. But after a year he left. Somehow things didn't work out as he had hoped. He didn't get on with the boss of the lab and he had a bit of trouble with one of his neighbours. So, with all his redundancy money that he hadn't touched, he decided to go travelling. His first port of call was to a place called Anchorage in Alaska. It was all right up there until the winter started. As soon as the temperature dropped below freezing, he went down to California. As you may remember he was a good guitarist and so he started playing in clubs in Los Angeles.

"It wasn't long before he started playing about with the owner of the club. She was a widow, rich and English, originally from Nottingham. Anyway, she soon invited him to move in with her into her luxury penthouse. It was a lot better than the hippy commune he had been living in since he had arrived there. Things went great for a time and then disaster struck. One afternoon he witnessed a road accident, which led to him being late returning to the club. It saved his life because just before he got back, an earthquake struck the place, killing his wife and two members of the band he had joined. He then decided he didn't want to live there any more. So he went travelling again, this time in South America.

"Then followed a year of escapades, adventures and more dices with death. He got thrown in jail in Bolivia for being drunk, met Robert Redford in Rio de Janeiro, was within an inch of being bitten by an alligator in the Amazon in Brazil, and was in Santiago on the day Salvador Allende's Government was overthrown by the Chilean Army. He finished up in Mexico City, where he won a small fortune in a casino and had it all stolen by a beauty queen who had led him to believe she was a property developer. Anyway, to cut a long story short, he finished up back in Cleveland with hardly any money, but every intention to write a book about his adventures. On his first evening there he called in what had been his favourite bar and who should be sat in there but Stephen Williams. Do you remember him?"

They certainly did remember him. He was an old chum of Basil Wilkinson's and had at one time been the company's Managing Director and a right pain in the backside for all those who worked in the Drawing Office.

"Unlike us lot, Joe had never had any trouble with him, because Williams had always been interested in what he had been doing on that X21 project. Anyway, after a few beers and a long discussion, Williams offered him a job at the new company that he had set up over there, working on his old pet project, but with some added assistance."

Ray then left the room and came back a few minutes later with four plates and a large casserole dish. He ladled out the food and told them that the beetroot had only been taken from the garden an hour earlier. Then, with the phrase, "Eat up lads, you're at your Auntie Val's", they started on their meal. Fifteen minutes later, their plates were all empty. It couldn't have gone quicker if a flock of locusts had descended on the table. Ray was clearly as good a chef as he was a brewer. He then proceeded to side the table, and on his return poured out more beer and continued with his tale about the adventures of Joe Platt.

"What I am going to tell you now is what Joe discovered from Williams about some of Basil's secret past. You know how arrogant Williams used to be when he was here? Well, he had always been different with Joe. Over there, they hit it off together, going out drinking and whoring every weekend. Now Joe could have supped for England, but Williams couldn't hold his ale too well. And whenever the ale loosened his tongue, he began to talk about things he should have kept to himself."

Ray took a long swig from his glass, wiped his face with the back of his hand yet again and continued: "Do you remember when Basil appointed him as Managing Director, we were all led to believe that it was because of his engineering background, qualifications and experience on project management? Some of that was true, but what we didn't know was that Stephen Williams had something on Basil from the past. Whether it was from their University days or somewhere else, or whether he was blackmailing Basil, Joe was not able to find out but it might have explained why some strange decisions were taken here, by Basil.

"You see, when Basil discovered a year after taking over the firm, that it was almost bankrupt, it was Williams who convinced Basil that the way out of the financial mess was for the company to be sold to Millers. What Basil didn't know at the time was that Williams was hand in glove with all the main directors of Miller's.

"The deal was very good for Miller's because they had just won a mega order in the Middle East and didn't have the capacity to do all the work at their clapped-out factory in Cleveland. So that's why we got all that work for Saudi Arabia here. It must have kept us going for nearly a year. It also provided Williams with an opportunity to get control of the projects that were running in the old Chemistry Lab. You see, Miller's were an engineering and construction company and with all the work they had on the order book, they weren't that interested in spending money on what Williams convinced them were long-term research programmes, like the X21 Project.

"So Williams set up his own company because, being a chemical engineer, he had a good idea of the potential for what Joe had been working on. A year later, Miller's moved into a brand new factory. As far as they were now concerned, the Ashurst site had served its purpose as all the backlog of work had been completed and delivered on time. Then Williams pulls another masterstroke. He convinced Miller's to sell the factory in Ashurst to the Northern Electrical Design Company, which was nominally based on the Isle of Man, as we later discovered. Miller's knew that Basil was the owner but they weren't bothered, because they just wanted to get rid of any involvement in Britain. Very cleverly, Williams had also told them that Harold Wilson's Government was going to nationalise the engineering industry and it would be best to get out while the going was good.

"Soon after, Williams's new company won a large order from the American military and went straight into full production. Joe reckoned if the work had been kept here, and Basil had shown a bit more interest in it, Ashurst might have become a boom town by now."

As he paused for another drink of beer, the four of them heard the front door being opened and into the room came an attractive young woman carrying a small baby.

"Hello, Janet. We are not making a mess. We are just doing a bit of Bible study," laughed Ray and before she could say a word, he turned to Charlie and said

"I'd like you to meet my girlfriend."

His words shocked them, it just wasn't Ray's style. He was well turned sixty and the woman was only half his age.

"Don't look so amazed Charlie. It's only my daughter and my dear little grandson."

He then introduced his three former workmates, she said she was always pleased to meet any of her Dad's old comrades and asked if they were planning the revolution yet again. Then she reminded him that he was babysitting for her the following night, went into the living room to collect some shopping and left, with the words:

"Don't forget to put everything into its correct hysterical context, Dad."

"She is so like her mother," said Ray sadly, then he continued, "Anyway back to Joe's life and times. A few weeks ago, Basil turned up in Cleveland and from what Joe could see, there was no love lost between him and Williams. After Basil had left, the two of them went out on the ale. They stayed most of the evening in a classy nightclub, with Williams spending time with a couple of right dodgy characters. When they had gone, Williams, in his usual drunken state at that time in the evening, told Joe that they wouldn't be seeing Basil in Cleveland or anywhere else again. 'That imbecile has just been measured for a coffin' were the very words that the man had used.

"Rather curious about the two characters they had been sat with, Joe commented that they looked a little out of place for the most expensive club in town. 'Don't ever cross those guys, Joe. And don't ever tell anybody you drank with them. In this town, even the Mafia quake in their boots when the McKenna brothers are around.' The following day Joe got the phone call to tell him that his older brother was dying. So he flew back home straightaway and arrived just in time for the funeral. That was last Thursday. And then he hears that Basil has gone missing. So he came over here last night to tell me what he knew and wonders whether he ought to go to the police."

"Just one question Ray, how come he came to tell you all this, why you?"

"A long time ago, I saved his life, when he was a kid. I'll tell you about it some other time, how and where. His Dad was also a big pal of mine when we both worked at Hilton's and before that we were in the Labour League of Youth together. So you see, we go back a long way. And although Joe was never interested in politics, he was beginning to smell a rat about some of the things being talked about either from Williams, or from Miss Blabbermouth."

"Who was she?" asked Charlie.

"She was in charge of the Wages Department and knew all about the financial side of Williams's new company. A couple of years earlier, she had had a bit of a fling with him before Joe had arrived on the scene. But Williams had treated her badly and she had never forgotten it. So when Joe turns up, she started knocking about with him, unknown to Williams. And she couldn't keep her mouth shut either, which as far as Joe was concerned, was another of her strong points."

"All this would all make a bloody good film," laughed Sam.

"I know and there's a lot more too: stuff that I've discovered over the last six months, quite independently from what Joe told me last night.

"If you cast your mind back a few months ago, you'll remember Basil splitting Wilkinson's into two. He called the part you work in Wilkinson's PLC (1982) Ltd and the other half became Wilco-Allison Products. At the same time, that firm Morgan Chemicals came into the picture. At first, they were just doing a bit of design work for Wilkinson's, then, right out of the blue they become the third part of this big new company.

"So I did a bit of digging around and found out that one of the directors of Morgan's was a woman called Heather Allison. That just happens to be the maiden name of Williams's second wife. I also found out from my contact in the States that the first Mrs. Williams died in mysterious circumstances while visiting Taiwan, where her husband once owned a chemical company, which has since been closed down.

"So let's get this clear," said Charlie. "Basil sells the firm to Millers in 1963. They use it to get all their backlog of work completed. They sell the Chemical Research projects to the new company that Williams set up. A year later, Miller's sell most of what they had originally bought in Ashurst to a holding company called Electrical Designs, which is based in the Isle of Man and controlled by Basil. Under his control again, this then gets allied with the Morgan Chemicals Company, which has the second Mrs. Williams as one of its directors. Soon after, Wilkinson's gets split into two, Wilco-Allison Products comes into being and I bet you are going to tell me that Heather Allison is involved."

"Good guess and there's more. What was one of the first things that happens after this character, Miles Darlington, takes over? Design work gets sent to the Southern Power Design company. And will you be surprised when I tell you that one of the two major directors in that company is none other than Heather Allison. Now, she isn't there because she is a pretty face or because she is married to Stephen Williams. She is a leading figure in the Republican Party in Ohio, has an elder brother who is an advisor to Henry Kissinger and another brother who works for the Pentagon. And the other

195

director of S.P.D. is a Sandra Czerny, who also holds a top job in a major American bank in New York, has a sister who works for the C.I.A and a husband who was based in the American Embassy in 1971, when the Army overthrew the Government of Salvador Allende.

"Well I don't know what this has got to do with it," said Charlie, "but it seems a right viper's nest."

"It does if Basil is going to get bumped off. It looks as though a complete takeover of the whole firm is being engineered, but I don't know why. There are also a couple of other things I am looking into. One is Basil's possible involvement with another chemical company in Taiwan and the second is the links that Williams has with a Christian fundamentalist group in Texas."

"How do you find the time and the enthusiasm to do all this, Ray?"

"You know that I've always been interested in politics and understanding how the world works and to whose benefit. That's why I spent so much time and effort helping Len get the union going at work and also being active in the Vietnam Anti-war Movement, as you know. Well the older I get, the more I want to do. Usually with a lot of folk, by the time they get to my age, they've had enough of it all. For me it's the opposite. And of course it's all very interesting too. I've got a few good friends in this country and in America who I've known a long time. And with the pace of things in the world now, every day throws up something new. But at the end, it all seems to boil down to one thing, powerful forces in America wanting to fashion the world in their image and in their interests."

"I'm not disagreeing with you Ray, good luck to you," said Charlie. "I suppose that you could say that you are trying to make the world a safer place for your children and grandchildren to grow up in, and mine too."

"Exactly, there were plenty people around in the early Thirties who did their bit to try and stop Hitler and if they had succeeded maybe there wouldn't have been the Second World War. Anyway as far as this little meeting tonight is concerned, it either didn't take place or, maybe better still, if anybody asks, we discussed Len's old idea of setting up an organisation for the old age pensioners. You see, I'm not doing anything illegal, just finding things out that others in authority might want to keep secret."

"OK," said Charlie. "This is the rebirth of the Ashurst Old Age Pensioners' League, It fell to pieces when Len died anyway. You are going to be the Chairman, I'll be the Secretary, Sam can write the monthly newsletter and Greeno can collect the stubs."

At that point there was a knock on the door.

"That'll be our Maud."

Charlie was right. It was Alice Eccleston, who immediately apologised for being late and then told Ray that she had heard a lot about him over the years and was very pleased to make his acquaintance. Shortly after, they left, but with Alan and Sam refusing the offer of a lift.

"Thelma's coming round for me," said Alan, "so we can drop Sam off, preferably off Belton Bridge."

"I didn't know Thelma could drive," said Ray.

"In their house, Ray, Thelma wears the trousers and drives the car. Greeno just drives her barmy, he's still nipping out every night to see what's pulling the milk train," laughed Sam.

"Do you want another, lads?" asked Ray as soon as Charlie had left them and, before they could even nod enthusiastically, two more pints of Donkey Common Hofmeister were put on the table before them.

"So you say that you once saved Joe's life. When was that, Ray?"

"It was when I was an apprentice at Hilton's. I was on my first date with a girl from the Wages Office. We went for a walk along the Sankey Canal, one Sunday evening. In the distance I saw a woman pushing a pram and holding a dog on a lead. Then a smaller dog appears, her dog started jumping up and down trying to get at it and she slipped and let go of the pram handle. It just rolled away from her and down into the water. She starts screaming 'My baby, my baby'. So without any more thought, I whipped my shoes and trousers off and jumped in. Luckily the pram must have dropped on top of something in the water, so the baby was all right. But where I jumped in, it was deep so I was soaked. Anyway, I pulled the baby out of its pram and lifted it up to its mother and then clambered out. By this time there were a couple of other people there and somebody else had run off to phone for an ambulance and the police."

"I suppose the girl was quite proud of you."

"Well not quite, you see when I was getting ready to go out, I couldn't find any clean underpants so I went out without any on. When I got out of the water, all I was wearing were my socks and a tee-shirt. The funny thing was that by this time, there was an old woman stood nearby and as the girl came up with my trousers, this old woman said to her 'I bet that's not the first time you've seen him like that.' 'It is,' she said, 'I've only been going out with him for ten minutes.'"

"And how long was it before she had another look at it?"

Before he could answer, Thelma arrived and the next half hour was spent with Ray telling her about incidents that he could remember happening during her first few weeks at Wilkinson's.

During the next two days, the door to Basil's office remained locked, except when a couple of men from the Serious Crime squad were in there. All the members of the senior management were interviewed, although in a most desultory way, after which the men from London departed without as much as a thank you or even a goodbye.

But there was still no sign of Basil. He had just disappeared from the face of the earth. Or was he dead and buried somewhere, just like would happen in some second-rate gangster film?

Were dark forces at work? Were elements of the American military or extreme right wing forces involved somewhere in the background? Had Basil somehow attracted those whose role might just be to protect privileges and power in a troubled world? Might Joe have to now tread very carefully: would it be even safe for him to return to Cleveland? Based on the content of various recent films that had been shown on the television , were the lives of people like Charlie, Sam, Ray and Alan now at risk?

It was easy to get paranoid about the whole affair, particularly whenever Sam answered the phone at home; he heard an unusual crackling noise as though it was being tapped. Two Americans were seen later that week knocking on doors in Scholes Lane in Thatto Heath, and then when Alan had made a detour past Ray's house on his way home from work, he saw that the milk hadn't been collected.

But although one set of ideas could be assumed, there was in these three cases three simple explanations. All Sam's neighbours in Winwick Road were experiencing poor reception, a fact acknowledged by BT. The two Americans who had been seen in Thatto Heath turned out to be members of the Church of the Latter Day Saints, trying to save the good people of St Helens from following false Gods and the wrong sort of Saints. The milk bottles on Ray's doorstep had been left standing there because, Ray had gone up to South Shields on the North East coast to spend time with one of his old trade union comrades and help him celebrate his sixty-fifth birthday in typical Geordie style, consuming the local brew which was almost as good as Ray's own Donkey Common Hofmeister. Of course, in his haste to follow up some more leads on the whole affair, he had forgotten to leave a note for the milkman.

23.

Basil's dark side

THE FOLLOWING DAY, Joe called round to see Ray again. They had a long conversation in which Ray told Joe to be a little more careful, to always watch his back and keep quiet about what they had discussed earlier in the week. He laughingly told him not to talk to strange men or strange women either and be careful what he said on the phone, since it might be tapped. He also let Joe know that Charlie, Sam and Alan knew about everything, after their little get-together on the previous night, but that all three could be trusted completely.

Joe was now showing a lot more interest in the whole affair, although neither he nor Ray had any idea what was going on, if indeed anything was going on. Ray said he would continue investigating the whole matter and would tell the other three if he had found anything interesting. Joe said that he would make up his mind in a week's time about whether to go back to Cleveland. Before that he intended to spend the next few days visiting his relatives. In his view, if it all came to nothing, it would have been an interesting experience, peering into the dark world of international high finance. But if something dramatic did emerge from what Charlie had described as "a right viper's nest", then Ray would no doubt make a lot of it. Joe was now intending to add it in the novel that he had started writing, based on his adventures in South America. While he had been there, he had learnt quite a lot about how American Big Business influenced events around the world, and who knows what might happen in other countries, even in Britain in years to come.

"Do you spend all your time doing this, Ray?" Joe had asked, stood in the back kitchen while Ray was making their third cup of coffee.

"No, I've got lots of other things to do during the week. I'm stripping down my old motorbike, I play for Queens Park Bowling Club every Wednesday afternoon, and go up there practicing at least twice a week, and babysit for our Janet whenever she wants me to and I go to an Italian cookery class every Friday morning at Lane Head College. And on Thursday evening, I usually have a game of snooker with the brother-in-law in Helmsley Conservative Club."

"I'm surprised they let you in there, with your political views."

"I don't tell 'em."

"So you are keeping yourself busy in your old age, by the look of it."

"To tell you the truth Joe, I don't know how I ever found the time to go to work. And now I've got a new problem. One of the women at the Cookery Class keeps suggesting that I call round and sample some of her spaghetti bolognese and I am getting the distinct impression that she means that we have it for breakfast."

"Oh, and the other thing, I've got to find at least ten minutes every week to do some of the housework!"

That was clearly untrue; the house, certainly downstairs, was very tidy, though with Ray's books taking up most of the space in both his front room and the living room, there wasn't much room for anything else to become untidy. Ray was one of those people who need no more than five hours sleep at night, so by eight o' clock every morning, he had already spent an hour reading a novel or a biography, made his breakfast, tidied the house, been to the paper shop which was a ten minute walk away, read the paper and done twenty minutes exercise. He was clearly a man who had organised a daily routine that helped keep him mentally and physically alert, although how all this might change if he had to include having breakfast at Tiffany's, or was it Theresa's, who could say?

Meanwhile, back in the Drawing Office, Charlie, Sam and Alan decided not to mention anything about their visit to see Ray. It wasn't that they couldn't trust any of the others, it might be paranoia on their part, but it wasn't really necessary, not at this stage. Then another little mystery reared its head. It concerned Mick and his new shoes.

The man from Platt Bridge had never been the slightest bit interested in fashion or even looking smart at work. His general view was that what he wore to go on his allotment was good enough for him to go to work in. The same clothes for growing vegetables in Wigan and working alongside vegetables in Ashurst, he would jokingly say.

Then without any warning or explanation, he suddenly turned up one day in a new suit, new to him that was and probably relatively new to the person who had donated it to that charity shop in Abram. What was clearly brand new, however, was an expensive pair of leather shoes, mauve in colour, ones which really did not go with his light-grey suit. What could be the dramatic departure from his habit of a lifetime? How could this flagrant waste of money be explained?

Could the answer be found in the fact that a month earlier the champion racehorse, Shergar, winner of the 1981 Derby, had been kidnapped and a ransom of two million pounds placed on its head? Had Mick and a couple of his mates from Platt Bridge carried out the deed and made themselves much richer in the process? What seemed to add further fuel to this view was the fact that Mick had also turned down the chance of working on two Saturday mornings, a sure indication that money was no longer a great problem in the Henderson household.

But when asked for an explanation, all that he would say was, "I've got plans."

Were these plans the ones he had drawn up for an extension to his kitchen or were they plans to go on holiday a little bit further afield than Colwyn Bay, where their kid, his brother that is, had his caravan? Did Mick have plans to go into the acting profession based on his experience of acting the fool over the last fifty years? But all talk and thoughts about this highly unlikely change of lifestyle came to an end when the news came through that Basil had been found.

It was now over a fortnight since he had disappeared. On the third day after the mystery had begun to unfold, his daughter Cynthia had made a rare visit to the factory and spent a long time in discussion with John Thomas, the Personnel Officer. Then she attempted to enter her father's office, though unsuccessfully as the two detectives from the Serious Fraud Squad, were still in there going through all the paperwork with a fine toothcomb. The next day, Basil's brother Cyril made an appearance in the morning, followed in the afternoon by the other brother Norman, both of whom sought but were denied entrance to the same office. Were they all looking for something in particular or were they just being nosy?

On the Thursday morning, the company solicitor arrived and spent an hour with John Thomas, signed various documents and agreed to the payment of a number of large bills with the company secretary. On the next day and oblivious to all that had just happened, the Sales Engineer, who covered the Middle East, had flown in from Cairo with the good news that he had just won a large order for Wilkinson's to install a mechanical handling and conveyor system for a chemical manufacturing plant at a place called Basra in the southern part of Iraq.

This provoked more discussion as Iraq had just entered the third year of its bloody war with its neighbour, Iran. For whatever reason, the Western powers were giving tacit support to Iraq, despite the Iraqi Government's record on human rights. A chemical plant for Iraq could easily be a place where weapons of mass human destruction, throughout the whole of the Middle East, could be manufactured.

The situation concerning the disappearance of Basil was now discussed daily at great length by most employees of both Wilkinson's PLC (1982) and Wilco-Allison Products Ltd. The mystery continued for another week. In the past Basil had often been off the scene often for up to a month. That had been when his role had been as the company's main salesman. Then he would have jetted off into Europe, the Middle East, the Far East or to America, North or South. As a matter of course, he would always telephone in to let the office know where he was, and also check up what was happening in Ashurst. On his return he would usually arrange to change planes at Schipol Airport in Amsterdam, because this would give him the chance to meet up with his friend Pietra van Poofen, who worked in the city's famous entertainment industry. But literally nothing had been heard from him.

The whole business seemed to have shaken up Basil's two younger brothers who, perhaps for the first time in their lives, were behaving in a very responsible and organised manner. Both were now coming into work every day, each had got themselves their own office and their own secretary and both had begun to show more interest in how the company functioned. Maybe it was just that Basil had dominated them over the years and prevented them realising their full potential, because he had always been a very difficult man to get on with.

Then came the news, issued in a statement by the Personnel Manager John Thomas, to a meeting of around twenty of the company's senior managers. It was the news that was becoming increasingly likely, news that indicated that a whole long period in the company's history had come to an end. Basil had been found dead in a house in Brighton. The cause of death was unknown, it was not in suspicious circumstances, possibly of natural causes but in unusual circumstances.

The previous day a group of six garages had been set on fire by kids in a quiet suburb of that South Coast town. By the time the Fire Brigade had put the fire out, the garages had all been damaged to varying degrees. In the end garage was found a car whose registration plates indicated the name of the owner was Mr. Basil Wilkinson. The garages were owned by a local estate agency that rented out properties in the area. Their nearest property was less than a hundred yards away and when it was visited, upstairs in one of the bedrooms was found Basil, lay dead on the floor, fully-clothed and holding a copy of the *Financial Times*.

Subsequent enquiries by the police revealed that the house had been rented for the last nine months by an American, of whom the estate agency had little knowledge. Immediately, Norman drove down to Brighton. He went first to the police station, arrived late in the day, made an arrangement to come back first thing the following morning and discovered where the house was where his brother had died. Having found a hotel to stay in, he had then walked round to see the scene of the crime, if it was a crime. His appearance round the back of the large terraced house coincided with the return from holiday of the next door neighbour, who immediately invited Norman in. A bit of an inquisitive person, he clearly wanted to know what had happened while he had been away and also to tell Norman what he knew about the house and its occupants.

So, well before the authorities found out about the 'Unquiet American', as Mr Brown called him, Norman learned more about the sort of company that his brother had been keeping. In Mr. Brown's opinion, the house was a right den of iniquity and the Yank was definitely trouble for somebody. He had the look of a gangster but was more probably military or C.I.A. The man didn't really live there on his own, because there were always visitors coming and going. Frequently, long heated meetings, involving four or five Americans could be heard and always dominated by the boss man.

Because of the layout of the back of the two adjacent houses, and because the windows were always open, Mr. Brown had been able to hear garbled bits of the discussions. It was clear that no smoking was allowed in the house, because every half hour or so some of the visitors would come into the yard for a puff and carry on talking. It was then that Mr. Brown heard more. Much of it was concerned with the Middle East, and although Mr. Brown couldn't understand most of it, hearing names and places mentioned that he also heard reference to on the news made him appreciate that his neighbours were not talking about their favourite holiday locations. Then one evening he had heard the cultured tones of an Englishman. That was unusual, it was the first time he had heard or seen an Englishman next door. However, from time to time, some very good looking English women from a nearby sauna club had turned up in the evening and stayed for breakfast. But it was obvious that they had not been invited for their conversational skills or their knowledge of international politics or the nuances of American government diplomacy. It was soon obvious to Norman that Mr. Brown had nothing but contempt for all that went on at number twenty-seven.

Mr. Brown went on to say that on the day before he had gone away, another very cultured voice had been heard from over the wall. Viewed from his bedroom on the first floor, he had seen a quite stunning English Rose. From his description of her, it sounded very much like Lady Phillipa Delcourt. Luckily, there were some of the company's publicity brochures in the boot of the company car that Norman had driven down in, and so Mr. Brown was able to identify the lady in question. Norman suspected that she and her brother were having some sort of an affair, but he couldn't quite see how she was involved in all this business.

The following day Norman went back to the police station but learned little more other than the investigations were continuing. After having formally identified the body, he was informed that no financial irregularities had been discovered as a result of the investigation into all the paperwork in Basil's office. It had at the time been considered necessary by the powers-that-be, that an investigation be carried out, but it had been based on information that was now discredited.

When Ray heard the news he arranged to see Charlie after work. Sat in Charlie's car, he asked him about the so-called graduate apprentice, who had earned the nickname, 'The Spy Who Came In With A Cold'. When they had rumbled his little game, they had discovered headed notepaper of the East Sussex Private Detective Agency. Ray had been in Ashurst Library ten minutes earlier and checked out the address. It was in Brighton, less than twenty minutes walk away from where Basil had died. Had the plot thickened or was it just another coincidence?

But then the whole thing went very quiet. At Brighton police station, Norman decided that he did not want to get too involved in the whole affair, so did not tell the detective who was dealing with the case what Mr. Brown had told him. Mr. Brown had in the past had a couple of brushes with the law, twice being accused of telling lies or making up stories in a couple of court cases he had been involved with. So both decided to say nothing and for a while the trail disappeared from the public gaze, except of course for Ray, who, without all this additional information, was still investigating things from a slightly different angle.

As things did go quiet, issues of a more personal or private nature took precedence in the lives of those who worked in the Drawing Office.

Sam was particularly concerned about his wife Carol. She was now waiting for the results of blood tests while his daughter-in-law was just about to go into hospital in order to make Carol a grandmother. Doing this would also turn Sam into a stepgrandfather, Paul of course only legally being his stepson. But Paul Holroyd knew that despite Sam not being his biological father, he could have not have been better brought up by any other person, even though Sam did come from Yorkshire and still didn't know how to differentiate between the fish knife and the meat knife, or which spoon to use for soup and which to use to eat his pudding!

Mick was also worrying on the medical front. He was becoming increasingly breathless when climbing up the stairs. It might be just a bit of an infection, but then again it might be heart trouble. That wouldn't be too unusual for a man now aged over sixty, who had not engaged in much physical activity since the time he had been a rugby league referee in his twenties, but then he had also been a big smoker.

Charlie's main concern was his house in Nutgrove Road. He had recently noticed cracks in the outside wall, a possible indication the house might just be sinking into the bowels of the earth, not an unusual thing in an area which had been built over the working of the old Ravenhead colliery.

Alan too was not immune from the progress of time. Although their house in Silkstone Street was as solid as a rock, facing no threat from subsidence, it still needed work doing to it. And he just didn't have the enthusiasm or the interest to do it himself and even less to pay somebody else to do it.

On top of all those particular personal concerns, they all faced an unknown future. Redundancy, short-time working and even complete closure were always possible at Wilkinson's. If that happened he had no idea what he could do. Maybe with all his experience, skills and qualifications as a design draughtsman, he might just be able to get retrained as a lollipop man or a traffic warden. That would definitely aid the country's economic recovery. Sometimes he worried that he might even have to move away, something he did not relish at all, certainly not with Robert in the fourth form and doing quite well at school after a difficult start.

In fact if he, or any of the others, had to move away from Ashurst, there was no guarantee they would find security elsewhere. An old mate of his had had to move to Basildon in Essex, after being unemployed for nearly a year. He had lived in digs and came back home every other weekend. Finally he had succeeded in selling his house in Wigan Lane and buying one half as big for the same price, about twenty miles from his work. After getting his children into their new school, one which neither liked, he had gone into work a week later to discover that the firm had been bought out by a company, whose first priority was to reduce the size of the workforce in order to be more competitive in a harsh economic climate. Since the rule of last in, first out was company policy, in his own bitter words, the lad had been well and truly shafted.

There were however other things going on in the minds of everybody in the Drawing Office and they were not all bad. For Alan, Charlie, Mick and Colin, there was the rugby to enjoy, both watching it on a Sunday afternoon as well as talking about it, what they had seen the previous week, what was going to happen next week and what happened many years ago.

The next fortnight was a busy one for Ray. He made a few long distance telephone calls, talked at great length with his pal in Newcastle and spent more time with Joe Platt. Joe had now decided to return to America. So Ray repeated his general advice to Joe to be super-careful, reminding him again that his phone might be tapped and his ingoing and outgoing mail might be opened. Super-cautious, even paranoid some might have said, he told Joe to memorise an address to send any mail to. It was Ray's sister, Staff Nurse Kavanagh, at Billinge Hospital, located in no man's land between Wigan and St Helens.

After Basil had been buried in the family grave at a cemetery in mid-Cheshire, Cyril began to show more interest in the running of the company. Then the daughter of their sister Cynthia, Penelope, called into work again. Was she going to make an unwelcome appearance? Hardly likely as she was now six months pregnant. But wherever she went, her equally devious solicitor boyfriend Nigel would not be far away. But at least Basil's widow, would not or could not get in on the act. When she had been informed that her husband had died, she responded by saying that she didn't know she had a husband. She was now settled in the asylum at Rainhill and sharing her daily life with her three new friends, a woman who believed that she was Zsa Zsa Gabor, a woman called Boadicea who kept asking all the staff if her horse was getting fed every day and a woman from Rochdale who liked to balance plates on her head and sing the National Anthem just before the main meal of the day. As far as Cynthia was concerned, the world outside was just one big madhouse of which she had no wish to concern herself about.

The following week, it was announced that, in view of the company's financial position and Basil's death, its organisation would be completely restructured, yet again with ultimate power being placed for the next six months in the hands of a Managing Director, appointed and installed by the company bank. Mr. Gray had a proven record of rescuing industrial companies that were facing financial trouble. Although his name was Gray, his favourite colour was red: red as in redundancy. That was his panacea for everything. He spent his first day talking with Norman, Cyril and Penelope and Mr. Darlington and three senior managers, then issued a statement that his reconstruction of the company would start with the dead wood at the top. The first one to go was the longest-serving member, John Steel, who had as much character as a padded cell with a voice that would have been eminently suitable for the era of the silent movie. As a result, on the occasion of his sixty-fourth birthday, he departed, along with a leaving payment of nearly twelve thousand pounds.

Four more nonentities at senior management level were eased out plus two foremen, who were allowed to retire early with full pension rights. In addition the next intake of apprentices was halved and plans to end the nightshifts in the two foundries announced. All this was achieved within the first week by Mr. Gray, who arrived every morning around seven o' clock from his house in Glossop and departed never less than twelve hours later.

A few weeks later a postcard arrived for Staff Nurse Kavanagh at Billinge Hospital and delivered to her brother Ray the same evening. It said:

Mary,

Glad to be back here although I am already missing my Mam's cooking. Met a nice girl from Manchester on the plane. Will see her again, I hope. Pretty busy at work, don't know how they managed while I was away. Now saving up for another trip to Alaska.

Love Joe

The following evening Ray showed it to Alan and explained its meaning.

"We devised a way to pass information. I'll not bother you with the details but on that postcard he is telling me that there have been some interesting developments, Williams is still very friendly and there are some new people on the scene."

A fortnight later another postcard arrived which when interpreted by Ray indicated that there were changes afoot at work and that Joe was a little worried.

Nothing was then heard for nearly two months, until a devastating piece of news emerged. Joe Platt's body had been found in a stolen car, which had been in a serious accident on a lonely stretch of highway a few miles out of Lexington in the state of Kentucky. According to the police report, he had been travelling at over one hundred miles an hour and had lost control while being chased by a patrol car. In the car, a substantial amount of cocaine had been found. Later, when his possessions were returned to his mother, they included a postcard addressed to Ray's sister at Billinge Hospital

As soon as Ray read it, he knew that Joe had become very worried about his situation. Unfortunately there was little that Ray could do about it. The incident coincided with all his time being taken up looking after his grandson, while his daughter was undergoing a major operation in hospital. But even if she hadn't been, what could he have done to investigate the matter? Maybe his contacts in America might have been able to do something, but what? As far as Ray was concerned, the whole thing stunk, especially since, to Ray's knowledge, Joe did not drive and had never given the slightest indication that he had ever had anything whatsoever to do with drugs.

24.

"Do a good turn when you can"

BACK in Ashurst, the pace of life for most of its inhabitants was much less fraught with danger and intrigue. That was particularly true for all those who lived in the Greenfield Old Peoples' Home in Dob Lane. No matter what time of the day it was, there would usually be about a dozen residents sat in the large common room. Jokingly, it was often called the Waiting Room because everybody in there would be waiting for someone to call or something to happen. Some would be sat there waiting for their next meal, often not quite sure whether it would be the midday meal or the evening meal. Others would be waiting for a friend or younger relative to pay them a visit. Poor Mrs. Hunwick would be sat there just waiting for her husband of no more than six months to arrive, still unable to comprehend the fact that he had been blown to pieces on the Somme nearly seventy years ago. And sadly some would just be sat there waiting to be called to the next world, if there is one.

Alan's Granny didn't spend too much time in there if she could help it. If the weather was nice, she would prefer to sit in the garden round the back of the house, or walk up to the bowling green at Lowton Bank or the railway line over the Stinky Brook. She also liked to spend time in her own room, listening to the wireless and watching the children going to school in the morning, and returning in the evening. Sadly all those in her family of her own age had now passed away. But there were still many younger ones who would frequently call in to see her during the course of each week.

Not like poor Mrs. Burrows, who hadn't had a visitor for over two years. That had been her son, whose visit had lasted no more than ten minutes, just long enough for her to sign legal papers that had made him rich. No one ever came to visit Mrs. James either. She had been born and brought up in West Glamorgan. At the age of eighteen, she had married a young man from Swansea. Then they had gone North, he to try his luck at rugby league playing for Widnes. But he hadn't been good enough and so he had finished up working as a check weighman at Sutton Manor Colliery, while Mrs. James had brought up two children in their council house in Gillarsfield. Her daughter had emigrated to New Zealand when she was twenty-one and soon after her son had been killed in the Korean War. A couple of years later, her husband had been run over by a bus, no more than ten minutes away from where she now lived, which all accounted for why she was all alone with just memories of her earlier life in a distant place to keep her company.

208

"DO A GOOD TURN WHEN YOU CAN"

Granny knew how lucky she was to have so many good relatives nearby. She quite enjoyed living in the home, because unlike some of the others who never went out, quite often one of her flock would turn up in a motor car and drive her round, to Rivington Barn or Pennington Flash or even as far as Southport if she felt up to it. And if she wanted to have a look at her old house in Silkstone Street, well, she only had to ask and one of the drivers in the family would soon take her there and back.

Her most frequent visitor was Alan's wife, Thelma, repaying the kindness that Granny had shown her in those never-to-be-forgotten first few weeks of 1963, during one of the worst winters in living memory. Thelma probably called a couple of times during the week and then over the weekend too, sometimes with Alan or Robert or Rebecca, and from time to time with all three. But whenever Thelma called on her own, as soon as she sat down, she would usually be greeted with the same simple question.

"How are the children?"

Then Thelma would tell Granny what Robert and Rebecca were doing at school and also what was happening to those who lived in Silkstone Street and who had once been her own neighbours. On most occasions, it would be a very pleasant way to pass the time, for Granny had many good tales to tell from her own life. But now and again sadness would, for a short while. dominate the proceedings.

One day as Thelma walked into the main room, one of the staff had told her that Mrs. Holding hadn't been too well that morning and had stayed up in her room. Thelma had dashed up the stairs, fearing the worst. She knew that Granny wouldn't always be with them but surely it couldn't be today that she would leave them. She opened the door very carefully and saw Granny sat by the window, with a photograph album on her lap and tears in her eyes. She smiled bravely as Thelma rushed over to her, kissed her on the cheek and gave her a big hug.

"What's wrong, Granny? Mrs Pennington said that you haven't been too well," she had said, even before she had thought of taking her coat off.

"It's all right love. I was just remembering some happy times."

Thelma waited quietly as Granny put the photograph album on the table, and patted the bed, indicating that Thelma should sit on it.

"It's our special day, you see, love. It's the day I first saw Ned. Nineteen hundred and seven, it was."

She wiped her eyes, smiled bravely and went on, "I am missing him, Thelma. I'm missing him ever so much."

Thelma took Granny's hand and stroked it and wiped the tears off Granny's cheeks.

"I wonder what he's doing now. I wonder if he remembered."

Thelma said nothing for a while and then Granny perked up and smiled at her.

"I'm all right now, love, now that you are here. I was just having a little weep for him."

"Where was it Granny? Where did you first see him?"

Thelma knew the answer to her own question. Granny had told her before on more than one occasion but it seemed an appropriate question to ask, but Granny didn't answer the question straightaway.

"Maybe I'll be seeing him soon. I hope he's all right."

"I'm sure he is, Granny and I'm sure he's thinking about you as well."

Thelma continued to stroke her hand and then, after a few minutes silence, she suggested that she went and got a cup of tea for them both.

Granny smiled and nodded.

"Yes please, love and a Blue Riband biscuit as well. I'm all right now."

Five minutes later Thelma returned with two cups and saucers, a pot of tea and Granny's favourite biscuit on a tray. As she walked along the corridor she again feared the worst, but as she opened the door, she saw Granny stood in front of the mirror, combing her hair.

Thelma poured out the tea, added the milk and sugar and then sat on the bed again and said, "Mrs. James was asking about you, downstairs."

"Did you tell her I was all right?"

"Yes, I just told her that you must have had a bit too much whiskey last night."

Granny shook her head and went on to declare how sad it was for her fellow resident, never having any visitors.

"I always like to have a word with her," said Thelma.

"I know you do, love. And I know she appreciates it too. She always looks forward to you coming."

Thelma knew that Mrs. James came from Merthyr Tydfil, not far from Tonyrefail where she had been born and not far from Pontypridd, where her mother was buried. She loved listening to her speak, for despite many years living in Lancashire, Mrs. James had still retained her strong Welsh accent.

"So, have you been looking at your old photographs?"

Now fully recovered, Granny picked up the album and opened it.

"Do you know who they are?"

It was a photograph of four lads aged about sixteen or seventeen.

"That's Ned, that's Old Bob, that's Albert Binns who lived in Peter Street and after all this time, I still can't remember who this one is. He looks a right little ragamuffin, doesn't he? They took that photograph at the Earlestown Races, just a few weeks before I first set eyes on him."

"Was that on the Whit Monday Walk?"

Thelma knew fully well that it was.

"DO A GOOD TURN WHEN YOU CAN"

"Yes, all us girls had met outside St Mary's school and walked down to Ashurst Parish Church. Then we went in the procession, all the way up to the field behind Pearson's factory. It's all gone now. We played some games up there and then we went to the little fair that they had. Ned was there with some of his pals, trying to throw hoops over a nail on a wooden board. He was quite good at it and he won a prize. It was a bag of sweets and he turned round and gave all us girls one. A bit later, we were walking round and I saw him again and he said hello and all the other girls I was with giggled at him. But I liked the look of him, even though he must have been the scruffiest lad on the field.

"A week later I saw him walking down our street and he smiled and I said hello and he asked me what was my name. And it wasn't long after that, that we started walking out together."

By now Granny had perked up, as she began to talk about the great love of her life. She wiped the last drops of her tears from her cheeks, put her hanky into the pocket in her pinafore, smiled at Thelma and continued. "He lived in Alfred Street. His father worked at Bank Top and his mother took in washing. He came from a big family and then a few weeks after we started seeing each other, his father was badly injured at work. I can remember it so clearly when he told me. He was only sixteen and him being the eldest, he had to help his mother bring up his brothers and sisters. And I was the same, because my mother had died when I was eleven and I had to be the little mother to my father and the rest of our family. So we had a lot in common right from the start."

Then Granny skipped a few years and began to talk about their early married life together.

"I can still remember how pleased Ned was when Doreen was born. He loved to hold her for hours on his lap and talk to her but when the war started, he went and joined up. A few weeks later he went away and then we didn't see him for four years. It was hard for little Doreen in those first few weeks. She kept asking where her Daddy was. How could I tell her what he was doing? And when it was all over and he came back, she remembered him straightaway. A year later we told her that I was going to have a baby and she asked if Daddy was going to go away again like he did before."

Then Granny laughed and said "I bet you've heard this all before, haven't you?"

"Yes, but I always like to hear you talk about the good old days."

"Ee, they weren't that good. Not with the General Strike and, after that, all the unemployment in Ashurst. It was terrible. Fresh air butties, that's all we had to eat sometimes. Other times it was lobbies. You just lobbed into the pot anything you could find and boiled it up. You wouldn't think we were living in a civilised world."

Then she talked about what had happened to some of Grandad's former mates from work, their neighbours and other relatives during those harsh times. It was like a history lesson, real history, not tales about Kings and Queens, who lived such different lives. Then she talked about what it had been like during the Second World War, how Ned had been an air raid warden, and how they had heard that their son-in-law, Doreen's husband and the father of Paul, Joan and Alan, had been killed in Italy in 1944. Then she talked about what Grandad had done with most of his spare time after he had retired from work at the age of sixty-five.

"I know he always missed watching Doreen grow up from being a baby. She was nearly seven when he came back from the war. So he spent a lot of time with his five grandchildren and they all loved him, but I think it was Alan who was his little favourite."

Then she broke off from her stories about her man, ones which she had always told with pride, and sadly repeated what she had said earlier.

"Ee, he was a good man. Everybody liked him and he liked you too, you know."

"I was a bit frightened of him at first."

"It was just his way. He often seemed a bit gruff with folk, but deep down he was good. Ee, he was worried about you in those first few weeks when you started living with us. And then when you were nearly better and the doctor had said you would be ready for work soon, I remember what he said to me one day.

"He took hold of that thin green coat you had and said, she can't go back to work wearing this coat in this weather."

Thelma remembered, how Granny had told her that she and Grandad would buy her a proper winter coat to go back to work in. Then the two of them had gone into St Helens a few days later and bought her a duffle coat in Helena House. And it had all been on Grandad's suggestion.

Then Granny talked about how things were after the war, how sad it was for Paul, Joan and Alan having no father at home and how good Grandad and Uncle Stan had been for the three of them. She talked about holidays they had enjoyed, paid from Grandad's wages, usually a week at Rhyl at that holiday camp. Then she went back to the time Grandad had been a prisoner of war for nearly four years, although he was much safer there than in the trenches. She had perked up completely now and carried on talking until they were interrupted by Mrs. Pennington, coming to make sure that she was all right and asking if she wanted to eat her tea in her room.

"No, I'll come down. I'm all right now and I don't want Mrs. James worrying, you know what she's like."

They had been talking for over two hours and Thelma hadn't even got anything in for tea. But nothing mattered as long as Granny was all right and of course Alan and the children wouldn't mind either, once they knew where she had been.

"Ee, it's nearly five o' clock and they'll all be waiting for you. Go on, get off home with you and get the tea on."

"I might get a Chinese takeaway tonight. That'll be the easiest."

"It won't be if you have to go to China for it," Granny had laughed. "I'll just be happy with a nice piece of English lamb and some potatoes out of Billy Fairclough's field."

As the two of them walked into the dining room where all the other residents were sat down, waiting to be served, old Mr. Burke said loudly, "We all thought you'd run off with the milkman."

Then almost in unison, they all said, "Hello Thelma. How are you? How are the children?"

A couple of days later, Thelma called round again. She had a bit of interesting news for Granny about an old friend. Granny and Mrs. Highham had both lived in Silkstone Street for most of their lives, Granny until she had moved into the home and Mrs. Highham until a few weeks earlier, when she had gone to live with her daughter in Leigh. Then a couple of Mrs. Highham's grandchildren had begun to clear out around eighty years of papers, valued possessions and rubbish. Mrs. Highham was indeed a hoarder. During the course of their efforts, the girls had found a few things that obviously belonged to Granny and had brought them across the street and given them to Thelma.

As her eyesight was now slowly getting worse, Granny had asked Thelma to describe whatever she had brought with her. Most of the things she was told of, she didn't want, though she told Thelma that Alan might want to have a look at them and probably add them to his collection. On one scrap of paper was written what was obviously a list of public houses:

The Swan	Baxters Lane	1910
Chester Lane Tavern	Chester Lane	1912
Red Rat Inn	Ellamsbridge Road	1927
Crown Inn	Clock Face Road	1930
Alexander Vaults	Fisher Street	1932
Crystal Palace	Waterdale Crescent	1935
Engine and Tender	Reginald Road	1938

Later investigation by Alan, aided by Charlie, revealed that they were the years that a number of pubs in the Sutton district of St Helens had closed.

On another piece of paper was a quite different piece of information:

Do A Good Turn When You Can

ONE SUMMER

King Frost
Gypsy Ballads
She's Not So Fair
It Is But A Cottage
John Swain. Lancashire Lyrics.

"What's this, Granny?" Thelma had asked.

Granny thought for a while and then smiled. "Oh, I remember that. It was some of his poems. The names of them. We learned them at school. They were really nice."

Then she put her hand over her mouth and said, "Let's see if I can remember it.

.

> It needs not great wealth a kind heart to display.
> If the hand be willing, it soon finds a way;
> And the poorest one yet in the humblest abode
> May help a poor brother a step on his road
> Oh! Whatever the fortune a man has or.

"Ee, I can't remember any more. That was the start of it. It was a long time ago."

"That's lovely, Granny."

"I think there were three verses of it. Mrs. Higham was good at it. She loved to say the words."

It was quite a moving poem and it clearly brought back more memories for Granny, as it brought tears to her eyes.

"Could you find it for me, love? You could ask at the library. I'm sure they'll know about it."

As soon as Thelma had made the tea and the four of them had eaten it, she walked down to Ashurst Library, but their historical section and collection of old reference books was quite sparse.

"Try St Helens Library. They have a lot of stuff in there that might be of help," suggested the woman on the counter, who it was said had been stamping library books since around the time that William Caxton had first started work on his printing machine.

So she and Alan decided to visit St Helens Library on Saturday morning. Within an hour she had found the book. It was actually called *Lancashire Lyrics, Modern Songs and Ballads* and had been published in 1862. In it she found a number of poems, not written by John Swain but by Charles Swain.

Carefully she copied out the words to the poem that Granny had repeated the first few lines of. There were two verses, not three. So on Sunday afternoon, while Alan had gone to the match, she had walked down to see

214

"DO A GOOD TURN WHEN YOU CAN"

Granny with the good news. As she walked into the main room, Mrs Pennington had told her that Granny hadn't been too well that day and had stayed in her room to eat lunch, although she had left most of it, quite unlike her. When Thelma walked into her room she found Granny sat there looking blankly at the wall. She smiled bravely and held out her hand and for a few minutes said nothing.

"I'm all right, love. I had a bit of a tummy bug. I was just thinking about Ned. I wonder what he's doing today. He's probably gone for a walk. It's a nice day."

Thelma waited for a while and then as Granny gave her that lovely caring smile, Thelma said, "I've got some good news for you. You know that poem you told me about, the one that you and Mrs. Higham liked? I've found it in St Helens Library. It was by a man called Charles Swain."

"That's right. That's the one."

"Do you want me to read it out."

Granny nodded bravely.

> It needs not great wealth a kind heart to display
> If the hand be willing, it soon finds a way;
> And the poorest one yet in the humblest abode
> May help a poor brother a step on his road.
> Oh! Whatever the fortune a man may have won
> A kindness depends on the way it is done;
> And though poor be our purse and though narrow our span.
> Let us all try to do a good turn when we can.
>
> The bright bloom of pleasure may charm for a while
> But its beauty is frail and inconstant its smile;
> Whilst the beauty of kindness, immortal in bloom,
> Sheds a sweetness o'er life and a grace o'er the tomb!
> Then if we enjoy life, why, the next thing to do,
> Is to see that another enjoys his life too;
> And though poor be our purse, and though narrow our span.
> Let us all try to do a good turn when we can.

"It was written a long time ago, Granny. Even before you were born."

"He must have been a nice man to write that."

"He wrote a lot of poems. Do you want me to read another?"

"Yes please love. You do it really well. Are all the people from Wales as nice as you?"

Thelma just smiled and replied, "And are all the people from Lancashire as nice as you?"

Granny smiled and held Thelma's hand more tightly.

"I'm so glad we looked after you. You've been just like one of the family."

Well of course Thelma was one of the family now, though legally only by marriage, but she knew what Granny meant.

"It's called *She's Not So Fair*."

She's not so fair as many there,
But she's as loved as any,
And few you'll find with such a mind
Or such a heart as Granny:
A maiden grace, a modest face
A smile to win us ever;
And she has sense, without pretence,
She's good as she is clever.

She's not so fine, as some may shine
With feathers, pearls and laces;
But oh, she's got, what they have not,
With all their borrowed graces.
Eyes blue and bright with heaven's light
That kindle with devotion;
A cheek of rose, a heart that glows
With every sweet emotion.

As she finished the last line, she felt the hand she was holding go limp. She dropped the paper she was holding and saw that Granny's eyes were staring blankly at the wall, her mouth had opened and straightaway, Thelma knew that she had gone. She continued to hold her hand and then picked up the first piece of paper and began to read out loud the first poem again. Its title really summed up Granny's whole life.

As she read, she heard the door open and into the room came Mrs. Pennington. Thelma turned towards her as she said, "Do you want a drink of tea, Mrs. Holding, and a biscuit?"

With tears in her eyes, Thelma replied, "Mrs. Holding won't be eating here again. She's just left us."

It might have been ten minutes or a couple of hours before the door was opened again. It was Mrs. Pennington along with Alan, the first one in the Holding/Greenall/Tabern/Pickavance family to hear the sad news that Granny had died. But she had left them peacefully, in the company of her adopted grandchild in perhaps the most fitting way possible.

She had been born Mary Isabella Tabern in 1891 and was one of five children, all of whom had now passed away. When she was eleven years old, her mother had died and so she had finished school and became the little mother for the rest of the Tabern family. In 1910 she had married Edward Holding and had two children, Doreen and Stanley, before he had gone to fight in the Great War. For four long years, she had thought about him everyday, as she brought up her two children. Then she remembered taking them both down to Ashurst Station, along with many other mothers, wives and sons and daughters to greet the soldiers on their return from the war. After that, they had had two more children, Norman and Eunice, and she had continued to be the heart of the whole family all through the Twenties and the Thirties. It was a time when unemployment and the depression dominated the lives of many people who lived in Ashurst and the surrounding industrial towns of South Lancashire. Then came the Second World War, with all the attendant shortages and rationing. During those harsh times, she had again helped both relatives and neighbours. Since then, she had buried her sisters Katherine, Doris, Hilda and her brother Eric as well as her husband's sisters and brothers Len, Thomas, Frank and his sister Doris. Well, she had not been able to attend the funeral of either Len or Frank. Len had died in 1978, in Sydney in Australia, where he had lived for most of his life. And Frank, like Norman Hunwick, who had also once lived in Silkstone Street, had been blown to pieces at Passchendale in 1916 along with many other men from Ashurst.

By 1962, as she and Ned were enjoying their retirement and being helped by all the younger members of the family, she had taken in the young Welsh orphan Thelma Johnson from Tonyrefail, on Christmas Day of all days, and cared for her for two months before she had returned to full health. So, it was quite fitting that it was Thelma who was there right at the end of Granny's life, holding her hand when she finally breathed her last breath. It was sad and very touching, sad but a lovely way to go, being read a poem written over a hundred years ago and called *Do A Good Turn When You Can*, which was something that Granny had been doing all her life.

Mary Isabella Holding
Born December 1891
Died October 1983
R.I.P.

25.

Friends reunited

GRANNY'S FUNERAL had been held on Thursday afternoon. After she had been buried in Windle Steps cemetery, everyone had gone back to Alan's home in Silkstone Street. The house had been the centre of the Holding/Greenall/Pickavance/Tabern family for years that looked like continuing. On many occasions, a family funeral had been followed by a gathering there. It was much better than everyone going to the Edinburgh Café or the Raven where at the end everyone would be stood outside, saying their goodbyes, all dressed in black and observed keenly, though in a strange sort of embarrassed way, by the rest of the world.

Alan went back to work on Friday and had answered the usual questions about the funeral, while the others had been respectful and made few humorous comments. When he had gone into the Wiring Shop, he felt as though everybody was looking at him, almost as though he had done something wrong. At lunchtime, he had gone to the Horse and Jockey as normal, but again the conversation was almost polite, with most of the chat being about Sunday's forthcoming home match against Bradford Northern.

When he arrived home, Thelma was still on the quiet side. It was hardly surprising, knowing how close she and Granny had been. As he ate his tea, he wondered just how long it would take before she returned to her old self. Then, after Rebecca and Robert had both gone out, Thelma asked:

"Alan, who are they playing on Sunday?"

"Bradford Northern," he had replied.

"I think I'll come with you."

It was not something that Alan had expected. He was almost sure that she would have wanted to go up to the cemetery.. But it turned out that she wanted to spend her first Sunday without any Granny to visit in a quite different way.

After he had eaten his tea, his mind went back to the first time he had taken her to a match at Knowsley Road. It had actually been arranged a few days earlier when the pair of them had been in the Masons Arms in Southport. With them had been, his mates Ken, Ronnie and Geoff along with their girlfriends Jenny, Dorothy and Sally. The occasion had been Wilkinson's Summer Dance at Southport's Floral Gardens, just one of the many social events that the Sports and Social Club used to organise. It was there that Dorothy had discovered that Thelma had never been to watch the

218

Saints before. So she had suggested that she came with them on the following Wednesday evening to watch them play Oldham.

That particular day, Alan had been working out on site at Cammell Lairds shipyard in Birkenhead and so, Charlie had taken Thelma and Ronnie to Doulton Street, where Dorothy's auntie lived. Alan had arrived later and gone straight to the chip shop to get their evening meal, taking with him four plates and a jam jar for their fish, chips and mushy peas. The house was no more than ten minutes away from the ground, and as soon as they stepped onto the pavement, they could sense the atmosphere building up. Once they were through the turnstiles and onto the terraces, Alan could tell by the way she kept looking round that Thelma's first impressions of the place were good. Soon after, Oldham had emerged from the tunnel to a great deal of cheering as the away team had brought a large following, many of whom were stood alongside them.

"What a noise," Thelma had said.

"That's nothing, you wait till the Saints come out."

"I thought that was the Saints. They do play in red and white, don't they?" she had responded.

"No, they'll be in a blue tonight. The home team always has to change when the colours clash."

And then there had been an enormous roar when the Saints had run out onto the pitch.

She kept quiet at first while she watched the early exchanges. As the game went on, Dorothy kept explaining to her what was happening and why the referee had blown his whistle. Alan had noticed how keenly she watched the action on the field, but he was also conscious of an Oldham fan behind them who kept shouting at the referee and bumping into her. Then another Oldham supporter pushed him back and said to Thelma and Dorothy, "He's all right, love. He's harmless. He just gets excited. He's as bad as this when he goes fishing."

Just before half-time, the Saints' Cumbrian forward Dick Huddart found a gap in the Roughyed's defence and made a forty-yard burst for the line, chased by half the Oldham team. As he ran, Alan remembered hearing her shout, "Go on, go on, go on, go on" with everybody else. Then he began to notice her smiling as she heard all the banter from the people stood around them.

"Prop, you call Watson a prop? I wouldn't let him prop clothes in our yard."

"Gerrum onside, referee. Bloody Murphy's been offside all night."

"Forward, that was miles forward. You must have left your glasses at home on the mantelpiece, referee. You could see that from here."

"Stiff arm, gerr him off. He's been doing that all night."

"You're a bloody disgrace, referee."

From time to time, from somewhere not too far away came a regular comment from a man that Alan only knew by his nickname, Move Up. He lived in Clyde Street, worked at Mather's Foundry and rarely ever missed a game. He had obtained his nickname by the advice he continually shouted out to the Saints team whenever one of their opponents had been tackled and was getting up from the ground to play the ball. Then he would bellow out, "Move up Saints, Move up," and with his arm he would indicate exactly what his team had to do.

Alan also remembered who her first favourite player had been. Although Tom Van Vollenhoven, Alex Murphy and Austin Rhodes had all been in the team that night, it was the smallest man on the field, the stand-off, Wilf Smith, who had caught her eye. Maybe it because he was on the short side, like she was. Maybe it was because of the way he danced around and avoided the clutches of men twice as big as he was. It didn't really matter though, because, as a result of her first visit to a rugby league ground, she had become hooked on the game.

The following week they had gone on the train to watch them play Bramley at Barley Mow and after that she had become a regular, now wearing her red and white scarf even on the hottest of days. Back at work on the following Monday she would then be heard discussing all the main points of the match with Big Joan, who used to run the Print Room. After a while she even felt confident enough to have a little dig at Mick and his support for the Saints' bitterest rivals.

But after they had got married and started a family, she stopped going although whenever Alan walked in to the house after he had been to a game, she always keenly wanted to know if they had won, who had scored and if he had seen anybody there. But then with the passage of time, her interest had waned a little.

Now she wanted to go again. It might just be for one match. It might be just something to take her mind of the recent sad loss that she and all the family had suffered. That might well be the psychological explanation for her request. But if it wasn't, it didn't matter. Alan would be more than happy to take her and the club would be more than happy to accept her entrance money.

Then he began to think about other people that he used to go with in the early Sixties, when the whole world was thrilled by the skills of the Saints three-quarter line that included the two South African wingers Tom Van Vollenhoven and Jan Prinsloo. There was Ronnie and Dorothy for example. Where were they now? He knew they had got married and gone to live at Helsby in Cheshire, but he had still seen them for a while though the last time now must have been over four years ago. Then there was Ken, who had gone to work in London. He had seen him usually at holiday times while his parents still lived in Seddon Avenue, but after they had moved he had lost contact. There was also Geoff, the fourth member of the group. He had emigrated to Australia in 1974 and from where he usually sent a card at Christmas.

He also remembered Eric Yates, the one whose trickery had led to Alan meeting Thelma on Christmas Eve outside the Co-op Hall in 1962. Eric was now moving up the ladder in the General and Municipal Workers' Union, and fairly often had his name in the paper, particularly when there was a strike brewing or some industrial issue that needed sorting out.

His mind also went back to those happy days at Lane Head Junior school. He remembered firstly Barry Winstanley, who he had last seen in 1949 and the tragic reason why he left the school. One morning, all the boys had been stood in line in the boys' playground, waiting for their teacher Miss Travis to tell them to walk into school. Alan had been stood next to Barry, who was crying. That was something boys rarely did in the sight of others and in Barry's case, never. After putting their coats in the cloakroom, everybody except Barry had walked into their classroom. Barry had gone to the office of the Headmistress and was never seen by any of his school mates again. Later that day, the class was informed why. Early that morning, Barry's dad, a miner had been killed in an explosion at Clock Face Colliery. Shortly after, Mrs. Winstanley, Barry and his two brothers left Ashurst and returned to Durham where his grandparents still lived.

But before he could think about any other old friends, Thelma was telling him to get the dinner on, as she wanted to be there in good time for the kick-off.

They parked in Doulton Street and had a look at the house of Dorothy's auntie. It was clear that she was not living there now. They crossed Dunriding Lane and walked straight up to the turnstiles. Alan remembered when they had played that game against Oldham in 1963, there had been long queues, but now the crowds were much smaller. They easily found a place on the terraces even had a crush barrier all to themselves, until they were joined by an old man who had probably been watching the Saints when they were once known as the Handrags, a description of them from a long time ago when they were not one of the most fashionable teams in the game.

He recognised a few people stood around him, but then when you stand in the same spot for years, you always do. He nodded to a couple of men who worked in the Assembly Shop at work. The game itself was quite a good one to watch. It was rather ironic that the nickname of the visitors was the Steam Pigs, quite apt really since although they had competed well until half-time, they just ran out of steam with the Saints finally cruising home by twenty-nine points to fourteen. And it was also a bit of a coincidence that one of the two players that Thelma had picked up on was the number six again, not Wilf Smith this time but Neil Holding, although the ball-handling skills of the loose forward Harry Pinner had also gained her seal of approval.

Just after they had passed St Helens Junction and were approaching Bold Power Station on the way home, Thelma suggested they called in The Junction for a drink. It was not a pub Alan had been in for a long time, although he did remember the four of them going in there after a match against Oldham. It was probably why she had suggested it.

On that occasion, there had probably been no more than half a dozen cars in the car park. Tonight it was nearly full, many of those being Saints fans who lived in Ashurst, Earlestown and Newton-le-Willows calling for a drink on their way home. They walked into the best room and then to their amazement, who did they see sat there but Ronnie and Dorothy.

"My God," exclaimed Dorothy. "I can't believe it. Don't tell me you two are still courting."

In situations like this, when people who were once very good friends meet after nearly fifteen years separation, where do you start and who starts first? And what could be made of the great coincidence, no doubt Charlie could include it in his One Hundred Great Coincidences of Our Time. First, there were the usual comments about how well each one looked, though clearly Ronnie didn't look that well. Then a bit of general chat among three of them while Alan went to get the drinks in. As he put the last pint in front of where he was going to sit, he heard Dorothy say to Thelma, "And how's Granny?"

After what had happened had been explained, and condolences rendered, Dorothy began to tell them what had happened to them since the last time they had been together. Ronnie had worked in the offices at Wilkinson's, while Dorothy had worked for Pilkington's at their Ravenhead Works. Shortly afterwards he had got at job at Prescot with B.I.C.C. and within six months he had been transferred to their factory at Helsby in Cheshire. Opportunities seemed good and they had bought a house there and, when Ronnie had started playing golf, she had started painting, both pastimes which had later led to them earning a small fortune between them.

It was through Ronnie's golf that he had come into contact with people he would not normally have got to know. And it was through becoming friendly with Harold that Ronnie had been encouraged to make a career move and had spent five years working in the oil industry in the Middle East. Within weeks of arriving in Saudi Arabia, a rather bored Dorothy had started painting again. What she liked to do was copy a picture of an old master but change the face of one of the characters in the picture to make it look like her husband or a relative or friend. Within a few weeks, she and an equally bored wife of one of the senior engineers had become good friends. On learning of Dorothy's talent, her new friend had asked her to copy a painting of the famous cricketer W.G. Grace at the wicket, behind which was seen the wicket-keeper and three fielders.

But the face of the great batsman was changed to look like that of her husband Nigel, while those of the four other cricketers all had the face of his mother, she being the main reason why the pair of them were not intending to return to Stow-on-the-Wold for at least another five years. Out of the mouth of the four were balloons containing some of Ma's favourite comments, like 'If I had my way, I'd flog 'em', 'I don't know why God allowed them to breed' and 'If my Arthur was here now, he'd show this Government what for'. As soon as others saw the end product, they all wanted something similar and all being extremely well off, were more than happy to pay good money for it. In this way Dorothy had earned a small fortune. So they had stayed in Saudi for five highly profitable years, before returning home with the declared intention of travelling the world.

Then Thelma had explained how they had spent the time since they had last been together, a time which, on the financial front, could best be summed up as being always broke on the day before Alan's monthly wage had gone into the bank.

Then Thelma went on to tell Dorothy that despite never having any money, money wasn't everything and they now lived in a nice terraced house in Silkstone Street, had two lovely children, good neighbours and other relatives around and of course, until last week, Granny.

"We never had any children," said Dorothy, rather sadly. "That was my big regret and only seeing my Mum and Dad once a year and never being able to watch our Ken's children grow up was the downside of living in the sun."

"So where are you living now?" Thelma had asked

"We've bought a house in Ormskirk, but we are having it rewired and redecorated at the moment, so we are staying with Dorothy's brother at Helmsley. That's why we are in here. You are lucky to have caught us."

They carried on drinking, Thelma on orange juice, like she always was when she was driving, Dorothy on gin and tonics and Ronnie on pints. As Ronnie got up to get the third round in, Alan asked who was driving the car. When Ronnie indicated that he was, Alan asked him if he knew there were rules about drink-driving in Britain.

"You must be well over the limit now."

"It's only a mile back to the house, so I'll drive through the fields so no copper will catch us."

It was the sort of comment that Alan would have expected from Ronnie, who had always held the attitude, if it's going to happen, it will.

A couple of days later, Ronnie and Dorothy returned to their large house in Ormskirk with an invitation to Alan and Thelma to come and visit them after they had returned from their visit to Florida for a month, a visit that might just make a tiny dent in their bank balance. But by the time Thelma managed to get someone to answer the Ormskirk telephone number, it was

ONE SUMMER

February 1984 and postcards from New York, California, Gracelands, Las Vegas, Denver and Rio de Janeiro had dropped through their letterbox. And it was not until after Easter that they had all met up again, with Ronnie able to tell them about one of the greatest coincidences of all time, all acted out on the beach at Acapulco on the west coast of Mexico.

26.

The last Christmas Eve

AS THE END OF 1983 approached, ideas began to be raised about how they should celebrate Christmas. Back in the 1960s, things would have kicked off around the first week in December. Various offices and departments would have organised a do, usually in the shape of a meal in a pub in Ashurst or maybe St Helens or Warrington. Sometimes if you were lucky you might get invited to some other section's do, if your girlfriend or boyfriend worked in that section. On odd occasions, a boss might even take all his section out one lunchtime to The Fleece or The Crimea, as a way of saying thank you to all who worked for him, although knowing what Wilkinson's managers were like, that was about as common as rocking horse manure.

The best celebrations always occurred on Christmas Eve. Officially work would stop at lunchtime. Most people would go down to the pub and for once it didn't matter if you were late back. Then it would be a case of finding out how to sneak into somebody else's office party, if your own section wasn't having one. As was always the case, many tricks were played, an old favourite being what happened to the apprentice, Benny in 1965. His foreman had told him to take a box of 2 B.A. screws to the Iron Foundry Pattern Shop and give them to the chargehand, Slack Alice as she was known. When he walked in there, she carefully opened up the box, then shouted out to the dozen or so girls who worked there, "Does anybody fancy a nice screw".

At that point, they all surrounded the young sixteen-year-old lad and proceeded to strip him naked. He didn't know if he was in Heaven or Hell. He decided it was the latter when Naughty Nora put all his clothes in a bag, attached it to the hook on the Foundry Crane and shouted to the operator to raise it to the roof.

On another occasion, the Chief Buyer Mr Large had been taught a fine lesson. Mr. Large, who was ironically only five foot six, practiced the noble art of hypocrisy with a brazenness that beggared belief. During the course of December, many sales reps would call in and leave a bottle for him. It was the accepted way of saying thank you for all the orders that he had put their way and hoping that things would continue in the following year. Two days before Christmas, his permanently locked cabinet was bursting. But not one bottle had been given to any of his staff, despite his professed belief to be a good Christian. On the Tuesday before Christmas Eve, he had placed all the bottles, at least twelve in number in three boxes, which he had sealed with tape.

Then he had put them under the table in his little storeroom, ready for his brother to collect later in the week. Unfortunately, on the Wednesday, he had been taken out to a slap-up lunch at a high class restaurant at Worsley on the outskirts of Manchester. This was unfortunate for him because it meant that he would be away from his office for a good three hours and unable to keep an eye on his Christmas goodies. In his welcome absence, the members of his department hatched up a cunning plan. They took three identical boxes from the stores, in which they placed a similar number of pop bottles full of water and then taped the boxes up using the same type of tape. What they had done was not exactly legal or lawful. But it was also a way of being cruel to be kind, because according to the factory rules, anyone found removing goods that belonged to the firm risked instant dismissal.

On Christmas Eve morning, Mr. Large came into work full of the good Christmas spirit and while the office celebrations were getting underway, he instructed a labourer to load the three boxes of booze onto a trolley and take them to the managers' car park, where his brother was waiting in his car. It would have been a sight for sore eyes to see their boss brought down to size when he opened up each box on Christmas Day and discovered that all that his family would be drinking that day would be corporation pop.

Another problem concerned the issue of drinking and driving. Everybody agreed that it was wrong to combine the two, but every now and again people did it. Back in the Sixties, not as many people had a car and more people still lived near enough to work to either walk there or catch one bus. But now the bus services weren't that good and many people lived much further away from work. However in some respects the situation in Wilkinson's Drawing Office had hardly changed since the Sixties. A good half of those who worked there could either still walk it or just catch a bus.

Officially it had been decided by the management that no alcohol would be consumed on the premises, and anyone found drinking would be immediately sent home. Work would cease at twelve and what any of the staff did after that was their own responsibility. As a result this Christmas was something of a sober affair, literally. That however didn't stop some of the old-timers calling in to wish everybody all the best and stopping for a while to have a snack. But it just wasn't how they had celebrated Christmas in the past.

"Nostalgia is not what it used to be," said Charlie. "It just doesn't feel like Christmas Eve anymore, what with Father Christmas getting the sack and no booze."

"Enjoy it while it's here," said Alan. "This will probably be the last time we ever work on a Christmas Eve."

His statement was right on two counts. Firstly, at most of the other factories in the town, it had been decided to make Christmas Eve a part of the Christmas holiday. But Wilkinson's, always being a little behind the times, hadn't caught up with everybody else yet. The second reason was that there was no guarantee that they would all be working there next Christmas.

"And of course we might all be dead," said Mick rather morosely.

"That's typical isn't it? Christmas is supposed to be a time of peace and goodwill to all men, and Mick is going on about us all kicking the bucket."

"We might all be dead if Ronald Reagan carries on with his bloody Star Wars programme," said Alan.

"Not you as well, I think I'll go and have a word with my mate Ronnie Garner. One thing's for sure, he won't be here next Christmas."

"Why?"

"He's retiring next month. You wouldn't think that he was sixty-five, not to look at him."

"Another good man gone, then."

"I think he'll be calling in from time to time. You get that with some folk. They just can't keep away yet with others you never see them again. Remember Joe Henshaw? He only lived in Herbert Street, you could see his roof from out of Mick's window. After he left, we never saw him again, did we?"

There was a very simple reason why they never saw Joe again after he left. He had died three months later. And if he hadn't died, he wouldn't be living in his old house now, because the Corporation had knocked it down.

"I remember Joe. I didn't know he had died. I wonder if he went to Heaven or Hull," said Yorky.

"Do you believe in life after death, Sam?"

"Greeno, I believe in life after death as much or as little as I believe in life before birth."

"I never used to, but when your close relatives die, it starts making you think."

"But if there is another life after this one, what age will you be when it starts? If you died tomorrow would you start again in 1983 as a newborn baby. And when you meet some of your relatives how old will they be? Will your Granny and your Grandad still be turned eighty or will they be younger as well?"

"I don't know, Charlie. I haven't a clue what it will be like or if it even exists."

"Heaven will be pretty boring if everybody has just turned into an angel and spends all day playing a harp and dancing on the top of a pinhead. You'd soon get bored with that," said Sam, in his usual deadpan way of speaking.

Then Colin chimed in with one of his usual contorted ideas. He was coaching the under-fifteens at Gillarsfield Rovers, getting quite friendly with the single parent mother of one of the young lads. And it appeared as though he was also becoming influenced by her quasi-religious hippy ideas.

"I'll tell you what my idea of Heaven is."

"Getting locked in Greenall's Brewery for a weekend."

"Better than that."

"Getting locked in Greenall's Brewery for a week."

"Better than that, even."

"Getting locked in Greenall's Brewery for a week with that new barmaid in the Nag's Head."

"No, my idea of Heaven is existing forevermore in a room sat in front of a computer."

"You little couch cabbage."

"No, it's not that. It would be a very special computer. On it, for a start you could watch any event from history, like the Battle of Hastings, or the Russian Revolution or the Normandy Landings or Napoleon's March on Moscow in 1802. You could watch any sporting event you wanted, like the first ever game at Knowsley Road or maybe a match between Heckmondwike and Brighouse Rangers in 1896 or any of the Saints and Recs derby games in the Thirties. You could watch Joe Louis boxing or the first ever Tour de France or that time in South Africa when Cyril Washbrook and Len Hutton were the opening batsmen for England and scored nearly four hundred runs between them."

"You'd get bored, just watching television all day."

"Ah, but there's more to my computer that that. You can also programme it so you can take part in what you watch. You could arrange to play in that Water Splash Final at Wembley in 1968 or be at Odsal when there were over 100,000 people for that replay between Halifax and Warrington. You could also set yourself up as a King or a Prime Minister and see how you would have acted in those circumstances and what a different world it would have been."

"You're bloody crazy," said Mick, "I've never heard ewt so daft."

"So what would you fancy doing, Charlie, if Heaven was like that?"

"For starters, getting locked in Greenall's Brewery for a weekend with that barmaid from the Nag's Head."

They all laughed as Charlie continued, "And can I have Sally who serves the chips in the canteen. She could cook our supper, make it three in a bed and then make our breakfast."

"Charlie, you can have her as many times as you want and whoever else you want."

"I'll have Brigitte Bardot as well."

"Like she is now or when she first started in films?"

"If it's all the same to you, both, if that's possible."

"Charlie, with my magic computer anything is possible."

But then in walked Dave Twist to wish everybody in the office all the best. After doing that, he then spent the next half hour with Charlie discussing the modifications to a control cubicle that had to be down on Liverpool Docks by the end of January.

Against the drone of his voice, Alan began to think about what Colin had said, daft as it was. Two things immediately sprung to mind. First of all he could programme Colin's magic computer so that Arthur John Greenall had not been killed in the war. Alan's life might then have been completely different, having a Dad at home, like most of the kids in his class at school. He also thought about the family tree that he had drawn up over the years. It went back to 1791 when his great-great-great-grandfather Albert Silas Holding had been born in a little colliers' cottage at Collins Green. One thing that he had never been able to find out was who were the parents and grandparents of this distant relative. With this computer at his disposal, he would be able to find out.

He could also programme the computer so that, beginning with Albert Silas Holding, he could observe all his ancestors in their daily lives. Perhaps he could make a film of it, all his relatives going back nearly two hundred years. How much he would have loved to surprise Robert and Rebecca when they had turned on the TV to watch *Top of the Pops* and seen that instead.

Then he thought about his wife Thelma who had never known any relatives until right out of the blue, when her cousin had turned up from Australia eight years ago. How much she would enjoy programming the computer and seeing, then talking to and hugging her own mother who had died in 1945, when she was only one. Thinking along these lines made him oblivious to what was going on around him, the possibilities of using such a machine were enormous; a bit like something out of *Doctor Who* with his Tardis.

"Greeno, are you still with us?"

It was Charlie, stood at the door, with his jacket on.

"We're going over to Ronnie Garner's office. Are you coming?"

Despite having worked his way right up to the top at Wilkinson's, Ronnie was still just one of the lads. Approaching sixty-five, but with the appearance of a man ten years younger, he was now looking forward to a life of permanent golf, crown green bowls and doing the odd bit of D.I.Y. "for ladies who live alone, rewiring the upstairs rooms in their house".

Despite the ban of any alcohol on the premises, their coffees were nicely laced with whiskey as Ronnie thanked all the electrical draughtsmen for their assistance and help over the years. He then asked them to raise their cups and remember absent friends and in particular Len, Stan and Horace who had all died, and others like Les, Tony, Grovesy and others, who had left for pastures new.

"I won't say I'll miss you when I've retired," he said, "and I don't suppose any of you lot will miss me."

They all knew he didn't mean it. He had always been one hell of a sociable guy, and a bit of a comedian too, although not quite in the same league as the former draughtsman Les Earnshaw or Tony Ellison, the chargehand in the old Rolling Mill.

"I know what'll happen. I'll leave here at the end of January. By the end of the February I'll be wondering how I found the time to go to work. By the end of March I'll have forgotten half your names and then about six months later I'll get a big shock that will bring it all back to me."

They all waited in anticipation of his next comment. He was on form and didn't give a toss now what happened at Wilkinson's.

"Our Maud will give me the *Ashurst Reporter* one Friday morning and say something like, 'Read this, I don't think you'll believe it'."

And then he lifted up an imaginary newspaper and read out the heading.

Big shock at Wilkinson's. Draughtsman
gets a drawing right first time

Then he walked over to Alan, rubbed his hand over his head and said, "Greeno, I always told you that one day you would get your name in the paper."

And for the next hour or so it was time for many 'Do you remember when...?' or 'Whatever happened to so and so...?'.

Everybody can have a bad day now and again, sometimes colleagues you work with can be a pain, sometimes some are totally uninteresting, even boring. And from time to time, they are almost evil, just like Walter the Fascist who was perhaps one of the worst people to have ever worked in their Drawing Office. But with the benefit of the gap between now and then, it was generally agreed that the majority of the draffies that they had known had been a good set of lads.

"Ronnie, do you ever remember that lad from Widnes, who worked in the Foundry? The one who'd do anything for a bet if there was money involved."

"Do you mean Tarzan? That's what we used to call him."

Few of those assembled had heard of him, not surprisingly because it was now over thirty years ago since he had been on the payroll.

"It was one Saturday afternoon and the foreman had gone to watch the Saints. One of the moulders bet him that he didn't dare go up the steps to the cranedriver's cabin, climb out along the frame and slide down to the box that was fixed to the hook. So he says he would do it if everybody who watched him put a bob in a kitty for him. Now he knew they were going to trick him, probably by lowering the hook about ten or so foot, because it was not possible to climb your way back up. And if that happened, he'd still be stuck in the box when the boss came back from the match to lock up.

THE LAST CHRISTMAS EVE

"So he agrees to do it and disappears. He comes back five minutes later and climbs along the frame and slides down the iron chain into the box. Oh, the other thing was he had to sing the first chorus of *God Save The King*. While he's doing that, the cranedriver lowers the hook about fifteen foot, everybody starts laughing and the driver says, 'I'll raise it if you give me half your winnings'. Tarzan shouts out 'Piss Off' and takes his shirt off and unwinds some rope he had wrapped round his stomach. He fixes it to a bracket in the box, throws the rope over the side, shouts out 'Abandoning ship' and slides down the rope to the floor. And that's how he got his nickname.

"I'll tell you another trick he once pulled. His mate worked for an undertaker in Dob Lane. One day he learns that a couple of Tarzan's neighbours were coming to sit by the coffin of one of their relatives who had just died. So he and Tarzan put another coffin in the corner of this room and Tarzan gets in it, and his mate screws the lid down. Now, the people who were coming weren't really mourners. They were pleased their uncle had died, they just didn't know who he had left his money to and so they wanted to give the impression they were really upset. So Tarzan's mate takes them into the room where the two coffins were and tells them to stay as long as they like. Then he taps on the coffin Tarzan is in, and leaves the mourners on their own.

"After a few minutes, Tarzan starts banging on the inside of the coffin and shouts out 'Let me out. Let me out. I'm not dead. Neither is the other fella.'"

As they laughed, Ronnie lifted a box onto his desk and told anybody who wanted any of the technical information sheets, reference books and catalogues, to take them, otherwise they would be going in the bin. As they were rooting through his material, Alan flicked through a copy of Wilkinson's 1954 Yearbook.

"You're not having that Greeno, but I'll show you a couple of things in it."

As they were looking at the many photographs, they saw one of the former foremen in the Winding Shop. Roger Ellison had been a rising star back in the Sixties. Unfortunately he had blotted his copybook a couple of years later after being found on night turn in a bed in the Works' Surgery with one of the nurses.

"Roger Ellison was just a creep. We were apprentices together. He was always out for number one," said Ronnie.

He laughed and went on; "I remember just after old man Wilkinson had his heart attack and we got that Managing Director, Stephen Williams. He sent an instruction out for all the foremen to meet him in the canteen one afternoon. Roger decides to turn up wearing his hard hat. But just before he left his office, one of his girls put a load of red powder under the strapping while he was out having a wash. He comes back from the washroom, puts the hat on and walks over to the canteen. While he's walking along, the powder starts falling into his hair and onto his forehead, so by the time he had got to the meeting, the hair on one side of his head was its natural blonde and the other side was bright red. We all lined up to be introduced to Williams and I was stood next to Roger. As soon as I had shook Williams's hand, Roger took his hat off, ready to shake the bosses' hand. It must have been the speed at which he did it, because what was left of the powder in his hat shot out and went all over Williams's best suit."

As they smiled at the tale, Ronnie continued: "His whole life was bound up with this place. He was never away from work. The amount of overtime he put in, he must have earned a bloody fortune. Anyway, it didn't do his retirement any good."

"Why?"

"Two weeks after he retired, he dropped dead in Nevin's supermarket. I tell you who I did see in Nevin's last week, another blast from the past, that test engineer who used to work in the old lab, Billy Eccleston. Was he a relative of yours, Charlie?"

"He bloody wasn't and neither was he a test engineer. He was only a labourer."

"Well he was always testing the patience of his boss, John Bradshaw."

"Do you mean Vesuvius?"

"How did he get that name?" asked young Jason.

"Whenever anybody upset him, he was always likely to erupt."

"He was so bloody slow was Billy. No matter what he did. I remember one Sunday afternoon, he was walking on the East Lancs Road up to Carr Mill to visit his mother-in-law and he got overtaken by a tortoise."

"I'm not surprised, so would you be if you'd ever met her."

"The best tale I heard about him was when he worked at Hilton's just after he got demobbed. He'd had a pretty hard time in the war, he'd been in a prisoner of war camp for a long time. Anyway, he goes back to work there and discovers that some things hadn't changed. The foreman in the assembly shop had been there all during the war and was still behaving like a tyrant. Most of the people in there were terrified of him. He was always telling people to stop talking and threatening them with the sack and generally being a right bastard. Anyway he was off sick for a fortnight and while he was away, the atmosphere had been much better, and of course Billy starts telling them all about what he'd done in the war. Egged on by Billy, they all start taking the piss out of the foreman while he's off and then Billy discovers that he had been a Mosleyite in the Thirties and had got himself a right cushy number all during the time that Billy had been away.

"So he decides that things were going to change. The day the foreman comes back, he has to go down to see his manager, so it must have been during the teabreak when he gets back. As he walks into the shop, it was the teabreak and everybody was talking and having a laugh and nobody sees him. So he shouts out 'Get on with you work'. But still nobody hears him. In a louder voice, he shouts out 'Silence' and then, when nobody stopped talking, he shouts out in his loudest voice 'Fire'. Not far from where Billy was stood, there was a bucket full of water and so without a second's thought, Billy picks it up and throws it all over him.

"Well, he went ballistic, particularly when the rest of the shop started shouting 'Sieg Heil' and then 'Out, Out, Out'. Not long after, old man Wilkinson had one of the accountants go through Adolf's so-called expenses and a week later he was sacked."

Ronnie then looked at his watch, told them that their keenness was appreciated but if they stayed any longer they would be working for nothing. It was just two minutes to twelve. So like a shot, they rushed out of the door, went back to the Drawing Office and still managed to get into the Horse and Jockey by five past twelve. And that was the last time any of them ever worked on a Christmas Eve again.

27.

The Hutton Report

"SO WHAT HAVE you learned while you've been at college?"

"Well Charlie, for a start I've learned that Pythagoras is making a comeback."

It was Hazel, their former tea girl pushing her old tea trolley round and earning a few bob over the Christmas holidays, From her first comment it was clear she had not lost her sense of humour or her clever use of language while she had been studying in Yorkshire for the last three months.

"Well, he might be in Bradford, but he isn't round here," said Mick. "What other little gems have you got for us or is that it?"

"I've learned that if you want to become rich, you shouldn't be a draughtsman. You should go into the finance industry because that's where all the money is."

"Phew."

"And on the literary front I now know that science fiction was not written for scientists and ghost stories were not written for ghosts."

"That's the spirit, Hazel," laughed Charlie. "I see the taxpayers' money is still being well spent."

"So what are you doing here? Haven't you any demonstrations to go on."
It was Mick again.

"I'm just selling my labour power and renewing my links with the industrial proletariat so I can better emphasise with the theories of Karl Marx on the production of surplus value."

"And how much are you selling your labour power for today and do you charge more at the weekend?"

"I'm also standing up for my rights as a member of the working class and as a woman and exposing the reactionary social attitudes of those wishy-washy Ashurst draughtsmen, who think that the class struggle is now redundant."

"If the new management hear you spouting all that rubbish, they'll soon make you redundant too," said Mick, not quite sure what she had just said.

"And then, I would call on you lot to down pencils and come out in support of a humble little tea lady, who is being victimised and ground down by a multi-national corporation, whose only raison d'etre and function is to maximize their profits."

"Hazel, what medication are you on now and have you got a bit to spare?"

"Hazel, give us some good news. Tell us you are not going back after Christmas."

"Hello Yorky. You'll be pleased to know that one of my new friends at college comes from the ancient Roman settlement of Mytholmroyd."

"Well I'm really pleased for you. Is it a man or a woman or maybe someone switching from one to the other?"

"It's a lad actually. He's our teacher's pet."

"Oh aye?"

"Yes, she keeps him in a cage during her lesson."

"So, how's your course? You have obviously learned something while you've been over there, even if it is only how to come back here. What subjects are you studying?"

"Education Studies, Organisation Studies, Sociology, Literature, South Asian Studies, and a bit of Philosophy. That's really interesting. We got introduced to Aristotle and Plato last week."

"I thought they were both dead," said Mick.

"What are all the other students like?"

"They are all right. Most of them are about my age, but there are quite a few mature students amongst us. A couple of them seem to know as much as the lecturers. And one of the lads plays for Bradford Northern in the 'A' team, you'll be interested to ignore."

"Hazel, Hazel, come quick."

It was Billy Mulholland, a draughtsman from the top of the office and an old friend of hers.

"It's worse than the Sahara Desert up there. Three of them have just collapsed from severe dehydration and the rest of us won't last much longer."

"You'll have to be patient, this lot haven't even got their bibs on yet."

She poured out their teas and proceeded to tell them a little more about her first term at the Bradford and Ilkley College. Then she pushed the trolley as far as John Battesby's office and spent another ten minutes talking to him before going into the Mechanical Section of the Drawing Office and offering them all a choice of cold tea or cold coffee. Later, anyone who went in the Works Canteen for their dinner would then see her again doling out the chips and then, halfway through the afternoon, she appeared again with her trolley.

"Does anybody in here know anything about Max Weber or Karl Marx? I could do with somebody helping me write an essay, contrasting and comparing their ideas."

"I could do an essay contrasting the ideas of Karl Marx and my Uncle Jack," said Alan. "Will that do?"

"I've got loads of work to do over the holidays," she went on, "I've even got to do a case study."

"Well you could take Mick as a good example of a nutcase," laughed Charlie.

"You could spend an evening in Jason's flat," said Sam, "studying his suitcase."

"So are you enjoying yourself?" said Billy Mulholland, who had known her a long time as she had been a friend of his daughter Claire and often been to his house when she was being brought up, or more accurately dragged up, in a prefab at Hyde Bank, by a mother who didn't really deserve to have such a nice girl for a daughter.

"It's really good. Most of the subjects are very interesting, particularly the Literature and Sociology. In fact one of my assignments over Christmas is to write a three-thousand word essay on the emergence of white collar trade unionism in the Sixties. From what I've heard you lot were a good example I could base my study on."

"If Brother Len was still alive, you would have been able to write a thirty-three thousand word essay on it."

"Do you still fancy becoming a teacher now that you've been there for a term?"

"I'll tell you at Easter. Straight after we go back, we have to spend a couple of weeks in a school."

"You'll be all right, Hazel. You've had plenty experience of dealing with children, after all the time you've spent with us in here."

Then she shocked them all when she continued to talk about her present life as a full-time student in far-flung Yorkshire.

"There's one other bit of news that you might all be interested to hear. I'm expecting."

She waited for what she had just said to sink in. She was a good looking girl and bright too, but if she was to enter the realm of motherhood at such an early stage in her life, it would surely put a stop, whether temporary or permanent, to her ever becoming a teacher. And of course she had no mother or grandmother to help her out.

"Yes, I am expecting to go to India in the summer."

She smiled and said, "You didn't think I was pregnant did you? I'm still as pure as a flake of snow on a midsummer night's dream."

What a way she had with words. Even when telling lies, she was good at it.

"One of my friends at college comes from Mysore in Hydrabad. She's going home for six weeks and I'm going with her."

"You'll be bloody Mysore if you start having vindaloo every day while you are there," said Mick. "You'd better start nicking some toilet rolls now."

Then he continued, "You'll have to learn to speak Indian, won't you or will they understand you if you just talk like Peter Sellers does?"

"Does your friend speak good English then?" asked Alan.

"Yes, she does. I'll tell you who she sounds like, Mario, who has the coffee bar in Bridge Street."

"You mean your Indian friend talks English like an Italian?" said Mick, in a rather puzzled voice.

"That's right. Mario has spent all his life in Bolton. My friend Sirindar has lived there since she was three, in a house near Bolton Wanderers' football ground. That's why she sounds like Mario. She's nothing like her cousin though, who is in the second year at college. I can't understand a word she says unless she speaks very slowly."

"Why. Is she from India?"

"No. She's from Glasgow."

Later on that afternoon, Billy Mulholland came down from the Mechanical Section to discuss a recent design change and when he had finished he made the comment that Hazel appeared to be enjoying herself as a student. "Did she tell you about meeting one of her relatives there? Another coincidence for you, Charlie."

One of the other students on Hazel's course was an Alistair Hutton, a forty-year-old former steelworker from Motherwell. Soon after meeting, and after she had told him that her mother's maiden name had been McGuire, he had half-jokingly said that they might be related. She then told him that her father had been brought up somewhere between Kilmarnock and Glasgow. She didn't know exactly where, he had never talked much about his past. Her mother had come from Arbroath on the East Coast of Scotland until her father, and what would have been Hazel's grandfather, had been drowned in a fishing tragedy in the North Sea just before the outbreak of the Second World War. So it was with that information that Alistair said he would check up for her.

Every term the students at Bradford College had what was known as Reading Week, a week during which they had a chance to read more widely or re-read their notes or catch up on coursework. Alistair had used the opportunity to return home to Motherwell and see his family. When he returned, it was with the news that his eighty-year-old grandmother had informed him that her late sister Alice, had had four children, one of whom had died as a result of an accident on a fishing boat within sight of Montrose Harbour, on the East Coast of Scotland in the summer of 1939.

The exchange of further bits of information and a couple of old photographs revealed that Hazel and Alistair were actually distant relatives. Moreover, before coming to Bradford College, and with much time on his hands after being made redundant at the now demolished

Ravenscraig Steelworks, he had begun to research his family tree. His thoroughness and perseverance had enabled him to get back as far as 1726, when one James Hutton had been born in Edinburgh. As Alistair researched more, he discovered that this member of the Hutton family had not only been a thinker, a gentleman farmer and an explorer. He had also written about the origins of the Earth, with material that had been powerful enough to influence Charles Darwin. This was something that soon began to interest Hazel.

"One thing I've become interested in is geology and the age of the planet and all that," she explained later that week.

"I know somebody who can tell you about the age of the Earth. It's Mick, well he is still living in the past."

"It's around sixty million years old," muttered the Wiganer.

"Was that a question in the quiz in your local last night?" asked Sam. "Or did you read it on the back of a beermat?"

"The origins of language is something else that I've begun to get interested in," continued the young student, "and how Neanderthal man communicated over fifty thousand years ago."

"You are really enjoying yourself there aren't you?" said Charlie. "Good for you. I'm pleased for you. You'll soon be as clever as me."

"Well, it's like a second chance I've been given. My mother was never much use because of her bad health and I know that my Dad tried his best but he was always working away. Now I just feel as though there's so much to learn and I'm still catching up. I don't want to finish up as brain dead as a draughtsman, present company included."

"Be careful you don't become a bookworm, Hazel. Do you have much of a social life? Do you go out much?"

"Oh yes. Every Friday night and every Saturday night. I often eat out as well, usually breakfast on a Sunday morning in somebody's flat."

"You rude thing."

"Well, it is the age of enlightenment."

"Not in Ashurst, it isn't. I don't think women have even got the vote here yet. How do you fancy becoming a suffragette?"

"A latter day Mrs. Spankhurst, eh?"

"What's your enlightened view on spanking?"

"I agree with it as long as I'm being spanked in a spanking new car."

Yes, she was good all round was Hazel and the lads in the Drawing Office, despite all the banter and the double entendres, treated her like she was one of their own. Well, after the departure of their old tea lady Joan from Leigh, Hazel was one of their own.

But then on the morning of her last day, the new works supremo decided that as part of the modernisation programme, tea breaks would be abolished in the New Year and the position of tea lady would be cast into the dustbin of history. New machines selling a wide range of beverages would be installed and a new step taken to ensure that the company kept pace with similar practices with the company's competitors across the globe. But the company saying that tea breaks would be abolished or outlawed or declared prohibited, was like earlier thinkers in the Church saying that the Earth was flat or that the Sun revolved round the Earth. And as Hazel was later to discover from her enquiries into the writings and thoughts of her ancestor John Hutton, the Earth did not really begin in the way that the traditional students of the Bible had believed.

On the first Saturday in the New Year, Alan and Thelma had bumped into Hazel in town. As a result the three of them had gone for a drink, giving Thelma the chance first to tell Hazel what Wilkinson's had been like when she had worked there and then to enquire what it was like being at college. Then Alan had asked her about her interest in Geology and what she had learned from her distant relative, John Hutton. Whether it was because John Hutton was related to her or because Hazel really had developed a keen interest in Geology, he wasn't sure. But he and his wife soon learned from Hazel about the importance of John Hutton's study into the origins of the Earth over two hundred years earlier, how he had worked out it was around 4.6 billion years old and how he should be considered as important to geology as Galileo and Newton had been to Physics and Darwin and Mendel to Biology.

Then Hazel had asked if either of them had heard of the Black Diamond Fields. Neither had so she proceeded to tell them that around 345 million years ago, the earth had entered the Upper Carboniferous Period. This had lasted for around sixty-five million years. The climate was hot and steamy, large river deltas formed swamps where huge subtropical plants grew. The plants died and decayed, eventually forming valuable coal seams.

Now in full flow after three pints, she proceeded to debunk the Christian teaching that the Earth had been created in seven days and was only six thousand years old. But when she started talking about the Greek astronomer Ptolemy but couldn't pronounce his name correctly, all serious discussion drew to a halt. So she changed the subject and asked Thelma if she knew the famous philosopher Charles Eccleston OBJ, and whether she was familiar with his Law of Coincidence. Thelma of course knew Charlie well, and both soon agreed he was one of the best, a sound guy.

"If he had had a better education and become a space astronaut, he would have gone far, that lad," Hazel had said solemnly. Then she declared that she would have to leave them as she was going on a demonstration, protesting about the evils of alcohol, and departed. Just before she left them, Alan asked if she was going to write a book about it, for she had made it all seem quite clear and easy to understand.

"Well I might do, when I come back from my trip to Boots this afternoon or from India in the summer. And I think I'll call it 'The Hutton Report' and get Oxford University to publish it."

"You could call it 'The Hazel Hutton Report'," said Alan, "that sounds a bit more sexy, or maybe 'A Journey Back in Grime, the uncovered history of Lancashire years ago'."

Then Thelma chipped in, "You could call it 'Hazel Hutton's Journey Back in Grime' or 'A Journey to the Black Gold Fields'.

"No listen, if what you said earlier about Wigan coal being called carnal coal, you could call it 'Carnal Knowledge in Wigan. Hazel Hutton's In-Depth Analysis' or even 'A Bit of Slack'."

"Alan, you're pissed. And it's only half one."

"No matter what you call it, I'll buy a copy as long as you sign it. It'll do for our Maud's present."

"Thank you for your suggestions. I'll get back to you in due course, probably after I have sobered up."

With that, Hazel went back into town to start the shopping she had hoped to have finished an hour earlier.

Back at work on the Monday, things were immediately quite hectic. Within ten minutes of arriving, the fire alarms went off, obliging everyone to leave the building. It was an actual fire in the old hut behind the Sand Wash, and with all the smoke billowing up into the sky it appeared a lot more dramatic than it actually was.

By the time they were back in work, Colin's wife had rung in to say he was sick. It was Sod's Law then, because he was the only one working on a rush job for a factory in Carlisle, so Charlie and Alan were given the responsibility to find out what he had already done and finish the rest off by Thursday at the latest. As a result it was not until they were all sat in the canteen, eating their lunch, that Alan's drink with Hazel was mentioned. Strangely, it was Yorky who mentioned her first when he made the comment that he had seen her dashing into Boots Chemists on Saturday afternoon, looking a little worse for wear.

"That's because she had spent the last two hours with me in The Fleece," said Alan.

"I hope Thelma didn't hear about it," said Mick.

"She was with us," and then he went on to talk about their student friend. "I don't know if she's on the right course, she seems a lot more interested in Geology than teaching."

"She talked to Thelma at first about what things were like when she was there. Then I told Thelma that Hazel was very interested in Geology. Of course, straightaway Thelma said she was but didn't know the first thing about it and so Hazel gives us the beginners' guide to ancient history; so she started off telling us about the Pre-Cumbrian Geological Period."

"Pre-Cambrian," chipped in Yorky.

"Well whatever, it was between 500 and 4,500 million years ago. Then she went on about how land masses can move over the centuries and how Britain was much nearer to the Equator a long time ago and how the study of magnetism in rocks can help the geologist today to plot that movement. Something to with the teutonic plates."

"Tectonic."

"This part of the planet was a great jungle of plants, giving off gases while they were living, then decaying and turning from plant debris into carbon-enriched remains buried under sand and mud for millions of years. And this slowly turned into what we now know as coal."

"Was all this before you got the first round in?" asked Mick.

"Ignore him, Greeno, carry on, it's interesting," said Charlie

"Well, then she went on about what conditions were like round here. It appears that the area that we now know as Wigan was covered by a shallow sea, with land to the North and South of it, and many rivers depositing tons of sand and mud into this sea which then silted up."

"Aye, and Wigan Borough Council still hasn't cleared it up," laughed Mick. "Carry on."

"What is interesting about Wigan coal was that it lay fairly close to the surface and so the first people who were able to extract it were the Romans. Also, Wigan coal was known as carnal coal. It has a very compact grain structure, burns well and gives off little smoke. In fact its composition makes it possible to turn it on a lathe and in 1893, a twelve-ton piece was sent to the Great Chicago Exhibition."

"Typical Wiganers, always making an exhibition of themselves," laughed Charlie. "Round here we just burn the stuff."

"I didn't understand a lot of what she told us but she was really enthusiastic. In fact she stirred a load of interest in Thelma, because as soon we came out of The Fleece, we had to go back into the library for her to get some books on it."

"Well if Wigan coal is so good, why is the Government planning to shut all its pits down?"

"I don't know that they are," said Mick, still clinging to his belief that the Government and the National Coal Board knew what was best. "They can't keep running pits that have hardly any reserves left."

"Like Cronton," said Alan.

Mick said nothing. "After a long period of unemployment, the new husband of his daughter had started work there a few months ago. But now rumours were circulating about massive cutbacks and closures, although it was believed that Cronton had at least another twenty years' reserves. But before that could be discussed and before they could learn any more about coal, whether loose grained or compact, whether lying deep or close to the Earth's surface, one of the shop stewards tapped Charlie on the shoulder.

"Have you heard the latest rumour, Charlie? There's a big meeting of all the nebbies this 'avvy. Redundancies are back on the agenda and we aren't talking of just a few dozen this time. You lot had better be ready for it. Don't forget we are all in this together."

Well it was bit more than a rumour. It was soon to become a fact that many more people in Ashurst were going to lose their jobs. But as far as Wilkinson's were concerned it was not going to be today. Tomorrow maybe, but not at this exact moment in time.

28.

"Say no to home rule in Ashurst"

COINCIDING WITH Hazel's departure came the installation of the vending machines throughout the factory. During the first week, the one outside the office of John Battesby had provided a wide range of beverages including warmish tea, watery hot tea, cold hot chocolate, hot mushroom soup with a dash of coffee and coffee with a hint of mushroom. By Wednesday, liquid was being provided in the shape of fifty-seven varieties of corporation pop. These included chicken-flavoured water, Bovril-flavoured water, tea-flavoured water and a real delicacy, coffee and tomato flavoured water. On Thursday came the ultimate irony, steam or smoke pouring out of the back of the machine which at the front was spewing forth large servings of cold water in small paper cups.

Fortunately nobody lost out financially, because the mechanism that took the money had stopped working so every drink that came out of the machine was free. On the second day, another bizarre thing occurred whenever anybody selected a drink the machine gave the recipient a ten pence coin. The thing was good for a laugh for a couple of days; well, it wasn't for John Battesby when late on Thursday evening, water had started leaking into his office and by the time he came into work on the following morning, to get to his desk he had to wade through a two-inch-deep pool of yellowish liquid in which were floating around small lumps of green sugar.

"Teething problems" was how the maintenance engineer from the Vending Company had described it. Not quite like everybody else had described it and when they all returned to work on the following Monday, the machine had been removed. To get a drink now, the machine outside the Wages Office had to be used. For anyone who worked in the Sheet Metal Section, this entailed a walk through the Mechanical Section of the Drawing Office, past John Battesby's office, through the Electrical Section and out through the door at the far end. Then there was a short walk through the Planning Office, Work Study, past the Meter Calibration Department and up the stairs to the second floor. Then it was into the Pensions Office, where the Manager had put an arrow on the side of a large cupboard indicating that the route to be taken by the thirsty was behind a row of drawers, which led the intrepid traveller out onto a landing, where there was no room for more than one person to walk along and so into the Wages Office. There was then, usually between nine and half nine, a queue to join before a drink could be

243

chosen, paid for and collected. After that came the long trek back to base, all of which meant that unless you ran like Billy Loo, you would be back at your desk a good five minutes later, drinking a warm version of a one-time hot drink.

It was not surprising that many people would say to themselves, "I wish Hazel was still here." Some even thought that the Never Lady was better than this trek, especially John Taylor who one morning had to make three visits to the machine before he could get his first drink of the day. On the first occasion he had got as far as the Work Study Office before one of his colleagues had caught him up to tell him he was wanted on the phone. On the second occasion, he had managed to get as far as the door into the Wages Office, before the same colleague caught him up again to give him the same message that he was wanted on the phone. On the third occasion, he had just managed to join the queue before the fire alarms went off and everybody had to vacate the premises for what proved to be a false alarm.

Even before Hazel had raised the issue of going into teaching, a frequent topic of conversation among those who had worked together for a long time was about how their various children were getting on at school. Sometimes there were similarities between their various offspring, such as a common interest in a particular subject at school, or a skill or talent in sport, or maybe just a good friendship. Sometimes there are other points of contact, like the children of two workmates going to the same school or later to the same University, taking up a similar apprenticeship on leaving school or working at the same company, or being fans of the same type of music or pop group.

Also of interest was the link between the child and its parents. Sometimes they would be very much like their mother or father: looks, voice, appearance or attitude, but on occasions a child would turn out in such a way that others might make the comment that 'You'd never think that that lad was his son, would you?'.

As they grew older, children would often drift away because of a row within the family or maybe move to the other side of town or even to another town for reasons associated with job, love, money or just a wish to see a bit more of the world. Often that was just how things panned out in life, although sometimes the parents might say with some regret that they wish they had had their time to go over again, because they would have brought their kids up in a much more enlightened way.

One man who came to realise that he had got his priorities all wrong was John Brown, an engineer in Wilkinson's Outside Contracts Division. While she was just a little girl, his daughter Janet had been the apple of his eye. But as she had grown up she had become a real handful, nothing malicious or nasty, just a girl who needed a lot of parental attention. John had left all that to his wife, since he worked away a lot on contracts all over the country and frequently abroad. But with all the money he earned, by the time Janet was in her last year at school, his wife had been able to give up her job on Ashurst Market in order to spend more time with their demanding daughter.

Then, John had been sent out to Hong Kong to supervise major alterations to a power station. He was eager to earn as much as he could, on what he had decided would be his last job abroad. The firm was keen to keep him on site, and offered to give John the cash that they would have had to spend flying him home for his two weeks holidays in the summer and similarly for the Christmas break. By the time that John arrived back in Ashurst, nearly two years later, he discovered that Janet was now a young woman about to get married and go and live with her husband in Stockport. At the wedding reception, he had to admit to his sister that he hardly knew his daughter now, so much had she changed while he had been away.

Perhaps a worse situation had been that of Ken Maguire, who worked in the Iron Foundry. He had two sons and a daughter and throughout his married life had always left all the responsibility for bringing them up to his wife. At work he was known as Mr. Overtime. Away from work he spent much of his time in the pub and at the bookies. When the boys were old enough, he began to take some interest in them, like showing them how best to analyse the current form of various horses that were running at Haydock or Aintree that week. But he never had much to do with what he usually referred to as 'the girl'. It was not surprising then that at the age of seventeen she had left home, something which Ken had responded to by telling anybody who asked about her that 'She'll come home when she's hungry'. Well she never did, and the next time Ken had seen her was in London, two years later, on the occasion of the 1979 Cup Final. On the Friday evening, he was staggering back to his hotel when a woman stood on a street corner had stopped him and asked if he would like to do some business. As he looked at her somewhat prematurely aged face, he realised that it was his own daughter, aiming to get hold of enough money to pay for her next shot of heroin.

Among the Big Four no such situation had occurred, although Charlie's early relationship with his firstborn had not been that wonderful. Paul Eccleston had been born towards the end of 1942. Stationed at the time at an Army camp in North Yorkshire, Charlie had been able to get a forty-eight-hour pass to visit his wife in hospital and see the new baby. But the next time he was able to see his young son was nearly three years later by which time Paul was walking and talking. Charlie's wartime service, first in North Africa and then in the Middle East, had been the reason for this gap, something that Charlie had always regretted.

By being in his official place of rest, but not asleep, Mick had brought two little Wiganers into the world. His son now lived at Spijkenisse in

Holland, a few kilometres west of Rotterdam, with his Dutch wife Elisia. His daughter lived four miles west of Platt Bridge at Up Holland with her husband, who came from Marus Bridge along with their three children.

Sam had not produced any offspring. But for most of the time he had lived in Ashurst, he had gone home each night to be greeted by two children. His first visit to the town had been to the wedding of an old shipmate in 1947. At the reception, he had met a widow whose husband had been killed in an explosion at Bank Top colliery. Going to one wedding often leads to another, it is said. It was certainly true for him and by marrying Mrs. Duxberry, he had become the stepfather of her young son. A couple of years later they had taken in the daughter of his wife's sister who, with her husband, had both been killed in a tragic car accident at Burtonwood.

Alan's wife Thelma was well known to all the older members of the Drawing Office, as she had once worked in the Print Room. She was now the mother of his children, Rebecca and Robert Greenall. Rebecca was nearly eighteen and preparing to go to University. Robert was still at Ashurst High School and had been blessed, or cursed, with a bit of a mean streak, which meant that on a bad day he could be big trouble to anyone who annoyed him. When he was really stirred up, the only person who could easily calm him down was Thelma, who sometimes had to get a small box from the kitchen to stand on and look him straight in the face in order to tell him off.

It is often said that at some point in their lives, everybody has fifteen minutes of fame. If so, Rebecca had already had hers. One day during the school holidays, she had had a row with her Mum and stormed out of the house aiming to go to see her friend Pamela, who lived nearby. Not finding her in, she had wandered onto Mount Everest, the slagheap that the firm Everards had bequeathed to the town just before it had been moved to the North East, where they had enough of their own industrial waste. There she had been chased by a large dog from which she had only escaped by running into an old hut, the last bit of Everards that had not been demolished or gone North.

Around three o' clock, she had slammed the hut door shut. Five minutes later, by which time she hoped that the dog would have run off, she found that she couldn't open the door of the hut. It was eight hours later before a man walking home after a night out in the Colliers' Arms had heard her cry for help. All that evening, half of Ashurst had been out looking for her. Her name had been on local radio and on the lips of many people in the town. And on the following Friday the full story, such as it was, along with a photograph of the four members of the Greenall family and the cat, had been splashed right across the front page of the *Ashurst Reporter*.

Robert had the potential to have a little bit more than fifteen minutes of fame. It would be as a result of his talent and ability on the sports field. He had played rugby league for Ashurst Schools against Widnes Schools at Naughton Park, scored three tries and kicked eight goals, had come first in the Merseyside schools cross-country twice and held the school record for the high jump and the long jump. But it was as a result of his battle with one of his teachers, that his name was to become best known.

Ashurst High School had once been Ashurst Grammar School, a school which Alan had attended in the mid-Fifties. Over the years some things hadn't changed, while others had. One good thing was that the Headmaster, Mr. Briggs, had gone and been replaced by Mr. Shacklady. He was quite different from his predecessor, who had ruled with an iron rod and a willow cane. Mr. Shacklady, originally a History teacher, just wanted an easy life so that he could continue his research into life in pre-industrial Lancashire. So for the first couple of years that Robert had been a pupil there, all had gone along quite smoothly. But that was soon to change with the arrival of a new PE teacher, Mr. Home, who originally hailed from Dover in Kent.

The weekly syllabus for Robert's class included Games on Monday afternoon, which for him and most of the class was the highlight of the week. From September to Easter, this had meant rugby on the first three weeks of the month and cross-country on the fourth. When Alan had been there, they had played rugby union but now, by popular demand, this had been changed to rugby league. In the summer cricket replaced rugby three times a month, with the fourth week given over to swimming in Ashurst's Victoria baths.

Just before the Christmas holidays, it was learned that their former PE teacher, Mr. Taylor, would not be returning to school after having suffered a heart attack earlier in the year. His replacement would start his duties in the New Year. On the occasion of his first session with Class Four, Mr. Home had been late getting onto the field. Keen to get playing, the lads had got themselves organised, with the keenest amongst them playing on the main pitch and the rest just mucking about, playing touch and pass with little enthusiasm. As soon as Mr. Home arrived, he called a halt to the proceedings.

"Whatever are you lot doing?" he had bawled out. "Whoever said that you could start playing?"

"We always used to when Mr. Taylor was in charge," said Robert. "He always let us organise ourselves."

"Things are going to be different now. I believe in the proper way of playing sport. That means that you get warmed up first; so you can all run once round the whole field, but before you start, let me have your names."

It didn't look too good. With Mr. Taylor in charge, the lads were allowed to do as they saw fit. With the new guy, it looked as though they were going back to being treated like schoolkids, which of course was what they still were. By the time they had returned from their run, another four players had been brought over from among the less enthusiastic.

"I'm not very impressed with your Maths either. Can't any of you lot even count? You were four players short."

Before anybody could begin to comprehend what he was on about, he continued. "Right, forwards, gather round me. I want to see what your lineout skills are like. The backs can practice running with the ball."

As they all stood looking at him stupidly, Billy Ashcroft asked quite innocently, "What's a lineout, sir?"

"Are you being funny, boy?"

"No sir."

Mr. Home pointed at the nearest boy to him and said, "You tell him what a lineout is, boy."

The lad shrugged his shoulders and continued, "It's when there's been a problem on the line and they have stopped running trains on that section of the track."

Jason Phillip's Dad worked for British Railways as a signalman at Helmsley Bank Signal Box and so he had a bit of knowledge about railway safety procedures. But the lad's answer did not impress or amuse his new teacher, who then pointed to each boy in turn and told him where to stand. Then he threw the ball to Robert and told him to get on with it. So Robert had passed it to the first one in the line who was on his side.

"What the hell was that?"

By this time the backs had returned and were stood around waiting to start doing something more interesting.

"All right, let's get playing a game so I can see if any of you are any good. And no more funny business."

It hadn't yet struck Mr. Home what was going on. Neither had it struck most of the lads, although one or two had a bit of an idea what was coming.

Two teams were selected, based on which House the boys were members of. The combined Birch and Willow House's team half-back kicked off, right into the hands of the full back of the combined Oak and Ash House's team. He ran about twenty yards before being tackled by an opposing forward, who quickly got up to let the full-back play the ball to one of his own team.

"Stop," Mr. Home bawled out. "Gather round and let me make one thing very clear to you all. When we come out here to play rugby, we play to the rules of rugby, not whatever rules you or your Mr. Taylor might have dreamed up in the past."

Mr. Home had obviously led some sort of a sheltered life down in the hop fields of Kent. It hadn't yet struck him that he was now living in rugby league land and that most of the members of class four were fans of the thirteen-a-side code.

Pointing at the full-back, he shouted out, "As soon as you had caught that ball, you should have kicked it into touch. From where you were stood, you could have easily made thirty or forty yards with a good kick."

Then, he had a go at his teammates for not gathering round their team mate and also at his tackler for so meekly moving away from the tackle.

Then he blew his whistle announced that the game would restart with a scrum. As the scrum went down, Mr. Home had to tell two more players from each side to join it, which they did with sheer amazement. Of course, as soon as the ball came out it went straight across the line through four or five pairs of hands until it came to the winger who unfortunately dropped it. Why none of them had not seen fit to kick it into touch, was then the basis for another long diatribe from Mr. Home.

Another scrum, another little passing movement and a tackle and another play the ball, which is at the heart of the game of rugby league but does not exist in rugby union. By this time, it was snowing heavily, so Mr. Home decided that they would all return to the dressing rooms, get changed and listen to him explain what was expected of them on a Monday afternoon.

He began by asking all those present to raise their hands if any of them ever watched rugby on the television or went to watch a local side. About half did.

Mr. Home pointed at the nearest boy and said, "Which team do you watch, boy?"

"The Saints, sir. We all do, except for Joe Wilson who's a bit simple and follows Wigan."

Mr. Home did not know who the Saints were but he had heard of Wigan before.

"Oh, I see the problem now," he said in a most patronising, condescending way. "That was why you were all behaving like a bunch of clowns out there."

Nobody spoke. Not one of the lads liked being called a clown, but Mr. Home was the teacher and no-one felt like challenging him for he was also over six foot tall, around fourteen stone and clearly an aggressive character. He was the complete opposite of Mr. Taylor, who would have been happy to let them all play croquet or ice hockey or watch the flowers grow, as long as they were back in the changing room by a quarter to four.

"Well, next week we'll be playing a much better game of rugby, so I suggest that you all make plans to watch *Grandstand* this Saturday afternoon. England and Scotland are playing in the Five Nations. It should be an excellent game. I'm really looking forward to it."

Of course none of them did, which disappointed Mr. Home no end. Then on the following Monday, the lads had to stay in the changing room for an hour while Mr. Home proceeded to explain the rules of rugby union. As soon as he had finished, he asked if anybody had any questions. Barry Phillips put his hand up, much to the surprise of all his mates.

"Do we have to play this game, sir? None of us like it. We want to play rugby league."

"I will treat that question with the contempt it deserves. Now get changed and let's spend the next hour playing some proper rugby."

As soon as the game got underway, whenever the ball emerged from a scrum or a lineout, Mr. Home was heard to shout "Kick it. Make some yardage, boy. Be expansive."

So, heeding his instruction, with the ball in his hands for the first time, Robert had booted it into touch. He had made about five yards, but the ball must have travelled more like fifty-five yards. At the ensuing lineout, Alan Shuttleworth had collected the ball and with the same degree of determination had made over ten yards with his kick to touch, although it must have travelled another hundred and five yards. The idea soon spread among all the others, and on every occasion that the ball was in a player's hands, irrespective of where he was on the field, he would kick it as far away from the field of play as he could. The war with Mr. Home had started.

The following week no rugby could be played as another heavy fall of snow over the weekend, followed by plummeting temperatures, made it difficult to even cross the school yard to the changing rooms. So they all had to sit in a classroom and listen to Mr. Home explain more of the rules of this foreign game. Then for the last hour he had decided to tell them about the history of rugby, although interestingly he never once mentioned the background to what had happened at The George Hotel in Huddersfield in 1895. He did however wax eloquently on the contribution made by the public schools to the sport and spent much time talking about one William Webb Ellis, the so-called inventor of the game of rugby.

Now Robert knew from his Dad that the game had not originated at the Rugby Public School where, in 1823, William Webb Ellis was supposed to have picked up the ball and run with it. He knew that rugby and soccer had grown out of what was formerly known as folk football and had its origins going back to the early part of the seventeenth century. The role of Webb Ellis was nothing more than a myth that had been created by the middle classes to justify their domination and keep out the growing number of the working class who wanted to play the game. But before he could say anything, Mr. Home caught Joe Wilson laughing to himself.

"What are you laughing at, boy? If something that I said is so funny, let us all hear it."

"I was just thinking that if Master Ellis hadn't gone to Rugby but to another public school, say Marlborough, then I would now be a red hot

Wigan Marlborough League fan. And I wouldn't like that, because I don't smoke."

As all the class burst out laughing, Robert made the point that it was a good job that Ellis hadn't gone to another public school, Newton Road Juniors either. But as he spoke, the bell went, at which point Mr. Home stormed out of the room.

"Nice one, John Pendlebury would have been proud of you," laughed Robert.

"Oh, I haven't finished yet."

And with that comment, Joe walked over to the blackboard, picked up a piece of chalk and in large letters wrote on it:

'Say No To Home Rule in Ashurst.'

29.

"Don't say a word, yet"

BY THE END OF January Monday afternoons had changed from being the best part of the week to the worst. They just did not like playing rugby union, neither did they like Mr Home. Then a second disaster occurred, one which completely ruined their Wednesday mornings. Their English teacher had been knocked off her moped outside Bold Colliery on her home on Tuesday evening. She was Miss Ramsbottom, the one with the long blond hair, luscious lips and nice legs.

As soon as she opened her mouth, you could tell that she came from Bolton. This made it much easier for her to instill in the class her own love of the written word and their common Lancashire roots. She was also a great impersonator and often imitated the various local accents as well as some of the other teachers and boys. In this way she was able to get difficult concepts across with great ease. Two other things added spice to her lessons. She had a great interest in old Lancashire dialect and would often use such words and phrases as doolally, barmpot, gallivanting, gormless, welly, sharri, tackle, fettle, rubbing rag, purring, lick, maiden, keep, flitting, over the brush, whoam, scorrick, ya fo and billy loo, into her monologues.

She was a great fountain of knowledge about Lancashire comedians and humour and would often tell them one of her famous 'Tacklers' tales', but only if they had all behaved or when one of the less than bright ones had made some valuable contribution to the class. She also had the ability to embarrass some inattentive boy with the instructions to 'Stop looking at my legs, young man and have a look at what we are all supposed to be discussing'.

Dianne came from quite an interesting family. On one side there were the Irish fleeing the potato famine in the middle of the nineteenth century, and on her mother's side was a distant relative called Arthur Twist, better known as the comedian Frankie Randle. Her mother hailed from nearby Farnworth, where the comedienne, one Hylda Baker, famous for her little saying, "Ee, she knows, you know", had grown up.

Her Dad was also a bit of a joker. Well he had to be, working for years in Leigh at the Anchor Cableworks, where one of his mates had been the famous Fifties comedian Ken Platt, he of the "I won't take me coat off. I'm not stopping" fame. So it would indeed have been very strange if Dianne herself had not had a good sense of humour.

252

"DON'T SAY A WORD, YET"

As Robert and his classmates waited for whoever would replace her, much of the discussion centred around who was going to visit her in Peasley Cross Hospital, with the usual comments thrown in that it would be nice to see her tucked up in bed in a nightie.

Then the door burst open and in strode her replacement. It was Mr. Home. A loud moan went round the room. But, as they were soon to be pleasantly surprised, it was a different Mr. Home from the Monday afternoon version they had all come to dislike.

"Well, boys, you will all be sorry to hear that Miss Ramsbottom has been involved in an accident and is now lying in a hospital bed. I'm also sure that you'll also be sorry to hear that I am to take her classes, probably for the rest of the year. Now I know that we have had a few differences of opinion, but don't let that carry on into this lesson. I'm sure we can all agree to speak the same language, by which, of course, I mean the Queen's English."

And with that seemingly reasonable start to the proceedings, Mr. Home began to talk about the content of the three books they were studying. He spoke about the life and times of the three authors and about other books that Charles Dickens, Ernest Hemingway and Emile Zola had written. Finally he changed tack and began talking about what he called the mechanics of language, defining the noun, adjective, verb, pronoun and preposition. He summed up what he had said by stating that they must all remember that words were a powerful tool in the sphere of communication. All that he had said was fairly clear and obvious, but his explanation of them was geared to helping them appreciate better what they read, be it in *The Times*, the *Radio Times* or the *Ashurst Reporter*. And he finished by stressing that they should bear in mind what he had said, when they themselves spoke, either to him or amongst themselves.

After the lesson was over and he had left the room, the general opinion of him was that he was quite different to what he had been like as the Games master and that what he had said was really interesting, though Robert, Joe Wilson and a few others were not totally convinced. For Robert it was just a gut reaction, while Joe reckoned that it must have been his twin brother that they had just met.

That night Alan had told his parents about how different Mr. Home had been and about the homework he had set them, trying to find out about the meaning of certain unusual words. On the following day, Alan passed on the news during the tea break, but when he mentioned that Robert's homework had been to find out what 'epistemology' meant, Mick had burst out laughing and said that the guy was probably just taking the piss.

The following Wednesday's English class wasn't quite as interesting as the previous week. It seemed as though Mr. Home had had to work hard to behave like a human the previous week. He continued with his 'travel through the world of words' before announcing that the following week they would begin an in-depth study of the first four chapters of the nineteenth century novel *Great Expectations* by Charles Dickens.

Then having listened to each boy's 'explanation' of what he had understood by the word 'epistemology', he wrote six words on the blackboard: Tradition, Freedom, Choice, Respect, Opportunity and Democracy.

"For your homework, I want you to write an essay of between eight hundred and a thousand words, based on these nouns and highlighting one in your title. They must all be linked in a common theme of your own choosing. I want to see some real effort go into this."

And before anyone could ask a question, the bell went and he walked out, leaving them all a little baffled, to say the least.

"I suppose I could write a piece that says in this country, our tradition of freedom of choice is part of our culture and democracy as long as we respect the fact that our opportunity to get a job when we leave school is virtually nil," said Joe Wilson.

"Can I just write that down?" said Billy Phillips. "I haven't a clue what he's on about."

"Well one thing is for sure," said John Evans. "He doesn't respect our traditions, like playing rugby league on a Monday afternoon. And we don't seem to have any freedom of choice in the matter either."

"You have just given me a great idea, Soapy," said Robert. "You've just made my day."

The afternoon was dominated by the news that Ashurst Council had approved a plan to allow the building of a new link road that would run from the top of Dob Lane to join the A621 down to Warrington. What was of particular interest was that St Mary's Girls school would have to be demolished to make this possible. This only fuelled the rumours that Ashurst High school was going co-educational, under the Council's new proposals for secondary education in the town.

Back at home, while eating their evening meal, Robert had reported on the day's news and outlined his plan for his essay. The following day Alan had talked about it over the tea break and the person it most interested was Mick, who proceeded to stay awake for the whole of the rest of the week.

"Well if this is what epistemology is all about, you can count me in. I wished they'd had clauses, nouns, subjunctives and past historic verbs when I was a lad. I don't think I would have finished up as a draffie."

"So what great plan has your Robert got?" asked Charlie. "From what you've said, he suddenly seems all enthusiastic again."

"DON'T SAY A WORD, YET"

"Something along the lines that in any decent country, where democracy exists, schools should respect the traditions of the area as well as providing every child with the opportunity to participate in the sport of their choice."

For the next few days various members of the office began to chip in with their ideas so that by Tuesday evening Robert, full of great enthusiasm, had just finished his essay. It was without doubt a bit of a masterpiece for Robert, writing essays had never been his strong point. It had also been typed out on next door's type writer and by Wednesday evening it had also been read by a couple of his classmates, who thought it was brilliant.

Alan took a copy to work to show Charlie and Mick and by the end of the day about thirty rugby league supporters had also read it. Later that evening, Robert told his parents that Mr. Home had collected them in and would be giving the top four a prize for their efforts.

He then read it again and of course noticed a few things that he could have done better. But it was too late to change anything, though it still seemed pretty good, certainly for Robert.

FREEDOM TO CHOOSE by Robert Greenall

Freedom is indeed a fine ideal. It is something that people over the years have had to fight for and even give their lives for. It is present at the heart of life in Britain today for few people are restricted as to where they can live, or where they can work. They have freedom to live their lives in a way that suits them and not in a way that just suits the authorities.

Freedom is also linked to democracy, the system of living whereby the majority has the right to choose the way they are governed and by whom they are governed. They exist because those who enjoy freedom are only able to do so because they respect the rules and laws that make it possible. And part of this general respect, is also the respect that the majority of the population hold for the monarchy.

But this is only true at a very general level. For example, it is accepted that everyone is free to drive on the public highway but closer examination reveals that this is not true. A driver has to hold a licence, which rules out people under seventeen. Neither has anyone the freedom to drive or park just where he pleases, just because it is convenient to him. Freedom has to be limited when one man's convenience may well prove very inconvenient for others.

There is also a positive side to restrictions on freedom. If given the choice, many pupils in this school would decide to opt out of cross-country every fourth Monday. Running across muddy fields in the freezing cold is not their idea of enjoyment. But having to take part in sport has benefits in the field of health and helps maintain a reasonable level of fitness in an age when many people are becoming couch potatoes.

ONE SUMMER

It is only with this in mind that one can look at where the issue of opportunity fits in. All people are encouraged to take whatever opportunities have arisen in their lives to better themselves. But this should not be done at the expense of causing hurt or lack of opportunity to others. Often an opportunity for one person to do something to acquire wealth may well restrict the freedom of another, an example being the landlord who turfs out existing tenants in order to bring in new tenants who are prepared to pay a higher rent. Such an opportunity for the landlord may result in a lack of opportunity for others to live in a way they wish.

Equally a large company may take the opportunity of a downturn in orders to reduce the size of their workforce and force those who remain to work harder for the same money, all in order to make higher profits. Equally at the same time, a group of workers may use the opportunity of a large order being won in order to force the company to improve their working conditions.

In the field of sport, the concepts of freedom, opportunity and choice are also found. For example an athlete may take the opportunity to give up his day job and turn professional in order to better his standard of living. But in doing so, he may well have given up the freedom to return later in life to the amateur ranks in his favourite sport.

Linking sport and education, different schools are often associated with different traditions, the public school of Eton being a good example. In our school rugby has always been preferred to Association Football, even though many pupils play soccer in the playground, though on a surface quite unsuited to playing rugby.

However, when a choice has to be made between the choice of rugby and the tradition of playing one form of rugby, a new contradiction arises. In the town of Ashurst, rugby league is a major part of the culture of the population. In the surrounding towns of St Helens, Warrington, Leigh and Wigan, it is more popular than football. Yet in relatively nearby towns like Bolton and Blackburn, the game has little presence, an unusual quirk in such a relatively small area.

Despite this fact, for a long time rugby union was part of our school's tradition. But then there was no opportunity for any pupil to exercise freedom of choice. The Headmaster alone had the freedom to impose on the school the game of his choice.

However changes were introduced when the school went comprehensive, most with the clear agreement of the new Headmaster. One of the first of the old traditions to go was the wearing of the masters' mortarboard and gown. They were rejected as an anachronism, with the full support of most of the younger teachers.

"DON'T SAY A WORD, YET"

Changes to the syllabus also meant that pupils had some degree of choice over what they studied. They could even switch subjects in mid-term, which would have been unthinkable when Mr. Briggs was Headmaster. He was more concerned to maintain his position by forever stressing the need for pupils to respect their teachers at school and their parents at home. But time has moved on and while his ideas were correct then and still are, there was another side to his coin, one which he totally ignored. Respect is like a two-edged coin, you can't have one side without the other. Teachers should respect their pupils and parents should respect their children.

One other feature of the new outlook in school has been the introduction of varying degrees of democracy. Following discussions between representatives of all those boys who were interested in sport and the Headmaster and sports master, it was agreed by an overwhelming majority that rugby league should replace rugby union.

But now a situation has arisen whereby the freedom of choice to play the rugby of our choice has been taken away with not one bit of democracy in sight. Tradition, democracy, freedom and choice are meaningless words if they are over-ridden by hypocrisy, bigotry and an unwillingness by those who wield the power, to show any respect to the wishes of their pupils.

The following Monday, although snow lay on the ground, the weather wasn't that bad that they couldn't go running. The lads came out of the school playing fields, ran half a mile down Wigan Lane, crossed over into the fields, skirted round the ginny green teeth, and on towards the old miners' cottages near Helmsley Bank Signal Box. Then they turned right and ran up and over the Montague slagheap, all that was now left of the old pit, then down past what had once been The Hotties at the back of Mather's Foundry. Then they jumped over what was left of the Stinky Brook, ran for a hundred yards up Billinge Road towards Hyde Bank and then cut across the fields and back to school. In a strange way, the whole run had been quite scenic, with the snow covering much of the countryside. As they returned through the playing field gates, they saw Mr. Home there indicating that he wanted them to continue round the whole playing field before returning to the changing rooms.

Tuesday dragged very slowly, the only bit of interest was when Billy Phillips nearly blew himself up in the Chemistry Lab. Tuesday night dragged too, not much on the television, not even enough homework to take Robert's mind off tomorrow. But finally it was eight thirty on Wednesday morning as he set off to walk the mile and a half to school. It was a long time since he had looked forward to being there. Might be a bit different next year, when there might be a load of girls in the class, he remembered thinking.

ONE SUMMER

There was no assembly on a Wednesday so bang on nine o' clock, in strode Mr. Home. He put all his papers on his desk, said that he had been surprised by the efforts of some of the class, and highly disappointed by the lack of efforts of others. Then he proceeded to read out the names of the best four boys who would receive a valued prize for their efforts.

"Fourth was Maurice Day, an unusual theme but easy to read. Third was David Webster, quite a historical piece well written with a consistent theme, but you need to improve your spelling. Second was Billy Phillips. I can tell you don't have much time for the monarchy but I can see you worked hard at it."

"Me," half-stuttered Billy. "It was rubbish. I only did it while I was having my breakfast this morning."

By now everybody expected that Robert had won first place, but it was not to be.

"And the first place goes to Keith Turner for a very well researched piece of work."

"What about Greeno's essay, sir. It was brilliant," shouted out Joe Wilson.

"I demand a recount," muttered Jack Pickford.

"Silence, this is not a circus. There is no need for a recount. What I do have to say is that I had to reject three of the essays; John Stainbridge never even mentioned the words democracy or respect in his pathetic attempt. Peter Shaw only wrote three hundred words, which consisted of little more than the definition of each word and Robert Greenall submitted more than a thousand words, which was the upper limit."

Then as he proceeded to give out the four prizes, which were tickets for the following Saturday's game between Sale and Otley, Joe Wilson, who was sat directly behind Robert, put his hand over his mouth and said "Don't say a word yet."

It was a good thing that Joe had done what he did. If Robert had responded, who knows how that might have affected the rest of his time at school. But by the time he had removed Joe's hand from his mouth, it was too late to do anything stupid as Mr. Home had disappeared sharply from the room. Not surprisingly, most of the class remained behind to discuss what had happened.

The general view was that it was time to fight back but what was the best way to do it? Joe appeared to know what was required and the first thing was for a few of them to meet at his house that evening and form an action committee. Like Robert's Dad, Joe's Dad was an active member of his trade union. In his case it was the Transport and General Workers Union, an organisation which his elder brother was also a member of. Bob Phillips's Dad was in the National Union of Railwaymen, John Stainbridge's Dad was in M.S.F, which had once been known in part as the old draughtsmens' union, D.A.T.A., and Ken Fowler's Dad was a miner at Gillarsfield Colliery and a militant member of the N.U.M.

That evening in John Stainbridge's shed, their meeting soon started. It was clear that what their various fathers did in their respective trade unions had rubbed off on their offspring. But it was clearly what had happened at Wilkinson's over the years and how the draughtsmen had fought Basil that had the most relevance. There, one of the ways that they had opposed Basil was to do exactly what he said, literally. There were many examples to learn from. But it was John Stainbridge, with his insistence that they had to claim the moral high ground, who gained the most support.

"What we have got to do is engage him in a discussion about the issue but on our terms and in the public eye," was how he had approached the matter. "We've got to show how he is unprincipled, a hypocrite and bad for the new democratic all-inclusive open ethos of the school."

"That's the first time I knew that the place had a democratic all-inclusive open ethos," said one lad. "I thought it was just a school."

"Maybe, but if we say it has, and if we convince Mr. Shacklady that we think it has and if Mr. Home continues to behave like he does, then Shaggers will be on our side."

"I don't want Shaggers with us. He's just a pain in the backside."

"Maybe he is but he's still the Headmaster and it's better if he supports us than opposes us."

"We could even get Mr. Bailey to support us. He may be a bit of an old fogey, but he's always trying to encourage us to learn more about our local history and our local traditions."

"What's history got to do with it? We are living in the present now."

"Maybe, but don't forget how bad it will look in the future if the school gets a bad name over an issue like this because in a few years time what we are doing now will be part of our history."

"I've just had a great idea." It was John Stainbridge again. "I know how to get some great publicity next Thursday and win the support of another teacher."

They all waited with for his suggestion.

"You know how Mr. Mitchell runs the Debating Society?"

They all did. It was his main interest out of school hours, though very few ever turned up to take part.

"Well, next week he is organising another of his stupid Balloon Debates."

A Balloon Debate was one where four boys took the part of some famous person and argued why they should not be thrown out of a hot air balloon because of the good that they had done for the world. At the last debate, the

259

four characters had been Winston Churchill, Joe Gormley, the Mayor of Ashurst and the editor of *The Sun*.

"Well, he has only got three suckers for his next debate, John Foster who is going to speak for Lord Kitchener, Dave Smith who will be Harold Wilson and Mike Evans who is going to be Les Dawson. Why don't one of us be Mr. Home?"

"Mitch wouldn't allow it."

"He has to otherwise he'll get exposed as a hypocrite as well."

"Why?"

"Why? Because as I was coming out of school today, I asked him if there were any characters in the world who I couldn't be if I wanted to take part. When he asked me to elucidate, I asked him, for example, if I could be Miss Ramsbottom or John Turnbull, the guy who tried to set fire to the Chemistry Lab a few years ago. In his words, he said anyone could be considered, even himself. So I then said if I could be the Headmaster and he replied 'Anybody means anybody'."

"So what do you suggest?"

"That one of us presents himself as Mr. Home and explains why he should not be thrown out of the balloon because he was the scourge of that heathen game of rugby league, because he believed that children should do exactly as they were told, because children should have no rights and everybody in Lancashire needed to be taught a lesson that they would benefit from in later life etc etc."

"And who is going to play him?"

"I've already asked John Duncan. He'd love to do it. He loves the sound of his own voice. He fancies himself as a bit of an actor. He doesn't like Home, even though he has never been taught by him and he leaves at the end of the year and hopes to go to Cambridge. All we have got to do is give him the bullets and he'll fire them."

It worked a treat. It was an absolute masterstroke. Over two hundred pupils turned up as well as seven teachers. Within the week, rugby league had been restored to the school curriculum and by the end of the term Mr. Home had left to take up a new position at a minor public school in Berkshire. There was even a bizarre twist to the whole event ten years later and at Twickenham, the home of rugby union, of all places. Mr. Home had been present for an International game between England and Scotland. There he had seen Joe Wilson outside the ground on the car park, with a large group of well-dressed people.

"Hello Joseph. I'm pleased to see you here. I gather that you must have finally learned from the previous error of your ways."

"Not really, ewd lad," Joe had replied in his rich Nook End accent. "I'm only here because my firm has sent me on a freebie. Free to get in, free champagne, a five course meal and a night out in London and I don't have to pay a penny. All I've got to do is stay awake while the headless chickens run round the field and be nice to everybody that I meet. But that doesn't include you."

And then to the amazement of all the well-heeled characters milling around, Joe had raised his clenched fist in the air and shouted out "No Home Rule in Ashurst. Rugby league forever."

30.

What might have been

WITH THE VICTORY of the boys of Ashurst High School over Mr. Home, the goings on there faded into the background until yet another of Charlie's contradictions appeared on the scene again. It happened a couple of weeks later with the arrival into the Drawing Office of the former apprentice, Tommy Wilson. Tommy had never had any great wish to work in the Drawing Office. He had always been a practical sort of a lad, always wanting to make something work by fiddling about with it. But due to an unfortunate accident, he would have to spend the next few months in the funny farm.

A few weeks earlier his foreman had told him that he would be working his last four months as an apprentice at Drax Power Station, which was located in sight of both North Yorkshire and East Yorkshire, just a bit too far to travel home every night. In charge of the job was the electrician Roy Penketh, who Tommy knew well. Along with Roy, there was another electrician, two fitters and the labourer Phil. With Phil on board a good time could be expected. He had the ability to behave like a magnet, although what he attracted was women, not iron filings. So when he began talking about the last time he had worked at Europe's biggest power station and had lodged with a playful widow called Stephanie, and all before they had even reached the East Lancs Road, Tommy knew he was going to enjoy his first trip into bandit country.

Unfortunately the van did not even get as far as Mosley Common. It was nothing to do with Roy's driving. It was all due to the driver of an ancient Morris Minor having a heart attack, resulting in Wilkinson's brand new van ploughing straight into the back of it. Three seconds later a speeding Eddie Stobart lorry had hit them up the backside. Fortunately, amongst the six of them, the only injuries were a few broken bones. Unfortunately for Tommy they all belonged to him, his right leg and ribcage. A 999 call saw the almost immediate arrival of a fire engine, two police cars and an ambulance which raced Tommy and the two fitters to hospital. By the end of the day the rest of the gang were all back at home in Ashurst sleeping in their own beds, Tommy was being looked after by a large Irish nurse and the man who had caused the accident was lying in the morgue. Two days later, Tommy had been released from hospital and brought home with strict instructions to take it easy, which was something that he was hardly in a position to disagree about.

WHAT MIGHT HAVE BEEN

It was during this time that he had begun to see what soon became the woman of his dreams, one who was soon to break his heart and his bank balance. At first he didn't know her name, her background or even where she lived; this was all because she had never seen him. And that was how, during his first few days in the Drawing Office, he began to tell his new workmates about Sandra. It was indeed a strange story, one that someone could make a film of, one with easily three or four endings to the tale.

Tommy lived in Manor Street with his mother, who worked at the supermarket in Bolton Lane. He knew that if he didn't get himself organised, and he would finish up watching crap TV shows all the time. So he worked out a plan which would include reading some of the books that had once belonged to his Dad. He also decided to spend time building model aircraft, and learning a foreign language, French, German or Italian, something which would come in useful if he could join the Outside Contracts Division when he had recovered.

He determined to get up every day at half seven, in time to have a few minutes' chat with his mother before she went to work. Then he would make his breakfast, wash and wipe up, read the paper just before she left the house and spend ten minutes planning the day. The best place to do this would be in the front room because, when the sun was shining, it would shine straight at him for a good hour. Sitting in there also meant that he could catch sight of the postman and his various neighbours setting off for work. It was also a time he would set aside for a bit of meditation, just an easy relaxing way to start the day. It was while doing this on the Monday morning, that he had first seen her.

That morning he had observed about two dozen people going past the house. If you discount all the males, the neighbours who he knew, and one or two others who he recognised from the Willow Estate, she was certainly the most attractive. Well she had to be, she was the only one left. On Tuesday morning he saw her again, this time carrying an umbrella as it was raining slightly, more like Billinge Mist than rain. On Wednesday she was obviously late, walking very quickly, the sound of her high-heel shoes resounding all down the street. On Thursday it was her footsteps that first caught his attention, for she was quite early. It was then that he caught a full look at her face. She looked about nineteen, dark hair tossed about in the wind, swarthy coloured skin and a distinctive style of walking. He then realised that he was quite attracted towards her. Friday confirmed that. It was a lovely day, and she was dressed to the nines and looked quite fantastic. Perhaps the place where she worked had a dress-down day on a Friday or maybe she was going somewhere after work. By now, he realised that he really fancied her, though he didn't know the slightest thing about her. He also knew that it was going to be a long time before he saw her again, all of forty eight hours; unless of course she worked Saturday morning, which of course she didn't. That wasn't surprising since there were very few people in Ashurst working overtime. There were not even that many working, some would say.

Over the weekend she was never out of his thoughts and then on Monday morning a disaster struck, for the postman knocked on the door with a parcel and he had to go into the living room to get a biro to sign for it. So he couldn't be sure if she had walked past during that couple of minutes.

On Tuesday she was there again as normal, only he didn't get a proper look at her as it was raining and she had her collar up and her umbrella obscured most of her face. Wednesday was another windy day and as she drew level to his window, though on the other side of the street, she brushed her hair back from over her face, so he only caught half a glance of it. But Thursday made up for the three lost days as she crossed the street right in front of him and he saw her face full on. Friday looked like being another disaster as she hadn't appeared by nine o' clock but suddenly she burst up out of Ross and proceeded to run all the way along Manor Street.

The only good thing about Saturday was the fact that there was a match to watch on *Grandstand* in the afternoon. By now he was walking without needing to use his crutches and so was able to mess about with his two nephews, who his sister Cynthia brought round every weekend.

The following Monday was another brolly day, Tuesday she was late again and ran past the house but on Wednesday she stopped right outside to remove a stone from her shoe. He must have seen her for at least twenty seconds and he really liked what he saw. Thursday was another bad day, with his next door neighbour Mrs. Healey knocking on the back door, wanting to give him some money that she owed to his mother.

Friday was obviously dress-down day and she looked great, pure class she was and now he knew he was falling in love with her. It was this that made the following week so hard to bear for he never saw her once. Where was she, was she on holiday or was she off work ill? Had she been made redundant, like many other people in Ashurst had been? And if she had gone on holiday, who had she gone with and if she had maybe gone with some other girls had she met somebody nice and fallen for a holiday romance? But then she might already be going out with someone, she might even be engaged, unlikely that she was married, though you can never be sure nowadays. But the following Monday she reappeared with a decent tan so it had been a holiday. She was also wearing a short skirt, which showed that the sun had also browned her nice legs. And Friday was a repeat performance, which made waiting another forty-eight hours a terrible cross to bear.

By now he was walking much more easily and was working out how to meet her. Plan A was to go down to the paper shop around twenty to nine, stand outside it until she turned the corner from Ross Street and then walk up it slowly and say hello. Do that two or three times and then maybe on Thursday or Friday stop and tell her that he had been watching her go past his house for weeks and could he take her out on a date. Plan B was to stand in the front garden as she walked past, but that wouldn't be much good if she was on the other side of the street and a car went past at the same time or if the weather was bad. Plan C was to find out where she worked by following her. Then if he knew anybody who worked there, he could ask them about her and Plan D was to follow her home, but since he had never seen her on her way back from work that was not an option.

He finally decided on Plan C. So on the following Monday he went down to the mini-market at the end of Manor Street and took ages to buy a Mars Bar as she was late going past. He had then followed her as best he could until she disappeared into Wood Street. On Tuesday he had stood in the phone box opposite the bookies in Clyde Street, then followed her along Hamer Street until she had turned into Oldham Street. Due to the difference in the speed they were going at, by the time he had reached there she had disappeared. She was clearly heading for the industrial estate there so there was a chance she worked at one of the firms that operated from there. That was what he discovered on the Friday for she went straight into Preston Printers, a small firm that employed about fifty people. Then he knew he had a great chance of discovering something about her since the mother of his old mate, Ronnie Sutton, worked there in the Personnel Department.

That night he had limped up to her house in Victoria Street. It was a bit embarrassing really for her husband had been in the front garden. He was a six foot two former second-row forward with Gillarsfield Labour Club, not really somebody to have to explain to that you wanted to talk to his wife about things of a romantic nature. Fortunately she was in the front room and told him to come in straightaway. As soon as he asked her about the girl, she knew who he meant. The girl was called Sandra and had worked at Preston's for about two months. She smiled when he told her why he wanted to know about her and what she thought his chances would be, or even if she could put a good word in for him.

"She's a nice girl but a bit on the quiet side. Her father was killed in the Falklands, though I don't think she ever saw much of him. Her mother used to be a staff nurse at Victoria Hospital, though I'm not sure if she still lives in Ashurst. She's also got two elder brothers, one lives in Scotland and the other is down south somewhere."

Then she carried on to say that although was very slight, she was not one to mess about with. It would appear that one of her main interests was judo, in which she had a black belt. She then gave him the good news that she didn't think that Sandra was going out with anybody.

"I don't know why because she's a really nice girl, if you don't mind doing all the talking."

Then she offered to do her bit as a matchmaker.

"I don't think she'd take kindly to you following her or even stopping her in the street and asking her for a date. Leave it with me and I'll tell her about what you've just said to me. But I'm not due back in work until Wednesday so you'd better call round on Thursday evening."

What a long week that had been for him, but finally he returned to hear what Mrs. Sutton had found out. And it was not good news.

"I'm sorry to tell you this Tommy, but she was made redundant while I was off and she finished last Friday. She told my friend Pat that she was going up to Aberdeen to stay with her brother. He's a dentist up there."

So, Tommy had gone home, told his mother about Sandra, borrowed some money off her and the following morning had caught the train north up to the Granite City. The following morning he went through the telephone directory, made a list of all the dentists and then began trekking round the city. Very luckily, the third dentist he had gone to was the one where Sandra's brother worked. Yes, the girl had turned up. She had stayed at her brother's flat for a few days and then left. Her brother wasn't working that day but a phone call to his house in Peterhead revealed that Sandra had now gone to London with the intention to staying in the Y.W.C.A. off Baker Street. He caught the train back to Ashurst to get hold of some more money and a change of clothes then caught the train to Euston. But when he arrived at the Y.W.C.A. he was too late. The lady on reception didn't know where Sandra had gone as she had left no forwarding address, but the girl she had shared a room with might know.

He spent all day waiting for Maureen to return from work, but it was worth it. Sandra was going to Dover where her other brother lived and, since he lived with his wife and five children in a small semi, Sandra had told Maureen that she would be staying in the nearby Youth Hostel. So that's where Tommy went next, but when he arrived there he was again too late. Sandra had only stayed one night and on checking out had asked the man on the desk how long would it take to walk to the cross channel ferry. To his question of where was she heading, she had replied, "Paris for a couple of days and then Rome."

With his money running out, no passport with him and hardly the slightest chance of ever seeing her again, Tommy had sadly returned home. It was with that 'interesting' story that he had joined the ranks of the many characters who had worked in the Drawing Office. Partly to ease the pain, Alan told him that it might just be a good thing, like the time in 1962 when he had arranged to go on a date with the bus conductress Helen Murdoch. On the Saturday afternoon he had badly torn his ligaments playing football and been unable to meet her. As it turned out, that had been a bad thing resulting in a good thing. Not that he knew it then, and probably not that she knew it then, but as a result of a one night stand the previous weekend she was pregnant. And so if Alan had turned up and started going out with her, and if she had been as good as her reputation was, within a month he would have been drawn into a situation that was none of his making. Then he would never have bumped into Thelma sat on the number five bus on Christmas Eve and his whole life would have been so different.

Charlie also told the tale about a choice he had had to make when he was much younger, one which had also worked out for the best. One of his mates at work was keen to set him up for a date with one of the canteen women. She always looked a bit rough either when doling out the chips, or even on a Saturday night in town. But nobody ever went out with her for her scintillating conversation, her dress style or her intellect. Her name was Penelope Wragg, and various four-line poems had been made up about her which invariably ended with the words 'a good shag'.

On the day in question the Saints were due to play a cup tie at Workington Town. As a result Charlie had chosen to go to Derwent Park. On the back seat of the coach returning back to St Helens over Shap Fell, he had become acquainted with a nice young lady from Duncan Street who he now lovingly referred to as 'Our Maud' , a St Helens way of describing one's wife.

Not to be outdone, Colin chipped in with a similar story. He had met a girl in the Co-op Dancehall and arranged to meet her on the following Wednesday outside Boots in Ashurst. He arrived around quarter past seven, fifteen minutes early. Half an hour later she had still not turned up, when a mate of his had walked past arm in arm with his girlfriend. When he told them why he was waiting there, she had asked him if he knew there were now two Boots chemists in the town. The girl may well have gone to the other branch, for he never saw her again.

Then Yorky came in with one of his classic tales. It was when he was still living at home, and his afternoon had been spent celebrating a big win his brother had had on the horses. He had arranged to meet a girl for their first date outside Burton's shop in Huddersfield. The shop had a large mirror in the window so anyone seeing a person stood outside on the pavement and their reflection in the mirror would think that there were two people stood there. Rather bizarrely, what Yorky didn't know was that the girl he was meeting was a twin and at the time they were both stood there outside the shop. On top of that, because of the amount of ale he had drunk that afternoon, Sam was seeing double and what with the speed of the bus as it went past the shop, Sam had to blink twice, because it looked liked there were about ten identical women waiting for him. He got off the bus and walked up to them, apologised for being both late and drunk and then taken his date to the pictures. He hadn't taken her home to Brighouse, just put her on the bus and arranged to meet her again later in the week.

Then they had gone for a walk and Sam had asked her if she had enjoyed herself the previous Saturday, despite him being in the state he was.

"Not really," she had replied. "I didn't feel too well so I just watched David Frost on *That Was The Week That Was* and then I went to bed."

"How could you have done that? You were in the pictures with me."

She smiled and burst out laughing. "That wasn't me. That was our Helen you were with."

But despite those tales, Tommy wasn't that amused. He still couldn't get Sandra out of his head. How can you find someone who might now be in Italy or even on the other side of the world? And so for the next month, never a day went past that he didn't think about her. Then one evening when he arrived home to the news that Mrs. Winstanley had left a message for him to call round. He was up there like a shot after his tea, to discover that Sandra had sent a letter to the woman who was ran the Wages Department and she had passed it on to Ronnie's mother.

"She's living in Perth now," Mrs. Sutton had told Tommy, whose first thoughts were that though it might be far, it wasn't as far as Aberdeen. But it was Perth in Australia she meant. So should he forget trying to contact her or was it worth making one final attempt? From other things Mrs. Sutton had said about her, she really seemed his sort of girl. But then while he was wondering what to do, starting to find out how much it would cost to fly to Australia and thinking about selling some of his vintage early rock 'n' roll records, another message came from Mrs. Sutton. By this time Mr. Sutton was beginning to get just a little suspicious, though in a rather humorous way. Tommy sat down in her front room as she told him that one of the girls that Sandra had been friendly with had just received a letter from Western Australia. Then she gave it to him to read. Five minutes later he knew that the he had to forget her.

Dear Christine,

Just a few lines to thank you for being a good friend and to tell you what has happened to me since I left Ashurst. I went to see my brother Frank in Aberdeen and then Paul in Dover. I spent a couple of weeks in Italy and then flew out here to Oz to meet up with my childhood sweetheart. John was so pleased to see me and me to see him. It was 1979 when I last saw him and we had quite a lot of catching up to do and it wasn't all talk, because now I am expecting his child. We are going to get married next month and live in Fremantle. He's a draughtsman with a construction company there, bigger than Preston's, though not as big as Wilkinson's. Give my regards to Tony, Jill and Linda, and to any hidden admirers I might have had and not known about. And if you are ever passing this way don't forget to call in and see me.

Love and best wishes, Sandra

With that brief note, Tommy was reminded of the old saying that 'it is better to have loved and lost than to have never loved at all'. During all the time he had been in the Drawing Office, he had been so bound up with his non-existent love affair and so, the next Friday lunchtime, he had insisted that he be allowed to buy them all a drink in the Horse and Jockey. As far as he was concerned this could be like a Wake, he had told them. It had been good while it lasted but then it had never really started. It had all gone on in his head. But he had got a great kick out of seeing her every day and suffered pain when she didn't walk past. Then over the next week or so, he began to come out of his shell and three weeks later his leg came out of its plaster. He also told them a bit about his family, including his nephew Joe who was still at school but was having trials with Wigan.

"Does he go to Ashurst High School?" Alan had asked.

"Yes, why?"

"Well that's a coincidence, because he is a big mate of my son Robert."

Discussing what the school lads had done to defeat Mr. Home helped to reduce Tommy's pain at losing something which he had never really had. He finally stayed another three months, by which time the broken bones in his body had completely healed up. It also gave him a proper chance to appreciate what draughtsmen did all day, having now mastered the art of using a 2H, 3H and 4H pencil and producing A4 drawings that even Mick could have said he was proud to have drawn.

A couple of months later and fully recovered from the accident, he had joined the O.C.D. and gone on his first job to a cotton mill in Accrington, then six months on a water treatment plant in Tunisia and a further three months at a chemical factory in King's Lynn. Nearly a year later he had married an Australian dentist who he had met while working in Shipley in West Yorkshire and was now living with her in Brisbane.

31.

Coal not Dole

"I SEE THAT Tony Benn was elected last night," said Mick, in a rather mournful voice. "Another upper crust toff come to save the world."

"Oh aye, and your Maggie Thatcher is the salt of the earth. Come to make us all slaves for the world," said Alan.

"Well, she has been prepared to stand up in the world for this country."

"Aye, and put thousands on the dole and bring back new levels of poverty and insecurity."

"I don't think your mate Callaghan ever did anything for the likes of us."

"Well, I wouldn't disagree with you on that one. But that's no reason for backing Thatcher. Not if you have to work for a living."

"Wasn't Callaghan the last Prime Minister?" chipped in Jason, the latest apprentice to spend time in the Drawing Office.

And before anyone could confirm it, the lad went on, "Another politician out to feather his own nest. They are all the bloody same."

Then Yorky gave his measured response to the current situation. "It's always been the same with most of them. It's just that it's more blatant now. The gap between the haves and the have nots is getting wider every day. I never thought I'd say this, but it just doesn't seem to matter whoever is in office now."

Politically there had always been sharp divisions among the draughtsmen. Mick was a big supporter of the new Government. On the other hand Charlie and Alan were strong opponents while the rest of them were somewhere in between or plainly just not interested.

"Well, say what you will, I don't think that Tony Benn going into Parliament will make any difference to the likes of me or you."

"The only person who ever went into the House of Commons with honest intentions was Guy Fawkes."

"Greeno, how many more times are we going to hear that from you? You're like a bloody gramophone record," retorted Mick.

"Well, it's true. Parliament is nothing more than the bosses talking shop."

Cough, cough.

"I, as the official returning officer for the dead constituency of Chesterfield, hereby declare that the votes cast in today's election are as follows."

It was Charlie in his best John Snagge Boat Race commentating voice, reading from his copy of the *Daily Mirror*.

Benn	Labour Party	24,633
Payne	Liberal Party	18,369
Bourne	Conservative Party	8,028
Maynard	Independent	1,355
Lord Sutch	Monster Raving Loony Party Last Stand	175
Bartley	Four Wheel Drive Hatchback Road Safety	116
Davey	No Increase in Dental Charges	83
Layton	Spare the Earth, Ecology Party	46
Anscombe	Death off the Road, Freight on the Rails	34
Nim	Yoga and Medication	33
Butler	Buy Your Chesterfields in Thame	24
Nicholas-Jones	Independent - The Welshman	22
Shaw	Elvisly Yours, the Elvis Presley Party	20
Hill	Prisoner. I Am Not a Number	17
Picarro	Official Acne Candidate	15
Cahill	Reclassify *The Sun* Newspaper as a Comic	12
Connell	Peace Candidate	7

Spoiled Papers		138,672

"And accordingly, with all the powders invested in me, I do hereby declare that the Spoiled Papers are duly elected as the said Member for Chesterfield."

Then he continued in a slightly more serious voice, "I just wonder what makes some people tick. I mean, what sort of a bloke would stand as the Elvis Presley Party or the Official Acne Candidate?"

"Was there going to be an Unofficial Acne Candidate?" laughed Alan.

"You can just imagine it, can't you? Him standing there on the platform in a church hall, explaining his policies and in storms the Official Acne Candidate, what's his name, Picasso, shouting out 'Eh, that's my spot'."

"I could agree with one of the fringe candidates though," said Yorky. "The Reclassify *The Sun* Newspaper as a Comic."

"He's probably a *Daily Express* reader," laughed Charlie.

"I thought Tony Bennett was a singer," chipped in the apprentice Jason. "What's he doing getting involved in elections?"

"Tony Benn, you pillock," said Alan. "He's no singer. He doesn't even use notes when he speaks."

"Not even when he's telling his butler what he wants for his breakfast in the morning," laughed Mick. "He's a Lord, isn't he?"

"He was. He gave it up."

"Well, he should have stayed as one. Who wants him in the House of Commons?"

ONE SUMMER

"Obviously around twenty-five thousand people in Chesterfield, it would seem, Mick."

Mick was a good draughtsman. Maybe not the fastest in the world, but his work was always carried out with the greatest attention paid to the smallest details. But when it came to issues of a political nature, he didn't let the facts cloud his judgement. Then when someone like Charlie or Alan tried to put things into a wider context, he would simply dismiss their comments as claptrap from the *Manchester Guardian* or the *Ashurst Reporter*.

Mick believed everything that was printed in his *Daily Mail* or reported on the BBC, except of course when it directly affected him or any of his relatives or neighbours, which happened later that afternoon.

Over the last few weeks, trouble had been brewing among the miners. Under the control of its new Chief Executive, the Canadian Ian McGregor, and firmly encouraged by the Government, the National Coal Board had begun acting in a very provocative manner. There had been numerous rumours of pits being closed and many jobs being lost. Mick, of course, in the abstract, believed that this was inevitable. Many pits were running out of their reserves or needed major investment to keep producing. On the other hand, North Sea oil was cheaper and easier to extract. A further advantage was that closing unprofitable and outdated pits would reduce the number of accidents and deaths that still happened underground. To him the Government strategy was inevitable and correct.

On his return from the canteen, Charlie told Mick that he had just heard that the N.C.B. had announced that they were not intending to re-open Gillarsfield Colliery. Just before Christmas, the roof had begun to cave in on the roadway that led to where the old Southport Edge pit had once been worked. At the same time, there had been flooding on the Henshaw face and earlier, in 1983, it had been estimated that the pit had no more than two years' reserves left. So the decision did not come as a great shock to those who were still working at this ninety-year-old pit. However, what did surprise many people in the town was the other news that the nearby Cronton Colliery was also to be closed.

What made matters even worse for all those who worked at Cronton, or who depended on their husbands or wives working there, was the fact that less than eighteen months earlier, information had been given to the Lancashire Miners' General Secretary, Sid Vincent, that the pit had another twenty years' active life in it.

The following week, the N.C.B. announced that it was abandoning the Yorkshire Main colliery at Doncaster. This had been opened in 1911, currently employed around 1400 men and in the previous year had made over £4 million profit. In addition, a £10 million improvement scheme for the washing plant had recently been announced. On the Wednesday, the

COAL NOT DOLE

N.C.B. announced that it was aiming to cut another 20,000 jobs. Closing another two pits in Yorkshire had lead to the Yorkshire miners' call for an all-out strike in protest, particularly when Arthur Scargill claimed that the McGregor plan was to reduce the manpower levels from the current 184,000 to 100,000 and to close a total of around seventy of the country's 171 pits. As a result, strikes in protest were called for on every coalfield, a decision that just happened to coincide with a decision by the N.C.B. to greatly raise the level of the redundancy payouts for those who were to lose their jobs.

Then Yorky began to dominate the discussions about what was now going to happen. Ever since they had known him, he had this knack of being able to forecast fairly accurately what would unfold in the future. He wasn't always right, although he was right many times more than he was wrong. Some of his predictions were spot on, like the time he had predicted that their old colleague, the war hero Stan, wouldn't live long after he had retired. Within six months of collecting his first pension, Stan had run for the Earlestown bus one morning, staggered up the stairs breathless, sat down on the nearest seat and dropped dead.

On another occasion, just before Thelma Johnson, had spent Christmas Day at the house of Alan's Granny, he had told his wife that he predicted the pair of them would get married and have two children, all of which actually happened. On another occasion just after Wilkinson's had been sold in unusual circumstances to the Miller Engineering and Construction Company in Cleveland, Ohio, he had predicted that within five years Basil Wilkinson would make a comeback as the works' boss. He did not however forecast that one day Basil would be found dead in rather unusual circumstances, although he did predict accurately that the Vietnam War would be over before the end of 1973.

At their Friday session in the Horse and Jockey, Sam began to tell the others what he thought the future would bring. That morning, Charlie had been talking about his son, who worked at Sutton Manor Colliery. Paul Eccleston was a very optimistic sort of a person, pretty much like his Dad, and a man who could never be considered a hothead. He always thought things through and then followed it up with suggestions which he knew that those around him could see the justification or logic for and so support them.

In the present situation, in Paul's view it had now fallen to the National Union of Mineworkers to stand up to the Government's economic policies, fight for the jobs of its members and their industry and at the same time expose the feeble nature of the Labour Party opposition. Paul also felt that many of the trade union leaders were going to be put to the test and would have to decide which side of the fence they wanted to be on: or in other words, to decide whether they wanted to be part of the problem or part of the solution.

Paul believed that the next few weeks would be crucial. The Yorkshire miners had given a lead and it was up to their colleagues from South

Lancashire to join them, along with those from Scotland, South Wales and Kent and at the same time for the miners in Nottingham to be given a sharp reminder that unity was strength and divided, they would all lose. Then once the whole miners' union was united, they would be in a position of strength and able to give leadership to a much wider audience who were becoming increasingly fed up with the growing unemployment that faced them, particularly in the industrial North.

"I don't quite see it like that, Charlie," Yorky had replied. "I'd like to agree with you Paul, but I don't think that things are so simple."

"How do you mean?"

"We've got a situation where neither Scargill or Thatcher are going to back down. Both have been spoiling for a fight to the finish and I know which side I hope is going to win, but I think that the Government has been preparing for this for a long time. Upping the redundancy payments is just part of it. Thatcher has probably already got the police and the Army prepared if things don't go their way. The newspaper editors will have been primed to ensure that all the news about the strike is presented from the Government's side and no doubt M.I.5 and Special Branch haven't been sat back doing nothing. I bet they have already got their spies and informants in place."

"On the other side, there are already splits and big differences within the N.U.M. The Nottingham and Leicestershire miners can't be relied on. They've already been told that their futures are secure, though they'll be fools if they believe a word of it. And I don't suppose that the T.U.C. will be much use once the going gets rough, just like they were in 1926."

"You are pretty negative today," said Charlie.

"I don't want to be. I hope the miners win. It sickens me to see what is happening in this country. You know yourself how many redundancies and job losses we've had in engineering. They have all been forced upon us and we just haven't been able to stop most of them. Happen the miners are the last group of workers who can stop the rot. But if I can work it out, so can the Government and knowing what Thatcher is like and what she stands for, she'll know too."

He paused for breath before his captive audience and then continued.

"I reckon we'll see a lot of dirty tricks over the next few weeks and months. No doubt the police will get loads of overtime, there'll be trouble on the picket lines and the papers will only report one side of it. Every day you read the papers or watch the news on the box, you'll get fed a steady diet of lies, untruths and sly innuendo. And that's why I'm not over-optimistic. I wish I could be. I hope my predictions are all wrong. But I can only tell you what I feel in my water. I just hope that I am proved wrong."

"You're totally wrong, Yorky. The workers united will never be defeated," said Simon Burnley, who worked in the Wages Office and who had been sat nearby listening. "You've no faith in the working class."

"Who rattled your cage?" asked Alan. "Three months ago you wouldn't even put anything in that collection we had for them dinner ladies who were on strike at Mather's."

Simon did not reply. He had only joined the union a fortnight ago, a few days after joining Ashurst Young Socialists. Despite his total lack of experience of the real world or the nature of industrial relations in Britain or any other country, he now believed that he had become a member of the only organisation capable of leading every struggle that could right every wrong faced by the British working class.

Back in the office that afternoon, the presence of John Wainwright, discussing changes to a control cubicle that was due to be delivered to Frickley Colliery in a week's time, made any conversation of a political nature impossible. Whether the cubicle would ever be delivered there or whether it would ever be connected up and used was not discussed. John was due to retire soon and for his last five years had lived in his own little world. He was the sort of person who, if he had been a waiter on the Titanic, would have still been brushing the crumbs off the tables, while everybody else was putting lifejackets on and heading for the nearest lifeboat.

After he had gone, Mick made a statement that showed in a roundabout way that the forthcoming dispute was on his mind. In his opinion both the Saints and the miners had one thing in common. They would both be out before very long. The miners would soon be out on strike and the Saints would soon be out of the Challenge Cup because the following Sunday they would face his team, the mighty Wigan, in the Third Round. Rather strangely, for once he was right on both counts. The Miners Strike of 1984, one of the bitterest disputes that the country had ever seen, was about to begin. And at Knowsley Road, before a crowd of over twenty thousand people, the Riversiders or Pie Eaters as they were often called, defeated the Glass Blowers or Pill Men by sixteen points to seven.

Later that evening Alan had gone next door to borrow a drill from his neighbour. Sat in the living room was Phil's mother, who had been staying with her son for the last four weeks. But she was more than a handful and had finally agreed to go and live in the Greenfield Old Peoples' Home. She appeared to vary between being utterly senile and reasonably alert and tonight she was clearly having a good day. In fact she was more than keen to chat with Alan, who she had known for all the time she had been visiting her son and grandchildren at number fourteen.

ONE SUMMER

"Alan, have you seen the news? The miners are going on strike. Ee, your Grandad would have loved to be there, and our Billy too. They would have shown them what to do. And about time too."

It appeared that there had been a documentary about the mining industry that afternoon on BBC2. A lot of vintage footage had been shown, including a photograph of a group of colliers stood outside the old Montagu pit in the early 1920s. Phil's mother was sure that she had seen her late husband and Alan's Grandad on it. They would have been in their early thirties then. It had clearly brought back many memories for her, some good and some bad. Just like his Granny, she would have lived through that long bitter struggle that the Lancashire miners had had to go through after the collapse of the General Strike in 1926.

No doubt she would be hoping that if there was going to be a strike, then it would be a short one and successful too, although it would not really affect her. Although it might just, if the Government decided the country could not afford to run old peoples' homes any more. Alan listened politely as she talked but when she mentioned the name Clement Attlee, he made a quick excuse and left. As soon as Phil's mother started talking about the man who had been elected Prime Minister in 1945 and who she had once met in Manchester, he knew she would be fully capable of rambling on about him until midnight.

Back at work on the following Monday morning a meeting of all the senior managers was held. There it had been spelled out in very clear terms what effect the miners' strike would have on the company. There would be no orders from the N.C.B. until the issue was decided one way or another. As a result the issue of redundancy and even closure reared its ugly head once again. And the way that fact of life affected people was emphasised most graphically later in the week on *Look North*, when it was reported that a twenty-seven-year-old father of two had committed suicide on Lowton Bank as a direct result of having his house repossessed by his building society, a situation brought about because he had been unable to find work over the last two years.

Various people reacted to the prospects of being laid off in different ways. Alan had been hoping to take the family to Brittany for a couple of weeks. Now it looked as though they would only get as far as Argate. Charlie had been saving up for the best part of a year in order to take his wife Alice to see her sister in New Zealand. But as he said, "Our Maud hasn't seen her sister for over twenty years so I don't suppose another year will make much difference."

When the prospects for the future were raised, Mick usually kept quiet. He knew that he was between a hammer and a hard place because not only could he not afford to be laid off, it was his great hero, the Iron Lady from Grantham, who was right at the heart of the problem.

"Well no matter what happens," laughed Yorky, "at least I've got my pension to look forward to. The buggers can't touch that."

But when he did come to retire, he and a lot of other workers like him discovered that the buggers could touch his pension. And in some cases the most unfortunate of them discovered that the buggers had done and they no longer had one.

32.

It's P45 time

"ERNIE CASE TELLS ME there's another meeting to discuss redundancies this morning," said Charlie, as he lifted the cover off his drawing board.

"If Darlington held a few less meetings, and did something useful for a change, there might be no need for redundancies," replied Sam.

"One thing is for sure. If they ever get rid of him, they won't need anybody to replace him," laughed Alan.

"He reminds me of a manager we had at Cross Fields," said Shaun. "One year he was off sick for about ten weeks. When he finally came back into work, one of the first things he did, knowing just how essential he was to the running of the place, was to ask the girl who sat opposite him, how many phone calls there were for him.

"Do you know what she said? She told him that there had only been three, one was from the library informing him that a book he had ordered had now arrived, one was from the cleaners telling him that his suit was ready for collection and one was from somebody on the Health and Safety Committee, apologising for being unable to attend the next meeting!"

Despite this little bit of humour, there was not the slightest bit of enthusiasm shown in the Drawing Office that morning. Neither was there much shown throughout the whole factory. Things had been made worse by the news that had been splashed right across the front page of the *Lancashire Evening Post* on the previous evening, that Wallworks had decided to finish trading at the end of November, putting another three hundred local people on the dole.

"So what's your prediction for our future, Sam?" asked Charlie.

"I don't think we have one. The Government isn't that much interested in heavy industry or engineering. More and more of that will get done in the Far East, where wage rates and costs are much lower and life is cheap. Here I reckon that they could well close us down, transfer a few staff and some product lines over the wall to Wilco-Allisons, offer a few key people a job at St Albans and sell the land off for housing."

"Maybe we shouldn't have been so militant, trying to get higher wages than the company could afford," said Mick; a comment he had often made in the past.

"Not that old chestnut again, Mick. I'd hardly say that this was the highest paid firm on Merseyside, would you?" retorted Colin.

"Mick, haven't you learned anything about economics? The other side of low wages is usually high profits. The bosses are only in business to make as much money as they can. Remember Basil, that was why he ran the place like he did. His trouble was that he could have made a lot more if he had behaved differently towards his staff."

"O.K. Charlie, I didn't really look at it that way."

"No Mick. You never do. You just read what's in your *Daily Mail* and repeat it. You don't think that they are neutral in any struggle that goes on between the employees and the employers, do you?"

Then Alan chipped in with his views on the matter.

"Papers like the *Daily Mail* always like to blame the likes of you and me, just for wanting a decent wage and a bit of job security. They are always going on about workers wanting wages that the country can't afford. When did you ever read it having a go at the big corporations for wanting higher profits than the country can afford? They like to tell us that money doesn't grow on trees. How do we know? They've never let us into their orchard."

Mick said no more on the subject. He knew that he was between a rock and a hard place. He was still a supporter of Mrs. Thatcher, but that support was beginning to wane. The day before his daughter had got married, her husband-to-be had been made redundant and hadn't worked since. So they had started married life with her as the breadwinner. But now she was pregnant and would soon have to give up work. How would Mick be able to help them if he no longer had a job? And his family's situation was the same as many other families that he knew in Platt Bridge.

"Do you know what? I think I must be going senile but I'm finally beginning to agree with some of the political stuff that Greeno has been spouting over the years."

"Well, better late than never, Mick. Would you like a machine gun or do you want to carry the banner?"

The following morning, many people clocked on fearing the worst. At half past ten, all the shop stewards and the senior managers were called to the expected meeting with, Mr. Grey. The start of his message to them was delivered in his usual cold, impassioned way, as though he had walked into a supermarket, surveyed the shelves and then told his butler to pick up whichever tins of food he wanted and reject every other item of food he didn't want.

But before he could get to the guts of his message, the one that would seal the fate of many local people, the fire alarms went off. This time, it was no false alarm, there actually was a fire, albeit a small one at the back of the Joiners' shop. But by the time all the employees were allowed back into work, it was too late for the meeting to be reconvened that day. Mr. Grey had to be on Runcorn Station by one o' clock in order to catch the London train.

So the suspense concerning their future had to continue until he returned North in a couple of days' time.

Not many ate their meal that day with much enthusiasm. A few played bowls afterwards, many sat on the wall on Warrington Road, some talking about the future, others just thinking about it. And the only thing that convinced the majority of employees to return to work early that afternoon was the fact that it had started raining.

Silence reigned in the office too. Talk about doom and gloom. Thankfully it was a Friday afternoon, so they could all leave at four o'clock.

Even the telephone didn't work for a long time either. When it finally did, it was Mick who answered it.

"It's for you, Charlie," he said, and as he put it on the table and walked back to his drawing board, he said, "I think it's Ray Hewitt. We're not going on strike, are we?"

It was indeed Ray, with an urgent message, and so later that evening Charlie and Alan found themselves back in Ray's front room. Just as they started to taste Ray's latest brew, his Sankey Stout, there was a knock on the door. It certainly wasn't Sam. He had been complaining about pains in his stomach all day and had gone straight home after lunch. Surprisingly, it was another member of the Drawing Office, Graham Healey, the Mechanical Section leader: not someone that Charlie would have expected to be involved in any of Ray's discussions or activities.

As soon as Graham had a pint glass in his hand, Ray began.

"I've asked the three of you to come here at such short notice because of what I was told this morning. Now you may not know this, Graham, although Charlie and Greeno do, but I've always been very curious about the way Wilkinson's was run, ever since when it was first taken over in 1963 and, even though, I don't work there any more, I haven't lost that interest. More recently, something else that has grabbed my attention has been the situation in the Middle East. Having plenty time on my hands, I've been able to read a lot and discuss matters with a few old trade union colleagues who, like me, want to understand just what's going on in the world today.

"Now one of my friends is a guy called Tariq, still a very active member of the union in London. He is an Iraqi Kurd, who came to this country over ten years ago. He is an absolute mine of information about Iraq and all the ins and outs of this Iran-Iraq war. It's not just a theoretical thing for him, either. His family has suffered both at the hands of Saddam Hussein and the Turkish Government because of their support for an independent Kurdish state. Anyway he has recently discovered that Saddam has decided to have a chemical plant built, just outside Baghdad and not far from the village where some of Tariq's family used to live. From another Kurdish friend, in Germany, he found out that the main contract has gone to a German company in

IT'S P45 TIME

Dortmund and, with a bit more digging, he discovered that some of that work had been subcontracted to Britain, and part of that had been further subcontracted to Wilkinson's for a mechanical handling system. But to keep it quiet, because Britain is supposed to be neutral, the order has been placed through a company based in Saudi Arabia.

"But now with the possibility here of industrial action to fight any redundancies, it has been decided by some mandarin in Whitehall that the actual work of building this plant is now going to be done elsewhere, possibly in Germany. But because of the urgency, they are going to use all the drawings that you lads have drawn. So what is planned is that sometime over this weekend, all the drawings will be removed from the Drawing Office.If that happens, there will be even less work for the shop floor. So it is in your interests to keep the drawings where they are. The other thing is there is every possibility that this chemical plant will be used to manufacture chlorine gas, which Saddam is using to gas Iranian troops in their thousands. this not something that any Government wants to be openly involved with.

"Charlie has already told me that all the electrical design work has been finished and prints sent off for final approval. But I don't know about the mechanical side, which is why I have asked Graham to come here. What can you tell us, Graham?"

"I certainly didn't know that this contract was for Iraq. All I do know is that Sherlock has been on my back all this week, trying to get the design drawings completed. But he keeps giving me things to alter on it. To be honest, I reckon he doesn't understand what he's doing. It's partly his fault that the job has fallen behind.

"We've finished the main part of the job. I told him yesterday that if he let a couple of us come in over the weekend, I could have everything ready for Tuesday. But he was adamant that there was absolutely no chance of anybody being in over the weekend. So you can take from that what you want. He also told me to make sure that every drawing was in the filing cabinet, in the right order, before I went home, just in case I won the pools and didn't come in on Monday."

"Sounds as though he was just making sure it would be easy to remove them, doesn't it?" said Charlie.

"He might just want to come in and run some prints off," said Alan.

"He won't be able to do that."

"Why?"

"One of the contactors in the print machine is knackered and they can't get a replacement before Tuesday. He'll be lucky if he even gets a light on."

"So what are we going to do?"

"Well, we can't do anything until Monday and it might be too late by then."

"One of us could go in tomorrow and hide these drawings."

"How are we going to get in? John Battesby always locks the office last thing on a Friday."

Charlie answered that problem with a big smile on his face.

"I've got a spare key. I always have had," and with that he showed them his bunch of keys.

"You are a clever bugger, but that still doesn't answer the question, what do we do?"

Then Graham made his first suggestion. It was based on something he had seen done, when he had worked in a Drawing Office in Manchester a few years ago.

"We had a similar situation when I was at that firm at Trafford Park. We knew that there were going to be redundancies announced soon, even though we had enough work in the office. One morning the Chief Draughtsman said that he wanted about twenty drawings drawn and checked by the end of the week. They were all panel assemblies, and pretty similar and easy to draw, so he gave the job to two junior draughtsmen: it was mainly copying work. On the Friday afternoon, he looked at what they had drawn and then told one of the lads to come in on Saturday morning, put a number in the title box on every drawing, and print off half a dozen copies of each.

"Now this lad hated his guts. He also knew that if there were any redundancies, he would be among the first to go. So he came in and did what the boss had said. The numbering system they had there was a very basic one. If it was an electrical drawing, it would have the prefix E followed by a number, if it was a sheetmetal drawing, it would be prefix S, P for pneumatic, C for civil and so on. By the time the lad had arrived at work, he had decided that he was going to leave anyway and was going to go out with a bang. The other thing was this boss always expected that his instructions be followed to the letter. But when he had told the lad to give every drawing a number, he hadn't said a different number, and the lad wasn't sure which suffix to use either. So what he did was give every drawing the same number. And do you know what number he chose, eh? P45!

"On the Monday, his mother rang in to say her son had been to the doctors, who had put him on the club for a week. At the same time, he wished to hand in his notice. I'm not sure, though, if she said anything about whether he had to come in for his P45."

"Look, it's not really a time for humour, but I'll just tell you a tale which might just give us another idea," said Charlie.

"It was what happened when my neighbour was working in Sheffield last year. He worked in the same office as this lad from Hull. He was a good draughtsman, even thought he was indispensable, but his trouble was that he was an alcoholic, a right piss artist, he was. On some days, he was still drunk when he came into work first thing in the morning. Finally his boss had had enough, called him into his office and gave him a final warning. Then he told the bloke that he had been checking what was on his drawing board, and suggested that the best thing he could do was to put a match to it and start again. Then he made some more insulting remarks about his appearance and told the bloke to piss off out of his sight.

"So the bloke went back to his board, opened his drawer where he always had a bottle of whiskey and took a large swig. Then he got a cigarette out, lit up, started smoking and brooding. At that point, his boss went out of the office, so then the bloke took the drawing off his board, crumpled it up and set it on fire with his cig. Nobody said or did anything, because they were all frightened of him once he started drinking. Anyway a few more drawings on his desk went up in smoke as well before the boss comes back and sees and smells what was happening. He walked straight over to this bloke and do you know what he said to him?"

"What?"

"You're fired."

"Eh, listen lads. I know it's all very funny, but there's serious business to agree on."

"There's no problem," said Graham. "Give us your key, Charlie. I'll go into work tomorrow and take all these drawings out of the cabinet and hide them. There must be over twenty thousand drawings in that place. He'll never find that dozen drawings if he searches for them all weekend. Luckily, I'm also going out on site first thing on Monday morning to that job at Avery Denison in Leeds, so nobody can get hold of me until ten at the very earliest, either."

But before Graham could drive to work, on the Saturday morning, he had to drive his wife into Warrington and then drop his seven-year-old daughter off at her regular Saturday morning dancing class in Helmsley. By the time he arrived in work, made himself a drink and opened the drawing cabinet, he discovered that all the drawings he had come to hide had already been removed!

And with their disappearance, the chances of the unions fighting any redundancies, whether voluntary or compulsory, was greatly reduced. Many years later, it became more widely known that the mechanical handling plant the three of them had played a part in designing had been used for manufacturing chemical weapons that were used in the first Gulf War. But by that time, much of the land on which the Wilkinson Engineering Works had stood for nearly two hundred years, had itself become something more like a bomb site as well!